Burton

CASTLE OF CARE

A vigorous tale of the Great Rebellion in a new and picturesque setting. The chief scenes are enacted at Conway, which town the Parliament carried by escalade after the last English stronghold had surrendered. Care is taken to afford an accurate background for a romance in which action and suspense, love and hate are interwoven. The reader, though absorbed in the exploits of the characters, is incidentally provided with a vivid picture of North Wales in those troublous days. The celebrated Archbishop of York, John Williams of Conway, is etched with particular fidelity.

CASTLE OF CARE

By

NORMAN TUCKER

Author of
"Night Hawk"

2nd Impression

London
ANDREW MELROSE, LTD.
*Paternoster House, E.C.*4

"Her Cafalier make no such feasts but have Irish rebels teares for her drink, and dine in the *Castle of Care*. . . ."

From "The Welsh-mans Propositions to the Arch-Bishop of Yorke, Commander in chiefe before Conoway Castle in Wales. . . . Printed in the Yeare of hir Cosen Taffies Carier, 1646." (Thomason Tracts E. 346–15. British Museum.)

MADE AND PRINTED IN GREAT BRITAIN, FOR ANDREW MELROSE, LTD., AT THE ANCHOR PRESS, :: TIPTREE, ESSEX ::

To
L. E. T. and A. M. T.

Castle of Care

CHAPTER ONE

In the late summer of the momentous year sixteen-forty-two a storm broke over England.

Through the darkness of the sultry night, John Heritage spurred his horse on to the limit of its strength. The great black beast was spattered with mud and foam. Occasional rumbles of thunder betokened the elements' unrest. Lightning played in the eastern heavens. It lit the skies over Hull, the vital fortress-town in which lay stored the arms got together for the Scottish campaign. It was the key to England's destiny—and the Parliament held the key.

For King Charles riding thither at the head of some troops found the gates shut in his face by Sir John Hotham and his son. "Unlucky town of Hull for thy Commanders' sake", laments an old Royalist. "A strong Cage it was to keep these unclean Birds from the Royal Eagle." So the King withdrew his injured Majesty, and all men knew what must come to pass.

A burst of torrential rain descended. It streamed ~~'s cloak~~ and from the heaving flanks of his

~~...~~ ~~...~~ hing three

"God's wounds, what a night !" cried Hogan with his customary lack of respect.

"Are the sentinels alert ?" inquired Holland. He never forgot he was an officer, and since his Grace of York had commissioned him lieutenant of Horse the week before, he saw the path of advancement shine clear before him.

"They are awake," quoth Hogan, tipping the water from his hat brim. "I have shifted Parry to the stables ; his matchlock is useless on a night like this ; and I have set Giles beside the palings. 'Zounds, he carried his pike as though it were a hay-rake."

Hogan slipped his sword-belt over his head and placed the weapon on a table from which he lifted a bottle of wine.

Holland pointed to the sword. "Best not discard your weapon," he said. "You are still on duty."

"I'll find it quick enough when it is needed," replied Hogan carelessly. He raised his glass. "Here's to his Majesty ; damnation to all scurvy Crop-ears, and God's luck to the lads who ride with him to the fight !"

Holland drank, and then seated himself before a table. "Come, Hogan, a game of cards to pass the time." He fell to shuffling the cards with the neatness and precision which characterized his every action.

"Let me open the window first," said Hogan, pushing back his chair, "though, Faith, 'tis as hot outside as in. The air comes like a blast from the pit." He flung open the window, then paused motionless beside it. From without came a low hum of voices.

"Come, Hogan !" Holland's voi...

"The cards are dealt and I ha...

the knave of spad...

"F...

"It must and it shall until I find some pleasanter source of meditation. Gad, man, she hath a neatly turned instep."

Holland yawned. "It would be edifying to discover your conception of military service."

"You shall have it—war : wine : wenches ! I'll fight for his Majesty, but Faith I must take my payment in the coin which pleases me best. Or, as our Grace the Archbishop would have it : the labourer is worthy of his hire. How say you ?"

"My desire," said Holland sententiously, "is to render his Majesty loyal service, venturing my life gladly on behalf of his crown and dignity. And if, in so doing, I may be deemed worthy of promotion——"

Hogan burst into a roar of laughter. "You and I are alike, lad, tarred with the selfsame brush. Each out to feather his nest : you in your way, and I in mine."

Holland rose with dignity. His fingers slid to his hilt. "I find your words uncivil, Hogan," said he ominously.

A knock sounded on the door.

"A monstrous opportune intervention," laughed Hogan. "Enter."

The sergeant of the guard saluted. "There is a woman, sir, at the gate desiring word with his Grace."

"Say to her the Archbiship is not at home," said Holland curtly.

"Wait, I will acquaint her !" cried Hogan, slipping after the retreating sergeant.

"Come back, Hogan !" Holland's voice fell on deaf ears.

In the shelter of the gatehouse stood a young woman, cloaked, and having a hood drawn well over her head. Her face was weary. A whisp of damp hair straggled across her pale forehead, but she did not appear uncomely. Hogan noted the full red curve of her lips.

Hogan bowed. "His Grace the Archbishop is absent from his palace," said he with the suavity he knew how to assume when occasion arose.

The girl looked distressed. "When can I have audience ? It is urgent. Where can I find him ?"

"Who can tell ? Let me serve as his deputy."

"I thank you, no," said the girl hurriedly. "I am——"

"Come, my dear, you will discover me more entertaining than his reverence, who, folks say, shows little partiality to the fair sex. What troubles you, little one ? Some confession, I'll wager."

"I desire neither your aid nor your presence," said the girl haughtily, as she stepped back into the rain.

"Stay, my pretty one, let me play father confessor to you. You cannot escape so lightly. . . ."

He slipped an arm about her waist ; then staggered as a small white hand smote his face with surprising violence.

He clutched at the girl, but nimble as a squirrel she evaded him and he floundered over a broken cobblestone.

"You little jade," he shouted, "I'll take payment for that." He reached forward, but his foot slipped on the wet ground and he measured his length in the mud.

There was a titter at his discomfiture from the soldiers of the watch. The girl lifted her skirt clear of her ankles and ran down the road. Hogan leaped furiously to his feet.

"Hogan ! Stay here. Come back, you fool !" Holland's angry command was ignored. Hogan was racing after the slim figure which was melting into the night.

Holland wheeled angrily upon the soldiers. "Who laughed ?" he demanded. As the grins faded he cried : "Get to your posts. Have done with this folly. Sergeant, see to your duties."

With head held high, Holland stalked to his room. He was aggrieved, humiliated at Hogan's behaviour. Moreover he felt such conduct would undermine discipline. There was the matter of the sword, now.

Ought he to have insisted on Hogan resuming it? The situation was embarrassing for, though he was now Hogan's superior, Holland was conscious of the fact that Hogan had seen service in Ireland and the Low Countries whereas he, Holland, was new to the game of war. He sat alone with his thoughts until his reverie was shattered by the sergeant's peremptory—"Guard, turn out!"

Holland donned his plumed hat and was straightening his belt when the sergeant tapped at the door. "Party of Horse approaching, sir, which I take to be his Grace and escort."

Holland stepped briskly outside, glanced down the road, recognized the dapple-grey mount of the leader, and ordered the gates to be flung wide and the guard to present arms.

For Dr. John Williams, the new Archbishop of York, was not one to dispense with ceremony. Few counsellors of the King stood so high as he. Indeed, now that Laud was in the Tower with the shadow of the axe already over his head, Dr. John Williams was virtually primate of England. There was little of the cleric about the alert cavalier who drew rein in the light of the gate-lanthorns. "The convoy, Lieutenant, hath it arrived?" he inquired as Holland raised his blade in salute.

"No sign of the munitions yet, your Grace, but one wain bearing equipment came in shortly before dusk. I had it unladen and despatched to the mill for corn."

"You did well. See to it the sentinels are alert. I hear disquieting rumours from Hull. Who aids you with the night watch?"

"Cornet Hogan, your Grace. He is inspecting the sentries."

"Ah, Hogan. I find him a zealous and active officer," commented the Archbishop as he rode past. Holland gazed at the retreating backs of the escort.

"Active, your Grace," he observed drily, "if not

zealous." Then bidding the sergeant leave the gate ajar lest Hogan should return, Holland retired once more to his room.   He was uninterrupted until brought to his feet by the rush of Heritage's reckless approach.

"Ho, there, open the gate !   I ride express."

"Give the word," commanded the sergeant as the great black horse pulled up almost on its haunches.

"To hell with words—'tis spurs you'll need !" shouted the messenger, and reaching forth a foot he thrust back the gate with a violence which stretched its guardian on the cobbles.   "They are come out of Hull, and march on Cawood !" he shouted by way of explanation to Holland, who emerged in time to see the black horse departing on its final canter.

Lights were shining from the mullioned windows ahead.

For days the Archbishop had been active munitioning his palace lest he should be called upon to hold it for the King.   Yet for all his goodwill Cawood Castle was but ill adapted for military occasions.   When the Archbishop visited his See in the Spring for the first time he found this erstwhile stately home of prelates in a most ruinous condition.   With his customary energy he took upon himself the task of restoring it to its pristine splendour.   "Industry was his recreation," says an old writer, "for he had not a lazy drop of blood in his veins."

Though the night was far advanced there was no cessation in the preparations, for the men laboured under the eye of the Archbishop, and no man felt the need of sleep less than he.   In his younger days, when his aspirations were hot within him, he trained himself to study while lesser men slumbered so that three or four hours a night for him would suffice. The Archbishop paused to survey the scene with some complacency.   A motley congregation was this miniature army of his : younger sons of neighbouring gentlemen, full of ardour and inexperience ; clerics, yeomen, tenantry from his broad estates. Scarce one had handled a firelock, yet they formed raw material which determination could weld into a force of some consequence, and John Williams, as all men knew, was not lacking in determination. The palatial floors were strewn with a medley of saddlery and bandoleers, bows and arrows, shoes, half-pikes, and stands of arms. Men working over bullet-moulds sweated at their task. The night seemed full of portents.

"Hark!" The clatter of hoofs caught the Archbishop's ear. They bespoke urgency as surely as the roll of a drum. "Mansel, see who it is," he commanded, turning to a young squire, "for, like Jehu, he rideth furiously."

But when Mansel looked forth from the casement, he saw nothing but the steaming withers of a foamspattered steed. Its rider was striding up the grand staircase, three steps at a time. He burst in upon the retainers, standing like Saul of old, head and shoulders above his fellow men.

"Ho, there, my lads, where do I find the Archbishop?"

There was an awkward silence.

"Your hat is upon your head," observed a suave voice.

"And your head is upon your shoulders—as yet," began Heritage, wheeling as he spoke. He checked his words. Standing before him was a slender but upright man of regal bearing, dressed in sumptuous but sombre velvet, relieved at throat and wrist by rich lace. In temporal contradiction the Churchman wore thigh-boots of soft brown leather and upon his hip, suspended from a broad brown leather baldrick hung a rapier with a richly chased hilt. No symbolic sword of the spirit, this, but a lethal blade, designed for the shedding of men's blood. But it was the man's face which arrested Heritage's attention. The noble, intellectual forehead carried calm dignity, but the dark eyes were piercing—

sharp as a fox's—an impression of vulpine keenness which was accentuated by a small, pointed silken beard. There was something commanding in the man's carriage which instantly demanded recognition. Heritage found himself doffing his hat. "Your pardon," said he less boisterously. "Do I address his Grace?"

Then Heritage threw back his head and a laugh danced in his eyes. "Lord, sir, I must be forgiven! I had not expected to find the Church militant."

"The Church assumes temporal weapons when her prerogatives are assailed," remarked the Archbishop curtly. "But your tidings, sir. The informality of your intrusion can only be explained by a message of urgency."

"The Hothams have come forth from Hull to raven for a prey," quoth Heritage. "I warn you to change your lodging and your country if you value your life."

The Archbishop's fair complexion paled, but instantly he recovered his composure.

"Sir John Hotham is a graceless traitor to resist his Majesty."

"He offered his Majesty entrance, but not the armed forces who were at his back."

"Nothing is more hateful than a malicious courtesy."

"Let that rest, sir. Young Hotham hath heard how your Grace hath railed against them. He is a rough piece and is provoked by your Grace's language for the disloyalty at Hull. When I had news of him, he was making ready to come with force enough to take Cawood Castle by five of the clock this very morning. He drew his sword before some gallants with a vow to cut off your Grace's head."

"I will withstand him," cried the Archbishop, his Welsh choler rising. "Mansel, see to the serving out of the arms——"

"It is folly," interposed Heritage. "He hath

ridden out from Hull with a score of hot-bloods at his
heels, and with them three score troopers——"

"He shall rue the day——"

"And half a battalion of Foot follow with field-pieces.
Cawood is unprovided, ruinous, undefensible."

The Archbishop was silent. If he possessed courage
he had likewise common sense. The flush on his
cheeks betokened the struggle raging within him, but his
impassive countenance gave no other sign.

"Make haste," urged Heritage, "else you are
sacrificed to the fury of a wicked dog. Think yourself
happy you can save your life. You are not equipped to
withstand a siege, and it is known the bulk of your
retainers have already joined the King's army."

"What you say is true," said the Archbishop in a
modulated voice. "I thank you for your warning.
Mr. Nightingale," he added, turning to a gentleman of
the King's Chapel who was in attendance, "hasten to
the gatehouse and bid Mr. Holland join me with every
man who bears arms. Bide you at the gatehouse and
when Hotham comes hang out a sheet for a parley,
saying you are prepared to surrender up the Castle
provided your life is spared.

"The remainder of you will assemble in the great
courtyard, each man bearing such goods as he can con-
veniently carry. Select only those things which will be
most acceptable to his Majesty's cause. Let every
horse be saddled instantly. Mr. Mansel, take this key
and pack my private papers. No time is to be lost."

The men scattered to do his bidding, leaving the
dining-hall deserted save for Heritage and the Archbishop. John Williams was calm of face, yet who
could gauge the force of this blow? It was not long
since he had ridden to York in defiance of both Houses,
and had been enthroned for the first time in the
Minster which should never see him more. Long had
he aspired to greatness, yet now when the pomp and
dignity so dear to his heart had come to him at length,

B

all must needs vanish in one short summer night. Well might one wonder what thoughts were passing through his teeming brain. At least there was no rancour against the monarch whose whim had thrown him into the Tower and stripped him of much of his wealth ; for in his Majesty's extremity, John Williams never hesitated to fling his all into the hazard : his castle and his lands ; his wealth—and he had amassed plenty—his dignity, of which he possessed even more ; asking no reward other than to be allowed to serve his King. And in this time of testing none could doubt but what the true man lay revealed. If John Williams had tasted power he had also tasted adversity ; he knew how to be abased as well as how to abound, and through both he had learned how to preserve his dignity unimpaired. "His gait was so stately," says an admirer, "that most persons mistook it for pride."

The Archbishop walked to the bookshelves and selected several tomes. "I pray you bear these to the courtyard for me. They are part of that rare inheritance bequeathed me by my first master, Lord Chancellor Egerton of ever-cherished memory. Some remembrance of him, at all costs, shall be saved from the wreck. My plate, thank God, hath already gone to the King's coffers."

The clatter of hoofs sounded in the palace yard. The cavalcade was assembling.

The Archbishop donned his plumed hat and allowed Heritage to place a cloak about his shoulders. With head held high he moved with stately tread to the grand staircase. Like the apostles of old he took with him neither scrip nor purse, nothing but his cloak, his papers and his belief in the divine right of kings. "He went away without a sumpter, nay, not with so much as change of Apparel," says the Chronicler, "and as for coin, he was sure no Highway-man would stop him for a Booty."

He stepped into the courtyard, where his followers

sat their horses. Slowly he closed and locked the door of his palace.

"Lay not up for yourselves treasures upon earth . . ." As a Churchman the words must have been familiar to him, though God knoweth hitherto he had shown little understanding of their meaning. If ever the force of the words were borne upon the ambitious Welshman, it must have been at this hour, yet the moment showed the mettle of the man, and his face was strong and calm with high resolve. When Heritage would have held his stirrup for him, the Archbishop waved him aside and sprang into the saddle with the ease of youth.

"You have locked the door, sir," said Heritage.

"Why should not I ?"

"You invite the soldiers to break it down and so put them in a humour for plunder."

The Archbishop shrugged his shoulders.

"Bethink you, the King's forces are not far distant," said Heritage. "His Majesty may resolve to retake the place when he learns of this indignity to your Grace."

"His Majesty hath weightier things to think upon. I would not distract him with any affairs of mine. Howbeit, take the key and unlock the door. I care not either way. It may be as you say, but my heart tells me I shall never see this place again."

The Archbishop touched his grey with the spur, and the cavalcade cantered into the black night.

CHAPTER TWO

HERITAGE waited until the noise of the departing horsemen faded into the night, then slowly he walked to the ponderous door and flung it wide. The rain had ceased and a pale moon was trying to pierce the lowering clouds with her sickly light. Within the palace the candles still burned in their sconces, flinging their pallid rays on a scene of mingled luxury and confusion. Heritage appeared in no hurry. Hotham's troopers were not yet due, and with his powerful steed tethered in the courtyard there was no cause for anxiety. Slowly he mounted the stairs. For a man of his bulk he moved with singular lightness : his footsteps evoked no echo from the deserted corridors. He paused and looked about him with leisurely curiosity.

His attention was attracted by a large portrait of the Archbishop, the gilt on its frame scarcely dry. He moved nearer to examine it. The painting was a copy —freshly executed—of the portrait which hung in the hall of Westminster School, of which his Grace was benefactor. It showed Dr. Williams as Lord Keeper, holder of the Great Seal of James I. Heritage passed on until he came to another portrait, faded, dark with age, yet still conspicuous by virtue of the crimson robes of the great Cardinal it represented. It hung as a reminder that Wolsey once dwelt in this place. Here it was that he received the last fatal message which assured him of his downfall. Their portraits hung upon the same wall—Wolsey and Williams—great men and all-powerful : lovers of temporal glory. Heritage's eyes turned slowly from one to the other, appraising them. Had Williams, like Wolsey, quitted the scenes of his splendour, never to return ?

Well might a man meditate on the uncertainty of power. Wolsey forsook Cawood Palace as a dying man : Williams had yet eight years to live ; years into which he crowded a wealth of heroic service ; in which he drank to the dregs the cup of suffering, and, by a last, spectacular, intrepid act, proved to the world that though princes might break faith, John Williams was a man of his word.

Slowly Heritage crossed the room, the floor of which was littered with discarded equipment. Muddied boots had trampled rich rugs from the Orient. Drawers had discharged their contents. The buffet was strewn with half-carved joints and dirty platters. Everything bore evidence of the speed at which the garrison had taken flight. Heritage's quick eye lighted upon a red-backed book among the debris. A glance inside revealed a strange combination of words and numerals. It was obviously a cipher code. He picked up a small bundle of letters, a hasty glance at which caused him to elevate his brows. His Grace, he mused, for a man of legal learning, was curiously indiscreet in his correspondence.

In the act of dropping them into his pocket he paused like an affrighted animal as his ears caught a sound. Silent as a shadow Heritage stole from the room.

The noise came from the hallway. Had Heritage waited longer he would have found the cause scarce sufficient to put a man to flight. It was no boisterous trampling of raiding troopers. The silence of the deserted palace was broken only by the sharp tapping of a woman's tiny heels.

"Is no one here ?" The voice sounded strangely weak amid the echoing walls. "Is his Grace at home ?"

The door of the dining-room was pushed timidly open. Into the room stole the girl who had already made her appearance at the gatehouse. She looked

about her with wonderment in her eyes until her gaze
fell on the laden buffet. Hurrying towards it with the
eagerness of one who had not tasted food for many
hours, she sliced a chicken, and eagerly devoured the
meat, revealing the whiteness of her shapely teeth.
A glass of ruby wine brought a touch of colour to her
wan cheeks. Her meal ended, she dropped her cloak,
and crossing to a hanging mirror she commenced to
arrange her disordered hair. Her improved appearance seemed to bring with it reassurance, for she
straightened her shoulders and looked about her with
a more independent tilt of her chin. Suddenly the old
harassed look crept back into her eyes. She stood
listening, her hand pressed to her heart, her eyes large
with fright. A heavy step sounded on the stairs. Like
a fluttered bird she scurried behind a curtain.

The tapestry folds had scarce ceased quivering when
into the room strode Hogan, hatless, dishevelled, none
too sober and plainly in an evil humour.

"Ho, there ! In the devil's name where is every-
one gone ?" He stared angrily about him until he,
too, sighted the buffet. Seizing a decanter he drained
it. Hogan became more tolerant. No longer he resented the deserted appearance of the apartment.
Placing a row of flagons before him on a table he drew
up a chair, and settled himself with the comfortable
assurance of one who contemplates a convivial inter-
lude. For a while he drank methodically. Something
attracted his gaze. Slowly he placed the tankard on
the table and bent forward, his eyes concentrated on a
black garment which lay heaped on the floor. He
picked it up and examined it. It was a woman's
cloak. A look of cunning crossed his face. "Come
out !" he commanded, staring about the room. "Come
out from concealment. 'Tis no use. I know jus'
where y'are."

Unsteadily he crossed the room, peering into the
window recesses, beneath the refectory table. He

paused, nonplussed, and shook his head.   Solemnly he regarded the room.   As he noticed a bulge in the tapestry a look of triumph crossed his face.   He tip-toed until he could grasp the curtain, tore it aside with a reckless sweep and rudely clutched the cowering girl.

"I have you, you jade !"

"Loose me—beast !"

"Nay, my pretty one.   No hard words.   A fine chase you've led me, but you shall find me mag-man-magnanimous."

He pulled her closer to him, bending his hot face over hers so that she turned away sickened by the wine-laden breath.

There was a quick movement.   Hogan sprang back with an oath, clapping his hand to his side.   He cursed as the warm blood wet his fingers.   The girl had plucked his dagger and plunged it into his ribs.   But his thick buff jerkin turned the point, and her puny strength had done no more than scratch his skin and further awaken the animal within him.

"I'll clip your claws for you," he snarled, and snatched a poker from the fireplace.

The girl essayed to escape, but her retreat was cut off, so she stood at bay, dagger poised.

"Stand back !"   But he moved towards her, wary as a fencer.

"Do not lay your vile hands on me.   The Arch-bishop will break you for this.   I am kin of his, do you hear ?" cried the girl, retreating.

Hogan laughed at her dagger and her threats.   With the ease of an experienced swordsman he struck the dagger from her grasp.   Flinging the poker from him he sprang forward, ripping the lace from her white throat.   "Now, you vixen," cried he, "you shall pay the price !"

His arms were about her, crushing her powerless. "God help me," she moaned, drooping.   "God—help—me."

"Let my help suffice!"

The words were calmly spoken. Hogan found his neck caught from behind in a crushing grasp and he was flung across the room so that he crashed among the fire-dogs. As he lay there breathing heavily, cursing, he found Heritage's great form towering above him.

Heritage turned to the lady with a stiff formal bow. "I heard your first cry, madam, and came back," said he simply.

"Beware!" she shrieked.

For Hogan had picked up the dagger and was poised to strike. Like a flash Heritage wheeled, warding off the blow with one hand. The other caught the descending wrist and wrenched the weapon from the nerveless grasp. It tinkled through the window glass as he flung the poniard far from him. Once again Hogan was sent reeling to the floor. But Hogan was a fighter, not easily quelled. To his feet he sprang, and his hand sought his hilt. A look of consternation crossed his countenance as he realized he had left his rapier on the gatehouse table.

"Damnation, I have no sword," he snarled.

Heritage stood, hands on hips, and mocked him. "The gentleman hath no sword," he laughed. "Had the gentleman a sword he would chastise me. Strike me, so he would!"

Heritage slid his own long blade from its scabbard and presented the hilt. "I am loth to have this soiled by your filthy fingers, but I would fain prove your mettle. If you seek a sword, pray try this."

Hogan took the weapon wonderingly.

"What are you doing?" shrieked the girl. "Are you mad?" But Heritage waved her back.

"It is a game I play," he said. He spoke coolly but his eyes were watchful. He draped his cloak about his left arm. Slowly he drew a heavy knife from his belt.

"Now," said he, his eyes never leaving those of his adversary. "Try to clip *my* claws."

Hogan's eyes blazed: he lunged. There was a flicker of steel as the knife diverted the blade. Ere Hogan could recover the cloak struck him across the eyes; he staggered blindly. The knife edge ripped his knuckles, causing him to drop the rapier. The cloak was whisked away. As he stood blinking stupidly, Heritage's fist caught him on the point of the jaw with stunning violence, stretching him yet a third time amid the andirons. This time Hogan did not move.

"I have every confidence his jaw is broken," said Heritage coolly as he sheathed knife and sword.

The girl came forward pale and trembling. "How can I thank you for your aid in my great necessity?" she said, speaking in a low voice which Heritage found full pleasing. "How can I offer to you my thanks for your goodness?"

"By quitting this place with all expedition," said Heritage curtly as he moved towards the door.

"I seek the Archbishop."

"He is fled."

"Fled?" The girl was bewildered.

"Ay! The Parliamentary troops are moving on Cawood Castle and are like to arrive any moment."

"Oh!" Her distress was pitiful. "What can I do? Whither can I turn?"

"Have you no friends?"

"None here, save the Archbishop. I have journeyed from London to join him, thinking to find security with him. Vain hope! Sir, can you not escort me to him?"

"No." There was more finality than courtesy in the reply.

"But you are of his staff?"

"A messenger only, come to bear him warning. I must return whence I came."

"Let me entreat you, of your chivalry, first to escort me to his Grace."

"It is inconvenient."

She flushed. "You are scarcely—gallant."

"I am a rough man, as perchance you have gathered. I have few regrets that I am no gentleman"—and he glanced contemptuously at the unconscious form on the hearth.

"You saved me from yonder rogue. I shall ever remember your service with gratitude. Can you not add one more favour, sir ? I am alone, as you see, and unprotected. Indeed, sir, my courage as well as my strength is nigh spent."

She raised pleading eyes to his. Heritage found the gaze hard to encounter.

"Come," said he curtly, and descended the stairs. "I was not minded to seek further acquaintance of his Grace, but I cannot leave you defenceless. Can you ride ?"

She nodded an affirmative. His powerful hands lifted her to the saddle of his horse. Taking the bridle, he walked down the lane at the rear of the building. As they reached the parting of the ways he dropped to the ground.

The girl was curious. "What are you doing ?" she asked, peering through the darkness.

"Feeling for the hoof tracks of the Archbishop's party. They are gone this way."

In silence he led the horse forward ; the girl dozed in the saddle. Presently, borne on the night air came a medley of sounds ; the shrill blast of a trumpet ; the noise of shouting.

"They have reached the gatehouse," said Heritage brusquely. "There is need to hasten. Dismount."

He swung into the saddle, offered her a stirrup and lifted her before him. Gathering up the reins he held her with such comfort as was possible, and urged his horse into a canter.

In this manner Heritage rode from Cawood Castle. It was for him a rare proceeding. Never before had he held a woman in his arms. He found the experience embarrassing—but not necessarily unpleasant.

CHAPTER THREE

THE girl must have been asleep. Suddenly she became
aware that the great black horse was motionless.

"What is it?" she asked quickly, opening her eyes.
"Hark!"

From out of the sable silence behind them, distant
but unmistakable, came the irregular clatter of many
hoofs.

"We are pursued?" There was alarm in her tone.

By way of answer, her cavalier lowered her gently to
the earth, leaped from his steed and opening a field gate
led the animal within. Closing the gate he took the
girl by the arm and guided her across the dark pasture
until a clump of high furze was reached. They stood
silent on the far side, listening, Heritage with his
fingers over his horse's nose lest it should whinny.
The hoof-beats grew louder. Over the hedge-top
dimly they could discern horsemen rising and falling
as they trotted past, a faint light reflecting from their
burnished headpieces. The soldiers rode two abreast:
sixteen in all. The hoof-beats faded and again the
night was still.

"We must not blunder into those rogues in the
darkness," said Heritage. "It is best we took cover
in these woods."

"What woods?"

"There are woods near by. I have heard the owls
calling." And so it proved. They came upon a
copse, but Heritage passed this by, heading for a larger
mass which loomed beyond.

The girl stumbled from weariness. "Can we not
rest here?"

"No.   It is windward of the road and sounds might carry.   Bear up a little longer."

His strong right hand supported her, affording her fresh strength by reason of his own.   He came to a wooded gully into which he turned.   The girl hesitated, deterred by the gloom, but Heritage led the way with unerring certainty as though possessed of a sixth sense.   Once they had rounded a bend he halted. He leaped the bank, and presently the girl heard a quiet slashing and he returned with his arms full of spruce boughs.

"A couch for you," said he softly.

"How could you see in the dark?" queried the curious girl.

"There is no need to see with the smell to guide me, and the feel of fallen needles beneath my feet."   He spread the fragrant boughs and covered them with his cloak.   "Rest on these," said he.   "You are weary and cold, but I will soon kindle a fire to bring you warmth and comfort."

"A fire?   But the Roundheads will see the blaze."

"Not as I make it.   Bide here while I seek touch-wood from the dry heart of some fallen tree."

She sat alone in the darkness, half fearful, until he returned carrying a bundle of dry sticks he had cut from the centre of a log where no rain could penetrate. She heard him digging.   There was the sound of flint and steel.   A spark glowed low down in the darkness. Heritage blew the tinder into flame and fed the blaze gently with tiny chips, coaxing the flame upward. When the fire burned, the girl saw it was at the bottom of a small pit he had dug with the aid of his knife.   He moved her couch to the edge and she found space for her feet between the fire and the wall of the pit.   He laughed softly at her satisfaction.   "The fire is below earth level and so cannot be seen from a distance," he explained.   "If we keep it small and feed it only with dry sticks there will be little glow or smoke. It is a trick the savages taught me," he added.

"Savages ?"

"Ay, the red-skins of New England. It is so they kindle their fires in winter when on the war-path and must needs have warmth to sustain them on a long vigil."

"Have you, then, been to America ?" The girl's weariness was nigh forgotten in her awakened interest. "Pray tell me."

But he shook his head. " 'Tis a long story and will keep. Meanwhile you are nigh dead with fatigue. I beg you slumber while you may." He brought her a blanket from his saddle-pack and spread it over her. He doffed his buff coat and rolled it for a pillow.

"You will be cold," she protested, but he shook his head. "I am used to the woods and will take no harm."

She lay back, contented, idly watching his nimble fingers fashioning a shelter of boughs over her. He unsaddled his horse, then leaned his back against a tree. Through her closing eyes the girl could see his massive form on guard, the fire's faint glow flickering on the high riding-boots with their big rowelled spurs. She could see his long straight sword, its businesslike hilt polished with constant handling. His face was lost in the gloom. A feeling of utter contentment and security stole over her. The strain of the wearisome day with its excitement, its privations, its dangers was put aside. She slept as one that had found peace. . . .

The sun was shining when she awoke, transforming into a sylvan paradise the wood which seemed so ominous a few hours before. A squirrel chattered from the branches of an oak. She lay watching the animal, and when he disappeared with a whisk of his bushy tail, her gaze wandered to a tiny tree-creeper which climbed the bark, nimbly as a feathered mouse. An appetizing smell aroused her to full consciousness.

She found Heritage, up betimes, watching her from the far side of the fire, before which some flesh was roasting, impaled on pointed sticks.

"A coney I snared," said the man in reply to her query, "and also a woodpigeon for your breakfast. You can hear his brothers crooning in the beeches."

"But how did you catch the pigeon?"

For answer he nodded to a short bow, newly fashioned, and some fresh-peeled arrows, their points hardened in the fire, and feathered with the dropped tail-feathers of a woodpigeon. "I have improved the shining morning hours," he smiled. "Now, as the food is nearly done, I advise you to go wash in the brook you will find north of yonder stricken birch."

They ate in silence. The meal done, Heritage burned all debris, feeding the fire with wood cut with a small axe which he drew from a beaded pouch on his belt. It had a long straight handle and a thin bright blade which, though small, was wondrous sharp.

"It is like no hatchet I have ever seen," said the girl watching.

"I do not marvel at that," replied Heritage. "It is a throwing-axe such as the savages call a tomahawk. They have great skill in its use as a weapon, and I, too, acquired some practice once when I was a captive amongst them, and was like to be adopted into one of their tribes as a warrior."

"How can they throw it?"

Heritage pointed to a beech bole. "Let yonder knot represent a man's head," said he, and with a quick throw sent the bright blade curving through the air. With deadly accuracy it was embedded in the tree.

The girl shuddered. "You would have killed him."

"I trust so," said Heritage in his direct fashion, "for had he been an enemy he would have desired our scalps and it is ever better to strike first."

He recovered his weapon, and resumed his task of filling in the fireplace. The girl watched fascinated as he removed all trace of their camp, scattering dead leaves over the surface.

"Was it the savages who taught you to move so stealthily?" she inquired.

Heritage nodded. "I have lived most of my life on the frontier," he said, "where a false step in the woods would bring death. When every tree bole may conceal a lurking savage it teaches a man to learn the craft of the woods."

"You are a strange man; I have never met your like," said the girl. "What are you called?"

For a moment Heritage was silent. Then he smiled. "The Mohawks called me The-Wolf-who-walks-by-Night," said he.

"I am no Mohawk; what may I call you?"

"My name is John Heritage," said he. "Suppose you tell me your name, and how it comes you travel unattended in these perilous days."

"My name is Maelys Wynn," said she, "and I do not travel alone from choice. My home is in Wales, near the old sea-town of Conway, but for some years I have dwelt in London with my Uncle, Sir Richard Wynn, of whom perchance you have heard."

Heritage glanced up quickly. "I have heard he is reported active for the Parliament. Are you, then, of his way of thinking?"

"God forbid," cried the girl vehemently. "I am for our good King and will have no truck with these threadbare cheats. Do you not know that my father, Colonel Hugh Wynn of Bodysgallen, is raising a regiment of Foot for the royal cause? I could not dwell in the city during this great sedition, so I ran away from my Puritan uncle. I went to London to learn the ways of the Court, but London now—ah!" She shuddered. "The prentice boys are wild: the trained bands are mustered: the Court is fled. Last winter they tore the robes off the Archbishop's back at Westminster when he withstood the mob. His Grace is kinsman of mine and has ever been good to me, for it is widely known that he is given to devoting most of his revenues to charitable deeds. Knowing he was in Yorkshire, whither he came to the King in defiance of both Houses, I set forth to join him, taking with me three men-servants. But one fell ill and the others deserted on the way, so I must needs finish the journey as best I might. Thus was I in sore plight when you came to my succour."

Heritage smiled a little sadly, and turned away.

A scream from the girl made him wheel. From out the brushwood at her feet slid a viper. With quick understanding Heritage stamped his left foot on the creature's neck an inch below the head, and bringing his right heel on the ugly skull he ground it to pulp. He caught the thrashing tail and flung the reptile's body into the undergrowth. "I have torn my boot," he complained. "I forgot I wore spurs."

But the girl stood with her face hidden in her hands. "Oh !" she moaned. "Oh !"

"You are not harmed ?" Heritage grew concerned.

"Thanks be to you I am safe, but it might have bitten you."

"Oh, 'tis simple enough when you know the way of it ! I have killed many thus in the bush," he said indifferently.

But the girl was unnerved and great shudders shook her frame. She clung to his arm, trembling. Presently she grew calmer. "You will think me a coward," said she with a wan smile.

"Not so. I have already seen you carry yourself well. I could desire no better comrade."

"You are generous—after my weakness. I never could abide a snake. Methinks it is a dread bequeathed all women by Mother Eve."

"Most of us have some particular fear."

The girl glanced up. "You can have none."

"On the contrary, dear lady, I have a fear which is like a living death to me—the fear of being shut in. It cometh, I suppose, from dwelling all my life in the open. Danger I can face as well as most men if I have God's good sky above me and the homely earth beneath my feet, but confine me within walls and my spirit wilteth. I am ill at ease in the streets of a town : I can scarce enter a cottage parlour without casting round for means of escape lest I be trapped. But come, comrade, let us not talk of fears, but rather of the brave road of adventure which lies before us."

He picked up saddle and blanket and strode down the gully. To her astonishment the girl saw a second animal. A sorry nag was hanging its head modestly beside Heritage's noble black. "I told you I had improved the morning hours," he laughed at her astonishment. "I went foraging for hay, and brought a mount for you as well—though I take no pride in his appearance."

He harnessed the nag for the girl, contenting himself with a rope and blanket for his horse. Cautiously he surveyed the landscape ere he allowed the girl to ride from cover. It was in this manner they passed onward, Heritage constantly seeking for signs of the enemy. At a fork of the road he gave a pleased laugh. "There go the tracks of the Parliamenteers," he cried. "The Archbishop's party turned this way and the enemy have missed them in the dark. Come, we can ride with greater ease now." They pressed on with lighter hearts until Heritage abruptly pulled the girl into a side lane. Dismounting, he sternly bade her stay with the horses. Noiselessly, he crept around a corner of the hedge. For some minutes the girl sat patiently. Then she grew restless, then curious. Tethering the animals she slowly followed Heritage's way. Down the road she came upon him standing deep in thought. His back was towards her, but though she trod softly, he heard her and turned swiftly.

C

"I bade you remain with the horses!"

His tone displeased her. "I go where I choose," said she, tossing her head. "I am no trooper to be ordered as you please."

"So long as you are under my care you will do as I bid."

She pouted. "I was curious."

"Then gratify your curiosity." Heritage stepped aside. There in the ditch lay a dead man, a Cavalier by his garb, little more than a youth, his face marble, his love-locks matted with blood.

Maelys would have withdrawn in horror, but Heritage would have none of it.

"I had wished to spare you the unloveliness of such a sight," he said, "but you chose to disobey me. I could tell by the signs there had been a skirmish, and it was in my mind to preserve you from this. But it is better as it is, for red war is in the land and the sooner you accustom your eyes to such sights, the stronger you will be. The time may come when you will be called to tend those you love when they are brought home maimed."

The girl turned away her head, but Heritage was adamant. "No, you shall face this. No faltering. Say to yourself—here lies a gallant lad who died for the cause he held dear. Honour him for so doing and pray that our ends may be as worthy."

She stepped resolutely forward. "You are right," said she bravely. "I am a soldier's daughter."

Maelys plucked a handful of late meadow-sweet and laid it on the stained tunic. "Poor lad," she breathed. She turned proudly. "I thank you, Captain Heritage, for teaching me my duty. Have you further—orders?"

"Return to the horses."

Without a word she obeyed. When Heritage rejoined her, Maelys noticed he carried a bridle and saddle for the spare horse. She noticed, too, that a feather now curled in his hat, and that a silken scarf was wound around his waist.

"Fine feathers make fine birds," she scoffed, though her face was still pale.

"I doubt if they become me," quoth Heritage. "I was never meant for a popinjay, yet one must needs follow fashion. If I had not had them, some other would."

"Tell me," the girl interposed, "how could you tell there had been a skirmish?"

"Why, it is plain enough. A pistol ball has furrowed the bark of that hedge-row ash. A broken sword-point lies in the mud of yonder rut. The ground is trampled; there lies a trail of blood; a gap in the hedge shows threads of clothing where men broke hastily through."

The girl looked around her. "It is so apparent when you make it clear: I never before met your like."

"Because I read as I run? 'Tis but a matter of up-bringing. On the frontier one learned to read signs or else he never returned to the settlements. I am less quick in other matters."

"Meaning?"

"I have no knowledge of the way of a man with a maid. I spoke to you harshly——"

"Ah, but you were right. It was I who was wrong. I disobeyed you—to whom I owe so much."

"My desire is to protect you," he said awkwardly. "If I am blunt of speech, I pray you set it down to my forest training."

She held out her hand with charming frankness, laying it upon his. He stared at the slender white fingers, so unlike his own great sunburned fist.

With a quick gesture he raised her fingers and clumsily brushed them with his lips.

Maelys laughed mischievously. "Are these your forest manners?" she cried coyly.

But Heritage, ashamed of his emotion, had spurred forward, blushing like a boy.

CHAPTER FOUR

AT noon they dined off food purchased in a hamlet. Near a wayside glade they sat in a welcome patch of sunlight, resting while the horses cropped the moist grass. Said Heritage: "We shall come upon the royal camp ere long."

The girl paused in her eating to look about her. "And now, pray, what signs are there for you to read?"

With a wave of the hand Heritage indicated the meadows. "Saving the grass, what is there that you can see?"

Maelys puckered her brows. Presently she said: "I see nothing."

"There is nothing to see," he agreed. "Not a cow; not a sheep; not a horse; yet it is good pasture land. You saw the farm we passed not long since? Not a hen scratched in the rickyard. See yonder cottage. There is not an apple left on the orchard trees, and from here you can see the white wood where the boughs were broken by those who gathered the fruit. There has been foraging all about here. An army is not far away, and it must be the King's for he is moving southward."

"It is all so plain when you explain it. I am ashamed of my ignorance."

"You are not ignorant. You have read other books: I have read the book of nature. Soon you will be safe with the Archbishop, dwelling among people whose tongue you understand, and I . . ." He paused and glanced down at her.

"And you will be rid of an unwelcome encumbrance?"

"I did not say so."

"But you think it."

"If you are an encumbrance, I do not find you unwelcome."

"So I am an encumbrance!" She pouted. "You say what you think."

"It was ever a way of mine. Is it wrong to speak thus to women? I am forest reared and have no taste for pretty tricks of speech."

"When a woman is comely she would fain be told so," said Maelys casting down her eyes. "So fair speech is not unwelcome to her ears on occasion. At least, so I gather. Being myself so plain and ill-featured it is not to be surprised that you should find in my face nothing worthy of commendation."

"Are you in truth uncomely? I thought I had never before beheld so fair a face."

The lady smiled contentedly.

"But then," went on Heritage, "I have no experience in such matters and my judgment may be at fault."

Maelys stamped her foot. "You spoil all. First you please me; then, in your next breath, you forgo all you have won. Is this your forest breeding?"

"Perchance it is. Little have I seen of women save the squaws and the wives of the settlers, who set more store on a woman who can cook, hoe the corn and load a musket than she who is set on pretty looks and foolish toys."

"Then I would have found greater favour in your eyes had I been a squaw?"

"You would have been more useful; for then you would have saddled the horses while I smoked and took my ease."

She was on her feet in an instant. "That I can do," she cried, but Heritage's great hand held her in a vice. "I did but chaff," said he smiling down on her.

So he saddled the horses and they rode in silence

until they reached the top of a rise. Heritage drew rein and pointed. The fields below were white with tents and gay with banners. There were hutments and waggons and horses, and in the centre of all a great canvas pavilion above which drooped the heavy silken folds of the royal standard.

Said Heritage : "I have brought you to the King."

The girl sat motionless, spell-bound.

"We part here," said Heritage abruptly. "Adieu, Comrade."

Maelys forgot the camp. "You are not going?" she cried hastily. "You will not leave me?"

"My service is ended," said Heritage soberly.

"But—I—the Archbishop may not be in the camp."

"It matters not. You will be among those who will be kind to you."

"Some—may—be—too kind."

Heritage recalled their meeting at Cawood. He shrugged his shoulders. "It would seem my responsibility is not yet ended," said he. "Come."

They rode down the hill. At a field gate a sentinel challenged them. The name of the Archbishop sufficed. Thus the wanderers came into the royal camp, but reached it a full six hours behind the Archbishop's party. The girl gazed about her in wonderment. It was a scene the like of which she had never seen before—the horse-quarters, gun-parks, waggon-lines. The companies of men at pike drill ; musketeers with matchlock and rest ; artillery tracks in the soft turf ; smell of trampled grass ; smoke from cooking-fires ; bright banners ; drum-tap ; trumpet-call, in one bewildering medley.

"Is it not a goodly sight?" she breathed, awed.

"This?" Heritage looked scornful. "It is miserable confusion. No discipline, no order. Why were we allowed to reach the hill-top without challenge from a vidette? See those oafs watering their horses in the only drinking water available. The noon meal is not yet cooked because no one thought to protect the firewood from the night's rain. The officers look brave in their plumes, but many of the men have had no shelter from the storm. The camp is pitched on a level plain and lies open to enemy attack. A daring raider could swoop down and carry off the King with nothing to prevent——"

"Oh!" gasped Maelys, horrified.

"Nothing to prevent them," continued Heritage grimly, "save the fact that the armies of the Parliament are cursed with even greater bunglers. If there are to be leaders in this war, it would seem we would have to fashion them."

He stopped a passing trooper who was coming from the horse-lines. "You have the cut of a stableman about you. Groom my horse and feed him well."

"Begging your worship's pardon, fodder is scarce——"

"Procure some if you have to steal from the royal quarters," said Heritage tossing the man a coin. "The beast's been overworked and deserves attention. And now, Maelys, I will endeavour to discover his Grace's whereabouts. Remain here where I can find you. Camp's no place for wandering. You comprehend? You are to stay here."

He strode in the direction of the King's banner. The Parliament might have the London trained bands and most of the county militia at their beck and call, but the King had the preponderance of Horse. Noblemen, squires, young men of good breeding, rallied to the royal cause, bringing with them the choicest horse-flesh in the shires. They were served, too, by retainers reared in sporting life.

His Majesty finding York too northerly for his purpose was moving nearer Oxford, beating his drums for volunteers. "King Charles his coming to York was not a progress of delight", comments the old Chronicler. There were some who showed no forwardness in respond-

ing to their Sovereign's call. Yet he had been
joined by many men of title, as the group which clustered near the royal pavilion testified. Wilmot was
there, intimate and trusted until his quarrel with
Prince Rupert made a rift in the royal council. Lord
Capel, his generous heart only equalled by his in-
eptitude as a soldier. Sir Jacob Astley—he of the
famous prayer before Newbury. Sir John Byron,
soon to be the first Lord Byron, one of the seven
brothers who came out of Lancashire to serve the King.

Heritage turned at an outburst from a sturdy,
choleric man who fumed at the fringes of the group.
"Why am I kept waiting by this priest who thinks
himself a soldier ? It is not right, I say, that I, who
have raised a regiment of Foot in Caernarvonshire, be
slighted thus. I tell you I am as good a man as John
Williams for all his mitre."

"How now, John Owen, what has soured you, old
fire-eater ? I thought his Grace was countryman of
thine !"

The speaker, a tall, swarthy, handsome man in his
early twenties, attracted instant attention by his
lavish apparel and haughty mien. Though he had not
been long on English soil, Prince Rupert was known to
all. Three years' captivity in Linz had paled his
cheek, but fired his martial ardour. As yet his baneful
influence on the royal cause was not suspected.
Terrible as a cavalry leader, his insolence and indis-
cretion were to undo all his valour achieved. As he
spoke, he stooped to caress his white dog Boye, his
constant companion even in exile. Colonel John
Owen raised his plumed hat but stood his ground.

"My countryman and neighbour, your Highness,"
he agreed, "but I take no pride in it. I am no neutral
of spaniel blood who will fawn as much upon a stranger
as upon their master."

"Do you question his loyalty ?" asked the Prince
sharply.

"I find no good in him," returned Colonel Owen. "Every day he grows more imperious and I have great hatred of his person and behaviour. I care not who knows it."

Prince Rupert laughed. Lack of respect for the Archbishop did not come amiss to his nature, for his Grace had more than once shown moderation in his views, and moderation was abhorrent to the German prince.

"Spare him, honest John, for the present ; there will be strife enough ere long for you valiant Welshmen without your falling out among yourselves. Wales is loyal, I hear."

"Staunch to the crown to the last man, your Highness. We would fight for it, an it did but hang on a hawthorn hedge."

A sharp command from the officer of the guard at the royal tent caused all conversation to cease. Halberdiers stiffened and officers raised their hilts to their lips. King Charles emerged. Calm of face he passed between the lines of saluting soldiers. Dressed in black velvet, the blue riband of the Garter brightly adorning his breast, he drew all men's eyes to him. Lack of stature was forgotten in the regality of his bearing. No king in history knew better than Charles how to look a king. It was a subject in which he was well versed. Behind him walked the Archbishop, hat in hand. Charles turned with a smile. "My Lord," said the King, "I commend you that you are no whit daunted with your disasters."

"I am a true Welshman, your Majesty," returned the Archbishop, "and they are observed never to run away until their general do first forsake them. No fear of my flinching whilst your Majesty doth countenance the cause."

"Yet you would forsake us and return to your native land, my Lord ?"

"It is not forsaking, your Majesty, but removing

whither I can the better serve your Majesty's interests, for the folk of Caernarvonshire are my own kith and kin, and will more readily harken unto me than to one who is a stranger to their ways and customs."

"Then God speed your Grace. Here is our seal manual for your safe passage. We thank you for the tender care you have shown in the advancement of our service, which we shall remember to your advantage. We pray you will in no wise abate your exertions. Adieu."

So the Archbishop took leave, "upon his bended knee, with tears running down his cheeks, and hearty prayers for his Majesty".

The King was not unmoved.

Muttered Colonel John Owen: "A few more sobs and slobbers will gain him the see of Canterbury."

Heritage overheard. "What we have just looked upon would arouse a feeling of reverence in the hearts of all men of decency," said he coldly.

The red blood rushed to Colonel Owen's face and his fingers twitched his sword belt. "You are insolent," he cried and paused. He found himself looking up at a massive figure which towered above him ; into eyes which held a steely intensity.

"It may be that I err," went on Heritage calmly, "but to me it seems becoming to the head of the Church to pray for his King's safety—even as the King's presence should be immune from brawling."

Colonel Owen breathed deeply. "You thrust in where you are not wanted," said he with an effort. "But what you say is truth—this is no place for going farther into the matter. As for that threadbare cheat, let him look to himself. The day will come when John Owen will put him where he belongs. At Ruthin free school he is not held so much greater than I ; and some day I will break his proud overweening spirit. If you be friend of his, say so to him from me."

And he stalked away, followed by his comrades.

"Lord, he's as full of anger as his buttons will endure," cried a voice at Heritage's elbow, and glancing down he looked into the merry eyes of a young Cavalier —eyes which somehow seemed vaguely familiar. "Heaven bless thee, Sir Goliath," went on the youth. "You have given him a bone to gnaw which is not to his taste. I am much beholden to you, sir, for his Grace is kinsman of mine and but for you I should have crammed Owen's words down his throat and thereby got myself arrested for *lèse-majesté*." He held out his hand. "Robin Wynn is my name," he said affably, "son of Colonel Hugh Wynn of Bodysgallen."

Heritage bowed and was silent for a moment. Then he said quietly. "I have some respect for his Grace of York."

Young Wynn heaved a prodigious sigh. "Then you are safe from my displeasure. I shall not chastise you. By my hilt, Goliath, had you been three feet nearer earth, I'll warrant John Owen had not been so respectful in the royal presence."

Robin Wynn, a merry youth, chattered gaily. "I came hither with a loyal message from the men of Flint," he said. "Roger Mostyn sent me. He is raising a regiment for the King at Mostyn. And now I am to ride courier for his Majesty. I am but awaiting despatches to Lord Ormond, Governor of Dublin Castle."

"You seem light of heart."

"Should I not be ? I sail from Beaumaris, which is but a stone's throw—albeit a long one—from my own home. Ah, to get back to lovely Wales again, away from drab Yorkshire ! To ride down the peaceful vale of the Conway where I know every farm by name ; to catch salmon in the river ; to hawk on the Ormeshead ; to listen to the surge of the sea ! But see, they summon me. I crave your leave."

He turned to go, but Heritage touched his arm.

"Before you ride from camp, pass by yonder hedge. There may be someone there whom you will be glad to see."

Off hurried the young courier, full of the joy of youth. Heritage retraced his steps. He could now take his charge either to the Archbishop or her brother. His task was accomplished. When he neared the spot where he had left Maelys, the girl was not to be seen. Angrily Heritage turned on the groom. "Where is the lady?"

The man paled before the fierce light in Heritage's eyes. "Your worship—she left—hurriedly—I know not whither."

Heritage was examining the ground for tracks. The heel prints were plainly visible. He followed a few yards, then stopped with a shrug of his shoulders. Why should he trouble further? If the girl persisted in disobeying, let her go her wilful way. He walked to his horse.

"I am most sorry, sir——" began the groom apprehensively, but Heritage interposed cheerily.

"The horse looks better for your attentions, lad," he said pleasantly, tossing a coin.

He vaulted into the saddle and left the camp. Slowly he rode up the hill which he and Maelys descended an hour before.

And his face was as expressionless as that of a Mohawk brave.

CHAPTER FIVE

As Heritage rode soberly to the north-east, the Archbishop with greater gladsomeness turned his dapple-grey to the south-west, whereby it will be seen their ways showed much divergence. His Grace, we are told, left some of his stoutest followers behind him, and kept a slender attendance to carry him to the furthest parts of North Wales. Those who rode in his depleted retinue were old retainers, six in number, with young Holland in charge of the escort. Who can tell what prompted the prelate to ride for Wales? It may be even as he told the King, that he could serve his Majesty better among his own people. At least he made good those words, for in the troubled years which ensued none laboured with greater zeal. But methinks it was a profounder impulse which turned the heart of the fighting prelate, now no longer young, to his native town, the ancient borough of Aberconwy.

It is said that save for one or two fleeting visits, John Williams had not been there since first he forsook the grey walls to climb the heights of power, yet in his heart of hearts he must have cherished a hope some day to return, for twenty years before he had bought himself the stately mansion of Penrhyn House, which lay in its pleasant park beside the Menai Straits near by the old city of Bangor. No, the call of Wales was to him even more profound than his loyalty to the King in his hour of trial. "It was the magnetic attraction of the town wherein he was born that drew him thither," asserts the Chronicler, "and a greater than he, King James, called it a salmon-like instinct to see the place of his breeding. By the circulation of a strange destiny he

45

was carried there in a rapture, or a whirlwind to spend a few years and to end his last days.

"Who", resumed the old writer, warming to his theme, "could better settle the distracted people of Wales than this person, and who did better deserve his help than his own flesh and blood ? He came not so much for refuge as to be a refuge to those true-hearted mountaineers, his kindred and allies. None could be more active in any place that owned the King's authority than he was there, in providing powder and ammunition, in sorting good commanders, in fortifying Conway Castle. So much did Wales gain by what Yorkshire lost."

So let us leave the Archbishop with his slender retinue jogging across the West Riding. Ahead of him on a swifter mount rides Robin Wynn, debonair, carrying despatches by the same route for Dublin Castle.

There were other riders following with John Owen's badge in their hats, but they kept from sight.

Meanwhile Heritage had his back to all these happenings. He had not ridden a league when he became conscious that far on the road behind him came a mounted man. Now Heritage was not of the disposition to rest content with an unknown horseman in his rear, so when he came to a convenient wood he hid his horse amid the trees and drew nigh to the roadway to lie in wait. The rider was slow of approach.

Presently Heritage stepped boldly into the road. The girl Maelys reined in with a cry of apprehension which turned to one of delight. "I've found you ; thank God I've found you !" Heritage noted she looked worn and anxious, but he did not unbend.

"You had found me with less pains had you remained in the spot wherein I set you," said he curtly.

She ignored the reproof. "I want you to take me to the Archbishop——" she began.

"Lord, save us !" cried Heritage with a mighty sigh.

"Madam," he resumed stiffly, "let me assure you that you possess qualities I admire. You have determination, resolution, pertinacity. Doubtless they will bear you far along the trail of life, but let me say unto you that I am no child to play hide-go-seek with. Find your Archbishop as you will, I'll be the fool of no woman's whims."

Her lip drooped. "You are—uncouth."

"Put it down to my forest manners," said he, turning away. "Get back to your camp and leave me to go my way."

The girl laid a detaining hand on his arm. "You think hardly of me—you have a right to—yet be not angry with me. I did not leave you to disobey you. Harken, and say if I did wrong. Some men passed me. They were angry, and because they spoke in Welsh they did not lower their voices. I was born in Wales and the years in London have not made me forget the tongue of Wales. They were plotting to bring about the Archbishop's downfall. They reviled him, saying he was no better than a Puritan because he withstood Laud and pleaded with the King to come to terms with the Parliament and not plunge the country into intestine war. They were all gall and jealousy. Let any tree grow tall in favour and the shrubs will complain. One swore horribly, saying his Grace was traitor at heart and would betray the King his trust."

"That sounds like John Owen."

The girl raised her brows. "It was Colonel Owen of Cleneney. How could you guess?"

"Go on with your story."

"I heard them say they would follow the Archbishop's party to the Cheshire borders, where there is strong sentiment for the Parliament, and there drive him into the hands of the Roundheads. If he is thrown into the Tower again it will kill him, for already his privations there have sapped his strength. Therefore, I entreat you ride with me to warn him."

"Madam, I have already proved that I have no ill will towards his Grace, but I have work to do. I have acted as I have done because I have heard it said that the Archbishop would have prevented this strife had but the King taken heed to his counsel." He stood thoughtfully regarding the pleading girl. A smile came to his eyes. "I have also heard it said that as clay is in the hands of the potter, so is a man in the hands of a maid."

And fetching his horse he turned its head once more towards the King's encampment.

.   .   .   .   .

Heritage pulled up so abruptly that Maelys, dozing from weariness in the saddle, all but collided with him.

"What is it now?" she asked dully, casting a glance about her. The weather had broken. For several days they had ridden through rain and cold, over the Pennines, across the flat plains of Cheshire, and they were now on a lonely moorland road which crossed the Welsh uplands. But for Heritage the girl would have fainted by the way, but he was ever steadfast, ever considerate, ever watchful. Thanks to him they evaded the skirmish when Holland and five troopers barricaded the road and held back a company of Roundhead infantry while the Archbishop and one retainer made good their escape. But for his skill the track would have been lost, but with unerring instinct he cast round until he found the direction the fugitives had taken. Now he sat staring at the mud.

"The Archbishop is ill or wounded," he said.

Wearily the girl looked at the ground.

"The grey turned into the lane which leads to yonder hall. A coach came out recently, drawn by farm horses. The grey has been left in yonder stables. Let us see the reason."

They rode up to the house, which belonged to the squire of the hamlet through which they had recently passed. The good lady welcomed them. It was true the Archbishop was ill ; not dangerously ill. An ague. He insisted on resuming his journey. Her men-folk had ridden to join the King and taken all saddle horses with them, but she had loaned his Grace a coach on seeing the King's sign manual, and also given him such farm horses as could be found. She would willingly have provided his Grace entertainment but he was eager to press forward.

"He is not easily vanquished," said Maelys.

"But you must enter and rest, my dear, your strength fails you," cried the châtelaine with impulsive generosity, but Maelys was unwilling.

"I must overtake him, the more so if he is ill. If you would aid me, I pray you get me his horse, for the wretched hack I ride is nigh foundered."

Thus they pressed on. Maelys endured in silence, but Heritage's vigilance never abated, his roving eyes were never still. Presently he said : "There is mischief afoot. Horsemen are following the coach. Ah, wait ! There is a watcher in the woods ahead. Pull into the shelter of this coppice as though we sought shelter."

He dropped from his saddle, slipped his swordbelt over his head and placed cloak and hat upon the hilt. Bidding the girl hold the hat so that it was just visible to the sentry, Heritage slipped noiselessly into the undergrowth. Maelys waited, her weariness forgotten, every nerve alert.

Heritage came creeping back, soaking from the wet grass, but well pleased with himself. "I have him safely trussed. Owen's men have held up the coach. They are not far ahead. Ride gently to the wood ; then stop, for we must see the pistols are primed. Can you fire a pistol ?"

The girl nodded. "I fear I do not aim straight. Robin tells me the only way I could hit a barn would be to go within and shut the door."

D

"Robin ?"

"My brother. He has ridden to join the King, I hear."

At the wood they drew rein. Heritage loaded the pistols with care and bade the girl keep them covered from the rain. He beckoned her to look from cover. Down the roadway, which was lined by walls of loose stone, stood the coach and about it clustered the horsemen, six in number. One held a pistol to the coachman's head ; another on foot was opening the door.

"A pick-purse trick," said Heritage loosening his sword. "It will be warm work, but I have the advantage of a shock charge."

She put out a hand to detain him, but he brushed her aside. "Take your pistols and creep behind the stone fence. When I ride forth, not before, fire at the rear horses. You ought not to slay the Archbishop at that range."

Heritage watched the girl take up her post. He flung aside his cloak, gripped his saddle with his knees, took a pistol in either hand and guided his horse into the roadway. The great black brute leaped forward.

"Bang! Bang!" from Maelys's pistols, and the clustered horses began to rear.

"Crack! Crack!" Heritage's weapons with deadlier aim brought two riders to the earth.

His hand swept above his head. The tomahawk whirled through the air and the man beside the door dropped with the bright blade in his skull. Out came Heritage's long sword and he rushed into the mêlée. Down went a horse at the shock of his charge, and he ran a trooper through the back as he passed. The black was reined on its haunches and plunged back into the fight. The two men who remained were fighters and closed on Heritage from either side. He was hard put, but would have held his own had not one of the fallen horses, lashing out in death agony, brought down the black. Heritage was thrown over its head, losing his sword and striking the ground with terrific violence. One of the men flung himself upon his prostrate form, but agile as a fighting cat Heritage wriggled clear and caught the man's throat in his terrible grip. But the second man had his sword point poised. There came an unexpected explosion and the man fell a crumpled heap in the mire.

Maelys dropped a smoking pistol and burst into tears. Heritage cast the limp body from him and sprang clear. Whipping up his terrible sword he stood at bay. But there was no need for further effort. He was the only man on his feet.

CHAPTER SIX

IT was a strange scene. The coach jammed against the wall ; the patient farm horses stoically accepting the untoward events as part of their day's work. Frightened riderless horses backing up the roadway. Groaning men in the mire ; a weeping girl and, dominating all, the mud-stained, blood-stained giant towering triumphant, sword in hand.

But Heritage had no time to spare for heroics. There were weapons to collect, horses to catch, wounds to bind. He busied himself while Maelys sought solace in the bishop's arms.

When Maelys emerged from the coach she saw no sign of Heritage. Evans, the coachman, pointed to the wood. Maelys found there a strange spectacle : a man bound to a tree with a tomahawk embedded beside his cheek ; Heritage standing a few paces off with knife poised. He turned at Maelys's startled exclamation. "Go back !" he said curtly.

"You shall not kill him," she cried. "Is your blood-lust not satiated yet ?"

"I am no Mohawk," said Heritage, "I do but reason with him." The girl demurred. Suddenly Heritage thrust out a sheathed sword. "Do you recognize that ?" he asked curtly. The girl stared—a cry of amazement burst from her lips.

"It hath our crest on it."

"Not many days since I noticed it in the belt of a young man for whom I conceived some affection. His name, it may interest you, was Robin Wynn. I am curious to learn how it came into this man's possession. Now will you return to the coach and let me resume

my—questioning? When this rogue tells me where
your brother lies, I will bring Robin to you."

Maelys, trembling, obeyed. By and by she saw
Heritage returning with the young Cavalier in his
arms. Despite a wounded thigh, Robin was in
irrepressible spirits, and laughed at his sister's tears.
Heritage closed the coach-door on the tender reunion.
He had other matters to think about. Rain was
falling again, turning the upland roads into a quagmire,
and the day was far spent. With only Evans to help
him he had to care for an ailing bishop, a wounded man,
and a weary maid.

"Drive!" he ordered Evans curtly, and the heavy
wheels revolved. Herding the captured horses before
him, Heritage rode with head erect defying the elements. Rain whipped the colour to his sunburnt
cheeks. He stared forward with proud disdain for
discomfort. It was a dreary road. The stone walling
ended, giving place to broad stretches of short cropped
grass, relieved by an occasional tuft of stunted gorse or
some grey boulder rounded by many rains. No
human habitation was visible. In the distance, dimly
discernible through the rain mist, the bold peaks of
the Caernarvonshire mountains thrust their bald
summits into the low clouds. "The West of Denbighshire is cold, hungry mountains, and ill inhabited",
laments a traveller of the period, and so Heritage found
it. The same writer later added, "But in the valley of
the river, the country is very pleasant, sweet, healthy,
and most fruitfull". But there were no signs of this
delectable land as yet.

For an hour the coach lurched monotonously forward.
There was no sound other than the resistance of mud to
wheels and hooves. The sufferings of the occupants,
jolted within the confines of the vehicle, could have
been little less than of those exposed to the elements.
At times Maelys would draw aside the leather curtain
which covered the upper door-frame in lieu of glass, to

gaze forth at Heritage. There was about him a
suggestion of steadfastness which communicated to
her the will to endure. Now that the loose horses had
accepted the way with docility, Heritage had dropped
back to ride beside the coach. Presently he bent from
the saddle as a slim white hand beckoned.

"His Grace is ill." At Maelys's words, he halted and
flung open the door. He found the prelate had
collapsed. Hastily he forced some cordial between
the pallid lips and chafed the white hands anxiously.
The Archbishop, who had hitherto borne his sixty years
with buoyant ease, looked suddenly aged. Those long
months in the Tower, and the strain of the Great
Rebellion, had told their tale. The spirit still was
willing, but the flesh grew weak.

"I—thank you. I—am—myself again. A slight
indisposition ; pray do not stop. It is the cold, I
think. The damp of River Thames seemeth to be in
my very bones."

"We will press forward, sir," said Heritage in an
expressionless voice.

"I would not add to your troubles, Goliath," said
young Wynn faintly, "but I think this wound hath
broken out . . ."

A touch revealed the truth ; the youth's jerkin and
breeches were moist with blood. "Don't sit staring,"
said Heritage curtly to Maelys. "Rip me some
bandages from your petticoat." With the ease of one
familiar to wounds, he placed a fresh pad on the injury
and bandaged it tightly afresh.

"He cannot endure this jolting ; neither can the
Archbishop," whispered Maelys.

"They will have to endure it !" Heritage shut the
door to find Evans at his shoulder.

"The nags is nigh foundered, sir."

"Turn them loose and help me harness the best of
the saddle horses."

"They'll be strange to the work, your worship."

"Then we'll accustom them. Haste!" The saddle horses fretted somewhat at their new role, but they were cowed by the elements, and Heritage was not in a mood to stand nonsense.

"Drive!" he ordered Evans, and himself rode beside the leaders.

They sighted trees, not a scattered clump but a dense mass, and Heritage took heart. They were reaching fertile land. The ground began to slope. Soon they would reach the valley; already the air seemed milder.

"Where is the nearest shelter?" Heritage asked the trooper. "We cannot make Conway this day."

" 'Tis but a couple of leagues to Gwydir Castle where dwell kinsfolk of his Grace, sir."

"Then forward, for God's sake, for both men are sorely in need of attention."

Familiar surroundings gave new life to Evans, and even the sufferers within the coach found fresh hope as they descended the hill. Through the leaves they caught glimpses of the river, in spate from the heavy rains, cascading over mossy boulders.

Dusk had fallen when the weary horses came down the winding, tree-fringed road which led to the gates of Lower Gwydir. As they drew into the curve before the main gate, a dog set up a barking, and a face peered from the tiny look-out window beside the gateway. Heritage barely glanced at the broad arch of carved sandstone, topped by a heraldic lion beneath which the carved "I.W." and the date 1555 recalled the great John Wynne who built the mansion in Elizabeth's day on the site of the ancient home of kings. His vigorous pull set the bell a-ringing and he hastened matters by rapping on the great doors with his sword hilt. The postern was opened and a frightened porter looked forth. "Fling wide the gates, his Grace of York is here, and is ailing!"

"Open, Caradoc, all's well. You remember me?" cried Maelys, hurrying from the coach. Lights were

twinkling. The sound of hurrying feet mingled with
the barking of dogs. The iron bars swung up, the
great gates creaked open, and Maelys with a cry of
delight ran into the courtyard.

"Gwydir, lovely Gwydir," murmured the prelate as
he essayed to remove his cramped limbs from the
coach. "I come among mine own people at last."

It may have been weakness; it may have been
emotion which overtook him : he would have fallen but
for Heritage's strong hand.

Instantly Heritage gathered the old man in his arms.
"Set me down," ordered the Archbishop indignantly.
"Plague take you, I will not be treated like a sick maid !
Set me down, I say !"

But Heritage paid not the slightest heed. He strode
through the entrance, all but colliding with Mr. Owen
Wynn, who came hurrying forth at the disturbance all
agog with excitement. "Your Grace, God bless my
soul. My dear and worthy master and kinsman.
Thrice welcome to Gwydir. I pray you are not ill.
This way, good sir, if you please."

And he guided Heritage to the great hall where a
fire burnt cosily in the wide grate.

Heritage, unceremoniously depositing the prelate on
a settle, stalked out. At his order a groom went
speeding along the straight half-mile to the ancient
town of Llanrwst, seeking a surgeon. Picking up
Robin Wynn, Heritage carried him tenderly into the
courtyard. "Straight to bed, lad, for you—which
way ?"

He bowed his head as he entered the side door,
turned to the worn stone spiral steps in the stair-
tower, and carefully bore the wounded man into one
of the bedchambers, where he looked to his bandage and
left him at ease.

When the tumult subsided, Maelys with gratitude
brimming in her eyes ran forth to render thanks to their
saviour, but Heritage was not to be found.

CHAPTER SEVEN

THE morn dawned joyously. Bright sunlight streamed upon the grey walls of Conway, setting the good folk early astir. Smoke from the chimneys rose straight in the crisp morning air. About the crumbling battlements of the castle jackdaws assiduously searched for their morning meal.

Heritage, rested and refreshed, stood in the doorway of the Black Lion Inn and looked forth complacently on the farmers who were already assembling, for it was market day. Some were already in the yard of the Black Lion, arguing at the weighing machine as to the price of hogs. His bulk filling the low doorway, Heritage looked curiously out of place in the little Elizabethan inn. Not far above his head a flat stone inserted in the wall proclaimed that the dwelling was erected in 1589. The "I.B.—E." which adjoined the date were held to be the initials of John Brickdall, a former vicar, and Em, his wife. Heritage had been glad enough to get a bed there when he rode his weary horse into the town the previous night. He stood in the doorway and pondered. He had ridden far from Yorkshire and had left no word of his intentions. This was not strange, for Heritage was ever given to acting as he thought fit, and restrictions were irksome to his free spirit. He could not make up his mind whether he would return. Slowly he extracted a letter from his pocket and regarded it thoughtfully. The seal, unbroken, bore the royal crest. It was King Charles's despatch to Lord Ormond. Heritage had abstracted it from the person of the man who had taken Robin Wynn captive. In the bustle of the arrival at Gwydir the previous night Heritage had forgotten its existence, and now he was at a loss to know what to do with it. With the courier wounded and the despatch in his possession, he felt an obligation thrust upon him.

A bell tolling in the belfry of the nearby church aroused him from his reverie. "Landlord," cried he, and the host of the Black Lion, who knew a man when he saw one, answered with a promptness he rarely displayed to casual guests.

"You called, sir ?"

"What is the quickest way to Beaumaris ?"

"Why, by water, sir, if the wind be fair. Or if the tide be out, to ride round the headlands and take ferry across the Menai Straits. If the tide be in there is the cliff road around Penmaenmawr headland, but mighty narrow and fearsome it is, and few dare face it save of necessity. Lastly, there is the hill road over the uplands, which is safest of all, but also longest."

Heritage glanced at the sky and noted the drift of the clouds. "I will inquire about a boat ; see that my horse is fed."

He walked down Castle Street, past the stocks at the corner and turned to the low gothic gateway which led to the quay. The gate was open and the portcullis raised. A couple of militiamen lounged on their pikes. Their presence was the only sign Heritage noted that Conway realized there was war in the land. Several boatmen were pushing off in small boats armed with long rakes, for the tide was at the ebb and they were for visiting the mussel-beds. Heritage looked up the river to where it swirled past the small wooded islet nestling under the castle walls ; he looked across the broad expanse of water to the eastern back where the rounded hills above Deganwy still retained a few fragments of the great castle where once kings of North Wales held their Court. He glanced down the river, past the curtain wall which thrust itself into the waters to protect the harbour from sudden attack. Nowhere was there a mast to be seen. The fisherboats, caught in the storm, had taken shelter elsewhere. Heritage turned on his heel and stalked back to the inn.

"There is not a sailing craft in sight," said he. "Saddle my horse. I must see the governor of Beaumaris ere nightfall."

"Begging your worshipful pardon, if it is the Governor you are wishing to see, why, Mr. Bulkeley's own son, Colonel Richard, is even now in town, having ridden over last night to have a word with the gentry at Plas Mawr."

"I will see him. Fetch me my horse. Where is Plas Mawr?"

"It lies but a hundred paces up High Street, your worship. There is no need for your horse——"

"Fetch me my horse."

Heritage settled his score, mounted and rode up the hill to the stately Elizabethan manor which raised its serried gables high above all other roofs in the town. The great hall dominated the town as truly as the castle had once done. It bespoke dignity and power ; from its grey walls its mullioned windows looked with superior calm upon the squat inns and shops which lined the slope of High Street. At the gatehouse he paused, turned to the right and rode to the upper door, where he fastened his horse to an iron ring. In answer to his inquiry the porter informed him that Colonel Bulkeley was dressing for breakfast, and bade Heritage enter and wait. Heritage entered, but was loth to wait. "Inform your master that a messenger from the King is here," he said, "and desires word with Colonel Bulkeley."

The message gave speed to the porter, for though the sober burgesses of Conway paid little heed to the momentous happenings in the land, the retainers of the great houses had caught from their masters something of the fire which was spreading now that war preparations were afoot. He showed Heritage into the

banqueting hall, where the refectory table was laid.
Heritage noted it was set for a goodly number of persons.
The servants who were placing the finishing touches
disappeared into the buttery as he entered, leaving him
alone. He seated himself on one of the fixed seats of
black oak and took stock of the room. It was worthy
of a man's attention. Above the broad hearth of
white stone, in which a newly lit fire crackled, the
ornate plaster overmantel rose to the very ceiling.
Here were the initials of Robert Wynn, the builder of
the mansion. There was no escaping the name of
Wynn, mused Heritage. In the centre was the quartered shield of the Wynns, displaying the three golden
eaglets on a green field which they inherited from Owen
Gwynedd, Prince of North Wales, and the three silver
fleurs-de-lis separated by a sable chevron, arms of the
scarcely less famous Collwyn-ap-Tangno. And sprinkled
freely in the decorative scheme were Tudor roses,
stags' heads, lions' heads, crests of the noble families
to which the Wynns were allied, all emblems picked out
in their proper heraldic tinctures so that the room was
gay with its reds and blues and golds.

The door opened and in bustled Mr. Maurice Wynn,
profuse with apologies. "You are up betimes, sir,"
he cried, "and I offer you pardon for our seeming sloth,
but indeed, we sat deliberating the King's levy until the
early hours and have scarce got the sleep from our eyes.
These are anxious times, sir, as doubtless you know
better than we. Take a chair, I beg you, and join us.
Come, this salmon, fresh from the Conway, should
tempt you."

"I have already broken my fast," said Heritage
quietly. "I desire to deliver a message to Colonel
Bulkeley, who tarries here, I am told, and then I will
away with all speed."

There was the sound of footsteps on the spiral steps
in the stair-tower outside the door and a group of men
came into the room. First, in the sober attire of

citizens, came Alderman William Hookes and Mr. Griffith Williams, nephews of the Archbishop of York ; Mr. Holland of Marle Hall, just across the river ; his next neighbour, Colonel Hugh Wynn of Bodysgallen ; dashing young Roger Mostyn, who was visiting his grandmother the Lady Mary Mostyn at Gloddaeth ; and last, the tall military figure of Colonel Richard Bulkeley.

All seated themselves save Colonel Bulkeley, who approached Heritage. "You desired word with me, sir," said he. "Speak freely ; we are all assembled here on his Majesty's business. I take it you come from the King ?"

Heritage produced the despatch. "The King's messenger who was entrusted with the delivery of this missive to Lord Ormond was set upon and wounded on the way."

Colonel Bulkeley took the letter and examined the seal. It was unbroken. A smear of blood crossed the paper.

"What is your name ; how came you by this ?" he asked abruptly.

"I took it from the man who held the messenger captive. As to my name, it matters not so that my task is performed. I give you this despatch of the King's, its seal unbroken, and bid you see to its delivery."

From without came the sound of a horseman arriving with haste. Mr. Maurice Wynn left the room. The guests paused in their eating to regard the two men who confronted each other.

"If you have carried this despatch this far, why do you not complete your journey to Ireland ?"

"Because I have no desire to do so."

"Those who ride for the King do not consult their own desires," said Colonel Bulkeley sternly.

"Sir," said Heritage. "I have come here at some inconvenience because it seemed a matter which concerned my honour. The missive is in your hands. Deliver it to Lord Ormond or to the devil : it is all one to me."

There was a strained pause. The door burst open and in rushed Mr. Wynn, a letter in his hand.

"News, news, gentlemen ! Hot news. His Grace of York is come to Gwydir. Hugh, your girl is with him, and Robin. Brother Owen writes in haste telling of the adventures which have befallen them, and of the aid rendered by one—Heritage . . ."

He paused. "Surely this is none other ? You are Captain Heritage ? Come, you are too modest, sir. It would seem they all owe their lives to you. When Robin was wounded——"

Colonel Wynn pushed back his chair. "Robin wounded——"

"A pistol ball in the thigh, sir. If the surgeon has had it out by this time, as indeed he ought, the matter should not prove serious," Heritage assured him.

"Gentlemen," cried young Roger Mostyn, leaping to his feet "I'm for Gwydir ! We can finish our business there. There is a story here which is worthy of our hearing more fully. Who will ride with me ?"

"My faith, I must see Robin at once, and that wayward lass of mine," cried Colonel Hugh Wynn. "Parry, saddle my horse at once !"

"And mine" ; "And mine," came a chorus from all but Colonel Bulkeley.

He touched the King's letter. "His Majesty's business comes first with me, my friends," said he. He bowed to Heritage. "The despatch shall be delivered by the first craft to leave Beaumaris."

"You will come to Gwydir with us," cried Colonel Wynn taking Heritage's hand in his. "As a father I am greatly beholden to you, and would learn from their lips what thanks I ought to offer you in full."

"I desire no thanks, sir," said Heritage slowly. "Now that my task is accomplished, all I ask is that I may resume my journey which, in truth, has been interrupted over-much."

"None of this backwardness, sir," cried Mr. Wynn, taking his arm. "You come to Gwydir with us. It would be a blot on the hospitality of the good name of Wynn were we to let you go thus."

So it came about that Heritage, against his will, came to Gwydir again.

CHAPTER EIGHT

On the following morn Heritage arose as soon as the servants were astir. He had slept but ill. Effusiveness was distasteful to him and he had been called upon to undergo much. As an honoured guest he had been overwhelmed by courtly compliment and assiduous attention. September was in a repentant mood. The day dawned with a radiant splendour ; the rains were over and gone ; the sun flooded the level lawns and set the birds twittering amid the trees which profusely surrounded the stately mansion. It brought Heritage out of doors with the dew still pearling the grass. He sauntered to the worn sundial in the centre of the formal garden which adorned the smaller court. His clothes had been furbished overnight and he presented a different aspect from the bespattered traveller of the previous day. He retained his sword, but of knife and tomahawk there was no sign. Crossing to the front of the house he paced the long terrace. The peace of Gwydir entered into his soul ; here was tranquillity. Trim paths wound between aged trees, luring him to the meads which led to the river. In this sequestered seclusion it seemed sacrilege to contemplate war. Heritage leaned his back against the trunk of a massive cedar of Lebanon and stood with folded arms and brooding eyes—thinking.

The tall chimneys of Gwydir rose with stately height against the morning sky. Behind one of the upper windows, Maelys lay sleeping, still fatigued from her privations. Heritage had not set eyes on her since the hour of their arrival.

His reverie was interrupted by the appearance of

Mr. Owen Wynn walking from the river, a brace of spaniels at his heels. He greeted Heritage cordially.

"You are early afield, sir," he cried. "I, too, like the morning hours. Why do men war when all the world is at peace?"

"I suppose it is because peace must be purchased at her own price," replied Heritage.

"Yes, yes. I forgot you are a man of war. After you retired last night, I visited his Grace in his room and heard from his lips something of your prowess. What a terrible warrior you must be!"

Heritage shrugged his shoulders. He was embarrassed. "I had them at a disadvantage—if you mean the rogues who held up the coach, and they were no real soldiers; merely the scum which collects about an army in the hope of finding easy pickings when the carcasses are strewn about. I am glad I have been able to render your niece some assistance in her plight."

"You speak modestly, sir, and I know little of such matters, yet it seems to me you acted with great courage and resourcefulness. But I am, as you gather, a man of peace, having learnt the gentler arts at the feet of no less person than his Grace, in whose household I had the privilege to serve.

"That was in the halcyon days when my good father, Sir John, lived. You have heard of my father, sir? Sir John was all but king of these parts. 'England, Wales and Llanrwst', run the old documents, for our power was such that we were a place apart. You have crossed our bridge, the same which Inigo Jones designed for us? No? It is well worth while your walking there before breakfast. It cost the joint counties a thousand pounds. It was Inigo, too, who designed the chapel which my good brother, Sir Richard, added to the church near ten years ago. There you will see the stone coffin of Llewelyn the Great. You will see, too, the pedigree of the Wynns back to Prince Owain Gwynedd. Pass on to the old town, and there you will

E

find the almshouses which Sir John erected in 1610, and the Free School, part of which he had built also and endowed. But there, I ramble on. I am a man of peace, Captain Heritage, and take interest in these matters. This rebellion is disturbing ; you do not think it will reach us here in this remote spot ?"

"A garrulous man ; proud of his family," thought Heritage, but he answered civilly : "The trouble is bound to spread, sir, and who can foretell where it will extend ?"

"My brother, Sir Richard, last year sent us by way of Chester several horse-loads of muskets, pikes, head-pieces, swords, bows and arrows with which to defend us should times prove bad, but I trust it will not come to pass."

"Sir Richard is a Member of Parliament," said Heritage suddenly. "Are you, then, for the Parliament ?"

"God forbid," said Mr. Wynn hastily. "I am loyal to the King. Yet I desire to obey our Parliament, too. Dear, dear, it is all very disturbing to a man who desires to live in harmony with his neighbours. Captain Heritage, how can one discuss bloodshed on a morn as fair as this ? Is it not better that man should turn from his folly and dwell at peace as I fain would do ?"

"There are others like-minded, sir, but men of arrogance and bigotry drive them to draw the sword to protect those very principles you desire."

The brazen clamour of a gong interrupted them and they turned towards the house. Mr. Wynn led the way chattering. "See this yew, Captain Heritage ; it is reputed three hundred years old. And yonder yew which still shows the marks where it sacrificed boughs to fashion bows. These cedars of Lebanon come from Syria. It is ever the fashion of our family, who are much given to travel, each to bring home with him some tree or shrub from the countries he has visited. There are rare trees at Gwydir."

"You keep waiting men who are sharp set," Colonel Wynn reproved them as they reached the breakfasting-room. "Good morrow, Captain Heritage. I am ever in your debt for your good will to my wayward girl. She is still a-bed but hath benefited much by her rest and sends you greeting. To-morrow you must ride with us to Bodysgallen and there recount to her mother all the adventures which have befallen you. By the way, sir, can I offer you a commission in the regiment of Foot I am raising for his Majesty?"

"I am honoured, sir, but I must decline. I serve in the Horse."

"Come with me," cried young Roger Mostyn, "and I'll see to it that you have a goodly troop."

Colonel Wynn shook his head reprovingly. "Roger, you do but raise a regiment, remember, and not an army. I hear you have over a thousand enrolled already."

"Nigh fifteen hundred ready to join his Majesty when he comes to Chester."

"Is his Majesty coming to Chester, then?"

"I had word only yesterday. The rebels are forward there and his Majesty thinks, and rightly, that his appearance will strengthen the royal cause in those parts."

Colonel Wynn spread some papers before him. "As Dick Bulkeley could not come with us, he passed his papers to me. His father would have come, but is at Baron Hill with the Commissioners of Array discussing the levy and how to set Beaumaris in a defensive state.

"Here is a letter received from Tom Salusbury of Lleweny setting forth that at a meeting of the gentry of the counties of Denbigh and Flint held at Wrexham it was agreed to levy £1500 to raise a regiment of Foot for the King's defence, and desires Bulkeley to spare him a score of lusty fellows. But this is what concerns us most, gentlemen : he bids us keep an eye on

Caernarvonshire, for it is said they bear a malignant aspect and the Puritans brag of a great party here as though they had designs for the Parliament. Know you anything of this?"

Alderman Hookes shook his head. "I dare swear all are loyal in these parts," he said. "There was that trouble with the recusants in Creuddyn last winter, but we rode out from Conway and overawed them, and since then there has been peace among all parties. I have no doubt that the Pughs of Penrhyn will stand by the King."

Heritage stood up. "These matters appear personal, gentlemen. I pray you excuse my presence. I will visit our wounded friend." He moved quietly from the room. Softly he ascended the spiral steps in the stair-tower and entered the bedchamber of Robin Wynn. From the canopied bed, Robin turned his head eagerly. "Welcome, Goliath," he cried, holding out his hand. "Lord, I am glad to have company, for I have slept but ill."

Heritage commiserated with him on his wound, but Robin cried, "I would not have it otherwise. Hitherto I did but play at soldiering, but now I have been fleshed I can bear my sword without it reproaching me."

"Did the surgeon extract the bullet?"

"The bullet, say you? I fondly thought he dug out a cannon-ball with a spade. Ay, 'tis a sweet, clean wound, so he saith, and he should know. It is not my wound which kept me awake. I have been robbed of my despatches, and know not what account to give to his Majesty."

"Set your mind easy on that score. I came upon them when I searched your captor, but in my forgetfulness I bore them to Conway with me, and not knowing I should see you again I bade Colonel Bulkeley undertake their safe delivery. He hath promised to bear them to Dublin as soon as the wind will permit."

"God bless you; you give me new life," cried Robin

wringing his hand. "I feared that in robbing me they were striking at the Archbishop. Was John Owen there ?"

Heritage shook his head. "No, Colonel Owen would not demean himself by undertaking such a task. They were but his paid bravos, and doubtless exceeded their instructions. I take it they recognized you as you rode towards where they were concealed, and fearing you would spoil their plans set upon you and held you hostage."

"You surmise as surely as if you had been present," said Robin. "They had me bound and concealed in a deserted sheepfold when you came to my deliverance."

Heritage rose. "I must pay my respects to his Grace," said he abruptly.

He made his way to the front wing and after tapping on a door waited respectfully until the Archbishop's voice bade him enter. He found the Archbishop flushed but better for a night's repose.

"I trust your Grace is recovering," said he. "I have called, sir, to place in your hands letters which I found on the floor at Cawood."

The Archbishop glanced quickly over the papers. "You add to my obligations. Is there any manner in which I can repay you for your services ?"

"I ask no reward. I have done what I have done because I have heard that your Grace, by wise counsel, endeavoured to persuade the King from taking the extreme step which has plunged the country into war."

"Say, rather, his Majesty has been compelled to protect his honour which was at stake ! For I tell you he hates the rebellion more for the indignity than the danger. Yet it is even as you say. I did, as a Christian, hope that conciliatory measures would prevail, but the King's ears were poisoned by advisers who foresaw their own advancement in the travail of the nation. Why do you ask ?"

"It was because of your Grace's tolerance that you were warned to escape from Cawood. It may be your

Grace's wise counsels will yet be needed by this unhappy nation."

His Grace straightened in his bed. "You speak strangely."

Heritage smiled and moved to the door. "I must not excite your Grace further. May the air of the Conway Valley speedily restore you to perfect health. If I can aid your Grace at any time, pray command me : I am your Grace's obedient servant."

Heritage passed out of the house and across the courtyard. In the stables he found his horse rested and refreshed. The animal had been groomed, the saddlery polished by men well trained in their work. Blanket and riding cloak had been dried and rolled. Heritage ordered his horse to be saddled.

"Is your worship leaving ?" inquired the groom.

"I wish to inspect the bridge and the Wynn Chapel, ere I ride to Abergele," he said.

"It is not a long walk to the bridge, sir."

"I shall ride."

The man said no more. Heritage's tone held finality. The groom touched his hat at the proffered coin and held wide the gates as Heritage slowly took to the road. High above him, banked with trees, rose the historic cliff, famed in song and legend, Carreg-y-Gwalch, "The Rock of the Falcon".

It was a green and lovely world on which Heritage turned his back as he rode slowly down the long, straight road which led to the river. "Gwaed-dir" might mean "The bloody land" ; that morning Gwydir was a land of peace.

At the roadside squatted a low grey stone building and from its border the bridge lifted its graceful arches over the chattering Conway. Beyond the old church on the farther bank clustered the buildings which marked the ancient market town of Llanrwst.

The horse took its own pace. The reins hung loose. The rider was heavy with thought. A clatter of hurrying hoofs sounded. His hand tightened on the reins. Heritage turned.

It was Maelys, bright-eyed, joyous.

"Whither away, Comrade ?" she cried, reining in her mount, a handsome beast borrowed from her uncle's stables. "May I not share your ride this jocund morning ?"

Heritage regarded her fixedly ; wonderment in his eyes. Hitherto he had found her winsome enough, but here was a new Maelys. A night's repose, a sense of security, the gladness of homecoming, had banished her cares as winter's dullness is shed at the coming of spring. Bright-eyed and radiant, she was altogether lovely. The girl was merry as the morn, but her joyousness evoked no response in Heritage.

"Lord," she cried, "you look as doleful as a Puritan. Would you not have me ride with you ? I vow you are not gallant."

"You cannot ride with me further," said Heritage abruptly. "Our ways part here."

Maelys's face lost its gaiety.

"What is it, have I offended you ?" she asked hastily.

"God forbid," he said. "I go back to report for duty. This is no time for dalliance. I have tarried over-long."

"Then tarry longer. We are greatly beholden to you. My father offers you a commission in his regiment ; if that does not suffice I will have his Grace speak to the King on your behalf. Come, I would rest happier if I knew your good sword was at my father's side when he rides forth to chastise those damned Crop-ears."

Heritage smiled grimly. "It may not be," he said.

"Stubborn man. You turn your back on sure advancement."

"I turn my back on happiness." Heritage's voice was expressionless but there was a look in his eyes which brought the colour to Maelys's cheeks. She laid her hand on his arm. "But you are not going yet." She grew reproachful. "You were riding away without a word of farewell! Am I not right?"

"Believe me, it is better thus."

Heritage was staring soberly across the river. The horses rested on the roadside sward. Idlers on the bridge turned curious eyes.

"How rare it is that duty and desire go hand in hand!" said Heritage reflectively.

"You are strange to-day," said the girl looking closely into his face. "I cannot read your mood. Why are you sad when all others are glad?"

But he would not answer her. Instead he put a question. "Have you cause for complaint against me? Have I failed in my care of you in any way?"

"I complain?" The girl was incredulous. "Why, you have been goodness itself. No word can give adequate expression to the gratitude my heart feels for all you have done. In my extremity you were my saviour. You saved the life of my beloved Archbishop; you gave back my dear brother to me. The remembrance of your kindness, your chivalry, will remain in my heart so long as life endureth."

Heritage smiled a little sadly. "I am glad you have not found my forest manners too uncouth," he said. "That you have spared a kind thought for me will abide with me through the dark days ahead. Goodbye, Maelys. We shall never meet again, but I thank God for the brief privilege of serving you." He took her hand in his.

"No, no, you shall not go. Stay with us. There is happiness here in the Conway's lovely vale once our good King hath crushed these accursed Crop-ears. Why must you go?"

Heritage gathered up his reins and touched his horse gently with the spur.

"Because," said he, "I am one of those damned Crop-ears."

CHAPTER NINE

A SOLITARY figure amid the moorland's vast expanse, Heritage lay beside a protecting rock and gazed down into the valley below. His horse, winded by the steepness of the climb, stood some distance behind the skyline regaining its breath.

"He who draws the sword against his sovereign must throw away the scabbard," mused Heritage. He smiled grimly as he looked into the valley. He could see Gwydir's tall chimneys rising with regal dignity amid the trim lawns and trees; the white roads along which weary horsemen were slowly returning. He had easily thrown off the pursuit which followed Maelys's alarm, as with blazing eyes she raced for Gwydir calling for aid. There had been delay in starting, for Heritage, foreseeing the possibility, had slit every girth in the stables while the groom was saddling his horse. He had ridden the road for Abergele, doubled back, forded the river out of sight of Gwydir, and had followed an old track which led to the plateau where the hills above Conway Valley merged into the foothills of the Snowdon Range.

He recalled how the girl had plucked her hand from his as though she touched an unclean thing. She had not spared him with her tongue. A burning loyalist, her gratitude to him was instantly forgotten in the light of the bitter truth. Heritage did not blame her; it was what he had foreseen.

"Come, Satan," cried he, mounting his horse, "there's work ahead of us, lad. Nothing so good as occupation to keep a man from fretting. Faith, you and I must sleep with one eye open, for every man's hand is against us now."

The short-cropped grass was as velvet beneath the hooves of the black. Heritage rode with chin up and a forced smile in his eyes.

It was strange country, treacherous country, with swamps and morasses. Heritage kept his eyes open for the dark green of rushes which showed where water congregated. Here and there were tufts of white cotton grass showing vividly against the gaunt outcroppings of rock which raised themselves like natural fortresses on every hand. Taking his direction by the sun, Heritage rode, not towards the English border, but in the direction of the coast.

At one place where the ground was trampled, he dismounted and stared hard at the tracks. "Cattle," he soliloquized, "though for a moment they had me perplexed. They have shod them for a long journey, Satan. Must be taking them to supply the King's army where it lies at Shrewsbury. We must bear this in mind, old lad, for these drovers are sure to know the quickest way to the border."

When he came to a monstrous upright stone, taller than a man and twice the girth, again he paused. Before it stretched a flat, circular arena. "This must be the Stone of Games ; I have heard him tell of it. We are nearing the place, lad—if the old man still lives."

Heritage regarded the spot with wonderment not unmixed with awe. Was it possible that a bygone civilization once held its sports before this Maen-y-Campau ?

Already the outlines of the hills on the Denbighshire bank were discernible over the mountain's rim. In the hollow of the hills he came across a low, squat church ; the ancient church of Llangelinin. Dismounting, he refreshed himself at a well in one corner of the churchyard. He tried the handle of the heavy door of the church and looked inside. He made no effort to remove his hat and frowned as he noticed the crudely carved altar-rails and the pictures of the saints in the stained-glass window. "Papist idolatory," he muttered. "The writing is on the wall!"

There was writing, too, upon the wall of the church. Above the arch of the eastern window there was painted in faded letters : "Fear God : Honour the King."

Heritage read it in silence ; withdrew ; led his horse to the incline's edge until he came upon a small cottage which blended with the landscape by reason of the natural stone out of which it was built. A dog barked and a man came to the door ; a man grey of hair and beard ; gnarled, wrinkled and brown ; his arms tattooed with strange designs ; gaunt of frame, but showing signs that he had been a stout fellow in his heyday.

Heritage dropped his bridle and strode forward. His roving eyes searched the man.

"Tom Jenkyns ?" he said.

"My name, sir."

"He who sailed with Raleigh ?"

"Ay, ay, I served under that great man ; bless his memory!"

Slowly Heritage drew his knife and laid the broad blade on his palm. "Do you remember this knife ? What memory does it stir ?"

The man stared hard. "Ay, I know it ; I've seen it, somewhere in my travels. Now where ?"

"Do you recall a night twenty years ago ?"

"Dear Lord, how could I ever forget that dread night ? But how came you by it, young sir ?"

"Do you not know me, Tom ? We were side by side that night when we avenged my father——"

The man gave a great cry and caught the giant by his arms, staring into his face. "Your father ? Ay, lad, you have his features. Curse my failing sight that I did not know ye. But what a man you've growed into ! Last word I heard of ye was that ye'd comed back from the Americas and was serving in the Low Country, and I said I should never set eyes on ye again. To think you should have sought out Tom Jenkyns ! To think ye should have found the way !"

"You talked so much about the place when I was a child at your knee that I felt I knew the way. I grew used to finding trails when I dwelt among the savages, Tom. It was always in my mind to seek you if ever I came to this land again, and when, against my desires, this trail led me to Conway I felt the hand of Providence was in it."

"How came you back, young master, if I might so ask ?"

"To strike a blow for the liberties of which we have been robbed. For years I have lived in the hope that justice would prevail ; for years I have prepared myself lest men should resort to arms ; and now the time has come."

"For which party do you stand ?"

"Which ? For the Parliament, the defenders of the people against wickedness in high places. Don't tell me you are for the King ? The Stuart whose father struck off Raleigh's head ?"

The old man looked puzzled. "Why, now you mention it, I did side in my mind with the King, seeing that my lad Watkyn, who is a drover, finds a good market in supplying the royal forces. But one side or the other, what does it mean to an old man who has seen his day and asks but to mind his own affairs for a few years more ? But I'm your man, young master, if only for the love I broe your father. What is the King to a broken sailor ? Who are you but my dead master's offspring ? My life is yours. Ay, ay, this warms my heart. 'Tis like the grand old days back again." And the sturdy veteran turned to conceal the tears which welled to his eyes. "But come inside, sir. My home is yours—humble though it is—but you must lower your head."

Jenkyns attended to the horse and then set about preparing a meal. The room was small. There was no ceiling. The walls stretched upwards until they met the rafters which supported the slated roof. Walls and shelves were plentifully adorned with trophies from foreign parts, souvenirs of the Spanish Main. A hanger, a pike-head and some pistols, all burnished and oiled, showed that the old sailor still preserved the tools of his trade.

Heritage inquired whether Jenkyns still worked.

"An old seafaring man can always turn his hand to odd jobs, master, and what with my boys' earnings I find enough for my humble needs. Is there reason for your asking, sir?"

"Yes. Do you understand masonry?"

"I mend my walls, that is all."

"Get a skilled worker to teach you. The Archbishop of York is coming to hold Conway for the King. He has it in mind to restore the castle, which is ruinous, and he will require masons. You are to labour in the castle—bearing in mind that the captives in the dungeons are likely to be men who suffer for the cause of religious liberty. You comprehend?"

"Ay, ay, sir. I will do as you say; and will the more readily get the work as the lads of fighting age will be required for the wars."

"Another matter. Do you know Mistress Wynn of Bodysgallen?"

"I knew Mistress Maelys, but she has been gone some years."

"She has come back. Watch over her and see to it no harm befalls her."

"What is the danger, sir?"

"I cannot tell, but when red war breaks loose it is an evil time for women. I cannot stay, for I have other work to do. Perchance fortune will bring me back to these parts, but first I must return to Hull. How can I send messages to you?"

"Send them by Watkyn the drover; he passes across the country freely. He is but now started for Shrewsbury to deliver cattle for the King's forces there, else I would bring him to you."

"I will pick up his trail and go to him ; the more so as my way lies eastward."

"Must you go, sir ?" asked the old man, who seemed loath to part with his guest. " 'Tis like having your father back on earth to see him again in your countenance. You have the same masterful way, if I may say so, though, by heaven, you have over-topped him in stature. Lord, there'll never be brave days like those when I sailed the Spanish Main as your father's gunner."

"I cannot stay longer. I left Sir John Hotham a week since with never a word of explanation. Being sent out from Hull on scout work, it came to my ears that the Archbishop's life was in danger from that hotblood Young Hotham, and having some respect for him, even though he be a Bishop, I warned him to flee. Now I go back to face the music."

"Reckon you can take care of yourself, master."

"I've weathered rough storms, Tom. If Young Hotham does not like my ways I'll take my services elsewhere. The Archbishop is too useful a man in the nation's counsels to lose his head because Hotham does not like his tongue. Well, see to my horse, there's a good fellow, while I take to the woods awhile. I must spy out the land ere I return. Yesterday my honour would not let me, for I was a guest. To-day they know my colours ; let them catch me an they can."

With a friendly nod Heritage strode from the cottage and vanished into the thick woods which cloaked the steep sides of the mountain where it sloped to the pleasant vale of Ro Wen.

CHAPTER TEN

SEPTEMBER reached its close. In the morning sunlight a haze hung over river and wall wrapping the ancient town of Conway in its misty light. But the town was bright with colour, and more animated than it had been for many a long year, for that day Colonel Hugh Wynn's regiment of Foot was to march to join the King. During the days that had slipped away since Heritage rode over the high moorlands of Tal-y-Fan on the track of the drovers, events had moved apace. Though no incident of consequence had occurred in Wales it was plain to all that a great battle somewhere in the heart of England was imminent. The King, after raising the royal standard at Nottingham—where a gale blew it down over-night—had drawn westward to Shrewsbury the better to recruit the 5000 Welsh levies he counted upon to strengthen his Foot. Sir John Byron had withdrawn his royalist troopers from Oxford to join the King there. Hither flocked the gentlemen of Cheshire and of Shropshire, magnificently mounted, well armed, ardent in their loyalty.

And now the men of Creuddyn were to rally to their King. Conway was gay with flags. They flew from castle turrets ; they hung from many a window ; they fluttered above the Guildhall, before which a dais stood. In the Castle Square burgesses crowded together gazing curiously at the soldiery assembled in hollow square for the leave-taking.

Already under the eagle eye of the Archbishop of York, now completely restored to health, Conway assumed a different aspect. Gone was its sleepy bewilderment. Guards at every "porth" and at the Castle drawbridge were well accoutred and alert.

Maelys stood in the Castle Square, bright as the September sunshine, in rapt conversation with a young officer who bore his left arm in a sling. It was Lieutenant Holland, the cynosure of all eyes. For he was the first man present who had fought the Roundheads ; the first wounded man to prove to the quiet citizens of Conway that war had begun. To the girl he appeared in the guise of a hero, whose self-denying heroism had enabled her beloved Archbishop to escape his pursuers. For Holland, though wounded and captured in the wayside skirmish, had effected an escape, and his arrival by water from Chester the previous day had set all tongues wagging. Holland was in no wise averse to this admiration. Stealing a glance at Maelys's animated face he found her fair to look upon. Holland was by no means blind to her beauty, neither was he oblivious to the realization that friendship with a kinswoman of the powerful and wealthy prelate was not to be despised.

It was not long before they discovered that he was distantly related to the consequential Hollands of Marle, who dwelt in the manor adjoining Bodysgallen. He had no need to exert himself to make an impression on the girl because her heart warmed to the young Cavalier who had rendered such service to the Archbishop whom she loved like a father. Holland, moreover, was a young man of culture, good to look upon, of pleasant speech and a very civil carriage. Never unmindful of the path of progress, Holland was not slow to reap full measure of the kindness accorded him, though he was too polished a gentleman to reveal too great ardour in the process. Rather, he strove to interest her in the gossip of the outside world, well knowing that the bearer of tidings is ever sure to find a ready ear.

"Would you had been with me in Chester last week to see his Majesty ride into the ancient city, Mistress Wynn," Holland was remarking. "I count myself happy that in escaping thither I did so when his Majesty chose to ride over from Shrewsbury.''

"They say the Parliamentary agents have been busy in the city,'' said Maelys.

"Ay, but they met with scant cheer. Sir William Brereton's town house was broken into by the mob, and others well affected towards the Parliament had their homes looted or their goods confiscated for the royal cause. Yet I owe the Rebels some gratitude, for it was their activity which fetched the King to Chester.''

"You saw the King?'' asked Maelys, her eyes bright.

"I was close beside him when he rode into the city on the evening of the twenty-third, having ridden out from Shrewsbury that morning escorted by two troops of Horse. The Sheriffs and Sheriffs' Peers rode out in scarlet to meet his Majesty with all their trained bands. The companies stood to their arms to entertain his Majesty, and the Mayor and Aldermen were on a platform in Eastgate Street, where the Recorder made a speech, though there was such a shouting for joy I think his Majesty scarce heard him. The following day all persons of the trained bands between sixteen and sixty years of age were summoned to appear before the King on Hoole Heath. I tell you, Chester is loyal.''

"Conway will not lag behind where loyalty is concerned,'' cried Maelys. "His Grace is putting the castle into a defensible state and is raising a troop of Horse for his Majesty.''

"Add that your father, having raised a regiment of Foot, leads them forth this morning,'' said Holland bowing.

A step caused them to turn. Gay in his Cavalier dress came young Robin Wynn, hale save for a limp of which he was more than a trifle proud. His eyes danced with excitement. "The regiment moves off as soon as Father—I mean the Colonel, arrives,'' he cried. "I go to the church to recover the colours from the altar, where they have lain over-night. Have you

F

seen them, Holland ? They are Maelys's own handiwork and never did a girl ply her needle to better
advantage. Look after her, Holland, till we come home
again."

With fond eyes, Maelys watched the gay young
gallant threading his way through the throng. She
turned to Holland almost eagerly to resume the conversation. Truth to tell she found the young soldier's
admiration a salve for her pride, which was sorely
wounded in the remembrance that she had ever shown
interest in Heritage. It annoyed her to find that, try
as she would to resist them, thoughts of Heritage persisted in intruding. Ardent Royalist, she resented
thinking of Heritage even to hate him. Holland,
however, spoke the language she was accustomed to
hear. He belonged to her world. He was like the
other young officers round about, gay in their new
uniforms, proud to be going to the wars. They were
cousins or kinsmen, most of them, for half the great
families of the district were related by marriage ties—
the Mostyns, the Wynns, the Williamses, the Bulkeleys,
Hookses or Hollands.

There was a movement in the crowd. The Mayor
was approaching, his red robes tipped with fur, eclipsed
in colour if not in quality by the Town Crier who pre-
ceded him, inflated by the greatness of the occasion.
In the Mayoral party came Mr. Thomas Bulkeley of
Baron Hill, soon to be created a peer for his services to
the royal cause ; his valiant son, Colonel Richard
Bulkeley, soon to be commandant of Beaumaris Castle.
Many other gentry from the surrounding manors congregated in the old town on that great day.

Richard Owen, who held the rights of the ferry from
the eastern bank, had never plied so brisk a trade.

On the level stretch of sward which lay between the
town walls and the river, the newly raised regiment
was marshalled. All eyes were turned on the river,
where, threading its way between the flag-bedecked

vessels, a barge from the Deganwy shore was bearing the Archbishop of York and Colonel Hugh Wynn.

The dignitaries assembled in the Castle Square paced to and fro, for there was a touch of frost in the air.

"They say," said Alderman Hookes, "that Brereton had his drums beat for volunteers for the Parliament in the market square at Chester and was like to be mobbed for his impudence if the Mayor had not given him shelter."

"I hear," remarked Mr. Holland of Marle, "that the Earl of Essex hath left London for his army, taking with him his coffin and his winding-sheet as a sign he will be faithful unto death to his Parliamentary masters."

But an excited whisper passing from the Porth Isaf or Lower Gate indicated the great moment had arrived. Maelys, on the dais, stood tip-toe and gazed down Castle Street. A fanfare of trumpets rang out, their brazen notes half silenced by the huzzahs which echoed amid the ancient walls. There came the stimulating roll of the side-drums. The rattle merged into a rhythmic tap, mingling with the tune of the fifes. Hats and kerchiefs fluttered in the air.

Around the bend, where Castle Street and High Street join, came the troops, at their head the Archbishop in his sombre suit of black, riding his favourite dapple-grey. Beside him with dancing plume and silken sash of the King's colour of "pale purple" came Colonel Hugh Wynn mounted on a white charger. His drawn sword glittered as he rode between the cheering ranks, head high, proud in the consciousness that he was serving his King. Immediately behind him rode his son, Robin, the pattern of young chivalry, bearing the silken staff-ensign of the new regiment. Maelys felt her heart beat faster at the sight. How she had worked over it, stitching and stitching the heavy silk and gold brocade until her fingers ached and her eyes grew weary! But it was all for the King's cause, and, now that its silken folds floated amid Conway's ancient walls, Maelys felt that it was a banner to be proud of. She had designed it herself, including the Cross of Saint George with the Dragon of Wales, and adding the Tudor rose, and the coat-armour of the Wynns, which displayed three golden eaglets on a green field, "or on vert"; arms of the royal Owain Gwynedd from whom they claimed descent.

Behind the colours marched the drums and fifes and then the new levies, trying to do justice to the occasion. They were a well-set band of young men, but closer examination indicated them ill equipped for battle. Not a pikeman had a corselet; many of the musketeers had no swords; some carried neither pike nor musket, but only pitchforks and cudgels. Yet their spirit was such that it was plain that if the King could not supply them with arms they meant to take them from the foe.

Into the hollow square they marched, the leaders raising their swords in salute as they passed. The Archbishop dismounted and walked with the regal dignity which ever characterized him to the dais, where he was met by the new Vicar of Conway, Parson Hugo Jones, and other clergymen from the surrounding parishes. They followed in the steps of their illustrious countryman as he ascended the platform. The Archbishop raised his hands, and hats were doffed and heads bowed as he offered a prayer for the King's Cause.

"Oyez! Oyez! Oyez!"

The voice of the Town Crier rang out. "Lords and Gentles and good people of Conway, I pray you silence while his Worship the Mayor readeth a proclamation received from his Gracious Majesty King Charles, given under his royal hand at Wrexham to his Commissioners of Peace for this County."

The Mayor stepped forward, scroll in hand.

"Trusty and well-beloved, we greet you well . . ."

The King's familiar salutation rang out on the frosty air.

"Whereas Rebellion is raised against us and forces are marching towards us, which hath already wrought a general distraction throughout this our Realm, to the great disturbance and grievance of all our good and well-affected subjects of whose wealth we are as tender as our own ; we are necessitated for the defence of our person and of this Kingdom and the religion and law established, to use all expedient means for our assistance at this time."

His Majesty referred to the "good affections and forward zeal" of his loving subjects in the Principality of Wales, and of Caernarvonshire in particular, and requested that all moneys raised for the defence of the Kingdom should be paid to Colonel John Owen of Cleneney to enable him to raise companies to bring to the royal standard.

The assembly was awed by this message from the King, but the Archbishop whispered to the Vicar : "Where is John Owen ?"

"Not here, your Grace. I understand he is with the King at Shrewsbury."

The Archbishop frowned, but he said formally : "Mr. Mayor, we look to you to conform to his Majesty's command and furnish Colonel Owen with these moneys."

The Mayor bowed.

At a signal the soldiers presented arms. The ensign was brought to the front by Robin Wynn, who kneeled in the Castle Square while the Archbishop consecrated the colours. Then his Grace addressed the troops, exhorting them with the fiery eloquence for which he was renowned to quit themselves like men and be strong for the King's Majesty. With benediction he terminated the proceedings.

The drums rolled. Words of command rang out. The troops formed. Robin Wynn returned to his post, and his sister, slipping quickly from the dais, ran to where her horse was held by a groom, and galloped to the Porth Uchaf or Upper Gate.

Abandoning the animal she climbed the outer stair to the ramparts. Built high on rising ground, the Upper Gate towers above town and countryside. The girl looked down upon the town with its houses which clustered under the shadow of the castle as though desiring protection or company, leaving the upper parts of the town overgrown with grass. From the shipping anchored in the river came a salute of guns. Maelys's eyes travelled past the drifting smoke to the farther shore where, though concealed from her sight, she knew her stately home lay among its green fields and pleasant woods. It all seemed well worth fighting for.

The drums were sounding in High Street. She could see the colours again, her colours. Nearer and nearer came the marching men. The guard at the gate presented arms. The drawbridge resounded to the tramp of feet. Maelys with a smile in her eyes and a sob in her heart looked down upon her father and her brother as they waved her adieu. Onward marched the column along the road which wound towards the inland hills. The girl waved again and again as the leading horsemen turned to bid her a fond farewell. The rear ranks dimly discernible through the dust cloud were passing over the final rise. She saw the flag raised in a last salute. . . .

Her courage took unto itself wings and she sank sobbing on the old stone stairs.

The town had grown suddenly still. The ships in the river were silent ; the castle artillery had fired its last salute.

The sound of a horse's hoofs aroused her. Maelys glanced quickly down High Street and dried her tears. A solitary rider came, his reins held in his right hand. His left was in a sling. It was Holland. Nimbly she ran down to greet him. "Where are you going ?"

Holland smiled. "To the wars," said he quietly. "I have asked the Archbishop to release me to serve with your father. I could not stay idle when brave blows were being struck."

"But you are not fit ; your wound——"

"My wound will be fit enough ere it is time to fight."

"Take care of Robin," she whispered.

"And your father—if they are not better fitted to care for themselves. Still, I will ever remember that you hold them dear. Adieu, Mistress Wynn."

"God's luck go with you," cried the girl impulsively. In her hand was the scarf with which she had waved her warriors on their way. Quickly she bound it across Holland's breast.

"Wear my favour—and God reward you."

Holland bowed low, looked into her eyes—then rode across the drawbridge in the wake of those who marched from Conway to do battle for their king.

CHAPTER ELEVEN

AUTUMN had finished painting the Vale of Conway. The rich woods of Benarth were losing their golden glory ; every gust sent showers of leaves whirling through the air. Watchmen on the walls of Conway shivered in the October blast and cast anxious glances at the distant mountains over which grey clouds were lowering. And worthy burgesses, comfortable in their great coats, spared a pitying thought for the soldiers on the campaign and breathed a prayer that the strife would be ended ere the winter storms began. Little was said, but one and all were anxious for news. Word had come that the royal army was moving on London, that the Earl of Essex had marched to intercept it and that a clash was inevitable.

Fires roared cosily in the broad hearth of Plas Mawr, which Mr. Wynn had placed at the disposal of the Archbishop while his Grace's house near by was renovated and made more worthy of being an archbishop's palace.

Day by day Maelys visited him, crossing the river from Bodysgallen in the hope of hearing tidings. News was the only thing that mattered. Each traveller arriving by the ferry from the Chester road, every person coming down the valley, was subjected to questioning as soon as he entered by one of the town's three gates.

"Nay, child, no news save that a battle is certain— in Warwick County, I believe," replied the Archbishop patiently in answer to the girl's inevitable question. "I have some gossip, though not the sort you desire. Your Uncle Owen writes from Gwydir that his cousin,

Anne Petrie, desires to sojourn there, being in danger day and night, by the report that young Hotham is coming to Chester. She holds that if he does, he will not be long in marching into this naked country."

"It is well you quitted Cawood," said Maelys, "for he hath followed you nigh across the breadth of England."

"I think this castle of Conway would give a better account of itself than Cawood. I am having it put in repair with expedition. But have no fear, if he cometh loyal hearts will bar his way. Think, girl, every castle in North Wales is held for the King— Hawarden, and Flint, Chirk, Holt, Denbigh, Ruthin, Rhuddlan, Caernarvon, Beaumaris, and this of Conway. It would cool young Hotham's ardour to venture farther."

A bell clanged ; there was a rush of feet ; Parry burst into the room with disregard for ceremony.

"Your Grace ! Your Grace ! A messenger from the battle . . ." and he almost dragged a mud-stained horseman into the apartment.

"The battle fought ?" cried his Grace, forgetting his dignity, while Maelys pressed eagerly forward.

"Yes, your Grace, under the great scarp at Edge Hill. I had been taken prisoner by the Parliamenteers as they advanced and lay in the hamlet of Kineton, where they left their baggage as they pressed forward. I could see much from my window, for the armies were drawn in battle array on the clear ground between us and Edge Hill. It would be two of the clock when the battle started. The King's troops quickly drove back the rebels' forlorn hope, and then, after some exchange of artillery, Prince Rupert charged. Ah, my Lord, those mealy-mouthed dogs cannot withstand our horsemen. His Highness on their left flank and General Wilmot on their right swept through them as though they were stubble. In a few minutes all I could see of their Horse was a few flying stragglers. Then our

lads were among their baggage waggons, reaping the
reward of their courage.   I was soon set free, and being
of these parts and knowing how your Grace desired news
I caught a riderless horse—and there were a-many
going for the taking that afternoon—and rode hither
without sparing spur."

"You did not await the issue, then ?"

"Nay, my Lord.   The Foot were yet at it with push
of pike when I came away, but it was but a matter of
time before we broke the rogues."

"Oh, glorious tidings !" cried Maelys, clapping her
hands.   "Shall I bid them fire a gun from the castle
and set the church bells ringing ?"

"Bide awhile, Maelys," said the Archbishop quietly.
He put some gold coins in the messenger's hand.
"Parry, see that this good man gets proper refreshment."

Maelys, her cheeks flushed, danced gaily to the door,
eager to spread the glad tidings.

"Get you home if you will, child," said his Grace,
"though there is little to comfort your Mother's heart."

"Comfort ?"

"Battles are not gained save by sacrifice."   Then
seeing the girl's face change, the Archbishop added :
"But there, I pray God hath shown compassion to those
you love.   It may not be long before a courier comes
with a full despatch.   When it reaches me I will hoist
a flag on the castle turret if the news contains good
cheer."

And with that the girl had to curb her impatience.
Donning her cloak, she was escorted to the postern gate
where she took the ferry to the eastern bank.   Thence,
by means of horses kept for the convenience of those
dwelling in the great houses near by, she soon reached
Bodysgallen.

The hours dragged ;   darkness fell.   Impatient,
Maelys despatched a groom to Conway, but the man
returned saying no word had been received.   There was
little sleep that night ; excitement, jubilation, appre-

hension alternating in the hearts of the women who rejoiced in the King's victory yet feared the price it might entail. When dawn broke, Maelys climbed the tower, which was the most ancient portion of her home. Bodysgallen is surrounded by luscious woodlands, but through the trees a ride has been cut so that a person standing in a certain position can see across the river to Conway Castle.

A commotion in the forecourt drew Maelys from her watch tower. She crossed the broad oak floor of the hall and opened the front door.

Climbing laboriously the broad stone steps which lead from the stable-court to the terrace, Maelys beheld a strange figure. She stared fascinated, bewildered, scarce recognizing the man, so broken and dejected did he appear. Holland had escaped the edge of the sword. His fine apparel rent, his face pale from suffering and fatigue, a blood-stained bandage about his brows, the man wearily ascended, supporting himself on a long staff from the upper portion of which ran a fringe of jagged silk. At the sight of Maelys, Holland straightened himself and saluted gravely, but there was no smile in his eyes.

Maelys's hot questions concerning the battle died on her lips. "Battles are not gained save by sacrifice !" The Archbishop's words sounded like a knell. The girl ran to Holland's side and guided his staggering footsteps towards a chair. "Thank you—Maelys." Madam Wynn hurried to him with a glass of wine.

"I beg you pardon me," said he with an attempt at his erstwhile courtesy. "I have ridden far and fast. I—came—hither first."

"Your wound ?" cried Madam Wynn, but he waved her aside.

"It will heal," said he wanly ; "what causes me anguish is that I must wound you——"

"Father ? Robin ?"

The questions were shot from agonized lips.

"The Welsh levies were cut to pieces," said Holland slowly. "Colonel Wynn is captured." He was silent.

"And Robin ?" cried both women.

"I am sure Colonel Wynn is safe, for I have spoken to several who saw him led away."

"But Robin, quick, the suspense is killing us."

"I have no good news of Robin. I saw him cut down. As I ran to his aid I, too, was cut down and trampled under foot so that I lost consciousness and only came to when night and weariness brought the strife to a close."

"Is there no word of my boy ?"

"None, Madam. I have searched everywhere."

"You could not find—his—body ?"

"Madam, there were thousands lying in the frost ! I had no hope."

Maelys sat hard-eyed. Her mother was weeping silently.

"I thought it a royal victory. Some liar said Rupert swept all before him," said Maelys dully.

"So Rupert did, but his men stopped for plunder and left our Foot to their fate. Wilmot avoided part of the rebel Horse in his charge ; why I know not ; and while he, too, went plundering, they fell on our flank and wrought our undoing. We fought for hours, but their pikemen were too strong for our ill-equipped lads and we broke and scattered. But it was the charge of their Horse whom Wilmot spared which undid us. And that fool Sir John Byron, who should have stayed in reserve, rode plundering after Rupert. They took our ensign when Robin was struck down. I had all but recovered it when a cornet of their Horse slashed the silk from the staff while another struck me from behind and down I went."

He picked up the staff on which he leant and placed it gently in Maelys's hands.

"I did my best," he said simply.

The girl stared uncomprehendingly at the staff. It

was cut and splintered and stained. She fingered the strip of ragged silk, and something about the fragment touched a cord of memory.

"Why, this is my banner!" she cried. "It is mine ; the one I made ! Is this all that is left ? Oh, they have spoiled my banner. I sewed and sewed until my eyes ached, and it looked so brave when it was finished, and now, it looks—oh—it looks—absurd ! . . .   Oh, so—absurd ! . . . "

And the girl burst into hysterical laughter which was more terrible than tears.

CHAPTER TWELVE

THE crowd, clustering on Conway Quay without the Lower Gate in the drab November twilight, looked across the broad waters of the river to where two merchant vessels were shaking loose their canvas. The watchers could see the seamen on the forecastles taking their places at the capstans, ready to up anchor and take advantage of the ebb-tide to set sail for Ireland. For Archbishop Williams, his spirits unaffected by Edge Hill's unsatisfactory scramble, was not a man to let grass grow under his feet, and already his thoughts turned to Ireland as a means of salvation. There were soldiers there, stores of powder and ordnance to be had for ready money. Now that the ships of the Parliament were blockading the port of Chester, his quick mind perceived that in Conway lay the King's best means of communication with his subjects across St. George's Channel. His astute brain, moreover, saw that Dublin was a profitable market for the farmers and miners of the Vale of Conway who were hard put to wrest a livelihood from nature. Ever active where the interests of his countrymen were concerned, the Archbishop set about opening up a new trade.

A sudden activity had stirred the sleepy town of Conway with the coming of the Archbishop from York. "Lawyers of Caernarvon, Merchants of Beaumaris, Gentlemen of Conway", ran the old saw, but now Conway had turned merchant, for the gentlemen were at Oxford with the King.

The crowd on the quay watched the departure of the trading ships with something more than curiosity, for many a good burgess had shares in the venture. If only the vessels could elude the watch-ships of the Parliament, which so far were not venturing farther south than Point of Ayr, there ought to be a quick market awaiting them in Dublin.

In Dublin the merchants were as anxious to receive the wares from Wales as the good folk of Conway were to send them. At least, so said his Grace, and he was in close communication with Lord Ormond, Governor of Dublin Castle.

Maelys stood aloof from the crowd. She stared at the ships, morose, hard-eyed, her mood grey as the river, the distant hills and the approaching night. Since the coming of Holland with the dire news from Edge Hill, Maelys's smile had left her face. Her grief for her brother and for her father she confided in no one. She went through life with a white face and brooding eyes which seemed at war with destiny.

Archbishop Williams, ostensibly watching the ships, stole covert glances at the girl's set face, and found his heart ache for her.

"Come, my child, the air is chill. Let us seek the warmth of Plas Mawr. Its comfort will be kinder than this keen wind from Carnedd Llewelyn which carries with it a touch of snow."

"I ask no kindness from life or nature," said Maelys.

His Grace was patient. "Your heart is heavy, dear one," he said gently. "One day you will see your parent again ; till then, let me be a father to you."

"He will die as Robin has died."

"Is that how he would have had you talk ? We who remain at home must show valour even as those who take the field."

"If only I could fight !" cried Maelys with a show of animation. "If only I could strike these sullen-proud ruffians ! I hate these accursed rebels who have spread desolation and dismay in our happy land. I have no name scurvy enough for them. Would that I could help to lay them low !"

"You can." His Grace's voice was quiet.

The colour leaped to Maelys's cheeks. "How ? I entreat you, tell me how."

"When Lieutenant Holland rode forth yesterday to rejoin the King, Studdart, my secretary, went with him, leaving me without an amanuensis. Take his place and I promise you that you shall strike the rebels in due time."

"Strike them with a pen !" mocked Maelys.

"A pen, child, can be sharper than a two-edged sword."

The Archbishop's voice was persuasive. Inwardly he was saying : "If only I can occupy her mind ; if only I can drive that dreadful hopelessness from her young eyes." But he said aloud : "I must have one in whom I can trust. Undertake this work for me— work with me—and you release a man for the cause."

Maelys turned quickly. "Then I will come," said she definitely. "Your Grace will find me a dull scholar, but at least a faithful one."

Side by side they passed under the worn Gothic arch which pierced the town walls, the guards at Porth Isaf presenting arms. Slowly they climbed High Street to where the terraced gables of Plas Mawr were silhouetted against the evening sky. The Archbishop led her to the room he occupied as his study ; the room which bore the name of Queen Elizabeth's room by reason of the great "E-R" which flanked the royal arms upon the ornate chimney breast. Here on the broad oaken tables was a litter of books and parchments. On the dark wainscoting maps were pinned. Maelys tossed aside her cloak. "Let me begin," she said briskly. "What orders has your Grace ?"

"Not 'your Grace', dear child, when we are alone. Let it be 'Uncle' for, with God's help, I mean to do my duty by you until your good father comes again."

Almost the tears came to the girl's eyes, but she fought them back. "You have more than done that duty already. There seems no limit to the goodness of your generous heart."

The Archbishop patted her cheek and laughed a little hardly. "Those who tore my robe from my back when I withstood them at Westminster seemed to think otherwise. By my Mitre, what with one party cursing me for being too much a Puritan, and the other for being too near a papist, I had little chance of pleasing anybody. But you are right, child, let us labour while there is yet time. To-morrow, remind me I must obtain more masons for the castle repairs. It shall be my own particular care until his Majesty can garrison it."

"But the cost—Uncle?" cried the girl picking up a quill.

"It shall be my own private charge," said the Archbishop.

"But, Uncle, you gave all your Yorkshire plate to the King's coffers."

"I should be but an ingrate were I to allow any question of cost to stand between me and my King in his hour of trial. Now here is a deeper matter. When any vital message is sent, we fear lest it should miscarry. So cipher is used lest our mail fall into the hands of the enemy. Here is the key. Persons of consequence are denoted by number. For example, the King is '60', the Queen '61', Prince Rupert '62'. Commit these to memory ; it is both safer and quicker. Here is a despatch brought by fisherboat from Dublin. Take the code and discover what Lord Ormond says."

As the girl bent obediently to her task, the Archbishop crossed to the fire-place, noting with satisfaction that already the features showed greater animation.

For a while there was silence in the room. Maelys lifted her head. "Lord Ormond asks for more grain. Is the war like to last long ?"

"When a domestic war seizeth a country rich in plenty and full of surfeits with continual ease, it never leaves purging those superfluities till all be wasted."

G

"It will outlast the winter, then?"

"It may last many years before we trample these petty tyrants underfoot."

"I should not have thought they could endure," said Maelys.

"None are so adventurous as those who dare not be cowards for fear of hanging." The Archbishop paced the room. "That is why I would have Conway set in good repair. If Chester remain blocked, I cannot see how his Majesty can maintain communication with Ireland save by way of Conway. And to Ireland he must assuredly look to replenish his forces. Lord Ormond and I are of one mind on it."

"Does his Lordship favour this trading, then?"

"It is to our mutual advantage. If he send me powder, of which there is great dearth, I will ship him beef for his soldiers." His Grace's shrewd eyes twinkled. "I have no doubt our hill farmers are glad of the market. Your uncle Owen Wynn writes me from Gwydir that the price of cattle is fallen by half in the fairs of late from what they were two years ago."

A knock sounded and Parry entered. "The coachman from Bodysgallen is arrived, your Grace, bearing a message for Mistress Wynn."

"Bid him enter."

The fellow, a grey-haired retainer, approached with deference and, after touching his forelock to the prelate, turned to Maelys.

"There have been strange goings-on at Bodysgallen, lady," he observed, taking the parcel from under his arm. "When Howell, the gardener, was in the sunken garden, he saw something lying near the sun-dial and on going to look he found this."

He spread on the table a broad silken flag. Maelys stared with unbelieving eyes. The silk was pierced and creased, and the white field was crossed by a brown bloodstain. But the embroidered designs were unmistakable. They were her own handiwork. There on the table lay the colours of Colonel Hugh Wynn's Regiment of Foot.

"It is the ensign you fashioned, Maelys," cried the Archbishop. "How came it there, my man?"

The coachman shook his head. "No one knows, your Grace, unless the Little People brought it in the night."

"This is no fairy gift. Was there no sign?"

"None, my Lord—save this." And he pointed to an imprint of a paw.

"Some dog hath walked across it."

"Look closer, my Lord. It is neatly drawn by a human hand; that is no dog track."

"I believe you are right," said the prelate peering.

"Now, will your Grace and Mistress Wynn don cloaks and follow to the courtyard?"

"You are mysterious, fellow," complained his Grace, but his curiosity was whetted. The heavy outer door swung open.

On the cobbles stood a white horse which pricked its ears as Maelys stepped forth.

"Monarch!" With a glad cry she flung her arms about the animal's neck. Quickly she turned her face to the coachman. The tears which had welled to her eyes at the sight of her father's charger were checked by the eager hope which rose within her heart. "Your— master?" she faltered.

But the man answered hurriedly, "Nay, Mistress, no word of the Colonel, sorry I am to say it."

"Then how came Monarch back?"

"No one knows, lady. I found him tied to a paddock rail."

"And no message?"

"No sign, save this." And the man pointed to the white flank which bore the imprint of a pad-mark.

"Magic and mystery," remarked the Archbishop. "Was the beast saddled?"

"As you see him now, sir. Harness well cared for. He has been in careful hands."

"But how came he there ?" persisted the Archbishop.

"Someone must have brought him and stole away quiet in the night," replied the man.

Maelys turned away, a sudden dread clutching at her heart. She heard the coachman's voice saying, "Whosoever he was he must have moved stealthily, for never a dog was roused."

But Maelys was living again the flight from Cawood : she could depict Heritage's noiseless movement through the darkened wood : she knew the stealth of "The-Wolf - who - walks - by - Night". A sudden rancour seized her. She would accept no favours from him ! He could bring the steed and the banner as tokens of his prowess, but he and his kind had robbed her of father and brother. The pent-up anguish of weeks was finding an outlet ; grief was turning to anger. Dimly she became conscious of the Archbishop's voice.

"You will be glad to see Monarch again, child."

"Where is his rider ?" was her retort.

"Who can say ?   But we know he liveth."

"They could spare the steed but not the master."

"Come, Maelys, let not bitterness oppress you. 'Tis the fortune of war. I doubt not his Majesty will effect an exchange and before long your father will roam the woods of Bodysgallen again."

But Maelys refused to be comforted. "I take no gifts from rebels," said she proudly.

"But consider, my dear. It was a kindly thought on some person's part. Accept the gift in the spirit of the unknown giver. The times are sad enough when a house is divided against itself, and a man dreads to hear another call surrender in his own mother-tongue. Nay, this warms my heart to find chivalry and courtesy can still flourish."

Maelys stood with bowed head. Presently she said in a low voice. "I will accept Monarch—only the horse."

So Monarch was led back to his own familiar stall,

but the banner Maelys would not touch. Wisely the prelate forbore from persuading her. Instead, he arranged to have the ensign replaced on its staff and carried with due pomp and ceremony to the parish church, where it was hung from the fine old rood screen to be a lesson and an inspiration to all.

After which the Archbishop preached mightily, exhorting all to "Fear God ; Honour the King".

  .   .   .   .   .

Maelys heard him not. She chose, rather, to walk the river path, pouring her woes into the ready ears of Holland. For that young man, promoted now to captain, had been sent back further to recuperate, for in his eagerness to rejoin the King he had set forth ere his wounds were healed. Stricken down on the route, he was brought back for further nursing, his chagrin at this ignominious home-coming being tempered by the sincerity of Maelys's welcome. Gallant and debonair, he appeared to her eyes as loyalty personified. In her hatred of all rebels she turned to this staunch supporter of royalty with a warmth which was the greater because it served to obliterate from her mind the thoughts of Heritage.

"Let these wounds heal, Maelys, and I swear I will not return to your side until I bring you word of your father," cried Holland ardently. In his earnestness he laid fingers on Maelys's arm and, finding she did not draw away, allowed them to remain. "Already I find Prince Rupert taking kindly notice of me, and I count on gaining his favour. I will speak on your behalf at the first opportune occasion."

She thanked him graciously and they walked in silence to the ferry.

"May I not escort you home ?" asked the gallant as he handed her into the boat, but she shook her head.

"I would be alone, my friend," she said. "You will find me but a doleful companion these days, I fear."

Holland bowed courteously. "I appreciate the greatness of your sorrow, Maelys," he assured her gently.

"You are a true friend—Claude," said the girl gratefully, giving him her hand to kiss.

Wrapping her cloak closer round her, Maelys settled herself in the sternsheets while the boatmen rowed briskly towards the landing place at Tywyn. A sabbath stillness had settled on the world. In the pale November sunshine a cormorant with outstretched wings sunned himself on a spit of sand. Redshanks and sandpipers busily probed for food along the river marge. All was peace. Would Colonel Wynn, peering from behind prison bars, look upon a scene one half so beautiful as this ? Maelys shuddered.

"You are cold, lady," said the steersman.

"The morning is chill," agreed Maelys with forced brightness, but she refused the jacket which the man with rough courtesy held out. "I will walk home, Hughes, and the exertion will speedily stir my blood."

Stepping ashore daintily enough, she ascended the hill, the exercise bringing her warmth and colour. Once on the crest she could see the grey gables and square tower of Bodysgallen rising from the leafless trees of its encircling woods.

The twigs spread grey as smoke, the drabness broken here and there by the dark green of holly or yew or ivy. The black cattle were still in the fields, for the weather was mild. Along the rutted lane she passed, alone in a silent, tranquil world. The beauty of the scene calmed her but did not bring her peace. She was conscious of no heart-ache. Rather a numbness seemed to have taken possession of her, dulling the agony of her loss. Father and brother, both sacrificed for the King's cause. And so early in the day, too ! If only she were a man ! If only she could have drawn blade and ridden boot to boot with Rupert's Cavaliers as they swept through the enemy pikemen, she could have found fitting outlet for the hate which smouldered within her. She hated these rebels, these scurvy knaves, authors of the land's miseries and depredations. She hated them . . . hated them . . . hated them . . .

She stopped suddenly as though she had been struck. Motionless as the tree beside which he stood was Heritage.

It was only when he moved to take off his hat that the girl realized that he was not a product of her fevered imagination.

"I desire brief speech with you," he said abruptly.

"Stand back, rebel!" Her eyes flashed. "Would you molest me here—in my own park?"

"I have endeavoured for days to gain word with you——" began Heritage unmoved.

"Run and hide lest true men make you rue your intrusion!" she burst forth. "I have no truck with rebels. Stand aside."

With chin high and hands clenched she stalked past on her way.

"But one word——" pleaded Heritage, but she would not heed. Maelys's heart was racing : hatred blinded all judgment. Her eyes swept the fields seeking some keeper or groom who could summon aid. To have him here, within her grasp, and to let him go free ! It was maddening. Yet what chance would a few grooms have against his terrible sword ? She must entrap him by stratagem. Fool that she was, why had she not thought of it before ? Perhaps it was not too late. Quickly she turned and ran lightly down the lane. It was deserted. "Captain Heritage !" she called. "Captain Heritage !"

He stepped from the hedgerow, and she bit her lip to think he had been so near at hand and she did not see him.

"I repent my haste—you—you took me by surprise," she said hurriedly. "I will speak with you if you wish——"

"I did but wish to tell you——"

"Nay, not here. Not here. Someone will see us. The moon is up at ten of the clock. Meet me by the old cell of St. Trillo on the shore near the weir. You know it?"

"A strange, awkward spot——" began the man slowly.

Maelys tossed her head. "I shall be there by ten. You may have speech with me then—if you dare come."

Heritage looked into her eyes. "I will be there," he said quietly.

.   .   .   .   .

Maelys stood alone upon the sloping bank of shingle listening to the monotonous lapping of the waves, waiting for the moon to creep above the distant headland of Penmaenrhos. Far off along the margin of the sea, a flight of ringed plovers were crying—a thin, eerie note. Against the grass bank rose the dark outline of the tiny stone cell of St. Trillo, its roof of rounded stones, its window niches devoid of glass. A hermit cell covering a sacred well, built nobody knows how many centuries before. It was, as Heritage said, a strange place for a tryst.

A pale glow crossed the eastern heavens. The moon was rising. Maelys watched, cold with apprehension and the chill of the night. The moon rose, throwing a path of primrose light across the face of the waters. She listened for the crunch of shingle which would herald Heritage's approach. There was no sound. Would he not come? Had he taken fright?

"I am here."

The words, quietly spoken, came from behind. She leaped with affright. Heritage had arrived, not from landward as she had expected, but walking the edge of the sea where the sound of his steps was drowned in the wash of the waves.

"Oh!" she gasped and was motionless, her voice

choked by the racing of her heart. He stood there
quietly, open and unafraid. He wore no cloak. She
noticed the tomahawk was missing from his belt, but
his long straight sword hung on his hip, terrible in the
moonlight. The girl's hands flew to her lips. A
whistle shrilled.

The stillness was shattered. From out the ancient
chapel of St. Trillo burst musketeers with matches
burning. From the bank above came running figures,
weapons glinting in the moonlight, pistols levelled.
From the direction of the Little Orme hurrying footsteps sent the pebbles rattling. Heritage leaped back,
hand on hilt, and glanced right and left. Verily they
paid tribute to his prowess. There was no dearth of
captors.

"Surrender !" The command was curt and emphatic.
"Come, you fool, it would be madness to resist."

Captain Holland, immaculate in his uniform, strode
forward, sword in his right hand, his left hand outstretched.

"Render your sword," he ordered.

Slowly Heritage slipped the belt over his head, took
the scabbard in both hands and with elaborate for-
mality handed the weapon not to Holland but to
Maelys.

She took it hesitatingly. Then she laughed a trifle
hysterically. "Take his knife, too," she cried. But
it was not to be found. Heritage had left it behind
him. Had he suspected a trap ? Maelys's conscience
smote her, but she thought of Robin and hardened
her heart. "You would affront me in my own home ?"
she cried. "Damned Crop-ear, rot in prison like a
better man than you is forced to do !"

She stared defiantly into his face. But Heritage,
serene of countenance, was calmly watching the cloudlets drift across the face of the moon.

CHAPTER THIRTEEN

MATTERS were going well for King Charles. Rupert's reckless daring had fired the spirits of the Cavaliers. True, the Londoners, fearing for their city's safety, had sent forth their trained bands to check his advance on the capital, but his Majesty found pleasant security amid the stately halls of Oxford while his enterprising horsemen pushed forward to within thirty miles of London. In the West Country, Sir Bevil Grenville, gallant as his illustrious forebear, rose in his wrath and smote treason with a heavy hand. Wales, ever loyal, was pouring a steady stream of pikemen to swell the Royalist Foot. Many a hardy Welsh squire, conservative of outlook and simple of faith, crossed the border prepared to die upholding the divine right of kings.

In Conway his Majesty had no more stout supporter than his Grace of York. He was a Churchman on Sundays, setting an example in his pulpit to every rector in the vicinity. On week-day he was statesman or general as occasion demanded, scheming with Lord Ormond how best to transplant the English army in Ireland back on English soil ; fortifying and victualling the ancient borough of Conway. Already the crumbling walls of the castle were rearing their battlements in rejuvenated pride. Many a neglected stone from the ruined pile of Deganwy Castle was ferried across the river to acquire fresh usefulness.

Faint-hearted dwellers in Flintshire, too near Roundhead Cheshire for their mind's comfort, resorted to the greater security of Conway's walls. Conway rejoiced and made what profit it could out of the commodities of which the Royalists stood in need. The tide of battle

seemed far away. With winter rains turning roads
into quagmires only occasional word came through of
the brave happenings in distant England. Couriers
riding from Chester to Caernarvon, or perchance to
Beaumaris as the port most convenient for Dublin,
were glad to rest at Conway ere they faced the perils of
the precipitous cliff road which skirted the massive
headland of Penmaenmawr.

One such messenger was even then taking comfort
in the Black Lion Inn. If he dallied over-long, it was
not because his despatches lacked urgency, but because
it pleased him to take his ease. For Lieutenant Denis
Hogan was ever one to set his own convenience before
the call of duty.

"Landlord, refill my tankard," cried he, thrusting a
pewter pot across the board table which ran between
the settles in the low-ceilinged tavern. Hogan had
chosen the common room because of the comforting
fire which roared in the grate. He was never fasti-
dious about the company he kept. He stretched his
booted legs and turned affably to the fisherfolk and
artisans who sat before the blaze, cosily as if at home.

"My lads," said he. "I've heard tell that Conway
ale was the worst in the land, and now I have proved
it."

"Ay," laughed a fisherman, " 'Cwrw Aberconwy,
gorau pei pellaf'—as the old saying is—'Aberconway
ale, the further off the better'."

Tom Jenkyns wiped his lips. " 'Tis good enough for
the like of us, your worship," said he with a meaning
look which Hogan was quick to interpret.

"You got under my guard there, you dog," Hogan
laughed. "So fill up, all of ye, and I'll give you a toast
—To the King's courage and to hell with all scurvy
Crop-ears."

The men drank deep and Hogan flung a silver coin to
the landlord.

"There's one Parliamenteer who'd relish some of

hell's warmth this weather, I'm thinking," said one of the men.

Hogan glanced up quickly. "Meaning?"

"That giant man they've clapped in the castle clink," replied the man. "They say it took twenty men to capture him."

"Twenty men—and a wench," added another with a leer.

"Speak respectful of your betters, Ben Humphreys," cried Jenkyns.

"Nay, I meant no respect to the Colonel's daughter," said the man hastily, for Jenkyns though old was still a fighter.

"What's the man's name?" inquired Hogan succinctly.

"Heritage, so I've heard tell," and Jenkyns looked at him keenly.

"Heritage?" Hogan puckered his brows. His geniality departed. He caught up his sword and rose. "Well, my lads, I'm for the Archbishop's Palace. Good luck go with ye."

Jenkyns finished up his ale and slipped out after the messenger. "Let me guide you, sir."

Hogan stood in the roadway and stared upward at the great round corner tower of the castle which overlooked the town. "Do you know the castle?" he asked abruptly.

"That I do, sir, seeing I am a mason that works on the repairing of it."

"Where is this man Heritage kept?"

Jenkyns pointed a gnarled finger to the left of the drawbridge. "See yon niche, sir? That lights his cell."

Hogan stroked his chin thoughtfully. "Well, let's find the Bishop," said he, and strode away, Jenkyns at his heel.

The old man showed the way to the Archbishop's Palace beside the northern wall. Outside the door stood a file of soldiers bearing half-pikes. The sergeant in charge, recognizing Hogan as an officer, gave a salute. Without a word of dismissal, Hogan left Jenkyns and went inside.

If Archbishop Williams was pleased to see his former follower he gave no sign of it. This was a formal occasion, and no one knew better how to preserve his dignity than his Grace of York. A long table drawn across the end of the room suggested a judicial bench. Several chairs were ranged behind it, the imposing high-backed chair in the centre indicating where his Grace intended to preside.

The remainder of the apartment was cleared of furniture. The stage, as it were, was set.

"You arrive opportunely, Mr. Hogan," said the prelate, exhibiting no surprise. "I compliment you on your freedom. When last I had word of you it was that you were in captivity."

"I escaped the rebels, your Grace, and have since taken service under Sir John Byron."

"I could have wished you happier choice," observed his Grace drily, for he was ever free with his opinions and cared little whom he offended thereby. "I will borrow your services awhile. I desire an officer to take charge of a prisoner's escort, and as most of mine have gone to the royal army I request you to undertake that service. The prisoner is lodged in the castle."

Hogan bowed. "The pleasure of your Grace's commission is the greater because I believe I have already encountered the prisoner."

"He is called Heritage."

"A notorious malcontent, my Lord. Let me extend my felicitations to your Grace on achieving his capture. He is one of the most violent men among the rebels."

"I was unaware of this."

"His powers are such that he was especially brought from New England by young Sir Harry Vane, to be a scout master for the Northern army. His cunning, learnt from the savages of the American forests, is such that he is of great value to the Parliament in providing their intelligences. Moreover he hath acquired a taste for civilized warfare by experience in the Low Country where he hath learnt the art from Swedish officers trained by the great Gustavus Adolphus."

His Grace bowed his head courteously. "Your coming is indeed opportune, Mr. Hogan."

"Bethink you, sir," interposed one of the men standing by. "If this man is in truth so dangerous, and withal so valuable a hostage, would it not be better to try him within the security of the castle lest he break away in the streets?"

The Archbishop turned a haughty gaze on the speaker "I do not wait on my prisoners, sir; they appear before me. Hogan, do your duty."

Hogan saluted briskly. "I guarantee he will not escape me, your Grace," he cried, and a moment later they heard his voice giving curt commands to the guards.

Small though it was, the incident caused a stir in the sleepy town. The soldiers, hitherto regarded as useless loungers, acquired a new dignity. Hogan, sword in hand, marched at the head of the pikemen, who, catching something of his martial bearing, bore themselves with better carriage. Up the incline to the castle they marched, across the drawbridge and into the barbican. In the Castle Square and the fields which stretched between it and the church an increasing crowd stood, heads thrown back, craning up at the castle to see what the outcome would be.

The drawbridge again resounded to the tramp of feet. Back came the soldiery. In their midst, bare-headed and bound by ropes, walked Heritage.

His gaze passed over the heads of the crowd. He seemed to be taking pleasure in the grey December skies and the cool kiss of the wind. To him it almost meant freedom. He breathed deeply and appeared content.

He took his place before the Archbishop. There was no lack of armed guards.

"You are John Heritage?"

The prisoner inclined his head.

"How came you here?"

The prisoner made no reply.

"You are a spy for the King's rebellious subjects."

"I am no spy." Heritage spoke at last.

"If you are no spy you are for sure a rebel, and as his Majesty's lieutenant in these parts I have power to detain you."

"You have already detained me."

"And shall continue to do so until this land, which belongs to his Majesty——"

"By what right?" cried Heritage.

"By the divine right of kings."

Heritage's lip curled: "Divine right of help-yourself; divine right of do-as-you-please; divine right of falsehood——"

His bitter words were cut short by a blow on the mouth. "You canting hell-hound," cried Hogan, "would you abuse the King's majesty . . ."

A thin trickle of blood coursed down Heritage's chin. He regarded Hogan coolly. "The injury to your jaw seemeth in no way to impair your speech," he mocked.

Like angry dogs the two men eyed each other: Hogan blazing; Heritage contemptuous. Hogan's hand dropped to his hilt.

"Order!" cried the prelate sharply. "Lieutenant Hogan, attend to your duty. I am competent to protect his Majesty's honour without your interference."

Hogan saluted and was silent.

"I advise you," said the Archbishop, speaking with the judicial evenness he doubtless acquired when Lord Keeper, "such unseemly conduct is prejudicial to your case."

"This is no time to dissemble," retorted Heritage.

"I drew the sword because every Stuart is incurably false. That perjured man Charles Stuart hath betrayed his country, and his subjects have been foully imprisoned, tortured and done to death for no other misdemeanour than that they stood for liberty of conscience. How many good men and true have languished in our gaols, have had their noses slit, their ears cut off, by the like of you ? You call yourselves servants of God, yet you kill men's bodies and curse their souls. No King, no bishops ! You whited sepulchres, the day of vengeance is at hand : the axe is laid to the root of the tree !"

The Archbishop paled with suppressed anger, but he had long since learnt how to curb his imperious temper. "It had been my intention," said he calmly, "to have dealt gently with you. I have received courteous usage at your hands ; why, I know not, but my worst enemies cannot justly call me ingrate. But you have slandered the King I serve, and vilified the Church I venerate. Your blood be upon your own head. I will break your Puritan spirit."

"Neither kings nor bishops can command the spirit," said Heritage, undaunted.

"Learn to revere your sovereign. A king must not be contented with a mediocrity of respect. Lieutenant Hogan, return the prisoner to his cell. Perchance time and those dank walls will cool his hot head."

Heritage calmly took his place between the files of soldiers, turned his back on the Archbishop and marched through the doorway.

In the street a curious throng still lingered. Foremost among them stood Tom Jenkyns. Heritage as he passed allowed his eyes to rest for a moment on those of his father's gunner. The eyes of both were devoid of recognition.

CHAPTER FOURTEEN

THE feast of Christmas came, but there was neither peace nor goodwill in the land. Still, good folks must forget their woes at such a time, so many a stout yule-log was dragged from the woods at Benarth or Gloddaeth to gladden the hearts of rich and poor. Mummers passed from door to door. True, their mirth was somewhat strained, and largesse was not what it had been of yore, but intentions were of the best.

Captain Claude Holland, still pale, was enjoying the hospitality of Bodysgallen. He helped Maelys to bedeck the portraits in the hall with bays and holly, and festooned with ivy the armour and weapons which adorned the wainscoting. He chatted incessantly, almost desperately, striving to make the girl forget her grief ; trying to banish the hopelessness from her eyes. Maelys, in her trouble, turned more and more to him. He had known her father, known Robin. He had been at their side in the gallant fight. The association seemed to link her closer to him.

Another thought intruded, though to none would she have confessed it. Ever and anon she caught a faint echo of a voice in the September woods—"I have a fear which is like a living death to me—the fear of being shut in. . . ."

And Heritage was shut in. In Conway Castle his great limbs were cramped ; his spirit fretting for the forest freedom which meant life to him. And she was the cause of it. But she would not repent. "I care not," she would whisper when alone. "I hate him : traitor, rebel, Crop-ear !" She would hold arguments with herself, trying to justify her action. Her ruse had been necessary. What chance had an ordinary man against him in open fight? But her conscience never wholly gave her peace. In her bedchamber she would lean on the mantelpiece and gaze at the sword which hung on the wall. It was Heritage's sword, much as when he had surrendered it to her—his captor —save that the hilt was no longer bright from much handling. With her kerchief she flicked some dust from the scabbard, then drew back her hand as though the weapon burnt. Perhaps it was this very blade which struck Robin the fatal blow? She stared stonily at the dumb sword and hardened her heart.

Yet it was the season of goodwill.

On Christmas morn she crossed the river early to worship in Conway church. Her mother, following custom, made her way to the ancient little church of St. Hilary, standing near the cross-roads at Eglwysrhos at the borders of Gloddaeth Park. Holland escorted Madam Wynn at Maelys's request. She wished to go alone to Conway, the girl explained, because the Archbishop would be there. Once they left the hall Maelys summoned a groom and bade him carry a basket of viands she had put ready. With some care she had selected pippins from the Bodysgallen orchard and oranges from the Dutch ship that came ashore in the great gale. But they were not for the Archbishop.

When Maelys stepped ashore at the town quay, a man moved forward and with rough kindness begged to carry her basket. She thanked him with a smile. "I would be glad indeed if you would have charge of it while I worship," she said. "I know your face full well; what is your name?"

"Tom Jenkyns, lady."

"Then wait near the church, Jenkyns, for I would like you to bear the basket to the castle when I come out."

Having worshipped, Maelys, with greater charity in her heart, crossed the frosty grass and made her way to the castle approach, Jenkyns following with the basket. The drawbridge lowered at her approach, for the Archbishop's protégé was known to all. She rewarded the sentries with a smile, crossed the barbican and rapped at the great door. She took the basket from Jenkyns and dismissed him.

"You have a prisoner—one, Captain Heritage ?" she said hesitatingly to the sergeant of the guard.

"Yes, lady. He is yonder," said the sergeant respectfully, pointing to the base of the tower immediately within the gate.

"How is—the prisoner ?" Maelys experienced some difficulty in speaking.

"No trouble, Mistress. His health seems good. He takes what exercise he can for hours, and then lies looking through the window niche. He seems well content to have this peep of God's sky, though I marvel at times what it is he ponders on. If ever he leads an attack on this town, he will not fail through lack of devising schemes."

"May I speak with him ?"

"Assuredly, Mistress, if you will but let me take precautions."

The main gate was closed and barred. Several musketeers with matches burning were posted in the courtyard and two guards with drawn swords stood at the entrance to the narrow passage which led to the cell. Maelys watched these grim preparations with a curious sensation. How would Heritage receive her ?

"You may go to the cell now, Mistress ; I have unlocked the door."

Daintily Maelys stepped down the sloping passage, catching a glimpse of the sky through a niche ere she reached the heavy iron-studded door with its massive key. It was ajar. Nervously she pushed it wider and stepped within. Heritage lay full-length on the slanting stonework which pierced the thickness of the tower where a niche admitted daylight. His chin was on

his hands.   Knowing his sharp hearing Maelys realized
he must have heard her entrance yet he made no move.
She placed the basket on the window splay near his feet.

"I have brought you—these," said she timidly.

For a moment Heritage did not move. Slowly he
slid back into the cell, stood upright, his head nearly
touching the joists of the room above. He spoke no
word. Maelys stole a glance at his face. It was
thinner, paler ; there were lines of suffering under the
eyes.   The expression was one of calm endurance.

"I thought—some delicacy—might be acceptable—
at Christmastide. . . ." Her words sounded strangely
futile to her ears.

"You are bountiful—unnecessarily so." Heritage
spoke in reserved tones.   "My life of frugality makes
delicacies needless—even at Christmastide."

"And I wanted to tell you—his Grace would have
released you—but for your rash words——"

"I accept no favours of him or any man."

"When I recall your goodness to me," went on
Maelys hastily ; "when I think of how you served me—
my heart condemns me that I should treat you as I
did——"

"Then do not think of it," he interrupted.

"I requited you ill."

"All is fair in love and war," said Heritage lightly.

"You are bitter : I do not blame you. Can you
believe I was bitter when—I—betrayed you ?"

She hung her head.

"May I observe that your presence here is embarrassing to us both ?" interposed Heritage. "His Grace
might find it unseemly. The trail I have followed all
my life has never been a smooth one ; I hold nothing
but contumely for him who treads the primrose path.
Set your heart easy ; I do not allow adversity to dis-
compose me.   Return to your own kind, Madam ; it is
unnecessary that you should waste your compassion on
—a Crop-ear."

He spoke lightly but there was a restrained intensity in his words which awed and terrified her. For a brief moment the ebullition reached the surface. "Crop-ear I am, and Crop-ear I remain, but by the living God there'll be cropped heads rolling ere this tale be told!"

He stopped abruptly, fighting to recover his composure. "I beg of you leave me," he said with forced gentleness. "I am no fit company for a maid of tender years."

Abruptly he turned his back on her. Maelys, wondering, moved to the door. Dimly she heard the portal bolted and barred. The sound made her shudder. She hurried into the light of day.

The guard saluted as she passed out of the castle. She walked slowly, perturbed, trembling. Across the barbican she went and across the drawbridge. The guards stared in silent curiosity. She did not heed them. As she reached the bridge's extremity she paused and stole a glance at the tower wall. She knew the niche which lighted his cell. Was he looking forth? If so, he gave no sign of it.

As her gaze descended some bright colours strewing the moat attracted her eye. She stared uncomprehendingly. Some oranges lay there. Then she recognized the pippins from her father's orchard and comprehension came to her with disconcerting suddenness. Heritage, hungry and desolate, but independent as ever, had flung from his prison window her Christmas offering of goodwill.

Flushed of face Maelys hurried away from the castle. Her pride was humbled. "I hate him," she whispered, "I hate him!" And her eyes again grew hard.

.   .   .   .

CHAPTER FIFTEEN

THE bells of Conway's ancient church rang in the new year. The burgesses were hopeful. War, as yet, had passed them by. Such reports as the couriers brought from the far south were full of comfort. Nearer home young Roger Mostyn at the head of the fifteen hundred men he had raised in Flintshire had taken possession of Hawarden Castle, and had strengthened the forces in Chester, where the Welshmen had indicated their disapproval of Sir William Brereton's espousing the rebel cause by sacking his town-house.

The Archbishop forsook Conway for the more pleasant environs of Penrhyn House ; that delectable spot which looks forth upon the entrance to the Menai Straits to where, on the Anglesey shore, his kinsman and neighbour, Mr. Thomas Bulkeley, dwelt under the ancestral rooftree at Baron Hill.

It was a period of feasting and goodwill. He is engaged, so his Grace writes to Maurice Wynn at Gwydir, in so many feasts and visits at Tom Bulkeley's and Sir William Williams's that it will be nine, ten or twelve days before he can leave these parts.

At Conway, Alderman Hookes is accustoming himself to the responsibilities imposed upon him by his prelate uncle. Horses are scarce and hay is only to be bought by the whisp at intolerable rates. Still, there is a feeling of greater security. The King's forces in Cheshire have thrashed the rebel militia, and a temporary truce, though "bare and poor", has been reached in that county.

Maelys, returning to her secretarial duties, crossed the ferry to Conway with Holland as her willing escort.

His presence was not wholly an act of gallantry. The old town's air of respectability was slipping away from it. Newcomers, many of them of no desirable type, were finding their way thither with no recommendation other than that they desired to fight for the King. More than one brawl had broken out in the quiet streets, and respectable householders looked askance at the rowdy gallants, newly come from the Irish disturbances, who swaggered and diced and caroused to the detriment of Conway's hitherto irreproachable morals.

Holland disdainfully thrust his way through the loungers who nigh blocked the Lower Gate. The girl blushed at the jests as they passed, and Holland fingered his hilt impatiently. A gentle pressure on his arm warned him that the time was not opportune for too great a display of dignity.

As they crossed the entrance to Castle Street, a gaily dressed gallant who had been lounging against the wall of the ancient house on the corner sauntered across the roadway close in front. Holland recognized an old comrade.

"Ah, Hogan," he cried with some semblance of cordiality, "back again?"

"Ay, back from Dublin by the last pinnace, and ridin' for Chester once I have broken fast."

Hogan as he spoke swept off his plumed hat to Holland's companion. Straightening his back, he glanced with pardonable curiosity at the girl. Her face seemed familiar. His brow puckered in an effort to recall where he had seen her before.

With Maelys there was no such uncertainty. With heightened colour she pressed onward. "Claude, this is no occasion for civilities," said she coldly, hastening up the slope of High Street.

Holland glanced at her curiously. "What is it?"

But she would not reply. He did not press her until they reached the Plas Mawr gatehouse. Ascending the steps to the terrace, he paused in the morning sunlight and laid a hand on her arm. "Something has disturbed you?"

"It is nothing—a recollection. Pah!"

"I claim a comrade's privilege; tell me."

She shook her head. Holland grew insistent. "It is something to do with Hogan? Ah, fool that I am! That night at Cawood! I had not realized . . ."

Catching up his scabbard he went leaping down the steps. "Come back," cried Maelys, reading his mind. "Claude, I beg of you not to be foolish. It is all forgotten. Claude!"

But he heeded her not, and she ran down the steps after him. Darting through the gatehouse doorway he turned and saw her following. "Bolt this door," he ordered the guard, "Mistress Wynn is not to come out." As he sped down High Street he heard the clash of the bolts which shut Maelys within the security of Plas Mawr. In his impetuosity Holland glanced neither to the right hand nor to the left.

Had he done so he would have noticed the man he sought was standing beside Plas Mawr's northern wall. Hogan regarded Holland's receding back with whimsical amusement. Coolly he walked to the guardhouse door and hammered thereon with the hilt of his sword. The smile on his face deepened at the sounds of altercation within. He glanced idly at the royal arms carved above the porch and the words *"Sustine Abstine"*.

"Bear and Forbear," he murmured ironically, as he heard the bolts shot back. Imperious Mistress Wynn was not to be withstood. The smile faded from Hogan's eyes. Maelys, hurrying precipitately out, all but collided with the object of her thoughts. Hogan's plumed hat brushed the cobbles.

"I crave a moment's speech with you," he said.

Taken aback, Maelys found no words to reply.

"It is but a moment since the enormity of my offence was revealed to me," said Hogan gravely. "I come, all contrition, to beg you to pardon one who finds it impossible to pardon himself."

Maelys's hauteur asserted itself. "Your conduct was inexcusable," she said curtly.

"Inexcusable, Madam, but not unexplainable," said Hogan blandly. "To my shame I had drunk so much that night that I was blinded to the obvious quality of—a gentlewoman."

"I will not listen to you," cried Maleys, breathing hard. Her hand was on the door. "It is intolerable to be insulted thus. Go—go—before I summon his Grace's men to scourge you through the streets. Had Captain Holland been with me you had not dared——"

"Oh, Holland!" Hogan cocked his hat rakishly. "I will settle Holland. You do not accept my regrets, Madam, so I bid you good day. I never apologize twice to man, devil—or woman." And Hogan swaggered down the road, scattering the onlookers who were assembling. Maelys hurried to the shelter of the gatehouse, detesting the curious eyes without. There she stood, biting her lips in an agony of suspense.

Meanwhile, Hogan strutted aggressively down the centre of the roadway, his eyes busy for a sight of his rival. At the door of the Black Lion, which he made his headquarters, he encountered Holland, who had gone there seeking him.

"By gad, Holland, that's a demned neat little filly you were parading," he said offensively; "had a fancy for her once myself."

"Damn you!" shouted Holland, and struck him in the face.

There were no formalities. Both men instinctively turned into the covered alleyway which led to the inn yard. Each threw aside cloak and hat, drew his blade and cast the belted scabbard from him. And there, on the rough cobble-stones, with the grey battlemented walls looking down upon them, the two men gave vent to their spleen. In sprang Holland, his bright rapier darting and thrusting so that Hogan was hard put to keep it from his heart. Once it ripped his shoulder, and Holland, ever chivalrous, forbore further attack. He leaped back, alert, but willing to accept this as satisfaction if desired. The drawn blood served but to arouse Hogan's fighting spirit. Swashbuckler though he was, Hogan was a born soldier and knew his trade.

"On guard, you fool," he snapped and his blade slid forward. At it they went, thrust and parry, parry and lunge, the swish of steel and their panting breath being the only sounds which broke the tense stillness. Men from the inn clustered motionless in the alley and watched with fascinated eyes. Suddenly their ranks were thrust apart and Maelys, followed by the gate-house guard, rushed up in time to see Holland's rapier whipped from his hand. Hogan's point was at his throat.

"Stop! Oh, stop!"

Maelys's agonized tones broke the silence. The two men stood, Holland pale and panting ; Hogan with a sneer of triumph on his hard face.

"Spare him, I entreat you," cried Maelys.

"Maelys," said Holland hoarsely, "go away. These are not matters for maids. I have lost and I must pay the price."

"I implore you, spare his life."

Hogan's sneer deepened and deliberately he pressed home the point so that a trickle of blood coursed down Holland's neck. Holland never flinched but Maelys was in tears.

"Madam," said Hogan crisply, "not long since you treated me with contumely and now you desire a favour. Had you accepted my apology this need never have come to pass."

"I was at fault," cried Maleys. "I accept your apology."

Instantly Hogan lowered his point. "Bedad, 'tis

plaguy public here," he cried. "A glass of wine at the inn with you, Holland," he said affably, and picking up the fallen rapier he presented the hilt with a bow to his late opponent.

Holland accepted it in surly silence. At the sight of Hogan advancing with sword still drawn the crowd scattered, and the three entered the inn. The landlord had wit enough to see they were undisturbed. Hogan fetched a seat for the girl. Standing with one foot on the settle he leaned forward and addressed her. His pose was carefully chosen, his words carefully selected.

"Madam," said he, "may I remind you that to err is human, to forgive divine ? On that memorable night at Cawood, I, being in my cups, would have essayed a little gallantry with one whom, in the darkness and because of my drunken condition, I assumed wrongly to be a camp-follower. Is it asking too much of you to believe that had I known you to be a kinswoman of his Grace, whose commission I had the honour to hold, I would have then treated you with the respect I now endeavour to accord you ?"

"But I might not have been his Grace's kinswoman," cried Maelys, shuddering. "Suppose I had been some other defenceless girl, what then ?"

"I am a soldier," said Hogan briefly. "I respect those to whom respect is due. What more can a woman ask of a man ?"

"I ask more of any who would claim my friendship," said Maelys softly.

"You are hard, Madam. I have sinned and I have paid the price. My folly cost me weeks in a Round-head gaol and no little ingenuity in effecting my escape. It has, further, cost me your good opinion. The latter I would rectify. I am trying to make amends. What more can I do to prove my repentance ? Have I not spoken fair ?"

"Your speech is fair enough," said Holland, speaking for the first time. Hogan flushed, then Holland hastily interposed. "I must not forget I owe my life to you. At least we must accept your explanation."

Hogan held out his hand, which Holland took without enthusiasm. Maelys, too, held out her hand. "We owe you a debt certainly, Mr. Hogan. You have acted with chivalry. I thank you. Gentlemen, the King needs your swords. I trust you never again to draw them against each other, but only in his loyal service. Come, Claude."

With a bow she passed through the door. Hogan crossed to the low window and watched them go up the street. When he turned away there was a cynical smile on his face. It was as though he felt he had gained more than a duel.

Holland walked in silence, for he was chagrined. Maelys was silent, for the episode had revived memories of the flight from Cawood—revived thoughts she would fain forget. It was a different Hogan she had encountered then, and she for one did not think the leopard could change his spots. She could remember the look in his eyes as he bent over her, ere Heritage coming noiselessly from behind had plucked him from her. Heritage. . . .

Instinctively Maelys lifted her eyes to the great round tower which dominated the town. There it rose, massive, silent, unchangeable, remorseless as when the first Edward had seen it built. It held Heritage in its cold clutch. Perhaps even then he was lying at the window niche looking with hungry eyes as she and Holland walked up Castle Street. Maelys shivered.

"Let us return to Bodysgallen, Claude," she said hurriedly. "The day's events have shaken me; I am in no mood for work. O that I had wings like a dove : then I could fly away and be at peace."

CHAPTER SIXTEEN

FEBRUARY came, and the snowdrops lifted their modest heads in the Bodysgallen woods. Maelys, escaping from her duties whenever possible, crossed to her home, glad to find freedom of body if not tranquillity of mind where the pleasant gardens caught the sunshine. The harassed girl found Holland's companionship a solace in her distress. The man's wound was healed ; his strength recuperated : he waited but the permission of the Archbishop ere he set forth to join Prince Rupert,who had, in January 1643, been appointed Captain General of North Wales and the adjoining counties.

Holland rightly judged that there was better prospect of advancement under the dashing young prince than in serving the loyal though aging prelate. Rupert, in fact, would have attracted his allegiance earlier had not inclination made him reluctant to leave Maelys's side.

Conway was bustling with activity again. In response to an urgent summons from the King, more men were being raised for the Spring campaign, and, harder task, more money collected for their payment. Maelys disliked Conway under war conditions ; she hated the disordered streets, the rowdiness, the incivilities. Moreover, the castle lowered over her like a thing of evil. She could not bring herself to look at it, but hurried past its towers with face averted, thinking of a captive languishing in its dungeon.

Maelys had been walking the sunken garden at Bodysgallen, searching for signs of Spring. As she ascended the steps, Holland at her side, a Cavalier was seen standing on the gravel sweep before the front porch. It was Hogan. Maelys recoiled a little. Hogan noticed.

"Still no forgiveness, Madam?" he asked quietly as he raised his hat.

"I have told you I have forgiven you," said Maelys quickly.

"There is no forgiveness in your eyes."

"Suppose," broke in Holland, "you tell us the reason of your appearing, instead of dwelling on Mistress Wynn's eyes."

Hogan raised his brows. "I have a message for Mistress Wynn," said he with unusual patience. They walked towards the house. As they entered Madam Wynn burst from the passage with an exuberance she had not exhibited for many a long day.

"Oh, Maelys dear one, what joyful tidings! What, have you not heard? Has not Mr. Hogan told you? He is safe, dear, safe!"

"Who is safe?" cried Maelys, turning pale.

"Your father, darling."

"But we knew he was safe, Mother mine."

"Safe, yes, but I mean free. He hath reached Chester and is being cared for by the Governor, who hath sent Mr. Hogan to acquaint us the good news." Madam Wynn held out a letter. Maelys recognized the shaky handwriting of the brief epistle:

To my dear and well-beloved wife, greeting.

I write to say I am delivered out of my Tribulations and hope shortly to see you face to face. At this time I lie abed with a distemper brought on by the exposures I have been subjected to, yet God be praised I mende apace. I have little strength to write you, save to desire you to sende hither our dear child, Maelys, the sight of whose sweet face will recover her Father more speedily than apothecary's draughts or surgeon's bloodlettings. The country, for the nonce, is rid of Parliamenteers, so with escort, which I beg his Grace to

*furnish, she may ride with safety. I trust Howells hath
pruned the burgamots. I have news aplenty for you, but
it must keepe till I see you. That this will be soon is the
prayer of*

Your truly devoted husband,
Hugh Wynn.

Maelys handed back the letter and embraced her
mother.

"Is my presence still unwelcome?" inquired Hogan.

"You are in truth the bearer of good tidings," said
Maelys with more warmth. "Let me change my habit
and I will ride with you to Chester forthwith."

"I, too, ride to Chester," said Holland quickly. "Do
not start until I have mustered the escort." And he
darted from the room.

And so they rode forth, Holland on Maelys's one hand
and Hogan on the other with a dozen well-armed
retainers trotting at their heels. Around the steep
headland of Penmaenrhos they went, keeping to the
sands, for the tide was at the ebb, rather than trust the
perilous track cut in the cliff face. Past Old Gwrych
and the market town of Abergele, past the castle of
Rhuddlan, which was held for the King, and on to
Flint Castle, which Colonel Mostyn had repaired and
garrisoned for the King at his own cost. The handsome
young Royalist received them gladly and gave them
hospitality for the night. On the morrow they set forth
as soon as it was light, and ere many hours were past
Maelys was in her father's arms.

Holland remained in the background, not a little
affected by the touching reunion. He was perplexed, for
in his distrust of Hogan he suspected a trap. He feared,
too, that this welcome act on Hogan's part might
advance that roystering blade in Maelys's favour.
Hogan watched the scene with satisfied smile.

Colonel Wynn lay under the shadow of a great four-
poster in the dwelling of the Mayor. He was wan, and

lines of suffering were drawn on his cadaverous face, but his eyes were glad. Maelys, a greater peace on her face than Holland had seen for many a long day, lay with her head on her father's pillow while her father's emaciated fingers caressed her silken hair.

"Child, child, you renew my strength," he murmured. "How have you been so long in coming?"

"We have not spared spur. We set off as soon as your message came yesterday."

"Yesterday? Did you, then, not get my first message?"

Maelys looked up quickly. "First message? Nay, this is the first word we have had save that you were taken at Edge Hill and were held in captivity."

The Colonel sighed. "I feared something had gone amiss. So great was my confidence in him that I believed him when he said he would get through, though the way seemed fraught with peril. Can he have forsaken me? Betrayed me? Nay, I will never believe it. Some evil hath befallen him."

"But, Father, of whom do you speak?"

"Whom?" The Colonel looked bewildered. "Ah, how could you know? This fever hath weakened my brain. Who but that strange man Heritage who brought you from Cawood. . . ."

"Heritage—Heritage . . ." Maelys sprang to her feet. "But, Father—I—do not—understand!"

"It was he who contrived my escape, who cared for me when this fever struck me down as he was guiding me to safety. With John Owen's men plundering on one hand and the Parliamentary dragoons patrolling the roads on the other, it was like to go ill with me had he not concealed me with some good folk, and ridden to Conway to fetch you to nurse me back to health. He must have been captured as he did not reach you— but what ails you, child?"

For Maelys was sobbing as if her heart would break.

"He came, Father, he came. He never broke faith with you—it was I!"

"You? How could you?"

"He came to me and I would not harken unto him. In my hare-brained folly I set a trap for him; being hard of heart at the thought of you in captivity, and now he is cast into prison . . . and he never reproached me. . . ."

She rambled on, sobbing.

Colonel Wynn endeavoured to rise but sank back. "This must not be!" he cried. "In which prison is he?"

"In Conway Castle."

"He shall not stay there another day if I can prevent it. Holland, fetch me tablet and pen. I must write the Archbishop. But for Heritage's care I should have died after the battle, for we were left uncared for, starving, till he came seeking me and carried me off in that masterful manner he hath."

"God forgive me," moaned Maelys. "He never showed me anything but kindness. Oh, this accursed war!" She fell to sobbing again. Suddenly she raised her head and looked about her.

"Where is he?" she asked quickly.

"He? Who?" asked Holland, turning.

"Mr. Hogan."

"He slipped out some moments ago. I scarce noticed."

"Ah! Something is wrong. Quick! I know it; I feel it! Find him."

"But Maelys——"

"Don't talk. Go! Ah! Those hoofs . . ."

"My dear girl, they may be . . ."

"It is Hogan. I know it. Don't you see? He hates him. He has heard you mean to release him. He rides to do him injury. Quick! Help me. We must ride and stop him."

She ran to the door, but Holland caught her. "Don't be foolish!"

I

"Do as I bid or never speak to me again. If Hogan hath not gone, there is no harm done ; if he hath, fetch our horses and after him as fast as we can spur."

"But your father . . ."

"Nay, leave me and go," cried the Colonel. "This concerns my honour. I would not have a hair of his head harmed."

Reluctantly Holland withdrew. Presently he came back with the horses and the news that a hostler had seen Hogan ride towards the water-gate.

"Then to horse, all haste, and after him," cried Maelys. "God grant we be not too late !"

CHAPTER SEVENTEEN

So they rode out of Chester and along the old road into Wales, leaving the Roodee and the flat river-lands behind them as they breasted the rise which was crowned by Hawarden Castle. Here they learned, as Maelys suspected, that Hogan had passed, riding hot-foot into Wales. The officer saw nothing surprising in this, being familiar with the sight of Hogan riding courier. But Maelys intuitively saw in Hogan's hurried journey only ill-portent for Heritage, his foe. So, not waiting for the escort, Maelys and Holland sped forward. They passed through pleasant country of wood and meadowland, and climbed the bleak ridge at Halkyn whence, across the Sands of Dee, they could see the sweep of the ocean, grey and menacing, with here and there a high-pooped ship thrusting her nose into the waves.

The air blew chill, and in many a roadside hollow the drifted snow still lay in murky patches. Holland glanced apprehensively at the girl, wishing she would seek shelter, but Maelys would have none of it. Her one thought was to make atonement ; her one dread that they would reach Conway too late. Studying the mud as they rode she endeavoured to distinguish Hogan's hoof tracks.

"What interest hath this man Heritage to you, that you should venture thus on his behalf ?" asked Holland.

"He cared for me in my need and I recompensed his kindness with treachery."

Holland grew argumentive. "I fail to see why you should reproach yourself," he said. "He was an enemy in our midst, and you did right bravely to outwit

him. Would that more rebels against his Majesty were
similarly placed!''

Maelys would not argue, but gave her horse the spur.
At St. Asaph they learned that Hogan had taken a
fresh mount. They did likewise, though the best horse
had gone and they benefited but little by the exchange.
But the animals though slow were fresh, whereas their
own beasts were nearly spent, for they had pushed them
hard. Holland urged the girl to eat, but she had no
thought for food. A little wine brought the colour back
to her cheeks.

"We do not gain on him," cried Maelys. "Claude,
I am a drag on your speed. Your mount is better than
mine ; ride on ahead.''

"And leave you, Maelys ? Never. There is folly
enough abroad to-day. But for your Father's behest I
would have had none of it.''

"What, not to aid me ?''

Holland bit his lip. "I had not meant that. What
I would say is——''

"It matters not. Waste no breath on words.
Ride !''

The suspense of that day remained long in Maelys's
mind. The interminable roads, the leaden-hoofed
horses, the dreary miles.

At the hamlet of Colwyn the country assumed a
familiar aspect and the girl's spirits rose accordingly.

Beside the stream in the dingle they pulled up
outside a small tavern and learned Hogan was nearly
an hour ahead.

"Give us swifter horses," cried Maelys. "His Grace of
York will pay your charges.''

And once again they changed mounts. Up the
narrow, tree-fringed highway they pressed, taking the
ancient way the Romans made ; then over the brow
and down, down the steep declivity to the hamlet of
Mochdre. In the distance they saw the silver glitter
of the Conway. "Ride !" cried Maelys again.

They knew the country now. Crossing the marshland by a causeway they raced their horses along the winding road on the farther side. Light was beginning to fall. In the distance they could see the outline of the ferry-house. Holland drew a pistol and fired to attract attention.

Men ran out at the signal and a boat was waiting when they dropped from their saddles. "Hogan? Has he crossed?"

"A horseman came half an hour since, lady," said the man pushing off. "He abandoned his mount and was rowed across."

"Row as you have never rowed before," cried Maelys to the boatmen, and sank back in the stern-sheets while Holland flung a protecting arm around her, trying to shield her from the cold with his cloak. The tide was on the turn. A strange vessel was swinging at her anchor in mid-stream. Her sails, loosely brailed, hung from her yards. Holland could count gun-ports in her high yellow sides. "What craft is that?" he asked curiously.

"Frigate, freshly come from Ireland, I'm told," said the steersman. "She came in with the morning tide. Already they've sent ashore a cask of wine with greetings from the Governor of Dublin Castle, and they say there's powder and guns in her hold for Conway Castle but that the Captain will not land them until he hath had word with the Archbishop in person."

"Ah, yes," said Holland. "And he is at Penrhyn House."

"Alderman Hookes despatched a messenger for him this morning; doubtless he will arrive before long."

They passed Yr Ynys, the little islet which lifted its brushwood-covered rocks high above the flood, and drew alongside the jetty opposite the postern gate. Holland threw the man a coin and bade him see to the horses.

Maelys almost ran up the pathway to the postern

gate. The guard were watching and held open the door.
"Just in time, Ma'am," said the sergeant, recognizing
her. "All gates close at curfew."

"Has Captain Hogan come in ?" inquired Maelys
breathlessly.

"Ay, Ma'am. Some time since. He went straight to
the castle."

Maelys hurried on, Holland beside her.

All of a sudden they stopped short. The jackdaws
came fluttering and crying from the castle walls as
the hollow boom of a heavy gun went throbbing on the
still evening air.

Passers-by paused to stare in amazed speculation.

"Whatever is that ?" cried Maelys. "A salute ?"

"I thought I heard a roundshot strike somewhere,"
muttered Holland. From the Lower Gate came
excited shouting. Again the thunder sounded, this time
a long irregular rumble. There was the sound of falling
slates, and a chimney stack rocked and crashed into
the street.

"By the Lord, they're firing on the town !" cried
Holland. "That was a broadside !" And catching
Maelys by the waist Holland dragged her to the
shelter of the massive town wall.

The town was awakening out of its stupefaction. A
trumpet shrilled its alarum. A drum rolled ; commands
rang out, followed by a ragged burst of musketry.

Holland dashed up the steps of a wall tower and
looked across the river.

There, with powder-smoke curling above her bul-
warks, and the flag of the Parliament drooping from
her main truck, the stranger from Ireland was dropping
downstream on the ebb tide. Even as Holland looked,
the dusk was stabbed by a dozen orange flashes as
another broadside hurled its roundshot against the
grey town.

Conway was helpless. It could only shut its gates
and man its walls. The effrontery of the attack seemed

to have paralysed the garrison. There was but one piece of artillery in the town and that was hastily dragged forth. But by the time it was brought to bear, and powder and shot found for it, the frigate was nearly out of range. After several attempts the gunners succeeded in putting a shot through the stranger's mainsail as she vanished into the gathering gloom.

"God grant she grounds on the bar," growled Holland, but the men aboard the frigate knew the soundings, and she found the channel with the ease of one familiar with the way. The musketeers who had been firing from the walls laid aside their pieces. They had done little damage ; the chief good was to their own self-assurance, for many had never been under fire before, and they had the satisfaction that at least they had hit back. Slowly Holland descended the steps.

"I never knew the like of it !" he confessed to Maelys, who greeted him with a bewildered look. Slowly they climbed to the castle drawbridge. It was raised, and it took some time to convince the warder that they had right of admittance, for the garrison was bewildered by the suddenness of the attack and the darkness. In reply to Maelys's question the sergeant of the guard said that Hogan had been admitted an hour before. They entered the inner gate and called for a lanthorn. Holland took this and the great key of the Clink and led the way, Maelys following close behind.

"Heritage ! Heritage !" called Holland as he turned the key, but there was no response. Slowly he pushed open the door and looked within. The lanthorn threw its pale gleam on the round, damp walls and finally rested on a huddled figure on the far side of the floor. At the sight of this Maelys gave a cry of apprehension.

"Go back !" whispered Holland. He knelt beside the motionless figure. The man's coat was tied over his head. Hurriedly he undid its folds and looked down upon the still face,

"Is—is it too late?" came Maelys's voice in a whisper.

"It is too late," said Holland grimly.

"Is he dead?"

"Not dead. See!"

Maelys crept anxiously forward, and looked down on the unconscious face of—Hogan.

She caught her breath and glanced quickly around the tiny circular room. There could be no hiding place. Heritage had vanished. She crossed to the window niche. Near by a flat stone projected from the wall, serving as a seat. To this a stout rope was attached. It led through the aperture and disappeared into the blackness beyond. Climbing over the window-splay, Maelys looked out. The stones on either side of the niche had been removed to form a passage wide enough for Heritage's massive frame to make its way. The dangling rope told the rest of the tale.

Maelys stepped back into the room. Holland, working over Hogan, who was slowly recovering consciousness, looked up. "You see," said he, "we were too late."

But Maelys made no reply. She felt almost resentful that Heritage should have gone without the aid she was now so willing to give him. Thoughtfully she passed from the room, and, calling two soldiers to accompany her, she made her way to the Archbishop's house. She found his Grace already there, having ridden into the town as the firing ceased.

He listened patiently to her story, tenderly congratulated her on the freedom of her father, and pursed his lips when he heard of Heritage's escape. "Perhaps it is as well," he said. "I bear him no ill-will; indeed he hath been large-hearted toward us. Having myself undergone the misery of imprisonment, it troubled me to contemplate him suffering there; yet duty to my King required that it should be so."

Evidently his Grace found that this duty was fairly

accomplished, for he gave no orders for Heritage's pursuit. For which omission Maelys, in her heart, thanked him.

"And now that you will have your good father back with you, I take it that I shall have to find a new secretary," added the Archbishop.

But Maelys begged that she might be retained. The work, she claimed, was agreeable to her taste, and her father would be away at the wars again, once he had recovered.

So the Archbishop, nothing loath, consented.

"Your Grace has done so much for me that I would be easier in my mind could I but give some little service in return," Maelys assured him. And so it was arranged.

"Sleep here this night," said the Archbishop, "and on the morrow return and acquaint your mother with all that hath transpired. I will despatch a messenger at once to set her mind at rest. But you must return speedily, for there is much work to be done. His Majesty is clamouring for more money and more powder, though where either shall come from passeth the wit of man to comprehend. This night's affray, small though it was, serves as a reminder that remote though we are from the seat of war we are not without our responsibilities."

With that they fell to discussing the attack. It was, said the Archbishop, a carefully planned affair. Maelys would notice that Heritage had been provided with a rope by some sympathizer without. The vessel had arrived at a time when the Archbishop was absent and when only one gun remained in the town, showing that those who planned it had good information of the state of affairs in Conway. The men on the ship knew the river, for the attack was made at the ebb tide, whereon the vessel would drift rapidly from range. Moreover, the attack was cunningly made at a time when it was still light enough to steer by yet dark enough for Heritage to slide down the rope into the castle moat unnoticed in the confusion.

Hogan's arrival, sinister as doubtless it was intended to be, might have wrecked the scheme but for Heritage's strength and resourcefulness.

"An unusual man ; a remarkable man, Maelys. Let us hope that he returns to Sir Thomas Fairfax and leaves us alone in these parts, for though I bear him no animosity I feel safer in his absence."

The following morning Maelys crossed the river for home. Holland was in attendance, more assiduous than ever, and Maelys, disturbed in mind, turned to him in the hope of forgetting the escaped captive.

Having told her mother the news, she made her way to her room. An exclamation caused her mother and Holland to hasten upstairs. They found her staring at the wall above the mantelpiece.

"It has gone," Maelys said trembling.

"What has gone, my dear ?" asked Madam Wynn.

"His sword."

The wall where Heritage's sword had hung was blank. Holland crossed to the window seeking signs but found none. Maelys stooped and picked up a curl of birch-bark, glanced at it and crushed it in her hand.

"What is that ?" asked Holland.

"Only a scrap of wood," said Maelys, partly exposing the fragment.

"Probably it dropped from him when he climbed through the window," said Holland. "He must have entered during the night. Have any of the servants heard anything ?"

But the staff knew nothing. Not a dog had barked ; not a thing was out of place. They searched for signs but found nothing save that on the white chimney facing in Maelys's room the rough outline of a wolf's pad-mark had been crudely traced in soot. Madam Wynn shivered.

"To think of that terrible man creeping about the

house while we slumbered. We might all have had our throats cut in our beds."

"Well," said Holland with a sigh of relief, "he is gone, and we are well rid of him. Take heart, Madam, we will never see the creature again."

Maelys said nothing. Her heart was beating rapidly. For pressed against the soft skin of her bosom was a curl of birch-bark. On this forest paper a knife had scratched the words :

"I SHALL COME BACK."

CHAPTER EIGHTEEN

High on the summit of the Great Orme, the westerly wind whipping their garments, Archbishop Williams stood gazing seawards with Maelys at his side. Some distance behind them several armed retainers clustered, all gazing seaward. Between them and the coast of Anglesey the sunlight glinted on the yellow sides and bulging sails of a small vessel which was hugging the Anglesey shore.

"Is she the *Griffin*, or is it Captain Lloyd in the *Swan*?" muttered the Archbishop anxiously. "Maelys, your eyes are sharper than mine. Yet Bartlett said he would run direct for Conway with word from Dublin Castle."

"It is the *Griffin*, Uncle, of that I have no doubt, and she is bearing up for Beaumaris. Perhaps Captain Bartlett hath despatches for the Governor there, for there is water enough for him to pass the Conway bar were he so minded."

"There is no sign of the pinnace for which I importuned. Our cause will make no headway, I fear, if Lord Ormond does not send us those loyal troops which have served his Majesty so well in Ireland during the troubles there."

"Perhaps there are troops on board, Uncle."

"There cannot be enough to be of any use; a few men are but a needless drain on our victuals. Come, child, it is futile watching longer. Verily this war is teaching me to possess my soul in patience—a quality I have been barren in heretofore, God wot."

He turned and walked slowly towards ground which sloped gently towards the little grey church of St.

Tudno, near which grooms were holding horses. As he reached his retainers, the Archbishop bade them set up a beacon on the summit, and to build them hutments there so that a look-out could be kept night and day.

"There are three sails to eastward," remarked Maelys, who had been gazing across the waters of the bay. The Archbishop strained his eyes, trying to discern the tiny grey shapes which broke the morning skyline. "God grant they be not the Parliament ships of war," said he. "Shall we walk awhile, child? The freshness of the air may clear my brain, which is growing perplexed; and the exercise will warm my blood."

So signalling to the grooms to follow with the horses, the two set off across the close-cropped turf, exhilarated by their altitude and the wide stretch of fair country which lay beneath them. "When I am here, Maelys, I can understand why the priests of Baal built upon the high places," said his Grace, looking about him with exaltation in his eyes. "Up here, I feel like a prince of the Church again; cooped within the confines of the town my troubles weigh upon me like a burden. I fear sometimes, child, that Conway is like to prove a Castle of Care."

They walked on until they reached a path which sloped gently towards a fertile hollow in which the white-washed cots of some smallholders crouched for shelter from the prevailing winds. Wild goats climbed nimbly up a craggy rock-face, startled at their approach. Below them a kestrel was gliding, its attention concentrated on a lower slope where gorse and stunted hawthorns found fertile ground amid the rocks. Suddenly the bird swooped: it flapped its jubilant way to the high rocks, its dangling prey showing dark against the sky.

"A lesson, my dear," observed the Archbishop. "When danger hovers, it is well to bide in a place of security. I have not done amiss in fortifying Conway. He that fears the worst prevents it soonest!"

"But why, Uncle? Is not the war going well for

his Majesty ? There is no danger of it reaching this
remote spot ?"

"A remote spot is not necessarily a safe spot. But
have no fear, child, the King's cause is yet strong in
Wales. Here in the North, every castle is in our hands."

"Then what disturbs you ?"

"How did you know I was disturbed ? I said nothing.
My secretary seems to know me too well ! Ere we came
out I had a despatch from Chester saying that Sir
William Brereton had worsted the royal forces near
Middlewich, taking Colonel Ellis and several hundred
Welshmen prisoners, and driving Sir Thomas Aston's
cavalry into the church, where they were wedged like
billets in a wood-pile so that no man could use his arms."

Maelys looked distressed.

At this the Archbishop laughed and bade her be of
good cheer. " 'Tis the fortune of war. Such a paltry
reverse will not deter the King from his purpose. I
had not troubled about it save that it brings the
Parliament within our borders, for they say now that
they are masters of the field in Chester. It was Hogan
brought me the news."

Maelys shivered. "I do not like the man," said she
in her forthright way.

"A good soldier, a reliable messenger, a brave man.
I am content with his service. But has he annoyed you,
little one ? These lads have rough ways with maids,
but I will see to it that they grow not overbold with a
kinswoman of mine."

The Archbishop eyed her keenly, and Maelys felt
herself colouring, but she made no explanation, saying
only, "I do not complain of his conduct."

"I hear good reports from Sir Nicholas Byron of your
friend Holland's conduct in Chester," said the Archbishop, turning the subject. "He was at the Middlewich
affair, and carried himself with greater valour than
many. It pleases me, Maelys, to see you show him
some partiality."

"I am proud to have his friendship," said Maelys, looking steadfastly ahead. "But had I not better call up the grooms, Uncle? We are near the foot of the path now."

And she beckoned the grooms. Before them stretched the sandy marsh—the Morfa Rhianedd, or Ladies' Marsh, tufted with grasses, and broken by sand-dunes beyond which the estuary of the Conway gleamed like a sheet of silver. Not far away, lapwings were tumbling and wheeling, filling the air with their cries.

They cantered across the sandy waste to the farther side where rounded hills and wooded valleys pointed the way to Maelys's home.

As they rode down the narrow road which led to Bodysgallen, a horseman drew out from a hedgerow's shade. "Why, it is Captain Holland," she exclaimed, and waved a greeting. "You did not tell me he was coming."

"I did not know, child. Perchance he is the bearer of tidings."

Holland, erect in his saddle, rode up with military ease, and swept off his plumed hat. After a deferential bow to the Archbishop, the young Cavalier bent over the hand which Maelys extended.

"You are unexpected, Holland. Is aught amiss?"

"No, your Grace. I bear good tidings. Fearing that Chester's security might be jeopardized, it was decided that Colonel Wynn, being fit for travel, should seek the safer and more bracing air of Creuddyn."

"Father? Is he at home?" cried Maelys.

"He was when I rode forth to seek you," smiled Holland, and drew back as the excited girl raised her whip and with a quick cut sent her mount racing along the road which led to Bodysgallen.

"Do we follow, sir? In more decorous a fashion?" asked Holland, smiling.

"Nay, let the tender reunion take place undisturbed. Come with me to Conway. I have work for you."

They left their horses at the ferry and were rowed across, entering the town by the Porth Isaf.

In silence the Archbishop strode up High Street, Holland at his heels, and entered his palace. He called for Hogan, and the lieutenant entering saluted and stood to attention, glancing curiously at Holland from the corner of his eye. The Archbishop seated himself behind a broad table. He drew a roll from a drawer and handed it to Holland.

"Know you aught of this?"

Holland examined the paper closely. "No, your Grace."

Hogan took the paper. His mouth twitched.

"You are permitted to smile, Mr. Hogan," observed his Grace drily, as he watched the man's face. Taking the paper, the Archbishop spread it flat on the table. It was a lampoon, cleverly drawn, depicting him complete with lawn sleeves, but with a bandoleer across his surplice and a matchlock on shoulder.

Across the bottom was written: "For his Grace his amusement." And it was signed by the imprint of a wolf's paw.

"This was found affixed to the outer door this morning."

"Impertinence," said Holland.

"It afforded me amusement," said the Archbishop. He touched the pad-mark. "You know what that means?"

"It is Heritage's symbol," said Holland. "He was in the town last night."

"So I gather. Gentlemen, your task is to find him. Good day."

In the street outside the two men paused and looked at each other. "A task I shall relish, but God He knoweth how we shall set about it," said Holland.

"Leave it to me," said Hogan. "At the tavern where I put up, I have met an old man, one Jenkyns, who brings me gossip. I will see what he can find out."

So to the Black Lion went Hogan, found his man

and sent him forth to inquire whether aught had been seen of Heritage. Jenkyns was gone some hours. He came into the town through the Mill Gate, and said he had word that a man who resembled Heritage had been seen in the woods above Benarth. "You will see his fire burning in a hollow beside the river when night falls," he said.

Hogan rubbed his hands. "I owe him a debt or two which I am desirous of paying," said he, and went away to choose men to his liking. He came back with half a dozen tall fellows, game-keepers most of them ; men familiar with the river and the woods. When night fell, he and Holland set themselves at the head of the men and entered the woods in single file. The world was silent. Down in the river, wild duck set up their gabbling. A curlew flew overhead calling eerily. Forward they crept towards the bend of the river which their informant had indicated, each man treading in the steps of the one who walked a couple of paces before him. Hogan led, stepping carefully lest he should tread on a dead stick or catch his clothing on a blackthorn's spines. There was no talking. An hour slipped away. Still they crept forward, the hunting instinct which slumbers in all men's breasts sustaining them. From the darkness ahead came a faint light, not a fire's flame, but the subdued glow of embers. Before them moved a dark object. Hogan loosened sword and pistol. "He's there," he breathed. He turned. "Holland, are you ready ?"

There came no answer. "Holland," he whispered, stepping back a pace, "can you hear ? Hell's furies ! Where are you ?"

Still no answer, and with a softly breathed curse Hogan commenced to retrace his steps. Yard by yard he crept back, fearful lest his quarry should escape, blaming Holland for not keeping in closer touch. His foot encountered something soft. Hogan pulled up abruptly, stooped and felt in the darkness as he heard a

K

muffled sound. A warm body lay there. Running his fingers nimbly over it, he encountered ropes. He felt the head and found it enveloped in a coat. Something about the posture brought to his mind an unhappy experience of his own in Conway Castle. Quickly he tore away the folds. Holland sat up panting for breath.

"I was attacked from behind," said he presently, and fumbling with the cords which bound him he rose unsteadily to his feet. "Give me your arm, Hogan, I've no strength left in me."

"What happened?"

"I know nothing save that as I followed you an arm took me around the throat and a mighty hand choked all sound out of me."

"Where are the others?"

"Who knows? Come and discover."

Back went the two until they found one of the keepers lying across the path, bound and gagged. Then they found another and another; and all told the same story of the stealthy attack from behind. One only admitted hearing a slight sound and this he had attributed to the comrade whom he imagined followed him.

Disconsolate they wended their way back to Conway. As they neared the Porth-y-Felin, Holland caught Hogan's arm. "Listen!"

From out of the woods came the sound of mocking laughter.

"He shall pay for this," snapped Hogan, "By gad, we'll scour the woods night and day. Sooner or later we shall catch him. A man must sleep."

Systematically they set to work. Every man in the district was pressed into service. Farmers and fishermen; sheep-graziers from the Eglwysbach hills, drovers from the uplands; grooms and gardeners. All of them men of the open who knew the countryside as they knew their own home. By day and by night they watched meadow and hillside, bridle-path and lane, seeking for signs of the unseen visitor. One bright noon a game-keeper came to Hogan saying that he had discovered the place where Heritage slept. In the thick woods on the Denbighshire bank of the river he had found a low shack built of boughs. There were the ashes of a fire, partly hidden, and the remnants of a meal.

That night they surrounded the place. At a signal from Holland the circle closed in, every man holding his weapon ready. A man tripped over a root, and from the shelter of the boughs came a slight movement. "Fire!" cried a man hastily and an irregular volley split the night air.

"Do you surrender?" cried Holland running forward.

There was no answer. Hogan paused to strike flint, and presently he walked stealthily forward with lighted lanthorn. "Stand ready with your sword, should he break cover," he ordered as he stepped forward and flashed the light into the shelter.

"Is he dead?" whispered Holland.

"Ay, dead as—mutton!" cried Hogan, and setting hands on thighs he burst into unrestrained laughter. "Hoaxed, by Gad," he cried.

Holland ran forward. There lay a mountain sheep, its feet tied, its wool stained with blood. And lest its presence should leave reason for doubt, about it was bound a Cavalier's scarf of pale blue.

Holland bit his lips with suppressed rage but said nothing.

"We'll score the next hand, never fear," cried Hogan, moving off. "Keep scouring the woods," he ordered the men. "Never abate your endeavours, night or day. A man must sleep some time."

So the men searched, but a week passed and no reward came their way. Meanwhile Heritage, having rejoined a boat which lay for him in a cove near the Little Orme, was comfortably settling himself in the cabin of the Parliament frigate *Crescent*.

As Hogan truly remarked, "A man must sleep!"

CHAPTER NINETEEN

AUTUMN of 1643 followed a summer the like of which his Grace of York was not like to see again.

Peace still spread her placid mantle over the Conway's verdant vale. Wars and rumours of wars continued on the Cheshire border, but the good burgesses of Conway never so much as glimpsed a Roundhead, and thought of them in the abstract as a force of evil, and not as men of flesh and blood subject to like passions as they themselves. The quay at Conway was ever a-bustle with vessels loading and unloading. Cargoes of food, which was getting scarce, and gunpowder, which was scarcer, were despatched to Chester at such times that the watch ships of the Parliament forsook the Point of Ayr. More cargoes were sent to Dublin; less now because of the market than to keep in the good graces of the Governor, the Marquis of Ormond, to whom the Archbishop turned in the King's hour of need.

My humble suyte unto your Excelencye (with thankes for all former favoures) is to give us creditt for 10 barels of powder to be brought for the use of this Countrye, by Captain Bartlett, and I will undertake to paye the money forthwith, with many thankes, wrote the Archbishop.

But men, more than powder, were what the Archbishop desired. Over in Ireland were five regiments sent thither by the King several years before to quell the Roman Catholic uprising which resulted in the massacre of so many of his Majesty's Protestant subjects.

And now Ormond had achieved a truce which left

these veteran campaigners free for the King to put to other uses. Month by month during that summer, Maelys, at the Archbishop's dictation, wrote letter after letter, urging that the Irish army be sent to stem the Parliamentary successes in Cheshire.

Over in Shropshire, at Wem, Colonel Mytton with three hundred men had beaten off Lord Capel with a force twelve times as large, and, it was reported, Roundheads were singing the doggerel :

> "The women of Wem, and a few musketeers,
> Beat the Lord Capel, and all his Cavaliers."

Elated at their good fortune the Parliament troops began to press seriously for the first time into Wales. Sir William Brereton, Sir Thomas Myddleton and Colonel Booth led the Parliament forces to Wrexham, where they quartered the night. From Wrexham they passed on to Hawarden Castle, which fell into their hands, whereat there was an outcry of treachery from amongst the Royalists. Flint Castle then surrendered with all the honours of war. Mostyn Hall suffered a like fate, four pieces of ordnance falling to the victors.

At Gloddaeth, the Lady Mary Mostyn anxiously awaited news of her valiant grandson. The Archbishop comforted her, despatched messengers to make inquiries and wrote afresh to Lord Ormond, bewailing the fate of the King's cause. To think that a force of less than two thousand men should thus invade territory which was strong for the monarchy was gall indeed.

"Write to his Excellency that if the English-Irish forces land here, they shall be waited on by two or three thousand Foot at least, and some three hundred Horse to the English borders," said his Grace.

"They will not come," said Maelys moodily, but the Bishop paid no heed.

"And ask his Excellency to spare me a hundred able

soldiers for the guard of this town and castle. They shall have good quarters. I care not what country they are of so as they come with arms and competency of ammunition."

But the disasters at Flint and Hawarden provided the necessary spur.

Maelys long remembered the tumult one late autumnal night when she was aroused by a clamour which sent her hurrying to her chamber door. Lights were twinkling in the darkened streets of Conway. Within Plas Mawr, where she slept, the candles were guttering in their sconces by reason of the draught from open doors.

"What is it ? What is it ?" she cried as she caught sight of the Archbishop, clothed with haste which was foreign to his customary immaculateness.

"They're here, child, they're here !"

"Who ? The rebels ?"

"Rebels ? No, dear girl, the soldiers from Ireland. There are twenty-five hundred of them landed at Mostyn, and more at Beaumaris who will be here to-morrow. Hogan hath just ridden from Baron Hill with the news, and we must work all this night to prepare for their welcome. The tide hath turned, and treason will never show his ugly head again in North Wales."

His Grace hurried downstairs, and Maelys, catching her wrap about her, followed close at his heels. A servant was busy heaping billets on the rekindled fire. Hogan, booted and spurred, stood with a wine-bottle in hand. He paused in his drinking to stare boldly at Maelys, who took cover behind the Archbishop.

"To your room, child, and attire yourself, the air is chill," ordered the prelate.

The next afternoon the walls of Conway about the Upper Gate were black with spectators when the vanguard of the Irish forces came riding down from the hills, having crossed from Aber by way of the old

track across the uplands, rather than face the dangers
of the cliff-road at Penmaenmawr Head. The Foot,
they said, were following later.

Maelys, who expected a victorious army, gazed speech-
less. Despite their tattered finery, the men were but
beggars on horseback, with never a whole piece about
them save their pistols and swords. Lean from hard
living, clothed in rags, some of them barefoot, they
clattered over the drawbridge into Conway, looking
about them with hungry eyes, as though they had
reached, at last, their promised land. At their head
rode several officers who, despite their threadbare
tunics, still preserved their dignity. They were men of
honour, gentlemen who held the King's commission,
and they did not forget it, but their bearing failed to
communicate itself to those who followed after. The
troopers carried with them an air of recklessness and
bravado, such as settles on men who have harried a
countryside. In the market square an ox was roasting,
and barrels of ale stood broached on the green. At the
sight of the beer the men broke ranks, and raced their
nags for the barrels, one of which was overturned in
the scuffle. With shouting and cursing they righted it
and baled out its contents in their battered hats while
their riderless steeds continued their roaming until
captured by bewildered burgesses.

"Barbecue!" cried a trooper, slicing at the ox with
his dagger and swearing as the hot meat burnt his
fingers. "Hey, my bully-boys, let the notches out of
your belts, we'll not sleep hungry this night, I'm
a-thinking!"

Maelys, somewhat aghast at the unseemliness of the
behaviour of those she had waited for as saviours of
the King, stood motionless on the high ground, staring
in mute amazement.

"A merry throng," said a voice, and glancing up she
saw Hogan swaggering towards her.

"A lawless crowd," said Maelys primly.

Hogan seemed none too sober.

"Ay, lass, they're soldiers, and my old comrades in arms. Gad, 'tis a happy strain o' luck that brings us together. It warms my heart to see them once again."

"Can you not exercise some restraint over your—ruffian—friends?"

"'Strewth, and why should I be so doing? Let the lads have their fun. They've earned it. If they fight for you, at least you'll not begrudge them a bite and sup."

"Their language is shocking."

Hogan laughed. "Wait till they warm to their task; they're cold from Irish starvation. I'll warrant there'll not be many wenches in Conway who'll go to sleep unkissed tonight."

"Lieutenant Hogan, you forget yourself," said Maelys, drawing away.

"So long as I do not forget you, sweet one," cried Hogan lurching after her. "Come, my dear, let us enter into the spirit of these revels."

He caught her by the arm.

"How dare you!" flamed Maelys.

"Don't tarry, my dear, I've played gentleman long enough. I'm a soldier; d'you hear? Not one of your bread-and-cheese warriors, like that milk-sop Holland. I've smelt powder in the Lowlands and in Ireland, and I'm capable of taking care of myself—and of you too, my pretty one."

He swayed towards her, but Maelys evaded him. Before her mind danced the remembrance of that first fateful night in Cawood Palace. She leaped away as Hogan grabbed at her.

"What is this? Explain yourself."

The cold dignity of the Archbishop's voice brought Hogan to a standstill.

"A little folly in honour of this glad occasion, your Grace," said Hogan unabashed.

"Keep your folly for your friends, you drunken dog!"

Hogan laughed. "Most undignified for a Reverend Father in God! Drunken dog, am I? But useful enough to run your messages; useful enough to fight to keep your Grace in wealth and power; useful enough to——"

The Archbishop's eyes blazed. "Arrest this man!"

Several retainers stepped forward, but Hogan flung them off and sprang back, whipping out his sword.

"What," thundered the Archbishop undaunted; "you dare draw steel on me! You'll rot in the dungeon for this. Drop that sword."

He strode forward, but as Hogan threatened him there was a rush from the retainers and a clash of steel.

"To the rescue, bullies!" yelled Hogan. "Hi, Kelly, Mack, Leary, to the rescue, old comrades."

From the barbecue came a rush of feet, and the throng scattered as a score of fierce rogues came bursting through, lugging at their swords.

"We're with you, Hogan. What's the trouble?"

"I'm to be arrested for wishing to buss a wench."

"By gad, you've a pretty choice, too," cried a burly fellow; "I'll kiss her for you," and he swung Maelys off her feet amid the ribald jeers of his companions. The retainers drew back before the circle of sword-points and the Archbishop stood alone but fearless.

"I order you to stand back," said he.

"Who's this perky bird, Hogan?" cried one of the men.

"I am the Archbishop of York, and I hold the King's authority," said the Archbishop staring coldly at the man. There was a moment's pause and then several officers came forcing their way through the ring.

"Can you not preserve better discipline than this, sirs?" queried his Grace with fine indignation.

"Put up your swords, men," cried the senior officer.

"Not if Lieutenant Hogan is to be thrust in the clink," cried the ringleader.

"Is that so, Hogan? For what cause?"

"For insulting my niece," said the Archbishop coldly.

"This is a serious matter, Hogan," said the Major. "You must submit to inquiry."

"By Gad," cried Hogan, "I know a better game," and bursting through the crowd, he flung himself into the saddle of a loose horse, and spurred over the drawbridge. He turned and blew a kiss to Maelys as he fled.

"After him," cried the Archbishop, but the Major laid a detaining hand on his arm. "With respect, your Grace, there are matters of greater import. I cannot have my troopers winding their mounts chasing over the countryside when their presence before Hawarden is of such consequence to his Majesty. If your Grace will but reflect, this matter will receive judgment when a more opportune time occurs."

The Archbishop bit his lip. "You are right, Major. I shall not forget."

And taking Maelys's arm he walked with dignity to his palace.

CHAPTER TWENTY

COLONEL WYNN, his health restored, waited at the top of the broad stone steps before his stately home at Bodysgallen. He was accoutred for war. In his rich apparel and plumed hat, he looked what in truth he was, a gallant and chivalrous soldier ; about his waist the broad sash of the King's colour—"pale purple". And now, on that short November day, he was once again turning his back on happiness and home to do his devoir. For the newly come English-Irish, having received food and clothing from the hospitable Archbishop at Conway, were ready to march for Chester to rejoin their comrades who were besieging Hawarden Castle.

It had been a time of turmoil, for the companies of Foot who arrived the day following had been even less apparelled than their mounted comrades, and the housewives of the district were hard at work knitting stockings for the barefoot crowd, and all good husbandmen sacrificed their suits to clothe the scarecrow warriors who had come to drive back the Roundheads. More orderly were the Foot than the roystering Cavaliers who rode ahead. Indeed, some of them had but little liking for their task. Having been engaged to fight Catholics they were reluctant to turn their pikes against fellow Protestants. With ill-feeding and arrears of pay many of them were in a mood which would have sent them over to the enemy on the slightest provocation. And so Colonel Wynn, and Claude Holland, recently made a Major by the newly created Lord Byron, were requested to accompany them along the road to Chester, not merely to act as guides, but to lend encouragement and to endeavour to mollify the discontented warriors.

"We must keep these lads in good humour, Holland," said Colonel Wynn, turning to his younger companion, who had just ordered their horses. "I hear Brereton and Myddleton have withdrawn from Mostyn, Flint and Holywell as far as Wrexham, whence the rogues have sent a coaxing letter to the soldiers landed at Mostyn, regretting they have not been better provided for and trusting they do not mean to take up arms against the Parliament. Fortunately the letter fell into the hands of Sir Michael Ernley, who sent them a reply which left little doubt as to their intentions, nor of their loyalty to his Majesty."

"I am glad to hear it, sir," said Holland, but his eyes wandered, for Maelys was coming from the house.

"I would I were coming with you, Father," said she, slipping her arm through his.

"It is a different Chester from when you last saw it, child. There have been fires within its walls, and destruction without. All hamlets which encroach upon its border have been demolished by order of the Governor, and an outer line of earthworks is thrown up beyond the walls. Our friends from Ireland have arrived none too soon. They will be welcomed in Chester, though God He knows howsoever they will be fed."

Holland tactfully withdrew, leaving father and daughter together at this hour of separation.

"A goodly man," observed Colonel Wynn, looking after the soldierly figure, "and one who is achieving much honour in the King's cause. Maelys, my child, he has asked me to give him leave to seek your hand in marriage. What are your feelings in this matter? These are troubled times, and it would set my mind at peace could I know you had your future provided for, and your safety assured."

Maelys coloured and looked steadfastly at the gravel.

"I—I—am fond of him, Father, though I had not thought of our friendship in this light."

"What answer am I to give him, dear?"

"I scarce know, Father," said she, laying her cheek on his sleeve. "At the moment I can think of naught save that I must part with you once again."

"I will not press you, but if you decide to hear him, as in truth I trust you will, remember you have my blessing on this union."

Holland came slowly towards them. "They are signalling from the castle, sir, that the troops are about to embark at the ferry. If we are to join them at Marle——"

"We had best be off," finished the Colonel, darting back to the house to embrace his wife, and then, descending the steps, he swung into the saddle of his lovely white steed and, bending, kissed Maelys's upraised lips.

"God guard my dear ones," he said softly.

"God guard you, Father, and—God save the King," cried Maelys, and the two women stood bright-eyed, waving farewell as Colonel Wynn and Major Holland, followed by their grooms, rode down the tree-girt lane.

"Can we not go down to the road and see them pass?" asked Maelys.

"Nay, dear," cried her mother, "one farewell is enough. I could not endure another so soon, knowing that I may never see his face again. But get you gone. Youth will have its way."

So Maelys, calling for her horse, rode through the woods, taking a short cut to the road which crossed the marshy land where once the river Conway flowed past Llangwstenin Hill.

And presently the forces came, plodding the muddy road to tap of drum, Colonel Wynn on his white horse conspicuous in the van, where he rode with several mounted officers who doffed their hats when they saw Maelys. She looked down upon the footmen, the pikemen and the musketeers, as they trudged stolidly along. There was almost a touch of pathos about these tattered warriors. Despite the efforts made to reclothe them, many were still but poorly equipped to face the November cold. A few waggons rolled behind drawing their equipment. For their food they must depend upon the hospitality of the country through which they passed.

Holland drew his horse from the ranks and sprang to earth as he saw the waiting girl.

"Maelys, this is sweet of you," cried he.

She held out her hands. "God guard my knight," said she impulsively. "Oh, Claude, I think it so fine of you to ride forth thus to risk your life for the King."

"I shall fight better for your faith in me." Then hurriedly: "Has your father said—anything . . . ?"

"Yes, Claude, but let us not discuss it now. Come back to me with honour and—and then, perhaps, we can talk of love. It seems terrible to think of peace and comfort when these ill-clad unfortunates are marching forth perhaps to death."

Holland drew her to him and kissed her tenderly, and she did not resist.

"God guard you," she whispered.

"With you waiting for me, how could I be other than safe?" said he, and, mounting, he spurred after the retreating column.

Maelys stood waving to him until the moving mass merged into the drab of the distant hillside, and then, remounting, she rode, not home, but towards the river.

She felt she must stifle sentiment in work.

Once more within Conway's encircling walls, she hurried to the Archbishop's palace. She found him engrossed with his papers, but he spared her a smile as she entered.

"Did you see them go, Maelys?"

She nodded her head; words were difficult.

"Cheerily, child. Your father will come back to you. The tide is at the turn. Here are despatches from Cheshire which say that the Roundheads are quitting Wales so fast that they have not even reinforced the garrison at Hawarden, which must now fall to our forces of a surety. Their fair hope of reducing North Wales is now lost."

The Archbishop picked up his papers brusquely.

"Is my secretary ready for work?" he asked. "In the excitement which followed the arrival of our friends from Ireland correspondence has been neglected. Here is a letter from Lord Ormond, giving notice of the timely want of the forces from Ireland, and begging us to furnish them with clothing and victuals. Write his Lordship that Lord Bulkeley at Beaumaris and ourselves at Conway have done what we could. Captain Bartlett awaits the answer. It amazes me how he and his brother run the gantlet of the Parliament ships without being taken. Perhaps it is because God is with us. Ah, this, my child, is of consequence. It cometh from his Majesty and is in cipher. Get the code, I pray you."

Maelys bent her head over her task. "It saith," said she presently, "that his Majesty is calling a Parliament at Oxford and bids your Grace attend."

The Archbishop rose, a flush on his cheeks, and something of the old fire in his eyes.

"They cannot do without me!" said he proudly. "My place is in the council of the nations. Give me a quill, Maelys, I will write with mine own hand, that I obey his Majesty's behest."

"But, Uncle, your health will not stand so great a journey at this time of the year. Bethink you, the roads are impassable in places, and much of the way lieth through enemy territory. It will not be safe nor prudent to go thither."

"Safety! Prudence! When the King calls? Maelys, dear child, you have lived long with me and yet dost not know me. To obey the King is God's law. I count my life as nothing if I can but aid his Majesty. And advise him I can, for this Colonel Cromwell who is making so great a stir in the Eastern Counties for the Parliament is a kinsman of mine, and if any man can read him, I am the man. He is little known, as yet, Maelys, but he is one to be reckoned with. It taketh a Welshman to understand a Welshman, and a Williams to know a Williams."

"A Welshman, Uncle ?"

"By descent, Maelys, and a Williams, too, even though his grandsire altered his name to the more imposing title of Cromwell. I shall go, child, I shall go. It may be that God, who hath so far seen fit to punish us for our sins, may allow me to be His humble instrument in ending this unhappy war."

The Archbishop with trembling hand picked up his pen and began to write.

So November merged into December. Hawarden Castle fell to the Royalist troops under Captain Sandford, that valiant if voluble captain of firelocks, and Colonel Roger Mostyn with five hundred of his Welshmen, aided by the newly arrived English-Irish. Sir Michael Ernley's forces were taken to Chester, where they were feasted and clothed by the rejoicing citizens. Lord Byron had arrived from Oxford to take command of Cheshire, Shropshire and North Wales under Lord Capel, as his Field-Marshal. The news, filtering through to Conway, gave his Grace of York scant pleasure.

"His Majesty is ill advised to place English soldiers over the old Britons who dwell in North Wales," quoth his Grace, "for they will serve their own kin better than a stranger."

Another Christmas passed. For the Archbishop it was a time of mourning, for he crossed the river to Llansantffraid Glan Conway, there to bury his sister— she who was wife to Sir Peter Mytton, **Chief Justice** of North Wales, kinsman of the Colonel Mytton so active for the Parliament.

It was the second Christmas Conway had known under war conditions, and those who worshipped in the old church praised God from thankful hearts that as yet war's horrors had not come their way. And yet the business of war did intrude on the time of goodwill, for the Archbishop summoned his nephews, Alderman Will Hookes and Mr. Griffith Williams, to meet their kinsman, Mr. Maurice Wynn, and the Sheriff of the County, Mr. Robert Jones, to attest a copy of an order under the King's sign manual, levying two hundred and fifty more men for his Majesty's forces, to be brought to Wrexham by the end of February.

Maelys was content. Her father and Holland had ridden over from Chester to spend the holiday at home, and the girl found relief from her occupation in the companionship of the young Cavalier. When the weather was fine they rode together, and the girl felt herself warming towards him, yet could not feel that she was wholly satisfied with her lot. Holland was full of his new experiences. That his mind ever ran on ambition was plain to see. It was said that Prince Rupert was coming to Chester. Some of the Irish had deserted to the Parliament. Lord Byron was planning to drive the Parliamentary forces out of Cheshire, and day by day parties of his Horse were scouring the countryside.

"The villains have torn down the organ in Wrexham's fair church, and melted the lead for bullets," said Holland.

"Lord Byron will punish them," quoth Maelys. "It must be good to serve under so active a leader!"

Holland was silent awhile. "Yes," said he slowly. "His Lordship is an ardent Royalist and a zealous soldier, but he has a strain of heartlessness in him which pleases me but little." Presently he asked the girl whether she had seen Hogan. She shook her head.

L

"I would I had been here when he was so offensive,"
said Holland. "I hear he hath gone south to join
Colonel John Owen."

"I am glad he hath rid us of his presence."

"I am more glad of his absence than of the company
he keeps. I fear that John Owen bears little goodwill
to his Grace, and Hogan's company will not mend
matters."

Holland returned to Chester and Maelys to her work.
With the new year his Grace made preparation for his
journey to Oxford.

Having dictated a letter to the Marquis of Ormond,
he himself wrote to the King of his impending
departure. The silence was broken only by the
scratching of the quills. The Archbishop read his
letter, sanded it, and sealed it with great care. He
looked up at an exclamation from Maelys. She had
risen to her feet and was staring at a letter in her hand.

"But what is this?" she exclaimed, horror in her
tones.

"Ah, I had not meant that for your eyes, my dear,"
said the Archbishop.

"I am sorry. I took it as part of my duty to read all
correspondence. I did not know that you did not wish
me to see——"

"I only wished to spare your feelings. War, at times,
is a harrowing affair, even for men. Give me the
enclosure, and the letter." The letter read:

May it please your Grace,
    *The letter enclosed is a copy of one seized by me
from a messenger despatched by the Lord Byron (in
sooth, a noble-man!), and as his lordship is now Governor
of North Wales, is seemed good to me to acquaint your
Grace with what manner of man is set over you. Lord
Byron his letter hath gone before the Parliament, I, as
scout master to his excellencye, Sir Thomas Fairfax,
having intercepted it in course of my duties. Should you,*

by any hap, encounter this villain Byron, I beg you tell him that I, John Heritage, if ever he cometh within my reach, will despatch his sinful soul to hotter flames than ever he forced these innocent unfortunates into.

I am, your Grace's humble, obedient servant,

John Heritage.

Scout master to his Excye. Sr. Thos. Fairfax.

Maelys with trembling hand put the enclosure on the table. It was the copy of a despatch sent by Lord Byron to the Earl of Newcastle, giving details of a barbarity in which it would seem his Lordship gloried. It told of the massacre at Barthomley in Cheshire, where his plundering troopers drove a handful of villagers and Brereton's men into the church tower. Under one Major Connaught, pews were broken up, heaped to the church door and fired. As the prisoners, smoked from their retreat, were forced to dash through the flames, they were stabbed and hacked to death.

I put them all to the sword which I find to be the best way to proceed with these kind of people, for mercy to them is cruelty, wrote Lord Byron.

"It is not true, surely ?" asked Maelys.

"I fear it is," said the Archbishop soberly. "In truth, I fear that Byron and these English-Irish have set a different complexion on the war in these parts."

CHAPTER TWENTY-ONE

In the raw, grey dawn of a January day his Grace girt himself for his long journey to the King's Court at Oxford, the last long journey he was to make until he set forth on that from which no traveller returns. The anxieties of the past years had taken their toll, and Maelys, looking anxiously at the pallor of his countenance, felt her heart fail her. "In assiduity of watching and an hundred vexations," writes his Grace's chronicler, "his strength and healthful vigour, well maintained to that time, began to fail, and from that year came forward no more."

But the spirit of John Williams showed no signs of failing, and calling for his horse, he walked forth from his house with a quiet resolution.

"Can I not dissuade you?" whispered Maelys. "It is the worst time of the year, and the way is beset with perils, both from the elements and from the rebels. Bethink you, his Majesty would not think of these things, else he would not have summoned you."

His Grace touched her cheek lightly. "You do not know me, Maelys. Child, my heart grows warm to think that I am still needed. I ride forth with confidence. If God will that the King listen to my voice, we may yet see peace reign in the land."

The Archbishop took with him four retainers, proper men, well armed, and rode for Chester, for the way across the mountains was blocked with snow. Word came from Chester of his safe arrival in that city ; another messenger came from Shrewsbury, and then silence.

In Conway, a quietude settled upon everything within and without the walls. What men remained were more concerned with cutting faggots in Benarth woods and seeking food wherewith to fight the cold, than with the distant war. From Chester, Holland wrote in high spirit telling of the arrival of more Irish, and of Lord Byron's resolve to drive the rebels from out of Nantwich, which now remained their only stronghold in Cheshire. Then came even more welcome word from Gwydir, that Edmund Williams wrote from Oxford to say his Grace was there in Oxford and was well.

The Archbishop took up his lodging at Queen's College. "He was received in Court with much grace," says his biographer, "where he saw his stay must be short, for that city could not long receive so many nobles and gentry as came to make a Session of Parliament."

His counsel to the King is on record. "Sir," said the Archbishop in debate, "my opinion will be strange and, I fear, unwelcome, if it please not, yet do not impute it to falsehood or fear, but to error and mistake. Your militia is courageous but small, not likely to increase, and then not to hold out. Your enemies multiply, and by this time your army hath taught them to fight ; they are in treaty with the Scots to make a recruit ; and the Princes and States beyond the Seas, to their shame, give them countenance. Their treasurers at Westminster boast that it costs them large moneys every month to keep correspondence with their intelligencers and spies about you. Your soldiers in their march and quarters are very unruly, and lose the people's affection everywhere. Out of these premises, I infer (and I engage my life to your Majesty's justice and my soul to God's tribunal) that I know no better course than to struggle no further, since it is the will of God, and to refer all to the pleasure and the discretion of that unkind and insolent Parliament at Westminster, but with the preservation of your Majesty's crown and person to which they have all taken an oath to offer no hurt or violence. But if your Majesty disdain to go so low, I am ready to run on in the common hazard with your Majesty, and so live and die in your service."

Says the chronicler : "The King received it with a smile, and said nothing."

Not so, many of the others, Rupert amongst them, who were hot for settling matters with the sword.

So the Archbishop travelled by easy journeys, being escorted through the troubled counties by a strong military guard as far as Worcester, which he reached early in May. He turned his face towards North Wales again, bearing with him, under the King's name and seal, instructions to garrison and hold Conway Castle and town for the Crown.

As the rigour of winter had passed, the Archbishop resolved to return by way of the upland passes. His Grace rode well in advance of his retainers, partly because of the mettle of his mount, partly because he chose to be alone with his thoughts. The road wound and dipped among the crags, bordered at times with dense clumps of trees. Deep in thought, the Archbishop rode forward.

Affairs at Oxford had not been to his liking. He found "things unfixed in the Court" and his Majesty "shaken by variety of counsels out of any settled resolution". Despite the bold plans made, his Grace detected a waning enthusiasm for the royal cause. Rupert, the dashing cavalry leader, was no courtier, and his arrogance and tactlessness spread dissention among the leaders. "Verily all are not a King's friends who follow him !" he soliloquized.

"Your Grace was saying . . ."

Startled out of his reverie, the Archbishop became conscious of hoof-beats in the mud behind, and unexpectedly the head of a great black horse came thrusting past his thigh. The Archbishop wheeled

in alarm, and found himself looking into the calm eyes
of Heritage.

"I fancied I overheard your Grace making an ob-
servation, the wisdom of which reflects your Grace's
profound learning."

The prelate cast a hurried glance backward.
Rounding a bend of the road came his retainers, each
with a buff-jerkined trooper riding at his side. No
weapons were drawn. It was a silent victory. His
gaze returned to Heritage. The man was leaner than
when last he saw him ; browner, as though he had
tasted hard campaigning, but he was aglow with
health. The Parliamentarian's eyes gave no indica-
tion of his thoughts.

"Your Grace returns to Conway ?" asked Heritage
affably.

"So I intended—should circumstances permit."

"It would be rank heresy to doubt fulfilment of
your Grace's desires." Heritage spoke as one who
nourished a secret pleasure.

His mood elicited no response. "I comprehend I
am in your hands, Captain Heritage," said the Archbishop abruptly. "What would you have of me ?"

"The privilege of riding awhile in pious company ;
the joy of your exalted converse, sir. If I recall
aright there were one or two points on which we
differed when last we met. Possibly your Grace
would care to continue your observations on my
backsliding ?"

"It would seem we meet opportunely."

"Scarce opportunely ! Your Grace does me little
justice. For the pleasure of this encounter I have
lain in wait many patient days."

"Your time will not be wasted if I can turn you
from the error of your ways." His Grace was recovering some of his self-assurance.

"Lord, sir, do you not yet appreciate there is danger
in plain dealing ? Your efforts are like to meet with

little better fortune than when you at Oxford endeavoured to perform an equally commendable office to the King."

"You are well informed, sir, of my doings," said the prelate drily.

Heritage smiled. "Mr. Thurlow's agents are everywhere—as you yourself drew his Majesty's attention to."

"What I said was for the weal of our unhappy country," said his Grace hastily.

"And drew upon yourself fresh enemies in consequence. Your Grace does not appear even yet to appreciate that virtue doth not quench envy, but rather kindle it. You forget there are men whose trade is war; if you seek peace, their livelihood is gone from them. The soldier that subsists upon pay and plunder had as lief die as lose his trade."

"That is a cap which might fit your own head!"

"A fair hit, your Grace," laughed Heritage. "But let it pass. My desire is to warn you that there are those who plot your undoing."

"Young man, I have suffered from the assaults of enemies all my life, and am as yet undismayed."

Heritage nodded his head approvingly. "You convince me I acted aright in preventing young Hotham from cutting off your Grace's head."

"If you cherish a design to turn me from my allegiance to the King by fair words, you may spare your breath, for my loyalty is pledged to his Majesty to the death. Our King is wise among wise men of the first magnitude, full of constant and great virtues, all of them pearls of clear water——"

"You misjudge me, sir," interrupted Heritage. "I assure you I deem you of far greater value to the cause of justice on your present side. His Majesty's other counsellors have not been conspicuous for their intelligence as yet—always excepting gallant Falkland—and your good King knows not sheep from goats.

But I bid you beware of John Owen. He hath the ear of the Prince, and after his courage at the taking of Bristol, he stands high. 'Tis said that Rupert is to get a knighthood for him."

"I have no fear of John Owen. His Majesty hath placed in me the constableship of Conway Castle."

Heritage nodded his head. "So that your Grace will be induced to spend even more of your wealth on the fortifying of the castle ?"

"What I spend in his Majesty's cause will be repaid me—I have his kingly word for it."

"The word of a Stuart !"

"You are insolent."

"God forbid ! Merely sceptical. I would give much to hear your Grace preach in Conway church from the text—'Put not your trust in Princes'."

"If you attend, sir, I will have them sing the Cavalier's Te Deum : *O Lord, in Thee have I trusted, may I never be a Roundhead.*"

His Grace grew serious again. "I would you had heard me preach on 'Fear God ; honour the King'."

"It speaketh well for Christian charity that the years your Grace spent in the Tower have not diminished your loyalty. Howbeit, when you discover your King is a man of straw whose word is blown on every passing wind, believe me, I am waiting to befriend you."

"You speak with the assuredness of youth. You may be more in need of succour yourself. I tell you, what doubtless you know, that his Majesty is preparing once and for all to crush this base rebellion. Already your armies are beaten."

"Beaten ? They are scarce flea-bitten."

"As for North Wales, every castle is held for the King."

"We will come and take them, one by one, as we require them."

"Your vainglory leaves me unimpressed, sir."

"Well, what of Cheshire, my Lord? Even at Oxford, you must have had word how we trounced your noble burner of innocents—your great commander, Lord Byron? You know that in the Namptwich fight we captured Sir Michael Ernley, Sir Richard Fleetwood, Sir Francis Butler, Major-General Gibson, Colonel Warren and Honest George Monck (who is the only real soldier among you), to say nothing of fifteen hundred men and six pieces of ordnance? There's less exultation about your English-Irish plunderers than there was a few months ago."

The Archbishop bit his lip. "I gather you were at the fight?"

"As scout master to Sir Thomas Fairfax I was there. My one grief is that your valiant Lord Byron ran for Chester with so great a zeal that I could not so much as come up within pistol range of him. He rode as though Satan were at his heels—as in truth he was."

"Satan?"

Heritage patted the neck of his mount. "It pleases me so to designate my horse."

"I little hoped to find such tangible proof that Puritans were in league with the Power of Evil."

"I called him Satan because I overcame him, your Grace—though it ill becomes me to argue theology with one of your eminent learning."

The Archbishop changed the topic. "If you were scout master to Sir Thomas, how comes it you remain here when he has returned to aid Lord Fairfax in Yorkshire?"

"Mainly because I had a mind to remain. I now serve Colonel Mytton. You have heard of him?"

"One of the Myttons of Halston, a kinsman by marriage of my late sister! Yes, he came to the forefront by his capture of Wem."

"Your Grace is like to hear more of him before many moons are past. I bid you take heed."

"We, in North Wales, are honoured by your attention, and I by your condescension."

His Grace's irony was wasted.

Heritage reined in his horse.

"Our ways part here, sir," said he abruptly.

The Archbishop raised his eyebrows. "Am I not,
then, a prisoner ?"

Heritage shook his head. "Your Grace persists in
misjudging me. Yonder lies Gwydir and, I trust,
safety, though I find mirth in the thought that you
are in greater danger from your King's men than from
ours."

"I fail to see the reason for this meeting."

"It pleases my humour. I am a man of strange
fancies. Some of Colonel's Owen's men had orders
to harass you in these hills, and I took it upon me to
see you suffered no molestation."

"You are solicitous," said the Archbishop. "I
cannot see how I have merited this attention."

"I have some respect for your Grace," said Heritage
lightly, "though if I followed my inclinations I would
hang all bishops as high as Haman. You happen to
be held dear by the girl Maelys. It is for her sake
that I endeavour to preserve you from harm."

The Archbishop frowned. "You speak with too
great freedom, young man. Friendship with Mistress
Wynn is not for such as you. Moreover, it may interest you to know, she is betrothed to Colonel Holland."

Heritage smiled. "Bid her to be in no haste to
wed," said he, gathering up his reins ; "it would grieve
me to be the cause of her widowhood."

He signed to his troopers, and cantered across the
moors.

.   .   .   .   .

On the morrow the Archbishop rode into Conway,
where his presence called for jubilation. To the good
folk of the town he was their benefactor and their

protector ; to the clergy he was their inspiration, and to the Welsh their deliverer from the encroachments of the English and Irish soldiers who now were rarely absent from the ancient borough. Maelys was overjoyed at his safe return. She spread forth the accumulated correspondence, and gave an account of her stewardship ; then listened with rapt attention while the Archbishop told of the grandeur of the Court at Oxford, of the King's appearance, of Rupert's appointment as generalissimo, and of the gossip of Court and camp. He showed the wondering girl the order, sealed with the King's seal, giving his "most reverend Father in God", order to make the castle and town of Aberconwy defensible. His Grace, with some deliberation, ran his finger along the lines . . .

You, having begun at your own charge to put the same into repair, We do heartily desire you to go on in that Work, assuring you that whatsoever Moneys you shall lay out upon the Fortification of the said Castle, shall be repayed you before the custody thereof shall be put into any other hand than your own.

And Maelys, who knew how the Archbishop had lavishly squandered his great wealth on the defence of the castle, sighed a sigh of relief.

"The word of a king," she breathed.

"You hold I do right to place my faith in his Majesty's word ?"

"Why, Uncle, could any do otherwise ?"

"There are some who claim to have doubts," said the Archbishop grimly.

"But they are rebels, Uncle ! Roundheads, stale and threadbare cheats, Crop-ears ! Having no knowledge of honour or loyalty ! You have no doubts ?"

"So great is my faith, child, that I intend by and by to send to all good persons in this district, bidding them bring their plate, jewels and valuables to the safe custody of the castle, which I shall hold for the King at all costs, until God vouchsafe to send us better times.''

Maelys's eyes shone with a great light. For the rest of the evening she sat at his feet, and listened to his stories of the adventures which befell him by the way ; stories enlivened by a piquant wit and touched by many a sally.

But the Archbishop did not tell her he had seen Heritage.

CHAPTER TWENTY-TWO

HOLLAND, looking from the castle battlements, said slowly : "There are pack-horses coming from over the Sychnant Pass."

Maelys sighed. "More of them?" She grimaced in whimsical dismay. "Ah, and I so wanted air and sunshine after being cooped in the tower all morning. What a tedious business this is, Claude, all this noting and checking and witnessing! And what queer things some of the folk bring in! I had one dear dame fetch me a chest containing nothing but silken gowns which must have appeared ancient when Elizabeth was queen. I' faith, they have interpreted literally his Grace's bidding to bring their valuables to the castle. Silver and gold and jewels, why, yes, but why should I make inventories of moth-eaten gowns and family portraits? I have had to get an upper chamber for the goods which would assuredly perish were they stored in the strong-room his Grace hath prepared in the base of the King's Tower. I suggested he gave them a discourse against storing up goods where moth and rust doth corrupt, but he only smiled and bade me finish my inventory. Who would be an archbishop's secretary?"

"But what an archbishop, Maelys!" said Holland, consoling her with an encircling arm. "If he stayed in his pulpit, both you and he would have greater leisure, but he was ever thorough. The last of the fighting prelates, Maelys. If he pledges his honour to protect these good folk's chattels, there'll be stern fighting about these old walls ere ever a Roundhead enters Conway."

"See," broke off Maelys irrelevantly, "there's a convoy coming down the Valley Road. I wonder if it is Uncle Maurice Wynn's valuables from Gwydir."

"'Tis well guarded," commented Holland, peering up the Valley Road. "I would ever trust your Uncle Maurice to keep a shrewd eye to his personal affairs."

Maelys ran nimbly down the steps which led to the great courtyard. The open space which a couple of years before had been a solitude given over mainly to owls and daws was a scene of activity. Around the walls, pent-houses stabled the horses of the garrison and housed the scullions and men of lesser worth. Armed men stood at the main gate, and others were at watch near the barbican, examining every person and load which came up the incline to the entrance ere they were permitted to cross the drawbridge. The neighbouring gentry were making their way through the throng, or pausing to run appraising eyes over the inventories which the Archbishop issued acknowledging the receipt of each article brought to the castle for safe keeping during the troubled times.

Maelys threaded her way towards the royal apartments where the bulk of the treasures had been stored and where, for many hours each day, she had been engaged in preparing list after list. Holland, hurrying after her, tried to dissuade her. "Maelys, consider your health. Come, there is no need to return to your labours yet. And recall, my leave from Chester is short, and I would spend the whole of it with you."

"My duty calls," said Maelys resolutely. "Get thee behind me, Satan."

"I shall have to administer a reproof to the sergeant of the guard if he hath admitted Satan to any castle of the King," said a quiet voice behind them, and wheeling, they beheld the Archbishop watching with a smile.

"Claude would tempt me from my duty," cried Maelys. "Admonish him, Uncle, and protect me from his wiles—lest I weaken."

"I was telling Maelys, my lord, that some fresh air and sunlight were necessary to her health, after being shut in yon dark tower so many hours."

"I dare say that your desire for her companionship is of more consequence to you than her health, young man, but I agree with you. I cannot have my secretary overstraining her eyes. Come, Maelys, I can get another to do the work this afternoon. I will set some of these clerics at it ; a little temporal responsibility would not do some of them any harm."

Maelys shook her head. "I am not one to look back after putting my hand to the plough."

"A most recalcitrant secretary," said his Grace, shaking his head. "Well, if you will not obey my orders, let me set you another task. There are several who have not yet sent their goods ; some of them near at hand. Take horse, both of you, and ride to remind them. There is Robertus Pugh of Penrhyn, bid him hasten ; Lloyd of Llangwstenin ; the Ladies Conway at Llys Euryn ; and, Holland, you might have a word with your kinsfolk at Pwllycrochan, though I fear all their plate hath long since found its way into the King's coffers."

And before the girl could demur, the Archbishop walked away.

The two looked into each other's eyes, and turned like children let loose from school. They walked through the royal quarters, crossed the royal garden where it overhangs the river, and traversing the narrow, covered way along the curtain wall at the mouth of the Gyffin stream, they descended the steps which led to the castle's private landing-place. Taking a boat which was moored there, they speedily crossed the river. A groom was despatched to Bodysgallen to fetch their horses while they walked at leisure towards Maelys's home.

May was merging into June, and at such a time the Vale of the Conway is enriched with a beauty almost too lovely to be borne. Afar off the outlines of Caernarvonshire's mountains might seem like a hard wall reared against the heavens, but within them all was tranquillity and restfulness. The broad river flowed within its verdant banks ; every hollow was rich with trees ; the luscious meadows held forth promise of rich crops of hay ; the sloping hillsides were patterned with hedgerows ; and all the world seemed at peace. Warmed by the noonday sun, Holland with Maelys at his side wandered up the winding lanes, while hedges of hawthorn and brier enclosed them in a world of happiness.

"It is good to be with you again, Maelys ; to walk at your side." The man's voice was tender. "How sweet it is to roam with you ; and to forget for a while the slaughter and the scenes of anguish with which, alas, every soldier has to accustom himself !"

Said Maelys : "When will it be over, Claude ?"

"If God send us good success now I shall hope for a speedy peace," he said slowly. "Prince Rupert, the only hope of this miserable estate, is at Chester, and I have heard him swear that the insolence of this rebel Parliament is no longer to be borne. He means ere long to fight one battle for the Kingdom of England, for the stake is no less—to strike them such a blow as they will never recover from. If that design succeed we may soon see the King in his full authority. What a leader Prince Rupert is ! Why, Maelys, he is no older than you, yet he is generalissimo of all his Majesty's forces. 'Tis life, indeed, to ride with him into action. Ah, the brave sight of the nodding plumes and the flutter of scarves and the sparkle of blades. Then the trumpet sounds, and we shout, 'For the King', or 'For Rupert of the Rhine', and boot to boot sweep down on the rebel pikemen and see them go down under our hooves or our swords. They cannot withstand us ; Rupert's cavalry are irresistible !"

His eyes glowed with pride as he spoke, and Maelys,

M

responding to his ardour, pressed his arm more closely through hers.

"The Prince will fight, you say?"

"He is planning to lead us to Yorkshire for the relief of York. Reports come daily that the Scots are marching south to ally themselves with the rebels, and York is endangered. But Rupert means to give both their deserts, and I, Maelys, am to command a regiment of Horse, part of which I have raised myself."

"Your regiment? Claude, you never told me."

"I concealed it for a surprise. Prince Rupert favours me and hath promised me much. I would fain have come to you bringing my sheaves with me when I came to ask you to be my bride."

A stillness seemed to fall. Maelys walked in silence as one bewildered.

"But I have grown impatient, Maelys, I—I grow tired of waiting, and now, before the battle, I must speak."

"No, no, Claude. Not just yet, please."

"Do you care enough for me, Maelys?"

"Oh, but yes, but—it is all so disturbing. Everything. The war; I am bewildered."

"But that is why there is need for someone to care for you. Your father agrees that your safety would be the more ensured if you were my wife, and I am to say that he approves of my speaking to you. . . . See, yonder he cometh. Pray ask him yourself."

And riding quietly down the lane on his white horse came a Cavalier who waved gaily as he saw them. Maelys's eyes dwelt on him fondly. A gallant figure in truth, with his plumed hat and his scarf of pale purple. Some distance behind came the groom with the led horses.

"I rejoice that the bird hath escaped her cage," he cried, kissing his daughter. "I was about to cross to Conway to intercede on your behalf, when Hughes arrived telling of your deliverance and seeking the horses.

So you are to ride to Llys Euryn ?   'Twill do you good,
Maelys, and though Claude here is in no need of saddle
exercise, I'll vow he'll not complain."

"Indeed no, sir." Holland became courteous. "Will
you ride with us ?"

Colonel Wynn looked fondly at his daughter. "I
think you can contrive without me ; I have a call or
two to make.   But I will save you visiting Lloyd as I
have to pass Llangwstenin and will be glad of an excuse
to drop in there.   God bless you both," and with a
cheery wave the gallant Colonel passed on his way, and
Maelys and Holland took their horses from the groom.

It was not a long ride to their neighbour at Penrhyn,
and soon the tall grey chimneys and stately gables of
Penrhyn came in sight.   Penrhyn in Crcuddyn, it was
often called, to distinguish it from Penrhyn House, his
Grace's stately home near Bangor.   The afternoon sun
was still on Penrhyn, lighting up the southern wall
of the old banqueting hall, which, even then, was worn
with the rain of centuries.   They left their horses at the
mounting-block, crossed the cobbled courtyard, and
entered the broad, low doorway.   From the cool,
dark room within came the owner.   Somewhat reti-
cent was Pugh, for since the trouble three years before,
when he was leader of the Papist outbreak, feelings had
been a little strained between him and his neighbours,
though now that he was wholeheartedly for the King,
as were most other of the Roman Catholic gentry,
most agreed that bygones should be bygones.   He
courteously placed chairs for them and heard their
story.

"I have sent my plate to his Majesty, and what
other things of value I possess I long since concealed
in a cave in the Little Orme, where I fancy they will
defy detection.   I thank his Grace for his kindly
thought, but I have no need for his good offices."

They took a glass of wine together.   As they walked
out into the sunlight of the courtyard, and made their

way to the horses, Pugh turned and looked seawards across the bay towards Penmaen Head.

"There was a Parliament frigate in the offing last evening," said he. "The *Crescent*, I fancy she was. We can see them beating off Point of Ayr often enough, watching the Chester shipping, but they don't often trouble us so near."

They bade farewell to their host and turned their horses eastward. Before them lay a broad stretch of morfa, broken by several streamlets as the Afon Ganol made its way to the sea. A little inland lay the farm buildings of Dinerth, with the doves fluttering about the dove-cote.

In joyousness they put spurs to their horses and raced across the smooth green turf, leaped the streams and dashed up the farther slope towards the ancient church of Llandrillo where it crowned the summit.

Before them, nestling at the slope of the gentle hill of Bryn Euryn, rose the tall chimney and limestone walls of Llys Euryn. A stately home still, but lacking the grandeur which once it knew when it was palace for the great King Maelgwyn Gwynedd. Here it was that Edynfed Fechan dwelt—Llywelyn the Great's commander-in-chief from whom Archbishop Williams claimed descent on the distaff side.

Here they dismounted and called upon the Ladies Conway, who professed that their goods were packed and ready, and that they needed but an armed escort for their conveyance to the castle.

As the two emerged, Maelys looked at the smooth pathway which led to the hill-top, and the spirit moved her to climb. "Come, Claude," she cried, "I will race you to the top. I love to stand on the summit of the green hill among the ruins of the old British fort, and to feel the breath of the breeze and to look far and wide like an eagle in its eyrie." She went off before he could remonstrate, and, nothing loath, Holland followed in pursuit. Ten minutes later, breathless and rosy-cheeked, they stood upon the rocky summit of the ancient citadel, and looked down upon the fair land beneath them.

"Yonder is Pwllycrochan nestling amid the trees," cried Maelys. "Shall we climb down this steeper slope and walk to it ?"

Holland smiled and glanced at his spurred boots. "I am scarce garbed for much walking," said he, "but if it be your whim, why, I never have the heart to refuse you anything."

"See," cried Maelys, suddenly pointing out to sea. "Yonder lie the rebel ships."

Holland looked. Far away, tiny grey dots on the face of the waters, could be seen the watch ships of the Parliament.

"Three, four, five," counted Maelys, "and the one beating off the Abergele Bay which must be the frigate of which Mr. Pugh spoke."

"Ay, and the others will be Richard Swanley's squadron, I surmise—his own ship, the *Leopard Regis*, and with her the *Swallow*, *Prosperous*, *Providence*, and the merchantman, *Leopard*. Did you hear that recently, with much scandal and insolency, they took seven barques out of Holyhead ?"

"Curse the Roundhead rogues !" cried Maelys. "The last time we tried to get a letter to his Grace of Ormond in Dublin it took nigh a month to reach him, so close was their watch."

With a shrug of her shoulders she turned her back on the offending men-o'-war and, finding a gap in the ruined ramparts, she commenced scrambling down the precipitous side of the hill. Presently they came to a belt of trees. Crossing the ravine—where once a Roman legion under Sempronius was ambushed—they found a narrow track which they followed until they came to the old steep road which ran from Llandrillo church up the hill and over the uplands to Llanrwst. Up this they walked, glad of the shade. They crossed

the narrow highway which, 'tis said, was built by the
Romans when they pressed down from Chester, seeking
copper in the Great Orme mines, and down this they
turned to Pwllycrochan.

Holland leaped the bank which ran beside the
sunken road and wading through the bracken to a fallen
tree seated himself upon the trunk. "Come, Maelys,
sit here and cool awhile. I've no mind to go a-calling
with a face like a lobster. My dear child, why do I
listen to you ? What other cavalier would have suffered
the agony and ignominy of walking when there was a
good horse to ride ?"

He laughed at his own discomfort, and side by side
they sat in the silent woods. Now and again some tiny
warbler would set up a thin piping or a bee would
drone past.

"Maelys," said Holland presently, capturing her
hand. "I have not yet had an answer to a question
which means much to me."

The girl was silent.

"Why do you not reply ?" persisted Holland.

Maelys looked up.

"I do not know," she said frankly. "You have been
true comrade to me ; I admire and respect you more
than any man—and yet—somehow—I—I cannot
answer you. It means so much to a maid."

Holland bowed his head. For a while they sat
silent. Far away sounded a soft rustling.

"Someone is coming !" said Maelys, who had the
quick ears of a wild animal.

Holland listened. "I think there is," said he. "I
believe I hear horses in the distance. I wonder who it
can be."

Idly he took a few paces forward and stood looking
and listening. Suddenly he stiffened. The girl saw
his face grow tense. He crouched, peering into the
green wilderness, then turning quickly came creeping
back on the tips of his toes, his face white and drawn.

His agitation communicated itself to the girl.

"What is it, what have you seen ?"

"Hush !" he breathed.   Then, clutching her arm, he forced her to cover behind the log.   Crouching beside her, he lay motionless.   The girl could hear the quick intake of his breath.   Here was a Holland she had never seen before ;   alert, keen-eyed, apprehensive.

"What is it ?" she whispered again.

Instead of replying he slowly raised his head among the bracken.   Maelys watched him anxiously.   She was conscious of the damp earth cool upon her knees.   A thorn was pricking her palm, yet she bore the pain unheeding.

"Look !"   Holland's lips framed the words.   Noiselessly she raised her head and looked over the green sea of bracken.

From the sunken road before them came the sound of a horse's hoofs.   They paused.   Between the tree boles, Maelys glimpsed the rider.

She saw a buff coat belted with an orange-tawny scarf, and above it a lean, brown face showing between the bars of a helmet.

A sickening sensation seized her as she realized she was looking at a Roundhead trooper.

CHAPTER TWENTY-THREE

THE trooper had his back to them. He looked down the slope where it stretched to the bay. Motionless, he sat scanning the landscape ; motionless, the two watchers in the bracken regarded him with anxious eyes. He moved his helmeted head and instantly the heads in the bracken vanished from sight. Maelys heard the horse move on. The leisured hoof-beats paused again. Through the screen of leaves Maelys could see the trooper halted at the cross-roads in the woods. After a while he moved forward, along the old highway, and vanished from sight.

Maelys breathed a sigh or relief. "Only one," she said softly.

Holland looked gloomy. "A scout," said he. "There must be more near by. They would never venture so far into our country unless they were in force. Come, let us get back to the horses. We must warn them in Conway without delay."

He crept forward through the bracken, Maelys at his heels. Up and down the sunken road they glanced, darted across its deserted surface and into the woods on the lower side. With many an anxious backward glance they crept through the trees. They neared the old road which dipped steeply downwards towards Bryn Euryn.

Suddenly, Maelys pulled Holland to cover. Down the hill was coming a body of horsemen. They rode two by two, keeping to the soft ground on either side of the road. Their buff tunics blended with the browns of the forest. Peering through the bushes which flanked the old road, the watchers could see them halt at the

cross-roads as the scout had done. There was no talking. At a signal half the party followed the old highway towards Mochdre, the remainder continued down
the hill. To Maelys, crouching breathlessly in the
bracken, every second seemed an age. Surely those
keen eyes would discern her. She became conscious
of the gaudiness of Holland's attire.

Slowly the horsemen rode past. They appeared
in no haste. They sat their horses silently, businesslike. Maelys caught glimpses of the spurred boots,
white with dust ; the sweat-ruffled coats of the bay
horses they rode. She dare not raise her eyes to see
what the faces of the riders looked like. Every detail
of the scene was impressed on her mind ; the trailing
ivy on the opposite bank, the rough earth with tree
roots thrusting through, the glossy leaves of a holly
bush. . . .

They had gone, lost to sight in the valley below, and
the last muffled footfall of their horses faded from the
still summer air.

Holland was on his feet. "We must see which way
they turn," he whispered, and keeping the hedge between him and the road he commenced a quick but
quiet descent of the slope. Maelys, her heart palpitat-
ing with exertion and excitement, was close behind.
At the bottom of the hill where there was another
cross-road they paused. There was no sign of the
enemy.

Maelys pointed to the trampled dust. "They have
turned towards Llangwstenin," she whispered.

With a quick glance to see they were unobserved
they darted across the road and plunged into the woods
which clothed Bryn Euryn. Here they grew more
daring and ran forward with less regard to silence
until, breathless, they reached Llys Euryn.

"The rebels are here," gasped Maelys as one of the
ladies came to the door.

Mistress Conway wrung her hands and looked helpless.

"But what shall we do ?" she moaned. Then turning to Holland, who came up with the horses, "Are you not staying to protect us, sir ?"

"Madam, one man against so many would but add to your misfortunes. They may not come this way. Hide your valuables and seek shelter in the vicarage."

"They desecrate churches," moaned the unhappy woman, but Holland gave her no further heed. Catching Maelys's rein he urged the horses into the open and headed them down the slope. They had galloped across the morfa not long since because of the joy of living ; now they spurred recklessly in fear of life. There was no sign of the enemy yet. They had the hill between them. They leaped the streamlets, sending the sandpipers fluttering for safety.

"Head for Gloddaeth," gasped Maelys, but : "Too late," replied Holland. "See," and glancing inland, Maelys saw a string of buff-coated horsemen riding towards Llangwstenin Hill.

So they made for Penrhyn, where they sprang from their horses, and shouted the alarm. A few retainers hurried out and began dragging farm wains to make a barricade across the roadway. Holland led the horses to the rear of the building and then joined Mr. Pugh and Maelys, who stood before one of the mullioned windows looking over the broad open stretch of sward, across which a score of troopers were advancing at an easy trot.

"They are too many for us," said Pugh grimly. "Escape while you can. We will try to hold them in check until you have a start. You may reach Bodysgallen by the Eglwysrhos road."

His advice was sound, and with a hasty handclasp Holland and Maelys took to their horses again, guiding them in the shadow of the trees to the old road which climbed the pass in the Little Orme. Fortunately the high roof of Penrhyn concealed them from their pursuers. Behind them a carbine cracked. Holland turned anxiously. "Quick! Pugh cannot hold out long."

"Keep to the fields. It is safer. They may ambush us," cried Maelys, so they rode in the open. The sloping meadows stretched far ahead. A distant shout sounded. On the hill above them a horseman was silhouetted against the skyline. Maelys rode faster. Suddenly she gave a cry of distress, and Holland, following her pointing finger, saw a sight which filled him with apprehension. Drawn in the shelter of the trees was a body of buff-clad horsemen and towards them, oblivious of danger, came a familiar figure on a white horse.

"Father!" cried Maelys. "Claude, save him."

"My dear, I cannot. It is too late."

"Then rescue him. I entreat you."

"It is too late. My duty is with you. I will save you if I can."

"If you care for me you will rescue my father. Go! Go!"

But Holland was obdurate. "He would wish me to protect you."

"I shall hate you if you do not aid him. Ah, see."

There was a sudden movement among the hidden horsemen. The white horse reared as they rode forth. Maelys saw the sparkle of a sword as Colonel Wynn realized his peril. Then the white horse and the scarf of pale purple were lost to sight in the russet mass. With a sob Maelys bent her head.

Behind them a trumpet sounded. She glanced back. A score of horsemen were in pursuit of them, stretched in a long line.

Suddenly Maelys's heart seemed to miss a beat. Far in advance came a great black horse, which gained on the fugitives with every stride. She did not need to discern the rider. She might have known!

"I shall come back! I shall come back!"

The words raced through her brain.   So this was the manner of Heritage's coming !

"Ride !" she screamed. "Ride !" The horses were stretched to their utmost. "Make for Maesdu. Old Parry has a boat drawn up on the sand-dunes. We will cross the river there."

But in her heart she knew if was futile. Remorselessly the horseman bore down on them. The thunder of hoofs grew nearer and nearer. Holland cast a backward glance and his face went white. His right hand crept to his saddle-holster and he drew one of the long horse-pistols. He turned in his saddle, took aim and fired.

At the explosion, Maelys winced. She ventured to turn her head. Heritage was still in the saddle, his face calm and unperturbed.

Holland drew his sword.   "Ride !" cried he now, and struck the girl's mount with the flat of his sword. He dropped slightly behind. Maelys ventured a second glance backward. Heritage was nearer now and gaining at every bound. He looked the same as before. The only difference was that he had drawn his sword, and at the sight of that long, straight blade Maelys shuddered.

Then came a clash of steel. To Maelys the result was inevitable. Holland was a good swordsman, but he was handicapped. His position was cramped. It was ill to fight when fleeing. He could not attack ; at best he could but guard himself from the sword of the pursuer. Holland experienced the feeling that Heritage was playing with him and the mortificaton infuriated him. He endeavoured to retaliate. There was a sharp swish of steel and the Cavalier's sword was struck to the ground.

"My dear Maelys"—Heritage's voice was cynical— "you should have chosen a more doughty escort."

Holland's answer was savage   He plucked the second pistol from his holster and thrust it in Heritage's face.

Maelys screamed. The report seemed to split her ear-drums. But quick though Holland was, Heritage was quicker, and his ready blade knocked up the barrel of the pistol so that the ball went harmlessly overhead.

Heritage rose in his stirrups and his great sword swung over his head. It came sweeping down. . . .

Again Maelys screamed. There was a sickening thud, the sound of a falling body; the girl's senses reeled; the sunlit day grew black about her.

.   .   .   .   .

When Maelys came to herself she was lying on the grass and Heritage was bathing her face with water which one of the troopers had fetched in his headpiece from a nearby pond. She could not have lain there long for the horses standing patiently by were still panting from the run. There was concern in Heritage's face when the girl opened her eyes, but the impassive expression instantly returned. For a moment she allowed her gaze to rest on him wonderingly.

Then she looked farther afield. She saw an irregular ring of russet-coated horsemen, each standing at his horse's head. So these were the rebels ! She regarded them curiously. Most of them were fresh-faced boys, sons of yeomen by their looks, well set, cleanly lads, somewhat serious. Their silence and discipline impressed her. Only one seemed to resemble the type of man she had expected. He was, apparently, a sergeant ; a man of middle age, hard-lipped, with fierce, intolerant eyes.

She turned from him and saw motionless on the sward the outstretched figure of Holland, lying near his bleeding horse. Her wandering senses suddenly concentrated.

"Beast !" she cried, striking Heritage across the face. "Murderer, you have killed him. Accursed Crop-ear, could not my loyal friend escape your fury ?"

She commenced to sob hysterically. Heritage looked a little puzzled, turned his head, and reassured her.

"He is only stunned by the fall," he said indifferently. "It was the horse I struck."

Maelys was relieved but unreasonable. "Brute that you are, you could not forbear to slay a harmless horse."

Heritage agreed. "It was a pity," he said. "The animal was valuable and horses are scarce. You must put it down to my forest manners. God hath not given me an unlimited patience and when he fired at me a second time I grew wroth. I was about to cut him down when I remembered that you held him dear. There was no time to check the blow ; all I could do was divert it, and so the horse took it in his stead."

Heritage stood up and turned to his men.

"Mount," he said curtly, and instantly every trooper swung into the saddle and sat motionless, awaiting the next command.

"Sergeant Pentecost, did you capture the hall over the hill ?"

"It pleased God to allow us to chastise the wicked," said the sergeant, speaking through his nose. "An accursed spot, it was, too, full of papists and idolaters, who had a chapel laden with images in the house. We have purged it clean."

"What have you there ?" Heritage pointed to an object strapped to the sergeant's saddle.

"One of the idols," said the man, uncovering the gilded figure of some saint. "I wrenched it from its niche, thinking it would serve for target practice, if it pleases your worship."

"Do what you will with it, so that you are not cumbered on the way back," said Heritage indifferently. "And now, do you take all the men but six, following the bank of the river until you come opposite the walls of Conway. You will rest your horses and open fire on the town from such points of vantage as you think proper, bearing in mind that your company is not to

scatter, and must move off in time to be at the rendezvous by the time the sun sinks beyond yon spur.
You are not to come to close quarters unless forced.
My desire is that you merely engross their attention
and keep them within their walls. You understand?"

The sergeant saluted. "And your prisoner, sir?"

"Let him lie there. The day is mild and he will
come to anon. Take his pistols, but leave him his
sword."

He took the weapon from the sergeant and thrust
its point into the ground at Holland's side. Six of
the best-mounted troopers had drawn to one side.
Heritage crossed to Maelys.

"Do you feel rested?" he asked curtly. She rose
without a word.

"What are you going to do now, burn Bodysgallen?"
she asked defiantly.

Heritage turned to a corporal. "Just beyond the
trees which cover yonder hill you will find a hall with
a grey tower. You will take three men and stay on
guard until sunset, seeing that no person molests the
house nor causes anxiety to any member thereof."
The man saluted and rode away with his troopers.

"I ask no favours from you," Maelys said with a toss
of her head.

Heritage picked up Satan's reins and mounted.
"I ask a favour of you," he said, extending a stirruped
foot, "mount in front of me."

"I refuse," said Maelys proudly.

"The lady's horse is here, sir," said the sergeant.

Heritage turned and looked at the man with eyes
which made the hard-faced sergeant step back a pace.
"Take your men and do my bidding. Interfere not
with affairs which concern you not. Ride on."

The sergeant saluted and led his men away.

Heritage turned to the girl. "Mount," he said.

Behind her, six troopers sat staring ahead with
expressionless faces.

"You will mount before me," said Heritage slowly, "or my forest manners will cause me to humiliate you by picking you up as though you were a naughty child."

He thrust out his foot again, and Maelys with a shrug of her shoulders did as she was bid.

"A captive has no option," said she. "All I ask is that you do not touch me more than is necessary. God save the King, and perdition to all Crop-ears!"

Heritage signed to the troopers, touched his horse with the spur and rode inland. Along lanes familiar to Maelys since childhood she thus was carried captive. They crossed the causeway the monks had built centuries before, and proceeded along the winding bank of the river, past the old church of Llansantffraid where the Archbishop's sister was buried, past the rocks at the river's marge where several coasting vessels lay dry on the sands, for the tide was out, until the road forked to the right. Down this lane Heritage turned, waded a brooklet, climbed the hill opposite between banks on which many wild-flowers grew, on and on until the road reached the river.

"There is no ford here," said Maelys.

"The road would not come here if there was no ford," said Heritage.

"I know there is no ford," said Maelys.

Heritage rode into the water. "I know there is," said he, "for I have already forded here. Yonder lies 'Cymryd'." He pointed to a quaint house at the river's marge.

"What of it?" said Maelys.

"I have a strong fancy for it," said Heritage. "I think we may live there when we are married."

His cool assumption made Maelys gasp. She bit her lip and said nothing. They turned down the river a little space and rode into the farmyard of the old grey stone house which had weathered the storms of centuries.

"You may rest here for an hour," said Heritage, lowering her to the ground. "I sent a messenger ahead to bid the good folk prepare for your reception. You will find refreshment within."

Without a word of thanks she left him and entered the building. In front of the wide fire-place a table was set for a meal. An elderly man bowed as she entered, and then left the room in silence. Maclys darted to the front door, opened it cautiously. Could she escape? Silently she tip-toed across the gravel path and on to the strip of lawn. Before her a path led to the river, where a boat was moored. She crept forward.

Suddenly she became conscious of the motionless figure of a Roundhead sentry watching her from behind a great cedar which threw its dark branches across the path. With a sigh she retraced her steps. . . .

An hour later, with resignation in her face, Maelys walked into the yard where Heritage was waiting. There was no sign of the troopers. She mounted in silence and they rode up the narrow farm lane which climbed the hill. Here and there they passed white-washed cottages where women, with children clinging to their aprons, came to the doors and stared in wide-eyed surprise. Heritage heeded them not. He came to a lane which led up the slopes of Tal-y-Fan.

"I wonder how old this road is," said Heritage suddenly. "It must have been here long years before the old church was built up there out of reach of the raiding pirates from the Irish seas."

Said Maelys: "That church hath the words you may recall—'Fear God; honour the King.'"

Heritage smiled. "I shall not take you that far, so you will not need to read them."

"I have no need, they are engraved on my heart."

Heritage turned his steed abruptly from the lane into a pathway which led to a great holly tree beside which a mountain brook plashed with pleasant sound. They dismounted, and he slipped the bridle from his

N

horse, allowing it to graze in the lush grass beside the stream.

All about them tall foxgloves rose like a wall of pink. Maelys stood watching her captor with expressionless eyes.

He walked slowly towards her.

"More than once," said he, standing before her and staring down into her eyes, "more than once you have been pleased to call me a damned Crop-ear. Did you realize the name was appropriate ?"

With a quick gesture he tossed his barred helmet on the grass and turned his left cheek towards her.

The girl saw that the top of his ear was missing.

CHAPTER TWENTY-FOUR

"You see," said Heritage casually, "there is but a portion missing. That was because they were generous ; they treated me gently because I was but a lad."

His voice held an irony which cut. He leaned his back against an elm, folded his arms and stood with his chin sunk upon his breast, deep in thought. Maelys stared at him curiously, a little awed.

"Don't you think," said Maelys, "that you could be more explicit. Who treated you thus ? Ought I to know ?"

"You shall know," said Heritage, without moving his posture. "I brought you here so that you should know." He turned to her quickly, a touch of fire in his tones. "You think," he cried, "that we have nothing to say for ourselves. You talk of us as though we rebelled against a noble king out of the naughtiness of our hearts. I tell you that what we do now is to draw the sword against tyranny ; we strive against oppression ; we fight for liberty of conscience ; so that our children may worship God without Star Chamber persecutions. What of your saintly Bishops ? Your busy little rat of a Laud and his kin ? Have they no better task before God than to spend their time devising nose-slittings and ear-croppings, pillory and prison for any of their fellow men who won't bow the head at their command ? There's only one of them worth a candle, and he is your Archbishop of York. He's filled his coffers to bursting by serving God and his King, yet he would have taken the middle way and preserved peace in our land if Charles Stuart had given a thought for anything but his own selfish pride."

"You talk treason," said Maelys coldly, turning her shoulder. "To clap religion into a quarrel is a formal foolery that every child can see through."

"I speak as I have suffered," said Heritage. "What do you know of the oppressions and the persecutions which have driven many a good man and true across the Atlantic to New England ? You have your home and your comforts, and servants to wait on you, and gallants to flatter you ; and it's fashionable to walk to your church and listen to a mumble of words ; but go over to Caernarvon and ask them what poor Prynne thought of it all after his ears had been cropped because he dared to write a pamphlet against dancing."

"And have you brought me here by force to offend my hearing with this abuse ? I tell you that I will hear no baseness of the King. Rather I will suffer as my brother and my father have suffered."

"Your father has not suffered as mine suffered," said Heritage slowly. "Listen, and I will tell you ; when I have done perhaps you will realize that I have cause for bitterness. My father was one of Raleigh's captains. Does that mean aught to you ? He was one of a different breed from the lap-dogs who fawn on you. There was a time when he sailed from Bangor, here, with old Sir Piers Griffith to fight the Spaniards, and later when Sir Walter set forth on that last mad venture to Guiana—into which he had been basely tricked by that Scotch loon, James—my father must needs go too. He came back with nothing but the clothes he stood in, and the fever germs from Orinoco swamps. We nursed him back to health, but Raleigh's execution—Raleigh's murder—left him a broken man. He aged quickly, but a few years slipped by in quietude. Then one day a churchwarden inquired of him how he never went to church ; and my father, who was never a man to choose his words, said that he for one would never bow down at the bidding of a King who must needs cut off Raleigh's head for no other reason than that he knew Sir Walter was the better man.

"There was little said at the time, but two days later in walks a Justice with his officers and reads forth a long rigmarole about blasphemy and treason, and then stalked off, leaving the officers to drag my father to the stocks. It was a damp, cold evening. I was but a boy of ten at the time, but it stands forth clearly in my mind and will do till I die. I besought them to have pity on his age and his honourable service for his country, but they took pride in humiliating a man they dared not have faced in his prime. Then one of them drew his knife and cut off both my father's ears, bidding him keep silence or they would slit his tongue likewise. I cried out at the piteous spectacle and, boy though I was, ran for the fellow and nigh had him on his back when his creatures saved him. At that juncture a coach drew up and two men got out, and one inquired the reason of the bother. He was a great man, I gathered by the respect paid to him, and I recall he was ablaze with silk and jewels.

"When they told him, he laughed and bade them slice off my ears likewise, crying that the whelp was like to be as vicious as his sire. With that the man with him, a lesser man in dark clothing, said : 'Nay, spare him somewhat, seeing he is but a lad ; just slice a tip as a reminder that he must reverence his King and up-hold his Church.' With that they passed on, and the ruffians worked their will on me as you see. I broke away and took to the woods, and presently found the cottage of one Tom Jenkyns, who had been my father's gunner. He was all for going to the rescue, but on second thoughts bided until dark and then set forth and freed my father by stealth. With fever and suffering from exposure he was nigh gone. We hid him and nursed him. He lingered two days, but the knife they had used had some distemper upon it and blood-poisoning set in so that my father died horribly in my arms.

"We laid him away, and then Jenkyns and I set forth. I ceased to be a boy that night ! We went to the village in the darkness and I got the knife which had done the deed. No man that had a hand in it kept his ears ; though what happened after I never learnt, for Jenkyns carried me to the coast ere the storm broke, and smuggled me across to Holland. There I found a colony of Englishmen who had fled the persecution, and ere long the one who befriended me set sail for New England, taking me with him. There I was reared in the frontier settlements, fighting the redskins, fitting myself by chase and war-trail for the time when the day of reckoning must come."

He paused, staring with brooding eyes. Maelys sat in awed silence.

"I discovered one thing. I learned the name of the grand gentlemen who looked on while my father was outraged. It was that general lover Buckingham—pardon me, I should say his Grace the Duke of Buckingham !—pampered panderer, odious and dishonoured ! He who strove to wreck this country, and debased it at home and abroad till the outraged nation would stand for his arrogance no longer. Yet I mourned when the assassin's knife struck him down. It robbed me of my right. Over and over again in privations and trials in the forests I had been sustained by the thought that some day I would meet his illustrious Grace of Buckingham, man to man."

Heritage slipped his hand to his belt. "Here is the knife that killed my father," he said. "I have kept it through my wanderings."

Maelys shuddered as he balanced the broad blade on his palm.

"Oh, I should not have used it as Felton did his," said Heritage proudly. "I am no assassin ! You recall the night on which we met ? Do you remember how I used my knife against Hogan's sword ? That was a game I have often played. I have pretended

that my adversary was his Grace the Duke of Buckingham, and I have fought as I would have fought had I
ever met him ; my knife of vengeance against his sword
and his skill.''

Again he paused. "There still remains the other
man," he said. "The man in black. I have been away
so long, I cannot find out who was with his Grace of
Buckingham on that day. As yet he is the only one
who has not suffered. If I had my way I would kill
even the dogs who witnessed my father's martyrdom.
Some day I will find the little man in black, and then—
ah, he shall only lose the tip of an ear—seeing he was
merciful because I was only a boy !''

He turned and looked at the girl. "You think me
bitter ? I am. There is gall in my heart. Through
long years I have brooded over the iniquity of my
father's death.''

"You—have—suffered," said Maelys in a subdued
voice.

He looked at her but her face was averted.

"I came back to the Low Country when I reached
a man's estate," he went on in lighter tone. "I had
learnt my woodcraft from the savages, but I knew
nothing of soldiering, so I took lessons under some of
Gustavus Adolphus's officers in Sweden, and I saw
service in the Lowlands. I was so sure this day of
deliverance would come. . . . I wonder why I tell
you this. I think it is because I would justify myself
in your eyes. We were good comrades for those first
few happy hours ere this accursed war raised a barrier
between us ! I think you will need my services again.
The Archbishop has many enemies. I would watch
over you, if I could, and him, likewise, for your sake.
Say to him that when the King breaks faith with him,
as he is bound to do, seeing that it is not in any Stuart
to keep his word—say to him that I will aid him to the
best of my powers if he but send for me.''

Heritage walked a few steps and pulling aside a screen

of leaves he pointed to a rough shelter of boughs beside the stream. "Here is my lair," said he. "I have dwelt here within reach of Conway more often than you realize. You know it now—should you desire to betray me—again."

A sudden flush mounted Maelys's cheeks.

"I should not have said that," he said hastily. "It was ungenerous. It is my forest manners."

He put his hands to his lips and softly imitated the cooing of a wood-pigeon. From out of the trees ahead a trooper stepped softly and walked towards them.

"Have you anything to report?"

"Nothing, sir, save Sergeant Pentecost hath ridden towards the rendezvous with his company. There has been no sign of any approach from Conway. The sheep have never ceased to graze, nor have the rooks moved from the elms."

"Good. Join the others and lead my horse to the road."

The man saluted and withdrew.

Heritage smiled. "They are learning rapidly, these lads of mine. I feel proud of my handiwork."

He paused and looked down upon the valley. "What a fair scene this is, Maelys, and what tranquillity is here! God knows why men must slay each other when all the world is at peace. The ways of God are past finding out. I suppose it must be. Rebels we are, yet people unborn will have cause to bless us for making their liberties possible. . . ."

He walked to the road, the road which is old beyond the count of time, and descended a little way.

"You will find your horse tethered to a gate just below," said he gravely. "There is also there someone who will act as escort back to Conway. Good-bye, Maelys."

"Am—am I free?" The girl was incredulous.

"You were never anything but free."

"Then—why—— "

"I so desired an hour of your company. Forgive my forest manners."

He bowed and stepped back. Slowly the girl walked down the hill wondering whether her horse was really there.

She saw it at the gate. Saw, also, a familiar white horse and beside it a well-loved form. "Father," she cried, running to his arms.

Colonel Wynn smiled happily down upon her excited face.

"Ah, 'tis too good to be true ! We are both free ?"

"Both free, child. So boot and saddle, and let's for home !"

But Maelys turned and was hurrying up the lane, her eyes aglow with gratitude.

"Captain Heritage !" she called. "Captain Heritage !"

But the silent woods gave back no answer. The roadway was deserted. Heritage had gone.

CHAPTER TWENTY-FIVE

"The war creeps nearer!"

Maelys looked up from her writing as the Archbishop entered the room. "Why, have Sir William Brereton's forces carried Rhuddlan Castle?" she asked quickly.

"Nay, God be praised, the garrison holds out," cried the Archbishop. "The ill tidings come from a quarter I less suspected. Caernarvon Castle has been carried by that villain Swanley—he who has infested these seas with his ships. They say he has taken four hundred men in the town."

"If Captain Swanley can carry Caernarvon, what hope have we?"

"Take your quill, Maelys," went on the Archbishop, "and write the Marquis of Ormond saying that if God for our sins continue these troubles, we will rely upon him for those hundred men to be lent to us."

The Archbishop paced the room. "It may be we will find greater security now that Rupert hath taken Liverpool."

Maelys was staring dreamily through one of the window niches.

"You are quiet, child; doth aught ail thee? Since your capture you appear to have lost some of your spirit."

Maelys forced a smile. "My spirits are as high as ever, Uncle."

"This man Heritage did you no hurt?"

"Hurt me? Ay, that he did; by his tender care."

"By setting you at liberty? Ah yes! Like as not he had no wish to be cumbered with prisoners."

The Archbishop dismissed the matter with a shrug,

and left the room. Maelys took up her pen but did not write. Unmindful of Captain Tom Bartlett aboard his pinnace in the river awaiting despatches for Dublin, Maelys sat dreaming. The grey walls of Conway's keep might encompass her, but her mind roamed the greenwoods. Ever since Heritage carried her off in his masterful way, the girl had been filled with a strange disquietude. Her peace of mind was gone, but she was not unhappy. Her unrest arose from a clash of loyalties.

It savoured of disloyalty to dwell upon Heritage with anything but rancour, yet she took pleasure now in every remembrance of him.

She was familiar with the homage paid by men, but their courtesy had never touched her like the direct ingenuousness with which Heritage rendered service.

But for the Rebellion . . .

Maelys picked up her pen quickly, conscious that the blood was mantling her cheeks. It was idle to speculate. For war there was ; horrid, tragic strife with bitterness increasing and the rift daily growing wider. She saw no light ahead save by virtue of the great battle which Prince Rupert meant to fight.

A knock sounded and Holland entered, booted and spurred. "I ride at once to join the Prince," said he, standing erect with his hat plume sweeping the floor.

Maelys rose and held out her hand. "Good fortune attend you, Claude," she said. "I pray for your safety, and—may you achieve the renown and preferment you desire."

A slight frown crossed Holland's brow. "You often speak of my advancement, Maelys, as though it was a desire scarce commendable."

"I—I could have wished you found your duty lying nearer here," she said.

"I must serve my King where his need is greatest," he said.

"I suppose you are right."

Holland shrugged his shoulders. "You think I desire promotion before all else ? Perhaps you are right.   If I desire success it is because I would offer to the woman I love something worthy of her exalted birth."

"A woman might find other things more worthy than titles, Claude.   But go your way.   I know I can count on you to do your duty.   It is true his Highness means to fight ?"

"Ay.   Rupert was never laggard, but when I left Chester he was raging.   They say in Court that the King grows daily more jealous of Prince Rupert and his army, and it is common discourse at Oxford that it is indifferent whether the Parliament or Rupert doth prevail.   Hearing word of this, Rupert was so incensed that he at once resolved to send in his commission and get to France.   His fury interrupted our march for ten days, for which I am grateful, for it gives me time to hasten here to bid you adieu."

"You leave at once ?"

"At once.   York is in sore distress and Rupert hath told Newcastle that he will succour him instantly. The King's letter, which I hear is indiscreet, hath put Rupert in fighting mood and fight he will, come what may.   I ride with Lord Byron."

"Return soon and bring me glad tidings of victory. God preserve you, Claude."

He kissed her hand and went.   Maelys experienced a sense of relief.   Ever since the encounter with Heritage, she was conscious that Holland resented the humiliation to which he had been subjected before her eyes.

She bent to her work, determined to drive all distracting thoughts from her.   So Captain Bartlett sailed in the *Confidence* with despatches for Dublin. Captain Swanley's watch-ships continued to patrol the coast.   The Archbishop rode to Gloddaeth, where he wrote "in this solitarye place" begging his Grace of

Ormond to send him one of the four or five pinnaces remaining in Dublin for him to rig out and man for service.

Then he returned to Conway to fume at Prince Rupert's appointing Sir John Mennes Governor of Caernarvon, Anglesey and Merioneth.

"The Prince hath chosen the creature with an eye to my humiliation," cried he in indignation.

"Do you think it rests with the Prince to do you ill ?" asked Maelys, and the Archbishop turned.

"A strange question from you, child."

"Captain Heritage," said Maelys with studied unconcern, "bade me say that you had made foes in Court who sought your downfall and that should you be in extremity he will endeavour to come to your aid."

"Captain Heritage can attend to his own affairs," said his Grace curtly. "I have the King's warrant for the custody of Conway, and neither Prince Plunderland—as I have heard his Highness termed—nor Mennes nor Byron dare over-ride that."

The hot summer days passed. Maelys still rode abroad, but with less assuredness than of yore. The peaceful lanes held now a possibility of lurking danger. Once, on her rambles, Maelys turned hastily and noticed an old man behind her. She walked towards him.

"Who are you ?" she demanded.

"My name is Tom Jenkyns, lady," said he, touching his hat.

"You seemed to be following me."

"Yes, lady. Times are dangerous, and I fear lest harm befall you."

"I have seen you before," said Maelys. "I thank you for your care."

The old man smiled and quietly withdrew. He did not intrude, but Maelys was conscious of his nearness. Often after that she found Jenkyns hovering near her on her journeys, and more than once, when streets were crowded and roisterers rude, his stalwart frame made way for her and protected her from insult. She grew to regard the old man with something akin to affection ; as one cares for a loyal watchdog, dumb but faithful.

Then one day a rider on a weary horse rode into the town by way of the Mill Gate. So haggard and war-worn was he that Maelys scarcely recognized the Cavalier as Holland. He rode past her in the street with unseeing eyes, and clattered up to the castle seeking the Archbishop. Maelys, scenting disaster, hastened thither and soon heard the tale from his lips.

For Rupert had received "a shrewd bang". On the moor of Long Marston, his fiery Cavaliers had at length met their match. Their valour proved unavailing against the stern discipline of the newly raised Ironsides.

"There is a new power in the land," said Holland soberly. "Victory seemed ours. We had broken Lord Fairfax and Sir Thomas, and the Scots Horse was in flight, when Cromwell's horsemen fell on our right wing. They broke Rupert's Horse, rallied and charged our centre. Newcastle's Whitecoats lie dead to a man about White Syke Close. Rupert's great fifteen-foot banner is taken ; even his dog, Boye, is slain ! It is Cromwell's devising."

"I knew it," said his Grace. "I told his Majesty that Cromwell hath the properties of all evil beasts, and bade him catch him by stratagem and cut him short."

"Lord Byron made an ill-judged move at the start," said Holland. "He moved his men from safe ground to advance across a slough where they were broken up in the mire by dragoons."

His Grace grew caustic. "Lord Byron," said he, "lost his Majesty the fight at Edge Hill, and was made a peer. Doubtless for this blunder he will be made a viscount, at least."

"Uncle," expostulated Maelys, "have a care what

you say. What if this should come to his Lordship's ears ?"

The Archbishop laughed, such being his nature, for his unwary discourses, says the historian, his passion and levity gave very great advantages to those who did not love him.

"How hath Rupert taken it ?"

"He is recruiting valiantly in Lancashire and Cheshire and looks to North Wales for help."

"Let him look elsewhere," cried the Archbishop. "Already he hath taken away my own regiment, and as for silver, all that North Wales now hath is that which lies unmined in the hills."

"How is his Majesty ?" interrupted Maelys.

" 'Tis said he finds the news but little to his liking. I fear the tide sets ill against him. The Court is split in factions. Poor Sir Charles Blount was pistolled not long since by one Langston in the King's very presence, which augurs ill."

"Let us pray for peace," said his Grace, "though I see small hopes of it."

An air of suspense hung over Conway, for Sir William Brereton was menacing Lord Byron in Liverpool and hoped to regain the harbour before winter, and with Liverpool again in rebel hands Conway's sea-borne trade would vanish.

The Archbishop had scant repose. One day he was at the quay remonstrating with the Sheriff for stopping merchants shipping corn to Ireland ; the next day stalking at the head of the town guard to disperse a brawl which had broken out.

Then came a body of troops clamouring for admittance. The Archbishop was summoned and the gates all closed.

Maelys found the prelate indignantly looking down from the battlements of the Porth Uchaf. Beyond the town ditch the commanders of the troops were arguing fiercely. They wished to be billeted in the town, but his Grace would have none of it. "No regiment shall be quartered on the inhabitants without assignment from the Prince or the Governor," he cried.

"We are royal troops and demand admittance!" cried the officer in charge.

"You can quarter in Gyffin," responded the Archbishop. "No one understands why you have been sent here, and we have scarce food for the inhabitants as it is."

The Archbishop was adamant, and the troops withdrew with ill grace. Maelys was summoned to write to the Commissioners of Array to lodge the Archbishop's complaint.

"Some enemy hath done this," said the Archbishop soberly. "Maelys, these troubles are no accident but a set design to bring about my undoing. But if my enemies think to drive me hence, I tell you I will not go."

CHAPTER TWENTY-SIX

From where she stood on the castle ramparts, Maelys could see the figure of a man sprawled in a patch of moonlight which lit up half of Castle Street, throwing the remainder into a shade more intense by reason of the contrast. The figure had not moved for five minutes now. The girl wondered whether the man was dead or merely stunned. The noise of the bickering had momentarily passed away, but she knew that before long it would break forth again. It was ever thus. At first these nightly brawls had terrified her, the drunken, cursing, slashing bullies who made hideous the erstwhile sleepy streets of placid Conway by their orgies ; but familiarity takes the edge off most things. Now her only care was for the safety of the Archbishop, for he would frequently venture forth into the streets to preserve order.

A woman hurried from the shelter of a house and lugged the body from the moonlight. Maelys could see her straining at the task. Surely the man could not be dead, else this woman had left him to lie in the kennel—but perhaps there was gold in his purse !

The girl lost interest in the moonlit road. She glanced up at the cloudlets drifting across the moon's face, noted the headpiece of the watchman in the turret silhouetted against the night sky, drew her cloak closer about her shoulders, conscious of the nip in the September air, and turned to pace the ramparts. It was a favourite walk of hers. Within the castle she felt shut in ; here she could look forth on the world.

She was continually alert, apprehensive, waiting,

O

speculating upon what the next hour would bring forth. From the height of the ramparts she could look down upon the town, could watch the mountain peaks for signal beacons, could gaze seawards for incoming ships, witness arrivals at the ferry or discern way-farers coming down the valley road. She felt an insatiable curiosity to know all that was going on in the world about her. And now there was so much unrest within the town she rarely passed the castle draw-bridge without escort. Holland was absent. He had followed Lord Byron to Montgomery Castle where the impetuous Governor of North Wales, undeterred by his frequent defeats, was confidently contemplating inflicting a crushing blow on the Parliamentary forces. The girl found herself half-resenting Holland's absence. For this she chid herself, arguing that he was fighting the King's battles. Yet in her heart the girl knew that Holland's loyalty was not unmixed with his craving for glory. He was brave and he was able, but she felt that he might well have remained at Conway serving the Archbishop in these dark, anxious days.

Instead, Holland chose to follow the fortunes of Lord Byron or Prince Rupert where rapid promotion was readier. The Archbishop was left much to his own devices. He had raised a regiment—and Rupert had requisitioned it. The young men of the place were of more hindrance than help, for they found the liberty and licence of war go to their heads like wine, and were ever alert for an excuse to break down restraint, or to wield the weapons which in peaceful days had to be kept more for ornament than use. The girl found irony in the knowledge that the unrest and sufferings Conway so far endured came not from the rebels but from the rakes and ruffians who called themselves Cavaliers ; who fought not so much for the King as against the puritanism which was hateful to them. Men of honour who served the King's Majesty found little in common with these plunderers, drunkards and libertines.

The worst of it was there were many clashes in Conway and the confines of it among themselves [the old writer informs us]. The raw soldiers now come into muster and pay, were malapert and crowed over their own friends that had not the honour, as they called it, to serve on Horse or trail a Pike. In some things the world is more civil than in ages past, but the longer it lasts our wars are more licentious and barbarous.

But while the Archbishop was "able to abate the rudeness of the common soldier by courteous treatment", he experienced greater difficulty in "thrusting back the ambition of those more than enough that would be commanders". Thus, we are told, "words of high language passed between him and some gallants before they would come down", finding that the valiant old Archbishop was "not to be outbraved by a buff jerkin and a feather".

"In all these contrasts the Archbishop prevailed, and broke through mutinies and high threats."

But it was an anxious time—as Maelys knew to her cost. And now the rioting had broken forth afresh. The night air was profaned by the shrieks and oaths and curses. There was the clash of steel ; a trumpet shrilled as the Night Watch was called out, the flare of torches lighted up darting figures in the dark alleyways.

Maelys bit her lip, turned hurriedly, determined to go to the King's Tower and dissuade the Archbishop from venturing forth as she knew he was bound to do.

Crash !

She paused in amazement, all thoughts of the riot forgotten. The signal gun at the Upper Gate had been fired and Maelys could see the white smoke curling about the grey towers lit by the light of moving lanthorns. Trumpets were sounding. The watchman above her was shouting. Amid the tumult Maelys caught the sound of horses galloping ; horses coming down the valley road at breakneck pace. She ran towards the wall which overlooked the Gyffin stream.

Below her lay the garrison mill, and beyond it the white road from the Mill Gate, the Porth-y-Felin, wound up the valley. Its pale surface was suddenly darkened by a moving mass which resolved into a body of Horse. Soldiers were hurrying to the ramparts, manning the walls. In the town the bickering died away, curiosity getting the better of the combatants.

Before the Mill Gate a Cavalier on a panting steed reigned up and shouted for them to open in the King's name.

"Haste, you slothful devils; they're at our heels! I am the Lord Byron."

Up went the portcullis. The great gates creaked open and the breathless horsemen came crowding into the town, hard on the heels of their general.

The gates clanged to. Not a moment too soon. Down the road swept another body of Horse who drew rein as they neared the walled town.

All save one, who rode dauntlessly forward.

"Bully Byron! Bully Byron! Stand and fight!"

Maelys paused. The voice was familiar. Someone put a torch to a beacon on the gate tower and the red glare lit up the scene. On road and sward were clusters of buff-coated horsemen clad in breastplate and barred headpiece. Before them on a great black horse, the leader was shouting defiance at the walls. "Bully Byron, the blood of those Barthomley innocents be on your head! Come out and fight!"

Maelys felt her flesh creep. She could see the musketeers levelling their pieces. One of them fired. How could they miss that massive figure? With a sob Maelys saw Heritage bend in his saddle, but it was only to place his horse between him and the walls as he rode from range. The shot called for an instant discharge of pistols from the Parliamentary Horse; and a volley from the carbines of their dragoons. The fire was returned from the ramparts. But Heritage was no fool to risk his men needlessly before a walled town.

At brisk word of command, the Parliamentary Horse wheeled and cantered into the darkness, leaving hundreds of curious eyes peering over Conway's walls after their retiring figures, and hundreds of ears straining to catch the sound of their retreat.

With a sigh Maelys turned. The town was a-bustle. By the light of torches she could see the horses of the pursued Cavaliers standing with hanging heads and steaming sides in the Castle Square while their masters thrust their way through the curious crowd and ascended the incline which led to the castle.

Maelys hurried down in time to see Lord Byron, his feather broken, his face streaked with sweat and dust, come stalking through the gateway, black-browed, vicious.

"You bear ill tidings from Montgomery, my Lord?" queried the Archbishop, greeting him civilly. "Has the day gone against the King's arms?"

"Would I ride hither with those ill-favoured curs yapping at my heels if we had not been worsted?" snapped Lord Byron. "Get us wine to swill this accursed dust from our throats, and food, for we have ridden far."

He stalked on, the Archbishop following close behind, amid a group of Cavaliers thankful to find the security of the castle.

Lord Byron flung himself into a chair and quaffed the cup of wine a servant held for him.

"Fill up," cried he. "Lord, what a ride! I know little of Church doctrine, your Grace, but I assert that the devil fights for his own. The rebel scum have given our lads as damned a thrashing as ever we got at Marston." He drank another cup. "The only saving grace is that we've sent Will Fairfax to perdition. Would to God we could do as much for his brother Tom!"

Maelys, staring fascinated from the background, felt her arm touched and saw Holland beside her.

"Our forces have been beaten at Montgomery Castle?" she asked.

"Sorely," said Holland. He was pale and bore signs of the conflict and the pursuit.

"You are not harmed?" asked Maelys quickly.

Holland shook his head. "I am not harmed, but I fear the King's cause hath received a blow from which it will never recover—at least not in North Wales."

The babel of voices around them was suddenly shattered by Lord Byron bringing his fist on the table with a force which made the glasses ring.

"I care not!" he shouted. "I am Governor of North Wales, and I say to you that troops shall be billeted in Conway."

"And I say to you, my Lord, that the town has not the wherewithal to victual them," replied the Archbishop with calm dignity.

"I shall march such troops here as I see fit," said Lord Byron.

"Then I trust your Lordship will make the necessary steps to see they are fed, for we have no provisions to spare, and the countryside hath long since been bled white."

"Argue not with me," cried Lord Byron violently. "I give orders ; see that they are obeyed. Your Grace is not in your minster now."

"Whether in cathedral or castle I serve the King to the best of my ability," said his Grace evenly.

"Meaning I do not?" Lord Byron was in a vile temper and made no effort to bridle it.

"I understand that if your Lordship had been as assiduous in obeying the orders of your superiors as your Lordship is in giving orders, several of his Majesty's disasters might have been averted."

There was an ominous silence. Lord Byron sat with twitching face.

"You are an old man and a churchman," he said

slowly, "else I had crammed your lying words down your throat. But take heed, John Williams. I am not the man to suffer an affront."

"Neither, your Lordship, am I," replied the Archbishop. "I hold the castle for the King, having put it into a state of defence at my own cost ; I shall see to it that his Majesty's warrant which I hold is not ignored."

Lord Byron deliberately filled his glass, and addressed an officer standing near. "Ride to Chester and request Colonel Mostyn to instruct three companies of the regiment from Lorraine to march to Conway instantly."

"This is a studied insult," said the Archbishop.

"I am glad your Grace has the wit to discern it. Your Grace will perceive that I am considerate enough to send you troops which, if not Welsh, are at least not English. Hogan, ride without delay. The rebels will not have crossed the river."

"Hogan !" said the Archbishop, looking up sharply. "That knave ?" He turned his eyes on his former lieutenant. His finger pointed fearlessly at Hogan. "I order that man's arrest," he said.

Lord Byron raised his brows. "On what grounds ?"

"Faith, my Lord, I did but venture a little pleasantry with the young lady yonder," said Hogan, unabashed.

Lord Byron gazed on Maelys.

"You show damned good taste, Hogan," he drawled. Lord Byron turned to the Archbishop. "I'll trouble you," he said ominously, "not to interfere with officers on my staff. Hogan, you waste time. Ride and have the Lorraines sent from Chester."

The Archbishop rose. He was flushed but still dignified.

"I shall not forget, my Lord," he said, and walked from the room.

CHAPTER TWENTY-SEVEN

On a January day in the year 1645 the men who were in the Benarth Woods lopping branches for charcoal paused in their hewing as their ears caught the sound of horses' hoofs coming down the frosty road which led down the valley to Conway. Watchers on the ramparts at the Upper Gate also heard the approaching cavalcade, and the guard turned out. It was nearing sunset and already the drawbridge was up. Before the company rode a horseman, fully equipped for war, and behind him a cluster of officers, a score of soldiers and then a disorderly rabble of hangers-on.

At the edge of the town ditch the leader drew rein. "In the King's name—lower the drawbridge and give us admittance."

There was a moment's pause from the guard, which incensed the waiting horseman who was evidently of a cholerous disposition. "Would you defy me ? Open, I say. I come from the King."

"Who speaks ?" cried the officer of the guard.

"I am Sir John Owen, Governor of this town."

"His Grace the Archbishop of York is Governor," came the reply.

"I carry the Royal commission," cried Sir John, brandishing a roll. "Admit us, or ill will come of it. I am not minded to stand here and freeze at the gates of my own town."

There was sound of parley within ; the drawbridge creaked slowly down and the horsemen clattered over the worn boards and into the town. The incident attracted some attention and already townsfolk were coming to their doors. Sir John demanded where the

Archbishop was to be found, and learning that the prelate was in his palace, which lay straight before him, the irate knight rode thither followed by two officers. His men, at a gesture from their commander, scattered to find warmth in the town's taverns.

Sir John dismounted, and followed by his satellites stamped into the Archbishop's palace without so much as a knock.

The Archbishop looked up from his writing as their spurs rung on the boards. "Who comes?" he called, and Maelys ran to open the door.

"I come!" cried the Colonel stalking into the room, his left hand on his sword hilt, his right holding his commission.

"Ah, it is you, John Owen."

"Sir John," corrected the Colonel with a twist of his moustache. "Your intelligencers have served you ill if you have not heard of my knighthood, John Williams."

"Your Grace, if you please—Sir John," came the imperturbable reply, and the Archbishop stared haughtily into the intruder's face. "You have been so long in camp, Sir John, that you appear to have forgotten the respect due to my high office; I will not say you have forgotten your manners, for I never recollect your possessing any."

"Better choose your words more carefully. I am Governor of this town."

The Archbishop rose to his feet. "What fresh affront is this?" he demanded.

"Dismount from your high horse, John Williams. I bear Prince Rupert's commission. Do you dispute this?" and the Colonel thrust the paper before the Archbishop's eyes. By the light of the candles the prelate glanced at the writing—writing with which he was only too familiar, having had frequent demands from the Prince for money, for munitions and for men.

"This is intolerable," cried the Archbishop. "Have I not his Majesty's own word that I shall remain in charge until the moneys I have spent are repaid me? I have spent my wealth for the King."

"And I have spent my blood!" retorted Owen.

"And the blood of others," cried the Archbishop. "Last word I had of you, you had led your regiment disastrously against the enemy."

"I care not for this windiness; here is his Highness's commission, and here is your new Governor. So pay heed, John Williams. There is a war carrying on, and the King needs soldiers to do soldiers' work, not a puling churchman. I am Governor of Conway."

The Archbishop stroked his beard thoughtfully. "You may be Governor of the town, as this saith, John Owen, but, before God, I remain Governor of the castle, for such has the King appointed me. Moreover, the good folk of the countryside have entrusted me with their valuables which I have stored there for safe keeping."

"I am Governor of both town and castle," cried Sir John with an oath. "Your treacherous utterances against Prince Rupert have reached his ears. Lord Byron likewise hath reported how you stir up your countrymen against the English."

"I shall hold the castle," cried the Archbishop, stepping forward.

Sir John whipped out his sword and presented it at the prelate's breast. "Not another step, old lad," he laughed. "I take charge of the castle, and you stay here, because, you see, you cannot go to the castle!"

"But I can!"

A fresh young voice rang through the room. There was a swirl of skirts as Maelys darted through the doorway, slamming the door behind her.

"After that wench. Stop her!" bellowed Sir John, and the two officers ran to do his bidding. But Maelys was already in the saddle of Sir John's charger, and with an astuteness culled perhaps from Heritage she drove the other horses before her as she swept down the street, leaving the shouting men to pursue her on foot. The good folk of the town came running out at the hubbub, but seeing only their beloved Mistress Wynn they stood aside as she swept by. Across the strip of sward which stretched beside the church she sped, leaving the squat white farmhouse on her right ; then up the incline which led to the castle drawbridge. "Haste ! Lower ! Admit me !" she yelled, and the guard knowing her full well did as she bade. Her pursuers, who had now been joined by some of their men, were at the foot of the slope.

"Quick ! Hasten !" yelled Maelys, and the men heaved at the windlass. Her horse was across ere the wood came to rest. "Up bridge," she cried, "quick, or it will be too late !"

The bridge climbed with irritating slowness and the foremost runner struck it with his sword as it rose out of reach, leaving a cluster of panting men standing at the edge of the perilous drop.

Maelys ran nimbly up the steps of a tiny guard tower, and laughed defiance at the bewildered soldiers.

"You shall rue this," cried the irate leader.

"Tell John Owen I hold the castle for the King—ay, and for the Archbishop ! And say to him, too, that if his Grace is not allowed to come hither without molestation I will turn the guns on the town."

The men withdrew, muttering.

Later in the evening a figure could be seen slowly ascending the slope which led to the castle. It was the Archbishop. On his admittance Maelys clung to him anxiously.

"You are not hurt ?" she queried.

"Nay, little warrior ! John Owen, boor though he is, knows better than to lay hands on me. Child, how can I thank you ? You have saved my honour. We

will hold the castle between us till I can get word to
the King."

He walked through the main gateway, across the
courtyard to the royal quarters where he had his
lodging. Maelys noted the weariness in his face. He
took his stand before the fire-place, leaning his arm
on the mantel-piece and gazing down into the glowing
coals.

"What does it all mean?" whispered Maelys
presently.

"I scarce know, child, save that persons have
aspersed me to Prince Rupert as an enemy to the
soldiery and a stiff defender of my nation and kindred.
Sir John Owen—who brings news of a garrison
intended for Llanrwst—looks big on me and this
place. He is very silent of his designs and lets nothing
fall to me save that he is come down with strange
powers and commissions from Prince Rupert for
martial discipline, even to life and death. He is to be
Governor of Conway, and, perchance, of Caernarvon
now that we have recovered it from the enemy. He
is to call by special warrants both Horse and Foot
from the Lord Byron's command to attend him."

"But what of the powers his Majesty gave you?"
asked Maelys amazed.

"I know not. I am afraid that John Owen means
to surprise this town and castle suddenly. I am so
discouraged, Maelys, and my mind bodes me of so
much trouble to these parts—if not to mine own
person—that I dare make no more provision but from
hand to mouth as not knowing how soon I must remove
from hence, or be driven."

And so the castle, munitioned and provisioned to
withstand the King's enemies, had to stand out against
those who came in the name of the King.

CHAPTER TWENTY-EIGHT

THERE were signs of spring. Daffodils were brightening the woodlands, and the winds from the Snowdon range had lost a little of their edge. In the woods and the hedgerows of the valley birds were blithe, but the coming of spring brought little solace to the dwellers in Conway Castle. The Archbishop's eye was as fiery as of yore, but his shoulders were stooping, and Maelys noted the spread of silver in his hair.

"My heart grows heavy for him," said the girl.

She was walking the castle ramparts with Holland, who had slipped through the Roundhead leaguer about Chester and had galloped to Conway for a brief visit.

"Owen's conduct is churlish and inexcusable," said Holland with unconscious dignity. Himself a colonel, he could speak now of the bellicose Sir John as an equal. "Now that Prince Maurice hath come to Chester as Governor of North Wales, there should be better order in these parts."

"Speak with his Highness, I pray, and have him turn out this odious Sir John. Faith, he glowers upon the castle as though we were the rebels instead of the King's loyal subjects, and I scarce dare venture down the streets of the town lest I should be given offence. Ah, Claude, you would scarce know the old town. But a few years past it was as happy, albeit as sleepy, a spot one could wish for, with nothing more disturbing than a neighbours' quarrel or rumour of trouble from the recusants in Creuddyn. But now, alas, there is no market day! No honey-fair! The fisherlads and the drovers have been driven to the wars. You scarce would tell this was a town in Wales, for the streets are given over to strangers; Irish mercenaries, and English troopers, and now to crown all come the soldiers from Lorraine under the Lord St. Pol so that we are become a bedlam. God knows where it will end."

"The King grows more hopeful."

"What? He scarce can have heard news from these parts. With Shrewsbury fallen, and now Hawarden, to that pertinacious Colonel Mytton, there lieth little encouragement here."

"But Prince Rupert is coming to shatter the leaguer about Chester, and with him Sir Marmaduke Langdale and General Gerard. Can you imagine the rebels withstanding the onslaught of leaders such as these? No, Maelys. We will drive them from Chester and then rally to the King's banner, for he plans to shatter the armies of the Parliament this summer once and for all."

"God grant it may be so," said Maelys. "But meanwhile I look to you to aid us here, for what to do I know not. Loyalty is a good thing, but when one loyalty pulls one way and another loyalty another way, a maid scarces know what course to follow. Must you return to Chester, Claude?"

"That I must. How goes Dick Lovelace's ditty?

"I could not love thee, dear, so much,
    Loved I not honour more."

"If you love me, Claude, you will stay and protect those I love," said Maelys in a subdued voice. Her kerchief was being twisted by nervous fingers. "Claude," she went on hastily. "Stay you here, and take charge of this castle. Whom have we here? An old churchman whom cares are killing, and a maid who hath naught to commend her save her desire to be loyal to her leader. Every day I fear me that some terrible thing will happen. The Archbishop says nothing, but I know he fears it too. We are all but prisoners in the castle. The drawbridge is never down ; the guards are never off duty. If the rebels were in Conway's High Street instead of Cavaliers we could not be more alert. Every time the Archbishop ventures forth I am distraught till I see him return lest John Owen do him injury. Stay and give us your aid.''

Holland looked distressed. "Indeed, Maelys, you grieve me ; would that I might stay by your side, but my duty calls me to Chester where there is danger to the King's cause.''

"There is danger here, both to the King's cause and to your friends. You can do your duty equally well in Conway as in Chester.''

"You do not understand," cried Holland.

"I understand that the Prince hath promised you knighthood if you serve him faithfully, now that he comes complete with powers to grant honours and rewards as well as impose levies.''

Holland flushed. "Maelys," he cried, a trifle haughtily, "you think I would set store on such things when it lies in my power to serve you.''

"It does lie in your power," said Maelys. "But you do not choose to see it. Will you stay here and aid us in our extremity ?''

Holland bit his lip and commenced to pace the rampart in his agitation. "I—I——''

"Nay, Claude, say no more. Your hesitation is its own answer. Return to your duty. You are right, you place your honour before your love.''

"But, Maelys, I hold the King's commission. Is it not right——''

"Oh, quite right. Nay, my friend, I do not blame you. You see your loyalty in one light, and I in another. I have no ill feelings.''

"I would not hurt you, Maelys. I shall exert myself on the Archbishop's behalf with all the influence I possess, I assure you. I beg of you to believe that I would serve you to the best of my ability.''

"I do believe it," said Maelys calmly. "I bear you no ill will. I only know now, Claude, that I do not love you."

"Maelys——"

"Let us not speak of it. There is work to be done. Return to your work, Claude. I wish you all the good will in the world. May honour and advancement come to you."

"You are not offended, Maelys ?"

"Offended ? Why should I be ? Because you set store on your obligation to the King ? I respect you very much, my friend, but I do not love you, that is all."

"I shall always value your regard, Maelys," he cried, raising her hand to his lips.

"God keep you," said Maelys in an even voice, and turned away.

Holland walked slowly down the steps to the courtyard and called for his horse. As he rode into the town he looked back at the castellated walls which towered above the street, but no farewell was waved as when he rode out to do battle at Edge Hill. Holland suddenly felt old, as men age rapidly in times of stress.

So Holland returned to Chester to find that Prince Rupert had not kept his promise to relieve the city, and that Prince Maurice, finding himself in dire straits, had followed after his brother, leaving the ancient city in the hands of Lord Byron and the valiant Colonel Roger Mostyn and the regiment of Welshmen he had raised on his estate. And all about them the ring of Brereton's army closed in.

Maelys looking down from the walls of Conway was conscious of some bickering broken out upon the quay. With apprehensive heart she hastened over the drawbridge and was running down Castle Street when she encountered the Archbishop.

"Oh, thank God you were safe."

"Safe, child ?" cried he, tucking her hand under his arm. "There is no one here who dare interfere with the Archbishop of York."

But she noted his face was pale and his breathing was fast. "Something is amiss ?" she asked.

"It is that John Owen, again," he cried. "Upon an alarm of ships (which I verily believe to be of his own making) he hath seized Lewis's corn, which lay ready for shipment to Ireland. I have persuaded him to return it, but if this goeth much farther our trade will be ruined and all our Welshmen beggars."

Maelys did her best to calm his distress.

"I will not endure these affronts to my people, Maelys," cried the valiant old prelate. "Sure I am it will destroy our market, and our people grow more and more discontented. At whose hands could they be worse used ?"

The Archbishop stalked indignantly up the street. He turned to the girl with sudden concern. "I would you were out of this, dear child," he said tenderly.

"I ask nothing but to be at your side ; to share your troubles and your dangers," replied the girl fondly.

"I am old and I have lived my life," said the Archbishop. "The young may die, but the old must, and the sands of my life are running out. But you, Maelys, you have glorious life before you. It is not meet that you should be called upon to face these hardships."

"So that I am with you, I rest content."

"It is not right," persisted the Archbishop. "The storm is brewing here, and it would be well to find some other haven whither we could resort if it break. My mind is made up. I will fortify my house at Penrhyn, and there retire if this intolerance continueth."

"But would you be safe there ?"

"As safe there as here. I will set to work by stealth victualling my house, and then retire thither when I

P

may do so with honour. But first I must see to it that the goods deposited in the castle are returned to their lawful owners, for I would sooner thrust an unprotected babe into a lion's mouth than trust that John Owen with the custody of this wealth."

The Archbishop entered the castle thoughtfully, followed by the girl. "I must send a messenger to my steward at Penrhyn," he mused. "Yet whom can I trust?"

"Send me, Uncle. I will go."

"You? Nay, the hazard of the journey is too great."

I have ridden farther. I beg of you let me do your errand. There is no one in authority you can trust."

"You say true," remarked the Archbishop. "It grieves me to let you take the risk, yet it may save you from a greater danger."

"Then I beg of you send a groom with a horse up the Valley Road to await me a league from here. I will go by way of the river stairs lest any should see me leave the town."

An hour later Maelys, landing on the bank of the river above Cymryd, watched the boat drop down the river, and turning her back on the Conway she plunged into the woods. Westward she walked, moving with such stealth as was compatible with speed. All about her young life was bursting from tree and earth. The freshness of the world sped her forward rejoicing, so good was it to be at large once more after months within encircling walls. The spirit of adventure was hot within her.

"It is good to be free," she whispered.

"Yet an escort might be advisable."

The words, softly spoken, startled her. She wheeled to find Heritage smiling at her.

"What are you doing?" she gasped somewhat irrelevantly.

"Following you."

"But—why?"

"I thought it desirable for your safety."

"How knew you I was in need of your—protection?"
Her tone was haughty, yet tinged with curiosity.

"I saw you leave the castle by the water-stairway,"
said Heritage, "and I imagined there was something
afoot. Is his Grace finding John Owen unwelcome
company?"

"How do you know this?"

"It is my task to discover what I may. I often lie
and watch the castle—whenever, in fact, my duties
permit me the freedom."

"But—why?"

"Because you are there; because I love you."
Heritage was direct as usual.

"No. You must not talk thus. I—I will not have
it. I forbid you ever to say that again."

Heritage smiled. "I love you," he repeated. "Come,
comrade, 'tis like old times to be out under God's
good sky together—with the trees about us and the
friendly soil beneath our feet. I will not disturb you,
Maelys. God knows your life hath been none so
joyous of late that I should add to your worries. Yet
I will escort you to your journey's end. Methinks a
rebel—a Crop-ear—might prove more wholesome
company than yonder Cavaliers. How think you of
the manner in which the King treats his loyal servant?"

Maelys bit her lip. "It was Prince Rupert's doing,"
said she stoutly, "and since his conduct caused him
to be deprived of his command, there is no little love
lost between his Majesty and his Highness."

"Ay. Prince Robber is not the man he was before
we rapped his knuckles at Marston. He hath played
false to that villain Byron at Chester now. Never
trust the word of a Stuart!"

"You need not think to turn me from my loyalty
to the King," said Maelys hotly.

"It stands between us—and happiness," suggested

Heritage gently. "When you know as much of Charles Stuart as I do——"

Maelys put up her hand. "Spare me, I beg you. Let me say this. I believe in loyalty. It was ever my creed."

"I, too, believe in loyalty, but loyalty to what? To a King you do not know? A King who breaks faith with those who serve him?"

"Let me be frank, then," said Maelys. "Even though you shake my loyalty to the King, which God forbid, yet will no man ever move me from my loyalty to the Archbishop. I love him; I love him. In the days of his affluence he gave me of his wealth; shall I desert him in the time of his poverty? Men speak hard of him; I have known nothing but tenderness and consideration. He hath flung away his great wealth to help the unfortunate. He is wearing out his precious life in the service of the King. And now he is ringed about by petty, vicious men who respect neither his age nor his rank, but only see in him an object for their spite. Though all forsake him, yet will not I! I have no hard feelings towards you, Captain Heritage; indeed, I am beholden to you for many courtesies; but if you think to shake me in my allegiance to his Grace, I tell you to your face that you waste your time. Had we met in happier times, it may be that I might have listened to you, but our paths run different ways."

"I never was given to following a beaten track," smiled Heritage.

"Then forsake your path and join mine," cried Maelys quickly.

"It may not be," said Heritage.

"What—scruples of loyalty—from you?"

"It is not that. A man must lead; a woman follows. It was ever thus since time began. Any other manner spells disaster."

"We waste time," said Maelys suddenly, "and time is precious. I must press forward."

"You go either to Gwydir or Penrhyn House," said Heritage. "There are soldiers quartered with your Uncle Owen at Gwydir Castle. You head westward, so I take it you go to Penrhyn. Have you a horse awaiting you on the road? If so I will fetch mine and see that no harm befalls you."

"I do not need your company," said Maelys curtly. Then in kinder tones: "I do not mean to hurt you; believe me, my friend, it is better that you should not ride with me."

"I shall follow at a distance. Are you afraid of my forest manners lest I should again try to woo you, or turn you from your loyalty to the Archbishop?"

"Nothing you could say will move me. I follow blindly where the Archbishop leads."

"You mean that?" asked Heritage.

"Utterly. Him I love; him I follow; though it lead to disaster or death. Let us not talk any more."

Heritage bowed his head. "Your high spirit makes me love you but the more," he said, and stepped softly into the bush.

That evening Maelys rode safely into the park of Penrhyn House. Her ride had been uneventful. She never set eyes on Heritage, yet all the while she was conscious of a feeling of security as though her way was guarded by an unseen protector.

CHAPTER TWENTY-NINE

"They're at the gates, your Grace !"

The cry of a retainer from the passage brought the Archbishop to his feet. He had not been well of late, and was taking his ease before the fire in the King's Tower of Conway Castle, glad of the warmth despite the arrival of the pleasant month of May. It was seven o'clock in the evening, and the day the ninth of May in the year 1645. For weeks now the feeling of tenseness in the old town had increased until it was scarce safe for the venerable prelate to venture forth in the streets without a guard. Almost every night there were bickerings in the darkened streets or the inns between partisans of the rival factions. Maelys, her mission fulfilled, had returned from Penrhyn House leaving the steward there laying in a stock of provision and ammunition and otherwise preparing the house to withstand a siege. Again and again she endeavoured to prevail upon the Archbishop to abandon Conway and retire to his own home, but he was obdurate. John Williams was never a man to run away, and he vowed that until he had returned to their owners the valuables entrusted to his care he would not quit the castle.

And now matters had come to a head. Maelys as she sprang to the door intuitively knew that disaster was pending. The Archbishop rose with what haste he could and hurried forth into the courtyard. As they reached the open, a hubbub of voices filled the evening air with steady murmur. The Archbishop with Maelys at his side hastened to the great gate where already the garrison of the castle were assembled, peering curiously into the bailey-court without.

The Archbishop shouted to the men to close the gate which they held ajar, and the massive oak swung slowly into place and the heavy bolts shot into their sockets.

"Maelys, run to the ramparts and look forth and see what is to do," commanded his Grace, and handing his keys to a trusted retainer he bade the man return and lock the doors leading to the towers. Maelys, nimble-footed, hastened to the battlements and peered down into the town, which was agog with excitement. The slope which led to the castle drawbridge was thronged with people. The drawbridge was down, and the wardens were standing with their backs to the wall, each guarded by armed men.

Before the main gate Sir John Owen, red of countenance, with drawn sword stood forth in front of the rabble and demanded admittance. Close behind him clustered a group of lusty fellows carrying crowbars and sledge-hammers.

"Open, in the King's name, or I will batter down your gates!" cried the irate knight. Then, catching sight of some muskets thrust through the embrasures which protected the great gateway, he shook his fist at the invisible musketeers and stormed: "Dogs, would you shoot at your Governor? Give way, I say, and open the gate. I come in the King's name, and I proclaim as rebel and traitor every man who does not do my bidding."

One of the men bearing a sledge ran forward and delivered a blow which shook the heavy oaken portal.

"Open! Open! I demand entrance in the King's name." Sir John was insistent. From one of the portholes the muskets were withdrawn and the pale face of the Archbishop looked down upon the disturbers of his peace.

"Why do you bring this beggarly rabble to assault the King's castle, John Owen?" demanded the prelate in a firm but quiet voice.

"Ha ! It is you, John Williams. I come as Governor of this town and castle to claim what is my own. I call upon you in the King's name to surrender your power to me. I give you one minute to open the gate, after which I will batter it down. Resist at your peril. Raise a hand to stop me and I denounce you as traitor to his Majesty and a hindrance to the royal cause. Open the gate, for the last time."

"I will not open the gate !" The Archbishop's voice was definite. Sir John gave a signal. The men with the crows and sledges, waiting like leashed dogs, darted forward and began to attack the gate. Musketeers with matches burning ensconced themselves in the little towers which protected the bailey-yard from attack from the town's side, and watched the castle walls ready to return the fire of any defender who should have the temerity to shoot.

The Archbishop's voice within could be heard ordering his retainers to lay down their arms.

"You may extinguish your matches, John Owen," he cried. "I will not fire on one who holds a royal commission. You come by force as a thief and a robber, and as such, before God, you shall be proclaimed to the King."

The prelate's voice could scarcely be heard above the clang and clatter on the gate. Soon, with a rending of wood the gate was forced back, and the attackers rushed into the inner courtyard, Sir John, carried along by the crush, among the foremost.

He swaggered truculently up to the Archbishop, who stood, looking somewhat frail, but with a quiet dignity of bearing.

"I demand to know by what right you refuse the King's Governor entrance to his Majesty's castle."

"My authority," said the Archbishop calmly, "is in the King's own hand. Read this, John Owen. What says his Majesty ? That I, having at mine own charge begun to put the castle into repair, am commanded to go on with the work with the King's assurance that whatsoever moneys I shall lay out shall be repaid me before the custody shall be put into any other hands but mine own, or such as I shall recommend."

The Archbishop paused impressively.

Sir John with a gesture brushed the paper aside. "Much hath happened since that time," quoth he. "I have Prince Rupert's commission as Governor, and as Governor I shall govern. So get you gone, John Williams."

"I will not go."

Sir John made a gesture, and two brawny fellows laid their hands on the prelate's shoulders. At this the Archbishop flamed. He flung off their contaminating touch.

"Stand back, you dogs! You dare to lay hands on my person! The King shall hear of this."

"Walk out, or be flung out—I care not which!" said Colonel Owen curtly.

"Then I insist that two of my trusted servants remain on duty among this rabble of grooms and beggarly people to see that the goods of the country be preserved from filching, and the victuals and ammunition which I have stored here at mine own cost suffer not from wasting and purloining."

At this Sir John's choler burst all restraint. "You dare term his Majesty's loyal soldiers a rabble of beggarly people? Your tongue was ever too long, John Williams. Get you out. Ho, my merry lads, burst me these tower doors."

The men needed no second bidding, and with shouts of delight they rushed to all parts of the castle, seeking plunder.

The Archbishop, shaking in every limb from anger and weakness, tottered slowly down the incline to the town, leaning heavily on Maelys's sympathetic arm. At the foot of the incline, like sheep without their shepherd, he found the Bishop of St. Asaph, the

Bishop of Bangor and a cluster of clergy awaiting him anxiously, and thus surrounded the prelate made his way slowly across the town to his palace, where a conference was held. The Bishop of St. Asaph was indignant. "Sir John is my own cousin germane," he cried. "I will expostulate against this dishonour done your Grace."

"I care not so much for myself, good friend," said the Archbishop, "but my mind misgives me when I think of the safety of those cherished and valuable goods which my neighbours entrusted to my care."

"It is no fault of thine, your Grace."

"It concerns my honour most nearly," said the prelate sadly.

The Bishop hastened to the castle, and presently returned to say that Sir John Owen had consented to suffer all things to be inventoried, and would furthermore allow the Archbishop to take away what he would, Sir John acknowledging all goods and ammunition to be rightfully his Grace's.

For which good service the Archbishop gave hearty thanks to the Bishop and went to his bed with an easier mind.

But on the morrow, Sir John, having slept on the matter, receded from all his promises. The castle was his and he would keep it and all it contained. Not a servant of his Grace's would be allowed to pass the portals. Not even the pleading of his own cousin, the Bishop, would move him to relent sufficiently to allow his Grace, who lingered under a great weakness and sickness, "either a little wine, to make him some cawdles, or so much as a little of his own stale beer to make him possets", which (laments the old chronicler) "all the country conceive to be very barbarous".

"No rebel in the country could deal more outrageously," cried the Archbishop. "Maelys, get your tablet and pen. The King shall hear of this."

And so the remonstrance to the King was drawn

up and sent by the hand of Captain James Martin to the King at Oxford, desiring his Majesty to repossess the Archbishop of the right of the castle, or, failing that, to place Sir John under the Archbishop's assignment, or, better still, to put in Sir John's stead "any other man of more moderation and less precipitancy".

So Captain Martin took the road to England, and weeks slipped monotonously by. Sir John at the head of a band of Horse scoured the district, rambling from place to place, and threatening to seize private plate and other valuables for his own use. Outraged squires rode to Conway to lay their protests before the Archbishop. His Grace heard them quietly without comment, and bade them wait. Then came Captain Martin, having penetrated the Parliamentary lines, bearing the curt message that the King would consider the memorial at more leisure.

And after that—silence.

The Archbishop, says the chronicler quaintly, "said nothing, lest he should have said too much".

Early one morning in summer a small cavalcade rode from Conway out of the Upper Gate and took the road for Penrhyn House. In the van rode a figure in black velvet mounted on a grey charger and at his side a woman. From the castle walls Sir John Owen watched the departure of his rival with secret pleasure.

Then with a smile on his face he turned and walked complacently into Conway, and seeking the nearest tavern shouted loudly for wine.

Thus the old order departed from Conway.

CHAPTER THIRTY

THE Lord Byron rode in sombre mood at the head
of his troops. Along the straight roadway which
comes from Caernarvon Castle they came, beside the
pleasant Menai Straits where the fair isle of Anglesey
lifted its pleasant meadows and groves above the
green waters, but his Lordship had no mind for the
beauties of nature. For Naseby had been fought and
lost and his Majesty was all but a fugitive. Only the
West held out for the royal cause. The King was at
Cardiff, but hopes were centred on Chester, and
Chester and the castles of North Wales were Lord
Byron's particular charge. Of the Royalist leaders
none had a definite plan. The Prince of Wales had
been hurried to France, and a vessel even then lay at
Beaumaris waiting, if the King thought fit, to convey
the Duke of York to the protection of Dublin Castle.

As for the King, there were serious thoughts of his
Majesty taking refuge in the mountain fastnesses of
North Wales, there to defy discovery by the Parliament forces until he could rally another army. Lord
Byron cast a gloomy glance inward to where the hard-
topped mountains stood in bold relief against the sky.
Their barren, inhospitable slopes promised security
but scant comfort, and his Lordship's thoughts set
them aside and returned to the ancient city of Chester,
where there was comfortable lodging at least, even if
provisions were scarce. Through the narrow streets
of the old city of Bangor rode the Cavaliers. Some
citizens collected with a dull curiosity to watch the
horsemen pass, though there was not much interest,
for such comings and goings between the adjoining
fortresses of Conway and Caernarvon were no rare

occurrence, and most householders were satisfied if none of the Cavaliers stopped for refreshment, for which it was their wont to forget to pay.

Once outside the confines of the city the troop drew near the village of Llandegai, and Lord Byron rode with baneful glance at the rich woodlands which comprised the park of Penrhyn House.

His lip curled. Suddenly he pulled his horse to the side of the road, and indicating the leading files to continue on their way unchecked he waited until some officers riding near the rear of the column drew near.

"Hogan !" he called, and a horseman drew out of the ranks.

"My Lord ?"

"Do you still cherish fondness for your reverend Father in God, his Grace of York ?"

Hogan glanced quickly at his leader, noting the cynicism in the saturnine face.

"It grieves me, sir, that his influence hath left so little impress on my soul," replied Hogan with simulated gravity.

"I am sure your heart yearns for his spiritual consolation, Hogan, and God knows your sinful soul is in need of it." His Lordship jerked his thumb to the park. "The old fox hath gone to earth yonder. How would you like to drink a glass of wine with him for old friendship's sake ?"

Hogan grinned. "A kindly thought, my Lord. Do I go alone ?"

"Oh, pick your companions ; his Grace was ever fond of boasting of his largeness of heart. But take your hospitality speedily, and see to it you do not tarry over-long. Tear yourself from his holy presence in time to rejoin us ere we reach Conway."

And with a supercilious smile, the meaning of which Hogan was quick to interpret, his Lordship galloped to his place at the head of the column. Hogan rode more leisurely to rejoin his companions. "Ho, there,

Pierre, you gay dog ; and you, Mack, and you, Leary, pull aside. There's game afoot, my merry lads."

The men pulled their mounts out of the line of march with an eagerness which bespoke familiarity with such excursions.

"What is it, *mon cher* Hogan ?" cried the Frenchman. "Is it wine or is it women ?"

"Or plunder, by gad ?" added Mack.

"You were ever a soulless dolt, Mack," retorted Hogan. "Wine this call, and perchance plunder the next."

"And the women ?" put in Leary.

"Ah, that I cannot tell." Hogan grew reflective. "There may be a chit of a girl there ; but if so she is for me. You understand ? I have a score to settle. Take any of the others, but this one is mine if it means fighting for her."

"Let us first view the little one, and discuss fighting for her when we see whether she be worth it," said the Frenchman coolly. "And now, what would you ?"

"A friendly call on the Archbishop of York," said Hogan, riding to the lodge entrance.

"Oh, pious pilgrimage!" sighed Pierre. "*Mon ami*, I always felt you were in need of guidance."

"Come, lads, there's no time to be lost," cried Hogan, and the four spurred their horses down the drive.

Maelys, sitting behind the mullioned windows of her boudoir deep in thought, heard the distant hoof-beats and raised her head wearily. Naseby had wounded her afresh, for once again the gallant Colonel Wynn, fighting in the forefront of his regiment, had fallen captive to the Parliament. And Holland, knighted only the day before the battle, had ridden in Rupert's slashing charge, but never returned and now lay buried in the long trenches where victor and vanquished were heaped when the tumult had passed away. The war was taking heavy toll of the girl. She would have been crushed had not her dauntless spirit upheld her.

The Archbishop, too, was deep in thought, for Naseby had been more than the defeat of the King's forces. The victorious Ironsides, carrying the Royalist position, had captured the King's coach and with it his correspondence—writing which cost the King more dearly than the loss of his troops, for it opened the eyes of the Parliament as never before to the type of man with whom they had to deal, and made hopes of a peace more remote than ever. So his Grace sat absorbed in affairs of state even as Maelys was deep in her private woe when the horsemen came sweeping across the lawn to the front of the stately house.

Both rose instinctively to their feet. Maelys went white.

"It is that beast Hogan," she breathed.

"Stay here, child. These men must not see your sweet face," said the Archbishop hastily. "They come for no good purpose !"

"Stay, dear Uncle, I will not let you brave them alone."

"My child, I do not fear what men can do unto me," said the Archbishop, and walked with dignity to the hall, shutting the girl in the room.

"Ah, greetings, your Grace ! We have called to drink a glass of wine with you."

"A dozen glasses of wine if necessary," said Mack, walking to the buffet and knocking the neck off a bottle.

The Archbishop regarded them in cold disdain.

"To your good white head, Monseigneur," cried Pierre, bowing very low, and raising another bottle to his lips. "Ah, the Church, the Church—I assert the Church has ever a good taste for wine." He smacked his lips appreciatively.

Hogan, too, drank. "Your welcome is not effusive, your Grace," he sneered.

The Archbishop spoke with deliberation. "I have often wondered why it was the King lost his battles ; I no longer wonder."

Hogan had the grace to flush. "Why, damn you," he

cried, "would you insult me?" He walked nearer, thrusting his wine-flushed face into that of the Archbishop, who moved never an inch.

"Your conduct," Dr. Williams said calmly, "is such as I would have expected of one of your breed. I thank God I so speedily rid myself of a cur of your type."

Hogan was staring hard at the Archbishop when a scream rang out from a distant part of the house. For the first time the Archbishop's face paled. "What is it?" he whispered.

"'Twill be Leary. He gave chase to one of the wenches as we entered," said Mack, helping himself to another bottle. "An amorous man, is Leary. Very soft-hearted where a wench is concerned."

But neither the Archbishop nor Hogan heeded him. Hogan had read the prelate's anxiety aright.

"Hi, my lads, that jade I desire is somewhere here. Keep this old bird on his perch while I have word with her."

He stepped forward, but the Archbishop interposed his body. "You shall not pass," he cried. "Stand back, Hogan! In the King's name, you shall not conduct yourself thus in my house."

"Stand aside," yelled Hogan.

"Out of the way, old man," added Pierre, clutching at his sleeve.

Hogan brushed past, but the Archbishop flung himself at him. "Never," he cried. "You shall not pass."

Hogan wheeled and dealt the old man a blow in the face which sent him reeling to the ground. His Grace raised himself on one elbow. He made a pitiable sight with the blood trickling across his silver hair. The fall had dazed him.

"Now for the wench," cried Hogan, springing forward. He had not far to go. A door was flung open and Maelys stood framed in the doorway, her eyes blazing.

"The wench is here," she cried. "You cowardly hound! Before God you are not fit to live."

"Fit to live and fit to love, Light of my Eyes," cried Hogan with a drunken laugh as he moved forward with outstretched arms.

"Stand back," cried Maelys ominously, but Hogan with a reckless laugh came on.

Up swept Maelys's right arm and a pistol flashed. Hogan, clutching at his shoulder, went crashing to the ground.

The echoes of the shot seemed to resound through the room, the silence of which was broken only by the panting of the wounded man. Hogan commenced to curse. "Get her, lads," he cried, and Pierre and Mack stepped forward.

"Rally! Rally, my friends," cried Maelys, and from adjoining doors a crowd of retainers burst in ; grooms and gardeners and keepers, carrying fowling-pieces and pitchforks, swords or muskets, as had come first to their hands.

Before so formidable an array the raiders faltered. "Get you gone," cried Maelys. "And you, dog, crawl to your kennel." Her little shoe spurned Hogan. "Go, go, bully. Striker of old men. Violator of a high priest whose shoe you are unworthy to kiss. Drag the vile wretch out of my sight, ere I have his blood on my soul."

And then, as the discomfited Cavaliers carried their wounded comrade out to the waiting horses, Maelys flung her arms about the dazed prelate and burst into sobs.

.   .   .   .   .

A month passed ; weeks of tension and anxiety. The Archbishop grew more silent. He wrote again to the King complaining of the treatment he had received, but no answer was forthcoming ; only a request that he should take himself to Beaumaris and there supervise the shipment of food and powder to Chester, which was now in sore straits. With a forgiveness which bespoke his Christian charity, without murmur he set about his task of despatching victuals to the besieged city with the whole-hearted zeal which characterized his every undertaking. Colonel Bulkeley raged when he learned of the outrage to his aged kinsman. Pacing the Castle Meadow one fair September day with the Archbishop he cried: "I vow to you, that if ever I lay hands on that miscreant Hogan I will hang him at Gallows' Point."

"His Majesty, God bless him," replied the Archbishop, "hath been very unfortunate in the choice of so many debauched officers."

But Maelys was not so complacent. Outwardly calm, inwardly she fumed at the indignity and injustice her beloved protector suffered. And when one day news came to Beaumaris that the King was coming to Chester in person, her mind was made up. To ride to Chester was now impossible, so close was the leaguer about the devoted city's walls, but in the Menai Straits lay Captain Bartlett's good vessel the *Confidence* which had year after year evaded every attempt of the Parliamentary watch-ships to catch her.

So by stealth Maelys went to her friend the doughty captain, besought him that he would carry her to Chester Water when next he sailed. And the captain, fearful of the risk the girl was taking, demurred until Maelys's mellifluous tongue persuaded him against his better judgment. And so it came about that, when the Archbishop was visiting his house at Penrhyn across the Straits, Maelys stole quietly on board. The Archbishop, watching from his grounds, saw the gallant little vessel beating off Priestholme to run the blockade into Chester. The thought of his duty thus fulfilled brought him some degree of consolation. He did not know of the fair passenger aboard.

Thus Maelys came to Chester.

CHAPTER THIRTY-ONE

FROM the busy decks of the *Confidence*, Maelys looked forth across the waters of the Dee to where Chester lay. The wharves were thronged with idle shipping, small vessels fearful of attempting to run the blockade. Persons were trooping down from the gates, eager to discover what provisions the intrepid Bartlett had brought them ; lean, haggard men, who bore on their cadaverous faces the marks of privations endured. Above the cathedral tower floated the royal banner, for the King was in the city. There were banners, too, elsewhere, fluttering bravely in the morning breeze ; and the streets and walls were gay with colour as brightly caparisoned Cavaliers, plumed and cloaked, made their way through the crowd. But Maelys, despite the outward show of brilliance, was conscious of a feeling of depression. The green turf of the Roodee, no longer given over to horse racing, was cut and furrowed. All about the city, making an outer line of ramparts beyond the circle of the Roman walls, ugly earthworks rose in unsightly outline ; and here and there bastions thrust the black mouths of cannon menacingly towards the Parliamentary lines. Every house and cottage which might harbour the enemy had been razed to the ground, and on every side were the black ashes of dead fires, charred rafters, splintered trees.

Across on the Welsh bank Maelys could discern the glitter of head-pieces as the Roundhead troops moved behind their earthworks.

The vessel dropped anchor in mid-stream, and Maelys was assisted by Captain Bartlett into a ship's boat and was rowed ashore. At the water-steps they were greeted by a fashionably dressed Cavalier. "Welcome, Bartlett, right heartily," cried the gentleman, "the more so as his Majesty arrived but last night and we would offer him better hospitality than most of us have enjoyed of late. You bring victuals, I'm sure."

"Ay, ay, Sir Francis, though no delicacies fit for a King."

"We have a King who is a soldier, and familiar with rough fare. But who is this lady who accompanies you ? 'Tis an ill place for the gently nurtured, with horseflesh for staple fare and dogflesh for savory."

"This is Mistress Wynn, daughter of Colonel Hugh Wynn, and kinswoman of his Grace of York," replied the captain.

Sir Francis Gamull bowed low. "I am charmed to meet you for your father's sake as much as your own, young lady, though it would give me greater pleasure were it under happier circumstances. May I ask if your stay with us is long ? For your sake I trust it be of short duration."

"I come but to speak with the King," said Maelys hurriedly. "Could you arrange for me to have audience with his Majesty, Sir Francis ?"

"It might be done. His Majesty is in good humour. Lord Gerard is here with the Horse and Sir Marmaduke Langdale is expected hourly. With their joint forces his Majesty looks forward to sweeping the rebels from the field. I will do what I can, young lady. His Majesty honours my house with his presence—in Lower Bridge Street, opposite St. Olave's church. But now, if you will excuse me, I must watch the unlading of these precious stores."

Left to herself, Maelys wandered into the city. A fine rain began to fall and she took shelter in the Rows, where she stayed awhile looking down on the passers-by. There were but few women, and most of the men were soldiers. Some of Rupert's Bluecoats ; a swaggering trooper from the King's lifeguard ; Colonel Mostyn's Welsh levies, citizens in homespun girt with sword and bandoleer. The streets were littered and unkempt. The carved woodwork of the ancient houses was pitted with bullets and roundshot ; many of the diamond panes in the windows shattered and stuffed with rags. In other places the black scorchings of fire showed. The faithful city had endured much. Less than four years before his Majesty had ridden into its streets with glitter and pomp, and had been received with all the colourful ritual and ceremony befitting the occasion. Then, the trained bands, well accoutred, were drawn up on either side of Foregate Street ; the Mayor and aldermen in their proper habits awaited their liege-lord ; banners and colours were displayed. Now, there remained only the stern business of war.

Maelys walked to Lower Bridge Street hoping to see the King. Guards were standing motionless in the street before the house, securing his Majesty against any alarm. Presently Sir Francis came bustling up from the river, eager to tell the King the good news.

Maelys touched his arm. "Ah, my dear young lady. A moment. I will ascertain if his Majesty will see you. Pray step inside."

The guards saluted as the knight escorted Maelys into his house. Maelys was left in a downstairs room. The minutes ticked by. Presently there was the sound of steps descending ; there were voices without ; a small, sombre figure with a blue riband brightening his tunic ; a dark plumed hat.

Maelys rose to her feet. It was the King. He turned and looked at her, and she dropped a low curtsy as the dark melancholy eyes rested on hers.

"This is Mistress Wynn, your Majesty, daughter of Colonel Wynn who was taken at Naseby."

"We have no word of him and can arrange no

exchanges," said the King, speaking in a colourless voice which still carried with it a touch of Scottish accent.

"May it please your Majesty, it was on behalf of the Archbishop of York I crave leave to speak."

"Ah! Has his Grace despatched the supplies from Beaumaris?"

"Yes, your Majesty. They have arrived this morning. But I would crave your Majesty to give heed to the petition his Grace sent regarding his displacement from the Governorship of Conway by Sir John Owen."

The King frowned slightly.

"His Grace has spent his wealth and toiled unremittingly on your Majesty's behalf. He grows old, sire, and this injustice is breaking his heart."

The King waved his hand. "We have no time," said he, and moved to the door.

Maelys stepped forward. "I entreat your Majesty . . ." But the King was walking past her, and an equerry rudely thrust her aside.

The officers followed after the King, all glancing curiously at Maelys. Only one, a gaily caparisoned middle-aged man, bent towards her. "I will have word with you later, little one," he said in a hoarse whisper. "You will find me more ready to listen to you. His Majesty was always over-cold where the fair sex are concerned."

Maelys shrank back in alarm. She saw the royal party enter the street, and the lifeguards form about the King. He walked slowly towards the walls. The girl watched, a dull ache in her heart; her brain numb. Her journey by which she hoped to achieve so much had proved futile. With sudden bitterness she felt the cut of royal ingratitude. . . .

Long sat the girl in the deserted room. Servants passed by the door, sometimes glancing within. No one disturbed her. With a feeling of despair she went outside and passed down the street. Somewhere behind her she was conscious of diversion ; shoutings, a trumpet's harsh note, the rhythmic roll of a drum. Men were running hither and thither. A mounted man brushed past her with never a care for her safety as he sped up the street. A rush of soldiers crowded her against the wall of a house. Presently she came to some steps, and mounting these she joined the throng collected there. She wondered what they were gazing at, turned her eyes to the flat stretch of country which spread beyond the walls but saw nothing save a troop of Horse marching towards the distant outworks. Presently she saw Sir Francis and him she stopped. "What is it ?" she inquired.

"Sir Marmaduke," he said, mopping his brow. "He was to have joined us here with the major portion of the Horse, but unknown to the King he hath engaged the rebels. We know not what to make of it. Sir Richard Lloyd hath just sent in a courier saying that he fears ill will come of it. They are out on Rowton Heath. Lord Byron and Lord Gerard are hastening to his support, but I fear it will be too late."

He passed on, and Maelys, scarce comprehending, continued her way along the narrow parapet. She came to the Phoenix Tower, the steps of which were lined with officers. At the top were clustered a knot of courtiers, their gay apparel showing brightly against the September sky, and a little apart a sombre figure in black who watched the distant field with an optic glass. Maelys looked over the wall as a man turned from his position.

"That damned Poyntz hath undone us," he shouted savagely, and broke away. Maelys could see horsemen racing towards the town ; troopers who rode without order, panic-stricken. Others were in the distance ; footmen staggering from wounds ; distant figures scurrying hither and thither like ants whose nest has been disturbed.

The man in black on the tower-top shut up his glass.

The courtiers stood aside. Slowly he descended the worn stone stairs, the melancholy brown eyes staring unseeing before him.

Men bared their heads. No one spoke.

King Charles had seen his troops defeated on Rowton Moor. . . .

.   .   .   .   .

Maelys long remembered that dread day. The trail of fugitives ; of bleeding, cursing, suffering soldiery. The disorder in the streets all night. Langdale, on whose dashing cavalry skill the King counted so much, was brought in wounded ; Gerard, also wounded, came in a vile temper.

Maelys timidly sought shelter in Sir Francis's house, and received it. She did not sleep. No one heeded her.

At dawn the streets were packed with horsemen.

The King came down fully accoutred for a journey. He gave Lord Byron his hand. "I must leave you, my Lord," said he calmly. "This blow is too severe to admit any recovery. If after eight days you see no prospect of relief, we give you leave to treat for your own preservation."

With a dignity which seemed to increase with each fresh misfortune the King walked to his waiting charger. He mounted, and, surrounded by five hundred Horse, marched over Dee Bridge into Wales.

Colonel Poyntz's victorious Yorkshire Horse hovered about the royal party, but that night the King reached Denbigh Castle in safety, where the Governor, Colonel Salusbury, received him gladly. Old "Hosanau Gleision" (as the Welsh called him on account of his blue stockings) proceeded to speak his mind, and (to quote Charles's own words) "never did a Prince hear so much truth at once". Then, to prove his loyalty, the doughty old soldier vowed that he would never deliver up the castle until his Majesty bade him do so—a boast which history testifies he nobly kept.

But Maelys only heard of this later.

At the time, Maelys, depressed and discouraged, turned her thoughts towards home. In the crowd a man brushed past her ; a man who turned and stared at her with evil eyes. His face was known to her ; it was the rake Leary, he who had been with Hogan when they broke into Penrhyn House. Quickly she slipped into a house, stole through the rear door into an entry. She heard footsteps following. She darted into another house and back into the streets— they seemed safer than those narrow alleys. She thrust her way through the throng ; her one desire to get aboard the *Confidence*. When she came to the water's edge the vessel was not to be seen.

"She sailed with the ebb, lady," a waterman informed her. "Her skipper was in a fine tear, seeking high and low for some passenger, but could find no trace of her."

Maelys, heavy of heart, made her way into the city, and sought the headquarters of Colonel Mostyn. Her brave young kinsman would see her to safety. But fresh disappointment awaited her. Colonel Mostyn had ridden with those who guarded the King.

As she looked through the window she glimpsed Hogan in the street. He seemed to be searching. . . .

Panic seized her. Escape from this dread city she must ! She would join the King's party. She coaxed an escort and set off in pursuit.

Once clear of the Flintshire shore a party of Colonel Jones's Horse, hot on the trail of the King, gave them chase. The escort scattered. Maelys found herself riding for the bleak uplands. Behind her galloped a party of buff-coated troopers. To her distorted imagination they seemed to be Hogan and his friends. Rain began to fall. Wet, weary, desperate, the girl rode—she knew not where. She had outdistanced her pursuers. Darkness fell. A sudden nausea seized her. Her senses reeled. Her weary mount, uncontrolled, walked whither it would. A glimmer pierced the gloom. A dog barked. Maelys staggered towards the light as the door of a smallholding was opened and a Welsh farmer called out to know who was there.

With a sob the girl collapsed at his feet.

He carried her within and handed her to the care of his wife. Presently the woman came out, concern in her eyes, to tell her good man that Maelys was in a raging fever.

CHAPTER THIRTY-TWO

MAELYS, returning from the wood where she had been gathering primroses, took affright when she beheld before the farm door several saddle horses.

Her desire was to avoid soldiery and she shrank to cover, but her precaution was of no avail. A young buff-coated trooper, the Parliamentary colours of orange-tawny about his waist, walked towards her and saluted respectfully. He showed no surprise at her presence.

"If you are sufficiently recovered, Mistress Wynn, I am to escort you to your home," said he civilly.

"On whose instructions?" she asked.

"One who shows concern in your welfare, Mistress," was his reply.

Maelys grew curious. "Is it—Captain Heritage?"

The man only smiled enigmatically.

"Was it he who sent the surgeon to me, and who was responsible for the delicacies I have received throughout my long illness?"

Still no answer. "If you will prepare for the journey, Mistress, we will set off. I am given to understand that it is no longer desirable that you should remain in these parts."

Maelys went to bid the good folk at the farm farewell, and to assure them of her father's gratitude. Her preparations were soon made. She mounted her horse and turned to the young Cornet who had charge of her escort. The troopers trotted ahead and dispersed in several directions.

"You *do* come from Captain Heritage," said Maelys emphatically, watching the riders. "I can see his

251

handiwork in the manner they take cover. He hath trained them to scout."

"I have also been trained to keep silence," replied the Cornet with a smile.

"Can you not give me tidings of what hath happened in the world? I have been so cut off that I have heard little save that Chester hath fallen."

"Oh yes! It was on February third that Lord Byron with colours flying and drums beating and all the honours of war marched out for Conway."

"And it was last September the King bade him hold out for eight days!"

"Both Lord Byron and Colonel Mostyn have conducted themselves with great valour during the siege. Several times we carried the outworks by escalade, but they beat us back. They were nigh starving when they surrendered."

Maelys grew more inquisitive. "Have you word of the Archbishop of York? I know he must be anxious about me."

"His Grace was long ago assured of your safety." Then he added drily: "His Grace hath other concerns to occupy his mind!"

The Cornet drew from his pouch a letter which he handed to the girl. She drew rein. The seal was already broken; the subscription in the Archbishop's own handwriting was addressed to the Marquis of Ormond. "It may interest you," commented the Cornet.

The Enemyes are retreated to theyr Quarters befor Chester, haveinge kept theyr Christmas in Flintshyre and Denbishshyre, and that without beinge once forced by our Forces, though they were 200 good Horse and 300 good Foote, well armed. Our Commander in Chief, Colonel Gilbert Byron, though chosen by our selves, yet lately married and verye indulgent to his Ladye, hath deceived our Expectation and done nothinge. I pray

*God the Count St. Pol, a verye valiant and active gentle-
man, who hath now undertaken to leade our little Armye,
doth not over doe it.*

Maelys looked up. "How came you by this letter?"

"It is our duty to apprehend messengers who ride
for the malignants," he said.

"But what of the Count St. Pol? Hath he met with
success?"

"With no better success than the others. We beat
him off near Denbigh—even though he was reinforced
by men whom Colonel Mostyn journeyed to Ireland to
raise—and chased them eight miles on their way back
to Conway. With Chester fallen, we are now investing
these piles of stones where your governors drink their
ale in false security."

So they rode forward, pausing once, to look across
the broad meadows towards Denbigh where Maelys
could see men toiling at a battery mount. The fair
scene was scarred by the new-turned earth. Above
the castle flew the royal colours in brave defiance. Its
Governor was "a verie wilfull man".

There was a puff of smoke and the thunder of a
heavy gun as a shot was flung against the Goblin
Tower. The "strong siege" had commenced.

Maelys, as she looked at the numbers of attackers,
felt her heart sink, but spoke no word. By a detour
they rode past Denbigh to St. Asaph, and thence by
way of the village of Bettws towards the Conway
River. Now and again they would pass a company
of Foot marching to tap of drum ; or a party of Horse
or dragoons scouring the countryside. It was impressed upon Maelys that without her escort her
chance of reaching Caernarvonshire would have been
scant indeed.

The girl felt her heart bound within her as, coming
to a sudden bend where the road fell suddenly away,
she found herself gazing down on the broad Conway

as it curved its way between green meads backed by woods which already showed promise of Spring. But she was given no time to admire the view. They descended the winding road to Tal-y-Cafn, where they crossed by the old ferry. The girl wondered whether she would be sent up river to Gwydir or down to Conway, but her escort pressed westward. Up, up they rode, climbing the narrow winding road which the Romans made to link their fort of Kanovium, on the Conway, to Segontium at Caernarvon. On the high plateau, following the narrow grass-grown road through the Pass of the Two Stones, they came upon troopers scanning the land.

They were General Mytton's men, surveying the route for his march on Anglesey.

It was late afternoon when the Cornet paused at the edge of the woods about Penrhyn House and bade her adieu. He accepted the girl's expression of thanks with a stoical smile.

"I carry out my orders, Madam," he said. Then, with a touch of courtesy: "I would they were always as pleasant."

He saluted, and was gone.

As she hastened eagerly up the woodland path which led to the house, a figure stepped from behind the broad bole of a beech.

"You!" she cried as she recognized Heritage. "What are you doing here?"

"Waiting for you, Maelys," he answered quietly.

"But how could you know I should come this way?"

Heritage smiled his enigmatical smile.

"I spend much of my time watching. The years I spent among the Indians taught me patience. I do not mind watching, especially when I watch for you, for then I reap my reward."

She coloured. "I forbid you to talk to me thus."

"I love you," he said.

"Hush! How dare you?"

"And did his Majesty receive you kindly?" he asked.

Maelys found herself colouring afresh. "I will not answer you," she said haughtily.

"I see I was right."

"His Majesty is great in his misfortune," she said proudly.

They walked in silence towards the house. As they came to the wood's edge Maelys stopped suddenly and stared in alarm.

The broad lawns were torn; the windows barricaded; brickbats and glass were scattered about the paths; the doors wedged with logs; eaves were charred from flames.

"Is this why you are here?" she cried fiercely. "You have captured the house. What have you done to the Archbishop?"

Heritage smiled.

"Tell me!" She shook him roughly. "Tell me!"

"His Grace is quite safe," said Heritage calmly. "Your misjudge me, Maelys; as, indeed, you have done before. This is the work of Byron's troopers. Thanks be to God, we arrived in time to rescue the Archbishop and they were beaten back. There have been eventful happenings since you were here."

Maelys scarcely heard him. "He is safe? You are sure he is safe?"

"Safe and well. You will see him anon."

She heaved a sigh of relief. "Then what are you doing here?"

"I—oh, I have been trying to protect the Archbishop from harm. A strange task, is it not? It is for your sake I do it. You are the first woman I have cared for, and I have not learned the way of these matters. If my wooing is strange, put it down to my forest manners."

He turned back into the wood and presently reappeared leading his great black horse.

Maelys walked towards him. "I would not appear ungrateful, Captain Heritage," said she in gentler tones. "I know I am much beholden to you, but I beg of you not to speak to me of love. It does but distress me."

"Have you not yet proof that Charles Stuart is unworthy of your devotion?"

"We will not discuss his Majesty. I have told you that my loyalty, above all, is to the Archbishop. Him I love. Him I serve. Him I follow always."

Heritage slowly mounted.

"Your resolve remains unchanged?"

"Nothing will change it. Where he leads I follow. Therefore what use to talk of love when you are for the one party, and I for the other? Can two walk together unless they be agreed?"

"You are resolute? You will follow the Archbishop always?" Heritage was looking down at her with a strange light in his eyes.

"My decision is unalterable. I follow the Archbishop!" said Maelys. "Why do you gaze at me thus?"

Heritage bent from the saddle, his eyes dancing with suppressed laughter.

"The Archbishop hath declared for the Parliament!"

He shook his reins and was gone.

CHAPTER THIRTY-THREE

THERE were uneasy minds among the dwellers about Conway during the fateful Spring of 1646. With Chester—the door into North Wales—captured invasion was inevitable. The taking of Ruthin and the investing of Denbigh hinted to the good folk of Caernarvonshire what would shortly come their way. For the moment Conway was ignored, General Mytton pushing his troops across the inland hills for the attack on Caernarvon, where Lord Byron and those who escaped the surrender of Chester, of Holt Castle, Beeston Castle, and Lathom House, were gathered with their backs to the wall.

"The amazed people", says the chronicler, "turn to the Archbishop, look upon his strong wisdom and grey hairs to stop the cruelty of the conqueror, and to lighten the yoke of their misery. The Archbishop calls some few to counsel with him, who agree to parley with Mytton."

Meanwhile, Captain Stephen Rich with the Parliament war vessels *Rebecca* and *Rupert* lay off Beaumaris waiting to force the passage of the Menai Straits.

There was bitterness among the Wynns, for at Allhallowtide the previous year Sir William Vaughan's troopers, fleeing to the mountains after their defeat by the Parliament troops under Mytton near Denbigh, fell upon Gwydir, stayed there five days, and on going rifled the house.

So it was when General Mytton passed that way in March, advancing on Caernarvon for his attack on Lord Byron, he found ready welcome at Gwydir, he testifying in a certificate to the cheerful "entertainment" he had been accorded by Maurice Wynn— entertainment which cost Maurice dear, for Sir John Owen sent out a party from Conway, on the Parliamentarian General's departure, and drove away all Wynn's cattle.

So when Mytton's mind turned to Conway, the Archbishop turned to diplomacy. "It is no time for the subdued to show their teeth when they cannot bite", observed his Grace.

.   .   .   .   .

On a bright August morning Maelys, returning from a ramble in Penrhyn Park, walked unconcernedly into the dining-room and stopped abruptly. There were strangers in the room. A glance at their sad attire indicated they were not Cavaliers. The Archbishop, who had been speaking, paused and all rose silently to their feet.

Maelys ran her eye curiously over the assembly, noting the papers and maps and sheathed swords which lay upon the table ; the serviceable buff coats and orange sashes worn by the men who bore the stamp of officers of rank.

"I—crave pardon ; I intrude," she stammered.

"Come in, child," said the Archbishop. "I would like to present you to Major-General Mytton, Governor of Anglesey and Commander-in-Chief in North Wales for the Parliament."

A man standing beside the prelate bowed solemnly. "This is Colonel Wynn's daughter—I might almost say my adopted daughter—and my secretary."

"With respect, your Grace," said General Mytton, "a secretary is undesirable at these deliberations which are *sub rosa*, but if Mistress Wynn cares to sit with us as your Grace's adopted daughter we shall find ourselves honoured by her presence."

He drew a chair to the table and extending his hand he guided Maelys to her seat. Indicating the other officers General Mytton introduced them—Colonel Carter, Colonel Twistleton, Colonel Glynne, Colonel Jones, Major Elliott, who bowed without speaking, and all resumed their seats.

Maelys stole a glance at the famed commander. Major-General Mytton, with whose name all North Wales was ringing, was not the type of man she had expected to see. The conqueror of Wem, Oswestry, Shrewsbury, Holt Castle, Ruthin Castle, Flint Castle, Caernarvon Castle, Beaumaris Castle ; whose forces were even then drawn about Denbigh Castle and Rhuddlan, had appeared to her as a relentless monster of a man. Instead, she found him possessed of a high and noble countenance and a polished manner which bespoke good breeding. His authority as a leader was obvious, yet despite his uniform he looked, what indeed he was, a kindly country gentleman who, for the sake of a principle, had caught up an unfamiliar sword and, possibly to his own surprise, found himself singularly adept in the wielding thereof.

And then Maelys sat in awe as the Archbishop began to speak. Of his eloquence on the judicial bench and in the councils of the nation she had ofttimes heard, but never before had her own ears experienced the convincing power of his tongue. Well might his Grace wax eloquent ! It was the crucial moment of his career, when life itself was the stake. A false move, an error of judgment, and all was lost. He must justify his past actions ; must ingratiate himself to his new masters. He spoke of the wrongs he had suffered : he pleaded his obligation to those whose valuables were entrusted to his care at Conway Castle. The King had given up the fight and called upon all his subjects to do likewise. What good purpose could be served by Sir John Owen's obstinacy at Conway ? "I see nothing in it," exclaimed his Grace, "but some fresh scheme by these sharks and children of fortune to gain for themselves fresh profit."

General Mytton listened gravely. "Then I take it we may count on your Lordship's support in the attack on Conway?"

Maelys gasped. "Attack Conway!" At her involuntary ejaculation the prelate slightly frowned as though he deprecated any interruption at such a moment, but General Mytton turned kindly: "Yes, young lady; and in return for his Grace's support, I have pledged my word that all the valuables for which he stands surety shall be restored to their rightful owners. Lord Byron's misguided arrogance in attacking his Grace has placed your kinsman's invaluable influence on the side of the Parliament." He bowed.

"You need not fear the issue, Maelys," added his Grace more complacently. "The people of Conway would as soon fight for a maypole as for Sir John Owen."

"Then, gentlemen, we attack the town of Conway," said General Mytton decisively. "I conclude that the operation be feasible, though full of doubt and hazard, and that it will not be effected without much loss, but with the blessing of God and by exercising our best skill I firmly believe that resolute men can achieve it."

He rang a bell. "Send Captain Heritage hither."

Maelys watched fascinated as the door opened and Heritage entered. He stood silently to attention, his great form towering above the others.

"We propose to attack Conway and carry the town by escalade without delay. It is essential that no word of our advance shall reach the town. The troops have rested well over night and can march at once. You will undertake to see that no single messenger reaches Conway to carry tidings of our advance."

Heritage bowed and withdrew. His eyes looked at Maelys; the girl fancied she read a meaning in the glance. When the assembly broke up, she hurried outside.

On the broad lawn a troop of Horse was marshalled ; silent, buff-coated troopers, some of whom looked familiar to the girl's eyes.

Beside Satan, Maelys's own horse stood saddled. Heritage gave the signal and the men mounted and took up formation.

"I thought you would like to ride with us. There will be no danger," said Heritage.

Maelys obeyed without demur. "Somehow, I never think of danger when I am with you," was her only comment.

The cavalcade rode at a brisk trot out of the park and took the road to Conway. Once in open country, Heritage halted his troop, and dividing them into parties sent some to watch the coast, some the roads through the passes and the others to extend along the uplands. The scouts dispersed with the noiseless alacrity of men who understood their task.

"Come, Maelys, we will go over the moors and watch lest anyone should slip through the cordon, which I doubt."

It never occurred to the girl to dissent. She found herself caught up in the toils of war and curiosity held her fascinated. She recalled the ride with Heritage on the night they met. Then his care of her had been a personal matter ; now the safety of an army, the success of an enterprise, lay in his hands. Neither spoke. Their mounts panted up the hill track and faced the broad upland moors. Heritage's eyes never ceased to rove. He picked his way from cover to cover, sometimes pausing, sometimes hurrying. Maelys followed every action in blind obedience. Just to be in his company brought her great content.

They came to a spur of the hills which looked down upon Conway, and Heritage, dismounting, tethered the horses in a hollow and sprawled behind the shelter of a clump of bracken.

"There are no preparations in the town ; I think we shall have them by surprise," said Heritage presently in a low voice. He pointed across the Sychnant Pass. Maelys after concentrating her gaze discovered a buff-coated form amid the gorse. "It is Trooper Willitt," he said.

"I should not have seen him if you had not pointed him out," confessed Maelys.

Heritage turned with a smile. "I am proud of my scholars," he said. "Our scout work is infinitely superior to that of the Royalists. It pleases my vanity to assume that our successes are not unconnected with that fact."

They fell silent again. The hours slipped away ; the sun at its zenith blazed down upon their motionless forms.

"If you feel the heat," said Heritage presently, "you will find a well yonder where the rushes show dark green. Only keep low and do not show against the skyline."

The girl discovered the well, and returned refreshed. Heritage still had his eyes fixed on the country below. "I suppose," he said slowly, "I ought to have fetched you water. You must blame my forest manners."

"You have your work. I understand," said Maelys.

"If you care to go to the western side of yonder rock, you will see a sight which I think you will remember."

Maelys went. Below her, in the pass, she saw an army on the march—men of the New Model Army wearing for the first time the red coats which were ever more to be the hallmark of the British soldier. Powdered with dust, drenched with sweat, they came, hard-featured veterans which four years' constant campaigning had turned into the finest infantry in Europe. Despite the hill they marched with ranks unbroken, their long pikes bristling ; muskets sloped ; resolute, terrible as an army with banners.

The drummers marched in front with their drums

slung behind their shoulders. There was no sound but the tramp of feet.

Heritage was beside her with the horses. "Captain Simkies with the Cheshire Firelocks is to deliver an attack on the North Wall of the town," he said. "He goes by way of the Morfa. It will be but a feint. I must lead these men to cover in the Benarth Woods until the hour for the assault is come."

They mounted, rode to the head of the column, which Heritage guided inland so that the wooded hills were interposed between the troops and the town. Ever and anon Maelys caught glimpses of buff-coated horsemen, the eyes of the army, scouting ahead, watching to see that no messenger carried tidings to the doomed town.

In the shadow of the woods the army halted and the men lay down amid the fragrant bracken to cool.

"I must leave you now. Remain here," said Heritage, and leaving Satan in the hands of a soldier he stole noiselessly through the trees in the direction of Conway. Maelys waited. Not far away a sergeant who was evidently an itinerant preacher had gathered a circle of soldiers about him and was exhorting them to quit themselves like men.

Elsewhere Maelys found another group busy fashioning ladders from young trees and from wood obtained from a nearby farm.

Suddenly a dull rumble sounded on the still air. The silent world became animated. Frightened birds flew twittering through the trees as a blast of musketry was carried down the wind. Trumpets were sounding from the castle walls ; drums were rolling the alarm. There were shouts and cheers and the irregular crackle of firearms.

All about her the red-coats were tightening their belts and resuming their weapons. The men with the ladders were running to the fore. All were marshalled on the road and went forward at a quick step towards the sounds of battle. Maelys, fascinated, followed. A soldier who had been detailed to guard her came behind leading the horses.

As Maelys stepped from cover an amazing scene greeted her eyes. The grey town which had been so familiar to her since childhood had assumed strange activity. The walls, seemingly but a shell of a long-distant past, were now a thing of moment. From every one of the twenty-one wall-towers rose the white smoke as hidden musketeers fired on the besiegers. Ramparts of castle and town were alive with people. Ever and anon a great gun would belch forth fire and smoke. The green sward without the walls was thick with moving figures. Red-coats were everywhere, like drops of blood in a green sea. Up went the ladders against the dark walls. Red-coats were filling the town ditch; others sprawled motionless on the ground. The ladders were too short. Through the drifting smoke Maelys saw ladders flung down, scattering their living load. The noise never ceased. Rocks were crashing on to the head-pieces of the Roundheads in the town ditch. Up went the ladders again. The attack grew more frantic.

Heavens, what was this? A great, strange, ungainly form came hurtling through the air, sweeping several ladders before it. Maelys to her amazement saw it was a horse. Another came. The besieged were flinging their chargers over the walls to stay the attack. Yet (as the old account hath it) "such was the resolution and gallantry of the soldiers, that though some were knocked down and crushed with horses, others cast off the ladders (which were ten yards high and yet proved a yard and a half too short) that they renewed the action, drawing up one another by the arm, till a considerable company were got over".

Maelys watched with fast-beating heart. Somewhere in the turmoil Heritage would be plying his terrible sword. She could see no sign of him. Red-coats were on the wall above the Upper Gate. Cheers were rending the air. The drawbridge was coming down. Captain Gethin's men had carried the gateway. There was a rush for the drawbridge from without.

Maelys, heedless of the flying bullets, began to run forward. Leading the stormers up one of the ladders she had seen a figure clad in black, conspicuous amid the crimson jackets. Helmet on head and sword in hand, Archbishop John Williams, last of the fighting prelates, was leading the stormers in their attack. Maelys, distraught, hastened towards him. Dead and dying lay about her but she heeded them not. The voice of a wounded fanatic was calling in agonized tones about the Day of Judgment. Up on the wall top, amid the glitter of blade and push of pike, the valiant old man was wielding his sword. He had learnt rapier-play in his youth, but though his spirit was young his arm had lost its cunning.

Maelys, caught up in the rush of reinforcements dashing to the Upper Gate, was swept aside as into the town rushed the panting, excited infantry. They were clearing High Street at push of pike. When the tumult died, Maelys timidly ventured inside. In the market square the Roundhead trumpeters were endeavouring to pierce the din. A group of discomfited prisoners stood with empty hands amid a ring of guards. In front of the farm below the Upper Gate the horse which had been grinding corn for the garrison lay dead in his tracks, killed by a stray bullet. Desultory firing from the castle announced that though the town was carried the castle still held out.

General Mytton, standing on the steps of Plas Mawr, ordered the guards to secure the town, and the prisoners were brought before him. A strange assortment, according to accounts. The attackers had "killed a corporal and a gentleman when they surprised the mainguard, wounded many, took a major, one Captain Wynne, an old cow-driver, four lieutenants, four ensigns, twenty-two soldiers of fortune and fifty townsmen in arms". They had also taken "one great gun, 200 arms, ammunition answerable, wine, corn and victuals good store, and considerable booty for the soldiers".

Was this the Conway of her girlhood ? Maelys asked herself as she gazed bewildered about the disordered streets, the bullet-marked window-frames, the wounded men ; and heard the shouting and the din of war. Was this her uncle's home against which she leaned ?

Then she saw Heritage's great figure striding among the red-coats, and she ran to him with a cry of relief.

He was smoke-stained and weary. "Thank God I have found you ; Maelys, you ought not to be here. I left you in the woods."

"I—I saw the Archbishop scaling the walls—and I was afraid."

"Come, we will find him."

Heritage, silent, led the way to a house near the river walls. "My dear," he said gently, "you must prepare yourself for a shock. The Archbishop——"

"He is not killed ?"

"Not killed, but wounded. He received a pike thrust in the neck. I trust it is not serious, but at his age——"

They ascended the stairs of the Black Lion Inn. There on a small bed lay the prelate, his throat swathed in blood-stained bandages, his face like parchment. But his dauntless eyes as he turned them to the door were bright. They softened tenderly as he saw Maelys, and the girl dropped weeping at his side. His white hand caressed the bowed head. "Oh, why did you do it ?" she moaned.

A smile came to the eyes of Dr. Williams. He fumbled in his tunic, and drew out a blood-stained paper. It was the lampoon which had been nailed to the palace door, showing him with head-piece and bandoleer over his episcopal gown. "I would have them—see—I—can—fight," he whispered.

Presently he fell asleep, and Maelys and Heritage stood motionless looking down upon the still, white face. Silently they withdrew and walked to the walls.

A sickening shriek of terror and a heavy splash caused Maelys to jump. "What is it?" she cried with white face.

"The Irish," said Heritage. "All Irish taken in arms are to be tied back to back and flung into the river."

"Oh, the poor creatures! But how terrible!"

Heritage shrugged his shoulders. "It is the orders of the Parliament to hang every Irish Papist taken in arms in this country."

Another splash made Maelys cover her ears. But curiosity was strong and she peered over the walls.

Along the curtain wall which thrust itself into the river, protecting the quay from attack from seaward, two red-coated soldiers were thrusting two bound unfortunates to the edge.

Maelys hid her eyes on Heritage's shoulder. "Oh, it is wrong; wrong!"

"Perhaps it is; they should not have come to this land. Their shedding of innocent blood is not forgotten. It returns on their own heads."

"You are hard."

"It is war. Come, Maelys, you are overwrought."

He led her into the town, which was now quiet. General Mytton was summoning the castle to surrender.

From the river came a final shriek and splash. The last ripples circled and vanished. The surface of the water spread like a mirror reflecting the glory of the setting sun. The vale of Conway was bathed in peace.

CHAPTER THIRTY-FOUR

THE dull reverberation of a heavy gun came rolling from across the river. It affrighted the rooks in the Gloddaeth elms and scattered them cawing into the bright sky. It caused the Archbishop to look up from his papers; it made Maelys lay down her quill. Their eyes met.

"The castle holds out," said the girl, "and General Mytton has ordered batteries to be thrown up. Captain Heritage was here this morning a brief while, and he tells me that Sir John is stubborn."

The Archbishop's fingers strayed to the bandage which swathed his neck. "I feared the castle would resist," he said with a nervousness which was hitherto foreign to his nature.

"Captain Heritage sets little store on it," said Maelys. "He says that already their flesh is near spent, though they still have some store of corn and beer. He is confident that the Parliament forces could carry the castle by scalada should the occasion demand, but General Mytton hesitates to shed blood when starvation must bring Sir John to reason."

"I like it not," said his Grace. His wound, though not severe, had shaken him. Perhaps he felt a gambler's apprehension, for having staked all on one throw he now awaited the turn of the card.

"Child, what think you of this Mytton—is he a man of his word?"

"He seemed to me a very kindly and gallant gentleman," said Maelys. "One who held his honour high, and would never break his troth."

"I trust so," said the Archbishop slowly, "and yet . . .

268

If he hands not over to me the goods in the castle it will go ill with me. Already some of our neighbours are accusing me of being basely backward in his Majesty's interests, though they were ready enough to fly to me to save them from the invader when peril threatened. I acted as seemed best. The Parliament troops were upon us, and what security hath the earthern pitcher against an iron pot ? His Majesty commanded that all his castles be surrendered. What profit therefore could be gained by withstanding them ? On the other hand, the restoration of these valuables to my neighbours who placed their trust in me is a matter which concerns my honour nearly. Had his Majesty not deprived me of the command of the castle, all might have been different. How wretched is the man who hangs on princes' favours !"

The prelate paced the room.

"Maelys, child, the die is cast. I must labour and pray that the Parliament win. Let them but relax their hold on our unhappy land, and the Irish will assuredly come hither and murder me. My security lies with the Parliament. I will come out boldly. Write, child, and say that it is my intention to preach a sermon in honour of the taking of the town."

"But, my dear, you are scarce strong enough, your wound——"

"An honourable scar. It should spur me. Let us have a fighting text, child. I shall preach from the 144th Psalm : *Blessed be the Lord my strength which teacheth my hands to war, and my fingers to fight !*"

"A goodly text, your Grace !"

The voice came from the doorway. Heritage stood smiling down upon them.

Through the open door sounded the distant rumble of artillery.

"Owen means to resist ?" asked the Archbishop anxiously.

Heritage nodded and leisurely seated himself,

stretching his long spurred boots as he took his ease.

"'Tis but child's play," said he. "It amuses our bombardeers."

"There is no doubt about the castle falling?"

Heritage was scornful. "I say again it is child's play. The fool is reasonably secure, and will hold out till we batter a breach, or until his waistbelt grows slack, and then he will cry truce and march out with honours of war, having shown the world he is a valiant fighter. He is destitute of relief. We hold the country now in the hollow of our hand. Denbigh and Harlech and Conway are the sole castles holding out for the King, and already they see the writing on the wall."

"What says General Mytton?"

"He hath summoned Owen to surrender. I heard him read aloud his summons before he despatched it with drum and flag to the castle. He told Owen that, now that it pleased God to give the town into our hands, he could do no less than put him in mind that his holding of the castle could produce no other effect than the effusion of Christian blood and the ruin of the country."

"And what answered Owen?"

"Faith, he kept the General, who gave him two hours in which to answer, waiting until next day. I have a copy of his reply with me." Heritage drew a paper from his pocket and puckered his brows over it.

"Read it, Maelys," said he. "I am not overfond of this scratching of pens."

"Sir John says," began Maelys spreading the paper before her, "'I wonder you should tax me with bringing misery upon this country which my conscience tells me I am free of, especially in doing my endeavour to hold it in obedience to his Majesty. Now you have gotten the town, I expect no other title from you than of the castle, which title I will maintain with my life. For the effusion of Christian blood, far be it from my heart, only I seek to defend myself and those that are with me. As for the ruin of the country, let the blood of those that lost it fall upon them that were the contrivers of it.'

"He goes on to say that he doubts that the King is in the Parliament quarter, and concludes, 'As for your summonses I shall hold this castle as long as it pleaseth God for his Majesty. Yet, if you shall accept of such conditions as I shall propound, which shall be honourable for us both, I will be content to treat with you only.'"

"The cunning fox," cried the Archbishop. "For all his valorous protestations see you not how he hath left a bolt-hole by which he can escape when the trap closes ? What said the General Mytton ?"

"Why, he said he would receive any propositions Sir John had ready."

"And what then ?"

"Sir John desired three days to prepare them, but the three days are past and gone."

"What says General Mytton now ?"

Heritage held up his finger. The distant rumble of cannon came down the still air.

"That is General Mytton's answer," he said. "The time of writing is over. We speak now from the mouths of cannon. The siege of Conway Castle has begun."

.   .   .   .   .

The yellowing of leaves came. Day by day the battle smoke curled above the grey walls of Conway Castle. It showed its misty patterns against the background of trees. The colourings of the leaves merged from green to gold, but the smoke from the guns drifted unchanged. Only the distant peaks looked down unmoved upon the scene. They kept the remorseless grandeur which was theirs since the dawn of time.

September passed.   The House of Commons is

assured by General Mytton that "the reducing of Conway goes on well". October comes. General Mytton, with greater matters to think about, leaves the leaguer in the hands of Colonel John Jones.

Possibly General Mytton is beginning to grow impatient, for the House of Commons is informed that he has planted "two pieces of cannon (very near) for batteries".

On November 18th, Sir John Owen surrendered.

The patience of the Parliamentary troops had become exhausted, and, the approach of winter rousing them to a fighting humour, it was borne upon Sir John Owen that the moment for discretion was at hand. For three months he had shown defiance. The Parliamentary battery on Benarth slopes had breached the base of one of his towers. The red-coats in the town had pushed their barricades almost to his very drawbridge. The men of the district were mustering for the final assault. Sir John hung out the white flag.

"And not the least time being spent in delay," writes the old chronicler, "the soldiers entered the Castle both by scalada, and by forcing the gates, assisted by the Archbishop's kindred and other Welch".

They took in the castle "seven pieces of ordnance, six barrels of gun-powder, good store of provisions and all their arms".

So Sir John Owen marched forth and retained his freedom for nigh two years, proving to be a thorn in the flesh to the Parliament, until he lost his liberty and nearly his head when he was captured in the abortive uprising which ended in the fight at Dalar Hir beside the Menai Straits.

Archbishop Williams was in a more tranquil frame of mind than he had been for many months, for it is on record that "Mytton kept the Castle—and kept his word to let the owners divide the goods among themselves, to which they laid title and could prove it".

"It is borne upon me that my judgment is still

sound, child," said the Archbishop complacently, "that my hand hath not lost her cunning."

But Maelys showed little enthusiasm.

"When will wars cease?" she asked sadly. "I cannot walk our lovely lanes, erstwhile so quiet, without encountering a gun-team, or dragoons, or a provision-train escorted by red-coated Foot." She pointed to the dining-room from which she had emerged, and quoted the Latin inscription across the fire-place: *"Give Peace in our time, O Lord; for there is none."*

"I fear me I took my text at the intaking of Conway from the wrong end of the Psalm, Maelys," said the Archbishop. He drew his chair nearer the blaze and turned a page. "Hear what the Psalmist saith:

" *'When our garners are full; when our oxen are well laden; when there is no breaking in and no going forth; and no outcry in our streets; happy be the people.'*

"I have hopes that the day is not far distant when the streets of Conway will resound no more to the din of war."

CHAPTER THIRTY-FIVE

NURSED back to health at Gloddaeth, the house of "his dear kinswoman", the gentle Lady Mary Mostyn, Archbishop Williams sat before the wide fire-place in the great hall and drew comfort from the blazing logs. The welcome flames made play upon the silver locks of the prelate, showed up the motto of the house picked out in coloured letters across the hearth, danced and flickered on the old minstrel gallery, and on the fresco over the dais where gleamed the royal arms of the Tudors with the red dragon supporter.

Despite his placid looks, which lent benign dignity to his countenance, the brain of the former Lord Keeper was as alert as ever, as General Mytton and the Parliament Commissioners found to their cost. For the Archbishop, it is recorded, "turned Mytton up and down with fine discourses and wrought him like wax so that the people thought they were in a dream when their League was made upon these conditions: That none of those counties should be compounded for delinquency, nor burdened with Free-quarter, nor have the Covenant offered them, nor be charged with taxes, but only in victual for Men and Horse in the Garrisons. So these Cambro-Britains were conserved by the cunning and dexterity of a Master-wit".

North Wales escaped better than anywhere in the land in the matter of sequestrations, and was "never much oppressed after".

. . . . .

The arras parted. Turning to see who entered, the Archbishop beheld Heritage standing there.

"You seek me ?" inquired his Grace.

"I seek Maelys," replied Heritage, "but as I cannot set eyes on her, I will speak with your Grace."

"I suppose you find yourself out of occupation now that Denbigh hath fallen. Old Hosanau Gleision put up a stout resistance, I hear, and would have held out longer but for his Majesty's express command. Is it right that rather than hand General Mytton the key he flung it into the moat from the Goblin Tower, saying that the Parliament had won the world now, and could make it their dunghill ?"

Heritage nodded, and put further gossip aside as irrelevant.

"I want to marry Maelys," said he bluntly.

"I dare say you do," said his Grace, stroking his small pointed beard. "If you saw to the release of her father, perchance you could discuss the subject with him."

"That will come to pass in due time, I have no doubt," said Heritage unmoved, "but I feel anxious so long as the girl goes about without a protector."

"I thought she was safe now that the Parliament holds North Wales in relentless grip."

"She is safe so far as our men are concerned. We are no violators of women. But your enemies are still active. That bully Byron hath fled to France—for which I am sorry for I was minded to try a thrust or two with him to settle that massacre—but Hogan and his rake-helly creatures are still hiding in these hills. And Hogan is not a man to forget an injury. Where is Maelys ?"

"She went out an hour since to visit her mother at Bodysgallen."

"I will seek her," said Heritage.

Heritage walked with brisk steps through the woods along the path which led to the adjoining grounds of Bodysgallen. He was ill at ease, yet knew of no cause for his foreboding. The naked trees rose in dark outline

against the grey sky. Heritage's quick eye discerned
the tracks of Maelys's shoes. Suddenly he began to run.
Half hidden by the roots of an oak lay a motionless
figure. Maelys? No, it was some man. The fellow lay
face downward on the cold ground, the back of his head
battered. Even as Heritage gathered the man in his
arms his eyes were searchings for signs. At the sight of
the face, Heritage groaned.

"Jenkyns, Jenkyns, old friend." There was a faint
flickerer of the eyelids. Slowly the eyes of the old man
opened. They gazed expressively into the eyes of his
master's son.

"Can you speak?" pleaded Heritage.

The pale lips moved but no sound came. The eyes
grew more eloquent. "You understand what I am
saying?" went on Heritage distinctly. "You were
struck down from behind while defending her?" The
eyes seemed to assent. "How many men? One, two,
three, was it? Three, then. Hogan was one? I thought
so. Nay, don't grieve, old friend, you did your best.
You want to tell me where they went? Never fret.
I will follow their trail. They shall not escape me. God
bless you. You have died for me and mine just as you
would have served my father. I shall never forget I
owe my escape from Conway Castle to your aid. I will
avenge you."

The eyes looked pleadingly into those of the young
man. "You want me to leave you? Never. I will take
the trail quick enough in due course."

Heritage never let his eyes move from the eyes which
gazed into his. Slowly the lids drooped. Heritage laid
the old man on the ground and reverently spread a
kerchief over the face. Then he became a man of action.
Quickly he picked up the trail in the damp soil of the
path, followed it to the road, found the tracks of three
horses, followed them at a run until he came to a break
in the hedge. He sprang over this and ran towards
Gloddaeth. As he reached the drive he pulled up and

whistled. There was a clatter of hoofs as his great black horse came trotting to his call. He paused only to examine the primings of his pistols and to see that sword and knife were in position. He thrust his hand into his rolled cloak, and drew forth a tomahawk which he stuck into his belt. Then, leaping into the saddle, he spurred for the roadway again. Bending low he kept his eyes on the tracks of the three horses and set off in pursuit. In his independence he never thought to summon aid. It was his task and he was content to attempt it unaided. The horses left the road and took to the open fields. They crossed the marsh where once the Conway flowed. One horse was heavy-laden. Up the tree-clad lane opposite went Heritage, every nerve alert. Were the men heading for the moors ? Presently they branched to the right. They were making for the river after a detour to avoid Llansantffraid. Past the old mill went Heritage. At his shout the miller came to the door. Had three men passed that way, one of them carrying a woman ? Yes. Heading for the river. Up the narrow lane went the black, and down again to the ford at Cerrig Groes. Heritage's eyes could see several horses tethered near Cymryd, on the western bank.

He plunged across the river and up the farther beach. Over the hedgerow jumped the black, across the fields, into a lane.

Heritage was conscious of bustle about the rear of the old grey house. He reined his horse to a slow canter. A long pistol barrel slid through an open window. A woman screamed. As the pistol cracked, the great horse reared, staggered a pace or two, and fell on its side. Heritage rolled on the ground and lay still, with the animal between him and the enemy.

"You shoot well, *mon cher* Hogan," cried a voice, and three men came running towards the fallen horseman.

There was a spurt of flame ; another—from behind the neck of the horse. The Frenchman fell dead. Up leaped Heritage. There was a sparkle of steel as the tomahawk, flung with deadly aim, curved through the air and split the skull of the second man.

Hogan paused irresolute, and turned back for another pistol. Heritage was running crouching towards him ; his long sword came sweeping from its scabbard.

"Coward !" he called, and Hogan turned. No one should accuse him of running away. Sword in hand he stood on guard.

Maelys, watching with fascinated eyes from the doorway, had no doubt of the issue. The fighting look was in Heritage's eyes. A sharp, quick hiss of steel, a parry and a vicious lunge which drove the hilt almost to the breastbone, and Hogan lay gasping on the ground.

His eyes opened in one last malevolent glare. "Your —damned—Archbishop—was—Buckingham's friend !"

Thus died Hogan, his tongue more deadly than his sword.

CHAPTER THIRTY-SIX

MAELYS, her heart warm with gratitude to Heritage, ran forth to greet her rescuer, but at the sight of his face her outstretched hands fell to her sides. He stood in the grassy yard, sword in hand, his head bowed. The three dead marauders lay unheeded where they had dropped. Behind him, the black horse, trained by his master to rear and fall when a pistol flashed, had risen to its feet and stood motionless, glad of the respite after the chase.

Maelys was frightened—not of the dead men laying where Heritage had struck them down, but of the look in his eyes.

"What is it?" she faltered.

"You heard what he said?"

"No."

"He said that the man who was with Buckingham at the time of my father's martyrdom was Archbishop Williams."

"But—but—that was so long ago surely, surely; you are not going to visit any youthful folly on his head now?" There was entreaty in her tones.

"An eye for an eye!" quoth Heritage. "When my father died in my arms I vowed that no one present should escape."

"But it may not be he; it is all so long ago."

"It must be him. Look back; Bishop of Lincoln, Dean of Westminster; friend of Buckingham . . . if I had not been so long absent from the country it would have occurred to me before that he might be the man. My eyes are opened."

"But all is past; forgive and forget."

"I neither forgive nor forget. Through these long

years the thought has sustained me. It has glowed like a hot fire within. Once, when I fell into the hands of the Mohawks, they tortured me. And when they stuck burning pine splinters into my flesh as I was lashed to the stake I endured because I knew that death must not come to me until my mission was fulfilled. Through all my travels I have kept this knife. Other things have been taken from me, but this I have protected for this day."

He drew it and stared at it in silence ; brooding. Maelys shrunk from him.

"You are mad," she cried. "Never speak to me of love again. Never let me see you again."

"Love ?" Heritage laughed. "I have lived among Indians. They hold vengeance is greater than love."

"Oh, don't, don't !" moaned Maelys. "I read your thoughts. Your eyes are terrible. You shall not touch him."

Heritage's laugh was bitter. "Oh, I shall not harm him. . . . I shall only serve as I was served. He was merciful because I was only a boy. Merciful ! I will be merciful too. . . . I will but slice off the tops of his ears."

He thrust his knife back into its sheath and walked towards his horse. Maelys ran after him. "Forgive me. I will give you anything if only you will let this pass. Do not lay hands on him. He is an old man and has suffered so. I will do anything for you ; marry you ; give you all I possess, only spare him."

Heritage brushed her from him, sprang into the saddle and spurred away. His remorseless eyes stared fixedly ahead. He gave no backward glance ; did not see the sobbing girl sink to the earth ; did not see her recover and spring to her feet and run towards Hogan's tethered horse. Heritage rode recklessly towards Gloddaeth. He knew not, cared not, that Maelys was behind him somewhere, riding for Gloddaeth too.

He left the spattered steed with heaving sides on the

gravel drive and strode into the hall. The steward greeted him without concern. Captain Heritage had visited his Grace before on important business.

"Where is the Archbishop?"

"His Grace has retired to his room, sir. He is weary."

Heritage mounted the stairs. With his customary caution he moved noiselessly now. The worn boards gave no hint of his coming. Gently he pushed open the bed-chamber door. The gathering evening threw the room into semi-darkness. The Archbishop was standing near the window. His lips were moving as though in soliloquy or prayer. The light of eventide fell upon his face, giving it a more intense whiteness as though death's fingers were already commencing their caress. Outside the hush of coming night had fallen over grove and meadow. The world was at peace. Peace, too, beautified the Archbishop's countenance. "I have passed through many places of honour and trust in Church and State," he murmured to himself, "but were I assured that by my preaching I have converted but one soul to God I should take therein more spiritual joy than all the honours and offices which have been bestowed upon me."

He sighed, and turned slowly towards his bed. Suddenly he started. "Who's there? Who is it?"

"It is I, John Heritage."

The great figure loomed out of the gloom, towering above the fragile form of the bishop.

"Ah! You fright—you took me by surprise. You carry an urgent message, I presume."

"Yes." Heritage's hand went to his belt. Slowly he drew his knife.

"I pray your Grace will take this knife to the steepest cliff of the Orme, and fling it to the depths of the sea. It is accursed!"

The door slammed and he was gone, leaving a bewildered bishop staring uncomprehendingly at a knife which quivered in the worn boards of his bedroom floor.

CHAPTER THIRTY-SEVEN

"Oh, you're safe ! Thank God you're safe !"

The Archbishop rose from his devotions ten minutes later as Maelys came bursting into his room. She flung herself sobbing hysterically into his arms.

"My dear child, what is it ? What has upset you ?"

"I am in time. I am in time. I was afraid . . . Heritage . . ."

"Heritage was here a short while since. What of him, child ?"

"He—did you no harm ?"

"Harm ? Why, no. He comes as friend now, I trust. A strange fellow. All he came for was to bid me cast a knife into the sea. Possibly it has some significance ; a token of a spiritual regeneration, let us hope."

Maelys sighed and said no more.

"But where have you been, dear ? You are distraught."

Then Maelys told him of her capture and the manner of her release.

"How complex are the works of the Creator ! A man of good impulses, this Heritage, yet a terrible fighter. Maelys, I am not wholly sorry we are on his side. Let us seek him and thank him for the service he has rendered you."

So they went downstairs, but the great black horse and his rider had vanished into the night.

.   .   .   .   .

The winter passed by ; and still another, silvering yet more the Archbishop's hair, adding touches of maturity to Maelys's sweet face.

282

For Maelys her sadness lifted somewhat, for her father was home again, released from durance vile to tread once more the pleasant paths of Bodysgallen.

The Archbishop was less happy, mourning the King's captivity ; dreading the impending doom, for, says his biographer, "from his fidelity to his Majesty, he never went back an inch".

Of Heritage there was no word. The girl sickened for news of him yet her pride would make no admission. The Archbishop read her inmost thoughts.

Hearing General Mytton was passing through Conway, his Grace made a special journey to the town.

"I would like to see Captain Heritage," said he.

"I, too, would like to see him," said General Mytton, "but at his own request he has been transferred to the Northern army."

"Could you prevail upon him to return hither ?"

"Should your Grace so desire, I could order his return."

"Then do so, I pray, and waste no time."

When June was flooding the countryside with sunshine, Heritage rode into Conway again ; an orderly Conway to which trade was returning, albeit slowly. Colonel Carter, who commanded the garrison, ordered him to Plas Mawr. Heritage was shown into the presence of the Archbishop.

"I am hurt, Captain Heritage, that you should have forsaken your friends so cavalierly."

Heritage held his head high. He looked older. "I am no fit company for your Grace. I have been possessed of a devil."

"I have advised you before, Captain, that it ill becomes you to argue theology with me. As a Prince of the Church I consider I have every authority to say that if the devil did once possess you, you have cast him out."

"I came to you that night to cut off your ears," said Heritage fearlessly.

The Archbishop raised his slender fingers and caressed one of the shapely ears of which he was justly proud.

"You may do so, my friend, if it will bring happiness to you and one I love."

"I am unworthy of her, sir."

"And therefore, I take it, the more likely to prove yourself worthy. Come, my friend, there is enough dolour in this unhappy country without making one heart sad unnecessarily. You have asked me once if you might marry Maelys. I do not think the maid is averse to such a proposition, and she needs a protector in these troubled times. God knows what lies ahead of us, for our King is like to die a blessed martyr, and England without a King is something I cannot contemplate. I tell you, my friend, we, in this island, look to a King to lead us."

"I'll subscribe to that, right willingly, your Grace—provided he be not a Stuart."

"Let us not argue that point," said his Grace drily. "As I look ahead, it seems to me that the time will come when King and Parliament will jointly rule this land with justice and dignity ; when out of all this turmoil and death and suffering, something bigger and greater than you and I have wit to see will yet be born. To do so, old sores must heal and old enemies become friends. It is not only sentiment which makes me favour your marriage to Maelys. It is only by thus reuniting these dissenting factions that we can ever hope to attain one harmonious whole. Come ; no more words ! You dine with me at Gloddaeth."

And Heritage, nothing loath, escorted the Archbishop to the ferry. Side by side the Archbishop's grey and the great black horse climbed the Tywyn Hill and cantered across the gentle park-lands which stretch between the road and Gloddaeth Hall.

Maelys, coming to the door to greet the Archbishop, coloured when she saw his companion.

"I have come to marry you, Maelys," announced Heritage. "We have dallied long enough."

There was a happier look in the girl's eyes than the Archbishop had seen for many a long day. "These are your forest manners," she cried with simulated dignity. "You ought to woo me first."

But Heritage put his arm about her and carried her indoors.

.   .   .   .   .

That hot June a few curious villagers pushed their way into the little old church of St. Hilary, where Christianity has flourished since the sixth century, for word had passed from mouth to mouth that a wedding was to take place. Maelys was there, very radiant, on the arm of Colonel Wynn. Her mother was there with Lady Mostyn ; and before all Heritage towered in his war-worn uniform.

The Vicar, a little flustered at the presence of the Archbishop, gave out the hymn and the old rafters caught up the strain. The villagers gazed with awe as the prelate stood at the altar rails. . . .

It was over. The curious had been herded from the church by the verger. Colonel Wynn and Madam Wynn had kissed their daughter a fond farewell.

Only the happy two and the aged prelate stood in the porch.

"I shall never, never, forget you," cried Maelys, tears in her eyes as she embraced the Archbishop. The old man smiled happily. "We have been good comrades," he said. "God bless you, child." And as she dropped to receive his blessing, Heritage, who had never bowed his proud head to any man before, knelt at her side.

The horses waiting at the lychgate pawed the ground.

"Come, Maelys !" Heritage grew impatient. "Adieu, your Grace ! I little thought I should ever be married by an Archbishop."

Joyously they hastened down the path to the waiting mounts.

"An Archbishop ?" The old man watched them with a tender smile in his eyes. "I—John," he whispered slowly and sadly, "Archbishop of York—that was."

Heritage mounted his great black horse and, reaching over, struck the second horse a blow on the withers which sent it careering across the field.

"Come," he commanded, and swung Maelys on to his saddle-bow.

"Whither ?" she smiled up at him.

"I was thinking . . ." he said slowly. "You remember the night we met ?"

"Could I ever forget ?"

"The shelter of boughs ; the fire in the night ?"

"And your cloak over me ?"

"There was a shelter I once built near the stream which runs below the old church at Llangelynin," said he, laughter dancing in his eyes. "I have used it often, there behind the old holly tree where the chatter of the brook lulls one to sleep. In the morning you wake warmed by the eastern sun, and harken to the cooing of woodpigeons in the elms ; and in June the foxgloves surround the meadows with a wall of pink . . ."

"I have seen them," she whispered.

"Rough lodging for a fair lady !" commented Heritage. There was an invitation ; a challenge in his eyes.

Said Maelys : "I love your forest ways."

THE END

BIBLIOGRAPHY

Calendar of Wynn Papers.

Hacket's *Memorial of Williams, Archbishop of York* (1692).

Royal Visits and Progresses in North Wales. Edw. Parry (1850).

Ancient and Modern Denbigh. John Williams (1856).

Transactions of the Honourable Society of Cymmrodorion (1927–28)—"John Williams of Gloddaeth". By Judge Ivor Bowen, K.C.

Oliver Cromwell. John Buchan.

Oliver Cromwell's Letters and Speeches. Carlyle.

Tourist's Guide to Caernarvon. Rev. P. B. Williams (1821).

Williams' *History of Aberconwy* (1835).

Proceedings. Llandudno, Colwyn Bay and District Field Club.

Carte's *Life of Ormond.*

Roland Phillips's *Civil War in Wales and the Marches.*

Archaeologia Cambrensis (1869).

History of the Great Rebellion. Clarendon.

Ambrose Philips's *Life of Archbishop Williams* (1700).

Historic Notices—Flint. Henry Taylor (1883).

Letters of Archbishop Williams. J. E. B. Mayor, Cambridge Antiquarian Socy. (1864).

Heart of Northern Wales. W. Bezant Lowe.

ANDREW MELROSE, Ltd.

PATERNOSTER HOUSE,
PATERNOSTER ROW, LONDON, E.C.4

Telephone:
City 3200 (Eight Lines

Telegraphic Address:
Literarius Cent. London

Mr. Földi is not only Hungary's greatest living author, whose novels appear simultaneously in many European languages, but he is considered by leading German, Italian, and French reviewers to be the "representative man" of Continental literature.

THE WORLD STRIDES ON   Michael Földi

Mr. Michael Földi is acknowledged as Hungary's foremost psychological novelist. This book is not a war book. The world happenings of the years 1912–18 form only the background of this human and engrossing love drama of two people who start out as medical students with dreams, ambitions, and aspirations, only to see them shattered in the maelstrom of the Great War. The scene is Budapest—the capital which is coming to replace Vienna as the city of romance in popular imagination.

This is a story of great emotions. It is a book of youth, and Mr. Földi's penetrating insight makes it not only a profoundly moving picture of a catastrophe of which the scars are not yet healed, but also a diagnosis of the present. The spectre of war still looms over Europe, and we believe that Földi's beautifully written novel is more timely now even than when it first appeared.

7s. 6d. net

BY THESE SIGNS   **Dr. Sinclair Touse**
Author of "Twin Strangers"

A powerful novel showing the workings of the great hospital and the devoted service rendered by physicians, surgeons, and nurses in alleviating the sufferings of humanity. It describe the vast amount of research that science is constantly struggling with, the obstacles encountered and successfully overcome the conquest of disease; and might truthfully be called "Microbe Hunters" in fiction form even though it is a love story that rises to the greatest heights.

No one is more capable of writing a story of such vital interest than Dr. Sinclair Tousey, one of America's most eminent surgeons and the greatest authority in the world on X-ray and radium.

In "By These Signs" the author of "Twin Strangers" has given the reading public a fascinating insight into the realms of the scientific and medical world which will long be remembered.

A truly outstanding novel.

7s. 6d. net

THE AFFAIRS OF WOMEN   **Davide Sernicol**
Author of "Love Wears a Veil"

The whole course of Amer Ebn Imram's life was changed by the affairs of two women. One was a Tuareg girl who, out of spite, sent him to a terrible death in the desert. The other was a rich English girl, the famous airwoman, Elaine Powis, who had been bitterly hurt by overhearing her so-called friend saying she would never marry unless she bought her husband with her millions.

She was flying solo over the Sahara, when she saw Amer and rescued him, and they made a bargain whereby they could help each other.

Elaine was delighted with their wild scheme until she met the gay, debonair André Labrant, only to realize that Amer stood between her and her happiness. Davide Sernicoli gives us vivid pen-pictures of desert warfare and desert justice, and then in sharp contrast, takes us to the Belgian coast.

7s. 6d. net

Two Sparkling Humorous Novels

THE CAT AND THE CURATE

Charles Gilson

Author of "Wild Metal", "Barry Royle", etc.

The Rev. Theodore Whitten lived alone—alone but for Susan, his Persian cat, who loved him. Theodore did not like to think about such things, but Susan obviously was strong on Sex Appeal. She was palpably feminine ; she used her paw like a lipstick ; she was modern in every way—independent, selfish, amorous, affected ; she frequently stayed out all night.

Contemplating Susan, the Rev. Theodore felt there were a lot of things that he should know and which he was sure, if she could talk, Susan could tell him. His red corpuscles wanted scope ; somehow sea air and celibacy didn't go together. He wanted Susan's advice.

This was the beginning of Theodore's phenomenal experience.

"Frolicsome farce, diverting and amusing."—*New York Times*.

". . . both pleasant and slightly shocking. The vast public which has lamented the passing of Thorne Smith might well look to Mr. Gilson to replace him."—*New York Herald Tribune*.

7s. 6d. net

RIVIERA RHYTHM
Lewis Helland

Here is a book with a real laugh on every page, almost on every line. This is no idle boast of the Publishers, but the opinion of the literary adviser who read the manuscript. The story concerns a small côterie of English people of the Smart Set staying at the same hotel on the Riviera, and their behaviour in their anxiety to reach a state of easy married bliss or to arrange it for their sons and daughters makes amusing, frequently deliriously funny, reading. Written in a light, smart, and brilliantly witty vein reminiscent of Keble Howard, "Riviera Rhythm" will have a strong appeal to all those who appreciate clever, unforced humour.

7s. 6d. net

THE MOVING MOON — **Barbara Vise**

A book of character, written by a new author who has an appreciation of words and their significance. Janet Quame is the *motif* of the story. She is a woman whose strange influence works—like a pirate loose on a foul wind on the high seas—among all she meets, plundering from each something which has been held precious; yet after each conquest she knows no victory. For Janet there is neither satisfaction nor rest from the jealous quest of her own elusive purpose. Among those whom Janet affects are Hugh Drufford, artist in temperament, passionate in his appreciation of beauty; Elizabeth Drufford, who can face life when there seems to be nothing ahead but the accusation of her daughter Daphne; Christopher Burben, who loses faith in many things. Janet Quame rocks the tides of life of these four people, but she, herself, is driven as the moon that moves across the sky.

Miss Vise tells her story with charm, and her delineation of Daphne's character is clever.

7s. 6d. net

WINTER CHERRIES — **Derek Temple**
Author of "Drums Over Africa"

"Winter Cherries" is the story of Daphne and Jim Tarrant, and that mystery of the flesh and spirit we call love.

Against a many-coloured tapestry of life in Kenya, with its atmosphere of brooding mountain and untamed forest, the author skilfully mingles the breath of the English countryside, and the fragrance of a Sussex dawn, together with an intense and objective insight into the reactions of the characters to circumstances that prove almost too much for them.

The characters portrayed are intensely human; the story is enlivened by flashes of humour, and the local colour is painted in with a lack of exaggeration that only makes it the more vivid, so that one becomes filled with a desire to go and see, to verify and experience life in Kenya as it is lived there today.

7s. 6d. net

PATERNOSTER HOUSE, LONDON, E.C.4

A MARRIAGE OF VENGEANCE
Julia Mowbray
Author of "A Woman's Ransom", "Within the Web", "The Path of Deceit", etc.

A story of passionate emotion which grips from the first chapter when Margot Lester, betrayed by Ivor Brandon, died by her own hand. In a moment of bitter anguish, Maurice Conway, who had hoped to make her his wife, swore he would be revenged on her betrayer, and strangely, terribly, he kept his word. How he won the girl Brandon loved and married her as part of his scheme of vengeance, and how, at last, happiness dawned out of the coil of sin and suffering, is told with all the power and skill at the command of this popular author. In saying this is Julia Mowbray's best novel up to date, we realize we are bestowing very high praise indeed, but we know that praise is deserved. Readers of every class and taste will be enthralled by this outstanding story.

7s. 6d. net

ASK NO QUESTIONS
Lyn Dean

This unusually good first novel, with a real professional touch about it, is the story of a death officially accepted as an accident, locally believed to be something very different ; and of a detective who doesn't want to detect. He is on holiday, and determined to remain so, but the old ladies of the neighbourhood insist on assuming that he has come there to investigate the tragedy, and pour into his ears all that they know or guess about it. Against his own will his interest becomes increasingly engaged and he begins to pay real attention to the information given him, until finally he rounds on the gossips and convinces them that the tragedy was a pure accident—being by that time overwhelmingly anxious to conceal the murder which he feels certain has been committed. The story grips one's attention from the first and holds it throughout.

7s. 6d. net

MURDER OF A PAINTED LADY **Harold Ward**
Mr. Harold Ward is one of America's leading serial and scenario writers.

Here is a detective thriller considerably above the average. It should prove extremely popular with that wide-reading public who appreciate a murder mystery that baffles, excites, grips, and—still baffles.

The story concerns the murder of a glamorous red-haired dancer. Scarcely have the detectives detailed to cover the crime got nose-down on the trail of clues than two further murders occur in the same apartment block in which the body of the dancer—"the painted lady"—was found. The discovery of the criminal comes with terrific surprise reminiscent of the late Edgar Wallace at his very best.

7s. 6d. net

THY HOUSE WAS CLAY   **Stephen Ronley**
Author of "Waters of Babylon", "They That Sow"

The kindly fate which veils the future gave no inkling of what lay in store for Frank and Ella Burgess—the wanderings, the sufferings and tragedy that they were destined to face together, on that mild October morning that marked the thirteenth anniversary of their wedding.

On such a note does the author open his latest and undoubtedly his greatest novel, "Thy House was Clay"; from such an opening does he relate the story of one man and one woman which might well be called the "Tragedy of a Father", for it is in actual fact the tragedy of Frank Burgess and his home-loving, courageous wife. From being a salesman in a large London store, with wife and family living placidly and in measurable comfort in Suburbia, the merciless code which shatters worlds and flings men on the scrap-heap drives him into the coal-pits of South Wales to provide the bare necessities of living. From salesman to coal-hewer sounds incredible; nevertheless, the novel is based on fact.

Mr. Ronley's gifts of characterization and understanding of the human heart combine to make "Thy House was Clay" a story titanic in human appeal that will be remembered and thought about long after other stories have faded from the mind.

7s. 6d. net

MOUSEBACK — **John C. Woodiwiss**

Author of "Death's Visiting Card", etc.

The solution of this intricate problem again launches Detective Inspector Hopton, C.I.D., into a series of amazing adventures.

"Mouseback" is another "super-charged thriller" in which the reader is carried forward at breakneck speed to a breathless conclusion . . . a crime of colossal magnitude planned by one of the coolest and most ruthless of Britain's enemies, Kurt Ernst von Mausbach, Ex-*Korvettenkapitän*, Imperial German Navy.

The finding of two bodies on a derelict cabin-cruiser in the Channel gives Scotland Yard its first intimation of the web of intrigue so craftily spun by a master plotter—the first intimation of the conspiracy whose repercussions are intended to rock the British Empire to its foundations, and which is only frustrated in the nick of time.

"Mouseback" is a worthy successor to "Death's Visiting Card". As in the author's previous story, thrill after thrill holds the reader's attention to the end.

"Mouseback" is a book you won't put down unread.

7s. 6d. net

THE QUEEN'S ESCORT — **Arthur Leonard Hall**

Author of "Rebels' Passage"

How many people remember that a Queen of England was once fired on by English ships when she tried to land in her husband's country ? Mr. Hall has chosen as the theme of his second novel the return of Queen Henrietta Maria from Holland with help for her husband, King Charles I, when her enemies made every attempt to prevent her from landing, and she finally spent the night in a ditch while the shot from the *Parliament's* guns dropped all round. Moreover, the landing took place at Bridlington in Yorkshire, one of the towns shelled during the Great War, thus linking past and present as one. The story, with its love interest, its action, and its setting, provides a theme to suit all readers.

7s. 6d. net

CLARE SINGLETON   **Bernard Hardwick**

Author of "Maiden Ladies"

Can a woman love and retain her independence ?

Clare Singleton, the heroine of this intimate and moving study of a modern business woman, thought that she could.

Secretary in a City office, and sharing a flat with a girl friend, she had reached her middle thirties : clever, cultured, and beautiful, still attractive to men, but rejecting all offers of marriage, remaining loyal to the memory of her lover killed in the War, content to be single rather than marry for the sake of a home, holding advanced ideas on sex and marriage, and proud of her independence, yet secretly hoping that one day the man of her dreams will appear.

Then Ewan Fenhouse enters her life, challenging her to put her ideas to the test, and stealing her heart. . . .

The resulting conflict is the central theme of this poignant, true-to-life story.

Mr. Hardwick writes with simplicity and deep feeling, and in his gently ironic yet sympathetic portrait of Clare, sincere and generous, facing adversity with quiet courage, the independent woman is seen at her best.

7s. 6d. net

WHO KILLED JEFFERSON BROOME ?
Helen M. Keynes

Author of "Murder in Rosemary Lane" (a Crime-Book Society recommendation)

This is a book for those discerning readers who like their Detection with a Difference. There is mystery, excitement, and detection, but the drama is enacted by creatures of flesh and blood, against a background of human emotions.

Dan Merrick loved a lady . . . but there were few to love, many to hate, and more to fear Jefferson Broome. Inspector Meryon, patient, shrewd, albeit fallible, finds the answer to the question "Who killed him ?" at the end of a thrilling chase.

7s. 6d. net

THE WRONG GIRL   **Rob Eden**

Trudy Vernon was only a clerk at the ribbon counter in Dana's Department Store. But she looked like Sharon Carr, a famous dancer in a popular show.

Sharon wanted privacy and Trudy wanted to meet Phil Dana, who would never see her behind a counter. So she consented to pose as the dancer. She was frightened at the risk—but it was only for a week-end, she told herself. How could she, at twenty, know that a week-end could mar two lives—that her resemblance to Sharon would throw them into a whirlwind of romance, adventure, and intrigue?

Here is a grand, up-to-the-minute story with a full quota of thrills and excitement, that rushes from country estates to Atlantic City beauty pageants, from millionaires to kidnappers.

7s. 6d. net

GUNSMOKE GIRL   **Clee Woods**

Author of "Riders of the Lost Valley", "Hoof Thunder"

Cole Tyler persuaded his family to give up horse-stealing and to move from Texas to Idaho, where they could do a legitimate ranch business. Not only did he want to straighten out his family, but he also wanted to be near Nan Hunter, whom he loved.

Between the Hunter and Tyler families there was bad blood because Hunter had stolen Brushopper Tyler's girl. When Cole Tyler's own family turn against him, he is caught between the cross-fire from both sides. The Hunter crowd are determined to drive the Tylers out of the country. And the fight is on.

In heavy clouds of gunsmoke and in breakneck riding through dangerous country, Cole Tyler fights to redeem himself in the eyes of his family, to clear up the old feud, to block the Hunter schemes, and to justify the loyalty of Nan. An open-range fighting tale that will keep you in a lather of excitement.

7s. 6d. net

FIRE AND HAIL   **F. J. E. Bennett**
Author of "The Prince Passes"

The little Polish Princess, Maria Clementina Sobieski, had one great ambition, to be Queen of Great Britain. So, when the Irishman Wogan came to her father's court at Olawa to ask her hand in marriage on behalf of his exiled master, King James III of Britain, better known as the Old Pretender, she was wild with delight.

The journey southwards, to be imprisoned by the Emperor of Austria, and rescued by Wogan, seemed thrilling, indeed, to the little Princess. And then her marriage—what a disappointment! For cold, formal James was no fit mate for the lively Clementina; he loved her deeply—but he was too stiff to show it.

Read the romantic love-story of Clementina Sobieski in this touching and well-written novel of Jacobite days.

7s. 6d. net

SPLENDID SURRENDER   **Kathleen Burke**

A love story in the most vital sense of the words, though it has little in common with the milk-and-water romances often so described. An English girl, young, inexperienced, alone, just waking to the facts of life, finds herself caught in the meshes of blazing passion under hot Eastern skies. The atmosphere of the East has been caught most wonderfully in this vivid novel, but against the tropic background a very human drama is played, a drama of human frailty as well as of human strength, picturing love in every phase—a love that gives willingly—a love that worships from afar—a love that is wronged and betrayed and misunderstood, yet lives on still. Kathleen Burke is essentially a modern writer, outspoken, virile, poignant, with uncanny skill in describing the heart of a woman. A book that has grip and thrill, passion and pathos, from the first page to the last.

7s. 6d. net

CARRIERS OF DEATH — **John Creasey**

Author of "Seven Times Seven", "Death Round the Corner", "Thunder in Europe"
"The Terror Trap", etc.

This is another of Mr. John Creasey's hair-raising stories of Department Z, the secret branch of the British Intelligence. The hero, Bob Kerr, is a worthy successor to other leading Department agents; the Arran Twins play important parts in the trouble that follows their efforts to get on the trail of Gregory Marlin and the men who are backing that astute broker, whose clients include many influential members of the Government. The story gets into its swing from the first page, and never slackens pace. The increasing threat from Marlin creates a tension in England, giving a suspense that few writers can create more effectively than Mr. Creasey. Move and counter-move follow fast upon each other, and Kerr fights ruthlessness with a greater ruthlessness, acting fast upon his thoughts with devastating suddenness. Complications tumble against each other, but never make the story confusing, and the well-drawn characters, both familiar and otherwise, are varied and strongly drawn.

"Follow Creasey for thrills" will be an even more apt slogan after this new book of breathless adventure.

7s. 6d. net

By the same author :

THE DEATH MISER	FIRST CAME A MURDER
MEN, MAIDS AND MURDER	REDHEAD
SEVEN TIMES SEVEN	DEATH ROUND THE CORNER

THE MARK OF THE CRESCENT

Cr. 8vo, Cloth Bound, 2s. 6d. each net

CASTLE OF CARE — **Norman Tucker**

Author of "Night Hawk"

A vigorous tale of the Great Rebellion in a new and picturesque setting. The chief scenes are enacted at Conway, which town the Parliament carried by escalade after the last English stronghold had surrendered. Care is taken to afford an accurate background for a romance in which action and suspense, love and hate are interwoven. The reader, though absorbed in the exploits of the characters, is incidentally provided with a vivid picture of North Wales in those troublous days. The celebrated Archbishop of York, John Williams of Conway, is etched with particular fidelity.

7s. 6d. net

SELINA'S SUMMER — **Janet Lynn**

Author of "Happy Rest"

This is a charming book which should appeal to all; it is a book of travel in Great Britain and on the Continent as seen from a South African's point of view. Those who cannot travel will enjoy this book, since by reading it they can visit in imagination many parts of England, France, and Germany. For almost the same reason this book will appeal to those who travel, as they may perhaps be able to map out an interesting tour.

This is by no means intended as a guide book; it is the diary of Janet Lynn's personal experiences when on holiday with her faithful old car Selina, and is written with quiet unruffled charm.

7s. 6d. net

Recent 7/6 Novels

THE MIGHT-HAVE-BEENS	**Anne Capelle**
MAGIC SHADOW-SHOW	**Sonia Cardine**
GOLDEN DUST	**Gertrude Charles**
THUNDER IN EUROPE	**John Creasey**
THE TERROR TRAP	**John Creasey**
ANTOINE, THE FEARLESS	**Gordon Grahame**
THE GENTLEMAN	**Gordon Grahame**
THE SHADOW-TREE	**L. A. B. Heney**
END OF A MARRIAGE	**Jane Hukk**
LAUGHING CABALLERO	
	Nels Leroy Jorgensen
HELL'S HARBOUR	**Herbert Patrick Lee**
THE GREEK VIRGIN	**Denis Meadows**
WITHIN THE WEB	**Julia Mowbray**
ROAD CLOSED	**Beatrice Murillo**
THE LAND IS DEAR	**Meta Mayne Reid**
THE DRAGON STRIKES BACK	**Tom Roan**
MISTAKEN LOVER	**Arthur Somers Roche**
THE STOLEN CONTINENT	
	Francis H. Sibson
TWIN STRANGERS	**Dr. Sinclair Tousey**
CLINGING SHADOWS	**Main Waring**
ALL THIS IS ENDED	**A. W. Wells**
HOOF THUNDER	**Clee Woods**
THE WINKING GOWN	**Muriel Wrighton**

A Grand Gift Book

KING EDWARDS OF ENGLAND

Elizabeth Villiers

Author of "Our Queen Mothers", "Love Stories of English Queens", etc.

A book of strange fascination and thrilling romance, proving again that truth may be stranger than fiction. As is usual in her work, Elizabeth Villiers takes a framework of solid fact, but on it weaves a fabric in which legend and tradition are mingled with history, thus changing dry-as-dust records into pulsing stories of high adventure and passionate love. Many of them told here are from unimpeachable sources and yet are little known. Who, for instance, can identify offhand that Edward of England, who loved and married a beggar maid? Or can say the name of the King in whose reign Godiva lived and who influenced her with his own fervour? In this book these stories are told in full with many others, all crowded with action and pulsing with the hot blood of chivalry. In gallant cavalcade the chapters move down the ages, bringing us to our own times and ending with a striking study of King Edward VIII.

The book is most beautifully illustrated, the photographs and reproductions of old engravings being not the least of its many attractions.

Demy 8vo, Illustrated, 7s. 6d. net

OUR QUEEN MOTHERS   Elizabeth Villiers

Author of "Love Stories of English Queens", "Alexandra the Well-Beloved",
"Women of the Dawn", etc.

The lives of all the Queen Mothers through 800 years, extending from Adelicia of Louvaine to Queen Mary.

Second edition

". . . A book of considerable interest."—*Methodist Times.*

Demy 8vo, Illustrated, 7s. 6d. net

PATERNOSTER HOUSE, LONDON, E.C.4

RECOLLECTIONS OF A LITERARY LIFE
"Rita"

With a Foreword by SIR PHILIP GIBBS, who writes :

"The story of 'Rita's' own life is beautifully done without egotism, and yet with self-revelation which touches one's emotions."

"Interesting reminiscences."—*Sunday Dispatch.*
"Has a pleasant fragrance."—*Daily Mail.*
"Disarmingly naïve."—*Lady.*
"A delightful book to read."—*Tatler.*

Large Demy 8vo, Illustrated, 18s. *net*

ANTHOLOGY OF ARMAGEDDON
Edited by Bernard Newman and I. O. Evans

This anthology is the most comprehensive, the most authoritative, and the most thrilling collection of writings on the Great War that has yet been published.

"I do not think that there is any better war book than this. I find it fascinating ; everything seems to be there. If anybody wants to tell a young man or woman what modern war in all its horror and humour and despair and monotony and courage is like, he could not do better than give this book. Every soldier had his own little war ; here is the 'little war' of a marvellously assorted company."—J. L. HODSON, the author of "Grey Dawn, Red Night".

First Cheap Edition   *Large Cr. 8vo,* 454 *pp.,* 3s. 6d. *net*

BOTH SIDES OF THE DOCK
Charles Kingston

Author of "Dramatic Days at the Old Bailey", etc.

"Can be cordially recommended."—*Times.*

"Seldom has the full extent of human villainy been displayed so completely . . . undeniably entertaining."—*Daily Mirror.*

"A panorama of personalities and incidents in the history of crime."—*Morning Post.*

"Mr. Charles Kingston has collected an amazing gallery of rogues to present to his readers in his new and entertaining book."—*Saturday Review.*

Demy 8vo, Illustrated, 16s. *net*

PATERNOSTER HOUSE, LONDON, E.C.4

JEN SHENG : THE ROOT OF LIFE
Mikhail Prishvin

English Version by GEORGE WALTON and PHILIP GIBBONS

With a Foreword by JULIAN S. HUXLEY, M.A., D.SC.

It is the story of the Manchurian Forests : of the search by two men—a Russian and a Chinaman—for the Root of Life.

The author had been called "another Grey Owl", and his book has been described as "the greatest nature-story since 'Green Mansions'". Extracts from **Professor Julian Huxley's** Foreword : "Mikhail Prishvin has written a nature-book of unusual and rare quality. He has an intense feeling about nature. 'Jen Sheng' is a book of great vividness, and has left a strong impression on my mind."

Illustrated by W. FAVORSKI, *the well-known Russian artist,* 5s. net

OLD TIMES AFLOAT : A Naval Anthology
Col. C. Field, R.M.L.I.

Author of "The History of the Royal Marines"

In the words of Sir Francis Bacon : "It may truly be said that the Command of the Sea is an Abridgment or a Quintessence of a Universal Monarchy." It is our Navy which has for centuries given us that Command, and all that concerns that historic Service must, therefore, be of interest to every Anglo-Saxon. Here in this anthology we have an "olla podrida" of curious items of the ships and sea-folk of days gone by. We read of the seamen of old, of the most famous ships of days gone by, of the attempts made by long-ago shipbuilders to protect them from the missiles of an enemy, of the fire-ships so dreaded in the seventeenth century, and of their development as explosion vessels, forerunners of the deadly submarine, mine, and torpedo. Here, too, are stories of the press-gang, Barbary pirates in our own narrow seas, our dockyards, and conflagrations ashore and afloat.

First Cheap Edition   *Illustrated,* 5s. net

PATERNOSTER HOUSE, LONDON, E.C.4

TWELVE ON THE BEAUFORT SCALE
Stanley Rogers
Author of "Ships and Sailors", "Sea Lore", "The Atlantic", etc.

Here is a storm book, a book of typhoons and tempests at sea, of peril and heroism, of ships and men in classical battles with the sea. "Twelve on the Beaufort Scale"—the hurricane number on Admiral Beaufort's storm chart—is indicative of the character of this book. Within its pages are first-hand accounts of some of the most terrible maritime storms in history, along with a description of the little-known centre of a typhoon, the character of gales and hurricanes, and the history of the famous Beaufort scale itself.

First Cheap Edition   *Illustrated, 5s. net*

THE ACHIEVEMENT OF HAPPINESS
Dr. Boris Sokoloff

This book on human happiness approaches the subject from the standpoint of an authoritative physician. Writing in a frankly autobiographical tone recalling Dr. Axel Munthe's "Story of San Michele", Dr. Sokoloff shows that all human beings possess the capacity for happiness and that a proper knowledge of our minds, bodies, and emotions can help us to achieve it.

"Every chapter bears the marks of a wise and instructed mind, whether it deals with the origins and nature of happiness, the nature of vitality, fatigue, 'the art of not-thinking', sex differences, the fighting instinct, or the connection between happiness and sexual and romantic love . . . this excellent study."—*British Weekly.*

Demy 8vo, 8s. 6d. net

SCOTCH : or It's Smart to be Thrifty
Compiled by Angus J. MacTavish
Edited by F. Gregory Hartswick
A Volume of 296 of the best Scotch jokes.   *2s. 6d. net*

The Westminster New Testament Commentaries

Edited by Principal A. E. Garvie, M.A., D.D. A Series of Commentaries on the Bible by Modern Scholars, designed for Teachers, Ministers, and Private Students.

F'cap 8vo, cloth boards, 3s. 6d. per Vol. ; leather, 4s. 6d. per Vol

S. MATTHEW **Prof. David Smith, M.A., D.D**
Author of "The Days of His Flesh"
Second Impression

S. MARK **Rev. S. W. Green, M.A**
Professor of New Testament Greek, Regent's Park Baptist College, London

S. LUKE **Rev. A. E. Garvie, M.A., D.D**
Principal of New College, Hampstead, London.

S. JOHN **Rev. Henry W. Clark, D.D**
Author of "The Philosophy of Christian Experience"
Second Impression

THE ACTS **Rev. Prof. H. T. Andrews, B.A**
New College, Hampstead, London.
Second Impression

GALATIANS AND ROMANS
Rev. Prof. W. D. Mackenzie, M.A., D.D
President of Hartford Theological Seminary, Conn., U.S.A.

THESSALONIANS AND CORINTHIANS
Rev. Prof. R. Mackintosh, M.A., D.D
Lancashire Independent College, Manchester.

THE CAPTIVITY AND THE PASTORAL EPISTLES
Rev. Prof. J. Strachan, M.A
(London.) *Author of "Hebrew Ideals"*

HEBREWS AND THE GENERAL EPISTLES
Rev. A. F. Mitchell, M.A
(Sheffield.)

THE REVELATION AND THE JOHANNINE EPISTLES
Rev. Alexander Ramsay, D.D.
(London.) *Author of "The Christian Citizen"*

MELROSE'S POCKET SERIES

F'lscap 8vo. Cloth. Gilt. 3s. 6d. net each.
Titles marked * are also bound in antique leather, gilt top and lettering, silk Register boxed. Price, 6s. net.

*ADVENTURES IN CONTENTMENT
David Grayson

25th Edition, reset and printed from new type.

The *Westminster Gazette* says : "It is full of the joys of healthy living, communion with nature, and the friendship of books."

*THE FRIENDLY ROAD   David Grayson

27th Edition, reset and printed from new type.
"A delightful view of simple experiences."—*The Times.*

*THE WOODCARVER OF 'LYMPUS
Mary E. Waller

22nd Edition, reset and printed from new type.
"A strong, human story, full of deep tenderness and understanding of the primary needs of the soul."—*Morning Post.*

*THE ROAD WANDERER Henry Shawcross
Third Edition.

". . . full of passion for beauty in Nature and for Human Justice. The book forms a grateful addition to the 'Pocket' Series."—*The Times.*

DEVONSHIRE IDYLLS   H. C. O'Neill
Sixth Edition.

The *Saturday Review* says : "Racy of the soil, quaintly and pleasantly reminiscent of days gone by. Miss O'Neill has a confiding way, and her work deserves an easy access to the reader's grace, as it has the secret of simplicity."

PROSE PICTURES : An Anthology
E. Margaret Jones, B.A.
Second Edition.

Compiled by E. Margaret Jones, B.A. From the writings of Michael Fairless, Richard Jefferies, David Grayson, Stephen Graham, R. L. Stevenson, and other famous writers.

PATERNOSTER HOUSE, LONDON, E.C.4

Melrose's Pocket Series (*cont.*)

*THE HAPPY FIELDS   E. M. Martin
Third Edition.

"He does not over-decorate his work ; there is no self-conscious display, no undue emphasis or exaggeration. The wistful harmony of a mind well attuned and modulated presides over all his meditations."—*Daily Telegraph.*

SHADED LIGHTS : On Men and Books
Anonymous

Third Edition.

"As satisfying as the lights of a homestead when we are lost at night in a difficult country."—*The Nation.*

THE LOWLY ESTATE   Cranstoun Metcalfe
Third Edition.

". . . This is the book to treasure on a well-handled shelf. It is in the true succession of Leigh Hunt and Lamb."—*Daily Mail.*

*CHEAPSIDE TO ARCADY
Arthur Scammell

Second Edition.

"Delightful essays, scholarly, with a rich imagination and a sense of colour that is always true."—*Daily Chronicle.*

A STUDENT IN ARMS   Donald Hankey
(*killed on the Somme, October* 12, 1916)

With an Introduction by J. St. Loe Strachey (late Editor of the *Spectator*).
Eighteenth Edition.

A STUDENT IN ARMS (Second Series)
(Being further sketches of "A Student in Arms")

Donald Hankey

With a Biographical Sketch by his sister.
Fourth Edition.

"Of a truth the world which can produce such a man as Donald Hankey is worth living in."—*Spectator.*

"A book, in short, that will add to the admiration and regret with which the author is spoken of in three continents."—*Punch.*

Works by Professor
J. ARTHUR THOMSON, LL.D.
(Late Regius Professor of Natural History in the University of
Aberdeen)

THE WONDER OF LIFE

With over 100 Illustrations, some in colour, by E. L. SHINNIE.

"This is the ideal book for the non-professional student. . . .
We can only marvel at the sure insight with which the author
has laid hold of the essentials."—*Glasgow Herald.*

"This remarkable book, with its clear style, its endless
'instances of the wonder of life', its remarkable illustrations,
some of them of exquisite colours."—*Contemporary Review.*

Sixth Edition   *Demy 8vo, cloth, gilt, 15s. net*

SECRETS OF ANIMAL LIFE

"As entertaining as they are instructive. Whether he is
examining the curious inexplicable life of the Cuckoo or Man's
arboreal apprenticeship, or the educability of the snail, he is
always a delightful companion."—*Morning Post.*

Third Edition   *Crown 8vo, fully illustrated, cloth, gilt, 5s. net*

DARWINISM AND HUMAN LIFE

With a Photogravure Frontispiece Portrait of Darwin, and
Twelve Illustrations by E. L. SHINNIE

"Professor Thomson is one of the most lucid and able
exponents of Darwinism."—*The Times.*

Fifth Edition   *Demy 8vo, cloth, gilt, 5s. net*

THE HAUNTS OF LIFE

Lavishly Illustrated by WILLIAM SMITH

"No one has done so much to create an intelligent and general
interest in natural history subjects as Professor Thomson."—
Daily Chronicle.

Demy 8vo, cloth, gilt, 5s. net

PATERNOSTER HOUSE, LONDON, E.C.4

Works by Prof. J. ARTHUR THOMSON (*cont.*)

SCIENCE, OLD AND NEW

This is one of the most varied, and certainly one of the most fascinating, of Professor Thomson's books.

Demy 8vo, cloth, gilt, 5s. net

NATURAL HISTORY STUDIES (School Edition)

Collected and arranged by the Author from his own works

Fully illustrated by WILLIAM SMITH

"You get, as you read, a sense of bees humming about the pages, of running water, of the wind among the trees, and of the scent of wild flowers."—*Star*.

Crown 8vo, cloth, gilt, 4s. 6d. net

THE CONTROL OF LIFE

"Professor Thomson is one of the few men of science who have become famous and yet retained the ability to see beyond the walls of their laboratories or studies."—*Daily Mail*.

Crown 8vo, cloth, gilt, 3s. 6d. net

MAN AND BEAST   Samuel Scoville, Jr.

With Illustrations by CHARLES LIVINGSTON BULL

"The stories deal with wild beasts of the jungle in life-and-death combat either with men or with one another. Well described, and Mr. Bull's excellent illustrations help to brighten the drama."—*Daily Express*.

"A wonderful collection of stories about wild beasts. A fascinating book."—*Yorkshire Observer*.

"The ever-growing public who delight in those romantically-told tales which impart knowledge of wild life and its ways will find something to satisfy in 'Man and Beast'. The author has the gift of powerful, dramatic narrative, and the illustrations are worthy of letterpress they accompany."—*Dundee Advertiser*

Crown 8vo, cloth, 3s. 6d. net

History

REFERENCE BOOK OF ENGLISH HISTORY
M. E. Hamilton Hunter and G. G. Ledsam

"This Reference History of England, which, wisely, I think, begins with the Norman Conquest, appears to me not only accurate and trustworthy, which is the first requirement, but to supply just the kind of information that one seeks in a book of the kind, and to give it a most convenient form.

"It was a happy thought to give brief biographies of celebrities at the end of each reign in addition to the historical sketch which follows the chronological list of events."—PROF. J. B. BURY, *Regius Professor of History, King's College, Cambridge.*

Crown 8vo, cloth, 550 pages, with Maps, Genealogical and other tables, 6s. net

AN EXAMINATION HISTORY OF ENGLAND
W. Nichols Marcy

"This brief, practical History of England has been used privately with great success in the author's brilliant career as a 'Crammer'. It is now for the first time published in the ordinary way, with a view to putting the book at the service of teachers, professional coaches, and private students preparing for examinations."—*School Government Chronicle.*

Crown 8vo, cloth, 5s. net

THE SYRIAN CHRIST
Abraham Mitrie Rihbany

"He has rendered admirable service to all Bible students. His work is of permanent value."—*Church Times.*

"Our opinion is that any preacher who studies the book will find it of infinite value in sermon-making."—*Christian World.*

Fourth Edition   *Demy 8vo, cloth, 6s. net*

Miscellaneous

A FIRST BOOK OF WILD FLOWERS

Margaret M. Rankin

Author of "A Girl's Garden", etc.

With over 100 Illustrations in Colour, by NORA HEDLEY

This book, of which six large editions have already been sold, is notable for the charmingly simple style of its text and the faithful excellence of its coloured plates which enables the reader to readily identify the wild flowers of our fields and hedgerows.   A seventh edition is now ready.

Crown 8vo, cloth, colour panel design, 6s. net

A COMPLETE LATIN COURSE

W. Nichols Marcy

"The greatest living 'Crammer' in the United Kingdom."

"Short cuts to learning are generally suspect; but Mr. Marcy does seem to justify the bold way he has thrown over tradition in the teaching of Latin, with consequent saving of the pupil's time and the teacher's temper."—*Evening Standard.*

Crown 8vo, cloth, 5s. 6d. net

THYREA (Memorial Edition)   John Ferguson

With Additional Sonnets, a Portrait, and a Biographical and General Introduction by the late ST. JOHN ADCOCK.

"In the poetry of the present generation no volume has had a more successful career than Mr. John Ferguson's 'Thyrea'. Its popularity, indeed, seems to grow with age.   There is in these sonnets, on a multitude of varying themes, an artistic morality, quiet humour, economy of expression, appropriateness of phrase, and a sweetness of cadence which are equalled by no sonnet-writer of our time : and for once at least a popular volume of poetry deserves its popularity when judged by the strictest canons of the critics."—*Aberdeen Press.*

"A marvellous literary work.   A choice and beautiful book."
—*Edinburgh Evening News.*

Fifteenth Edition   *Crown 8vo, cloth, 3s. 6d. net*

ANDREW MELROSE'S
3/6 *Novels*

Romance, Mystery, Adventure and Wild West

Cr. 8vo, Cloth Bound, with Attractive Coloured Wrappers

......JENNY ESSENDEN . . .	Anonymous
......PALLUDIA . . .	Anna Robeson Burr
......SIMON IN LOVE . . .	L. C. Douthwaite
......THE BLACK CHALICE . . .	Cedric Goodall
......WHISTLING WIRES . .	Pelham Groom
......THE PEACE FIRE . . .	G. M. Hort
......MURDER ISLAND . . .	Leland Jamieson
......IT TAKES A MAN . . .	Elizabeth McFadden
......THE FOG . . .	William Dudley Pelley
......DRAG	William Dudley Pelley
......DEATH FOLLOWS THE TRAIL	Michael Poole
......*THEY THAT SOW . .	Stephen Ronley
......WATERS OF BABYLON . .	Stephen Ronley
......THE SORTING VAN MURDER .	Mander Ross
......*IN THE DAYS OF HIS YOUTH	
	E. H. Lacon Watson
......*BRIDE IN SHORTS .	Arthur Noël Wheston

* Latest Titles

PATERNOSTER HOUSE, LONDON, E.C.4

ANDREW MELROSE'S
"Red Jacket" 2/6 Novels

Cr. 8vo, Cloth Bound, with Attractive Coloured Wrapper

Miriam Alexander

The House of Lisronan
A 250 Guineas Prize Novel

Phyllis Austin

*Self-Accused
*Valentine
*The Lovable Lunatic

John Creasey

The Death Miser
Men, Maids and Murder
Seven Times Seven
*First Came a Murder
*Redhead
Death Round the Corner
*The Mark of the Crescent

Jessie A. Davidson

*Dawn
A Romance of Malaya

Sinclair Drago

Women to Love

Jackson Gregory

The Bells of San Juan
Judith of Blue Lake Ranch
Ladyfingers
The Splendid Outlaw
Six Feet Four

H. Rider Haggard

Mary of Marion Isle
Allan and the Ice-Gods
The Treasure of the Lake

George Ingram

"Stir"
**(A Book Society Recommen-
dation)**

* Latest Titles

PATERNOSTER HOUSE, LONDON, E.C.4

"Red Jacket" 2/6 Novels—*Continued*

Nels Leroy Jorgensen

El Coronel

Marius Lyle

Unhappy in Thy Daring
A 250 Guineas Prize Novel

Cleveland Moffet

Through the Wall

Julia Mowbray

A Woman's Ransom
*The Path of Deceit

Margaret Peterson

The Lure of the Little Drum
A 250 Guineas Prize Novel

Blind Eyes
Tony Bellew
Green Stones of Evil
Dust of Desire
Just Because
The Love of Navarre

Arthur Somers Roche

The Case Against Mrs. Ames
(Crime–Book Society Selection and story of the film)

Constance Smith

Secret Drama
A 250 Guineas Prize Novel

Smokeless Burning
Just Impediment ?

Norman Tucker

Night Hawk

Patricia Wentworth

The Astonishing Adventure
of Jane Smith
The Red Lacquer Case
A Marriage under the Terror
A 250 Guineas Prize Novel

A Little More than Kin
The Annam Jewel
The Devil's Wind

* *Latest Titles*

PATERNOSTER HOUSE, LONDON, E.C.4